TO BE LOST IN HIM...

For the briefest of moments, she wondered how it would feel to bare her skin to that enormous, frightening-looking monster. Get him to hold her, maybe let her disappear into the steady beating of his heart.

Would her body shock him?
No.
No, he looked like nothing would surprise him. Not even her.

UNDER HER SKIN

ADRIANA ANDERS

sourcebooks
casablanca

Published by Sourcebooks Casablanca, an imprint of Sourcebooks, Inc.
P.O. Box 4410, Naperville, Illinois 60567-4410
(630) 961-3900
Fax: (630) 961-2168
www.sourcebooks.com

Printed and bound in Canada.
MBP 10 9 8 7 6 5 4 3 2 1

*To Z. This book would not exist
if you'd never been born.*

1

> Old hag in need of live-in helper to
> abuse. Nothing kinky.

UMA READ THE AD AGAIN.

Jesus. Was she really going to do this?

Yes. Yes, she was. She'd come all the way back to Virginia for the hope its free clinic offered, and if this was the only job she could get while she was in town, she should consider herself lucky to have found it. *Especially*, she thought with a wry smile, *since it's one for which I'm so qualified.*

The smile fell almost immediately. Everything was moving so fast. Not even in town for a day, and here she was, standing on a stranger's front porch. The house, thankfully, wasn't even close to the haunted manor she'd imagined. Then again, who knew what waited behind that chipped red door?

Taking a big, bolstering breath, Uma slipped the newspaper clipping back into her pocket and knocked.

There was a light *thunk* on the other side, followed

by what sounded like footsteps, a scuffling, and then nothing. She waited, trying to hear more over the drone of a nearby lawn mower, and thought of all the reasons this was a horrible idea.

Abuse? *Abuse?* How could she possibly take this job in the shape she was in?

But as usual, the desperate reality of her situation pushed all arguments aside. Food, shelter, money. There was no arguing with necessity, even if this place felt off.

And the situation was perfect. No one could find her here. In theory. She was pretty sure her new employer wouldn't be phoning up any references or doing a background check. The woman must be desperate too. She'd practically hired Uma over the phone, for goodness' sake.

Someone should have answered by now.

Uma knocked again. Hard, her hand starting to tremble.

Something moved in her peripheral vision, startling Uma into a gasp. The curtain in the front window?

The cloth twitched a second time. The woman was watching. Making Uma wait out here, overdressed in the unseasonable heat, sweat gathering along her hairline. Okay, fine. She could see how it made sense to check out a stranger before letting her in. She'd give the lady a few more minutes to finish her perusal. If only she could get some air. Just a little air in this stifling heat.

When there was no response to her third knock, Uma panicked. According to the oversize watch on her arm, three minutes had passed. Three minutes spent standing on a porch, enduring the scrutiny of a self-proclaimed *abuser* who represented her only chance at a job. Not the auspicious beginning she had hoped for.

It was all so familiar too. Maybe not the exact

circumstances, but the feelings she lived with on a daily basis—insecurity, worry, fear clawing at her chest, crowding her throat so each inhale was a struggle. Before they could overwhelm her, she shoved them away and walked down the rickety porch stairs and around to the side of the house, where she could gather herself unseen beneath the first-floor windows. She needed to *breathe*.

Uma took a shaky breath in, then out, another in, before biting into the meaty pad of her thumb. The ritual was safe, easy to sink back into, the shape of her teeth already worn into her hand. *Just a little while*, she thought. *Until I sort myself out, and then...* Then she had no idea what. She had nowhere to go, nothing left to aspire to.

One step at a time. That was her life now. No planning, no future.

She was vaguely aware that the lawn mower drew near, no longer background noise, buzzing close and echoing the beat of her heart. She'd have to push off this wall sooner or later, but the warm clapboard was solid against her back, and along with the sharp smell of freshly clipped grass, it kept her right here, present, in her body. A few more breaths and she'd move. Time to decide whether she'd head up to the house to give it another try or cut her losses and take off, find something else.

Yeah, right.

The problem was she wouldn't be cutting her losses by leaving—she'd be compounding them. How on earth could she go back on the road with the gas gauge on *E* and ten bucks to her name?

Strike that. After this morning's breakfast, she had only $6.54.

Uma sank down onto her haunches, the ground squelching under her heels, and squeezed her eyes shut so hard that black dots floated behind the lids.

She had nothing left—no home, no job, no way of making money, no skills but one...and Joey had destroyed any chance of pursuing her true livelihood when he'd smashed her cameras. Doing that, he'd destroyed *her*. Six months later, she was still trapped.

If she let herself feel it, there'd be no shortage of pain, inside and out. As usual, her wrist under the watch was raw, and her skin itched everywhere. It must be psychosomatic. It couldn't still itch after all this time, could it?

Visualizing his marks on her skin was enough to make her hyperventilate again. And the tightness was there, that constriction that had left her constantly out of breath these past several months. She'd thought the miles would clear the airways, but they hadn't.

And now she was back. Back in Virginia. Shallow breaths succeeded one another, pinching her nostrils and rasping noisily through her throat. Joey was close. Two hours away by car. Way too close for comfort. She swore she could feel him looking for her, closing in on her.

Something cold and wet swiped Uma's hand, snapping her back to the present. She opened her eyes with a start, only to come face-to-face with a *dog*. A black one with a tan face, floppy ears, and pretty brown eyes rimmed in black, like eyeliner. It smiled at her.

It was something else, that dog, with that sweet look on its face. Like it gave a crap. Weird. The expression was so basically human, it pulled back the tunnel vision and let some light seep in. The dog nudged her chest, hard, and pushed its way into her arms in a big, warm tackle-hug. Uma had no choice but to hug back.

Its cold nose against her neck shocked a giggle out of her. "Oh, all right. You got moves, dog."

"She does," said a deep voice from above.

Uma's head snapped back in surprise, sounding a dull *thunk* against the clapboard. Oh God. Where had *he* come from?

"She's a barnacle."

Uma nodded dully, throat clogged with fear. *Stop it*, she berated herself. *You've got to stop freaking out at every guy who says two words to you.* She tried for a friendly smile. It felt like a grimace.

The man just stood there, a few feet away, looking at her. She waited. He waited. He looked like a big, creepy yard worker or something. Tall. Really, *really* tall.

"Gorilla," he said.

"What?"

"My dog, Squeak. She's a guerrilla fighter. Thought about callin' her Shock 'n' Awe."

"Squeak?" She stared up at him, craning her neck with the effort. She was wrong before. To say he was tall was an understatement. The man blocked out the sun. With the light behind him, it was hard to see much, aside from the big, black beard covering half his face and the shaggy mane around it. His voice was deep, gravelly. *Burly.* It went with the hair and the lumberjack shirt. You didn't see guys like him where she came from.

"Wasn't her name originally. She earned it." When he talked, the words emerged as if they hurt, purling out one slow syllable at a time. As if being sociable was an effort. Yet, for some reason—for her—he was trying.

He waited, probably for her to say something in response, but she'd been running too long to be any good at repartee. She'd turned into more of a watch-and-wait kind of girl.

The man finally continued, tilting his chin toward the house she was leaning on. "You her next victim?"

Uma winced, embarrassed. "Guess so."

He lifted his brows in semi-surprise before turning to the side and stuffing his hands deep into the pockets of jeans that had seen better days. They were stained and ratty and littered with what looked like burn holes.

Backlit by the sun, his profile was interesting, despite the bushy lower half of his face. Or maybe because of it. He looked like something you'd see stamped into an ancient coin—hard and noble. The scene came easily into focus: clad in something stained and torn, wading into the thick of battle with his men, sword in hand, face smeared with enemy blood, and teeth bared in a primal war cry. Her hands came to life, itching for a camera.

She blinked and emerged to see him as he was: a filthy redneck with a rug on his face. He was intimidating, to say the least. Not the kind of guy she'd choose to work in *her* yard—not looking all roughed up like he did.

But this new phase of life was about taking back what Joey had stolen. It was about *courage*, and because this guy was so intimidating, Uma decided to face him head-on. Show no fear. Another rule for this new self that she was constantly reinventing: no more letting men intimidate her.

"Help me up?" she asked.

After a brief hesitation, he complied. His grasp was

rough and solid, ridged with calluses in places and polished smooth in others. For a moment, after pulling her up to stand, he didn't let go of her hand. Instead, he turned it over and eyed the crescent her teeth had left behind.

She fought the urge to snatch it away.

He raised his brows but finally let her go without a word. Burning with the need to put some distance between them, she took a hurried step back.

"Thanks," she said as he squatted down to scratch Squeak roughly under the chin. The dog's eyes closed in ecstasy.

Forcing herself to steady her nerves, Uma caught his gaze and held it. He was even scarier without the sun behind him, skin marred by a shiny, white scar along his hairline and a dark bruise on a cheek already peppered with errant beard hairs. His nose was crooked and thick, no doubt broken in a barroom brawl or something equally disreputable. She envisioned him in a smoky basement, duking it out for some seedy underground boxing title. Carved squint lines surrounded eyes that were a cool blue.

Or…*oh*. No. She realized with a start that his left eye was blue and the right was dark gold. She was instantly thrown off-kilter. Which one was she supposed to focus on? She blinked and turned aside, uncomfortable with the way he so effortlessly unsettled her.

"I've…" he rumbled, coming up out of the squat to tower over her again. She waited for him to continue.

"You've…?" she finally asked after the silence had stretched too long. She wondered if she was as off-putting to him as he was to her.

"Ive. It's my name. Short for Ivan."

"Oh. I'm Uma." She gave him her real name without thinking. "You mow the lawn here?"

"You could say that." His eyes crinkled. What little she could see of his mouth turned up into a surprisingly warm smile. "Figure I might as well mow her lawn while I'm doin' mine."

She looked at the house behind him. "*That's* your place?"

Her surprise must have been obvious, but he didn't react, just gave a single, brief nod.

"Wow. Nice." The house *was* nice. *Really nice.* Incongruously…civilized. He looked like the kind of guy you'd find chopping wood by his cabin in the boondocks, not maintaining the lawn of his lovely old farmhouse.

It was straight out of *Southern Living*, nicer than some of the places she'd photographed.

The caricature she'd formed in her head of this man melted partially away to reveal something a little softer, less defined. It didn't jibe inside of her, but she'd been running on stereotypes and first impressions and messed-up *wrong* impressions for so long that her instincts clearly needed a reset. Another thing to add to the growing list of upgrades for Uma 2.0.

He nodded, face serious, but she thought she could detect pride beneath the gruff exterior.

She caught sight of a bright-red tricycle in the drive beside a clunky Ford pickup. Kids. Probably a wife. Her perception shifted yet again, and he didn't seem half as scary as he had a moment before. Wow, she couldn't straighten her life out at all, and *this guy* seemed to have his shit together. So much for first impressions.

Uma briefly wondered what he'd look like without all that fur on his face.

She took in the house, the trike, the coziness of this sweet mountain town. A town so small that elderly ladies hired you right over the phone without even asking for references.

That reminded her of why she was here: the ad. *Maybe not such a sweet town after all.*

"Well, I'd better get to it." She kept her hands in her pockets, not wanting to risk another touch of his rough skin.

"Yeah. Don't wanna piss her off." Was that a joke?

She gave Squeak a quick pat on the head and turned away from man and dog. His voice stopped her after a couple of steps.

"Hey, Uma." It came out rough, and he cleared his throat. "You ever need a break, come on over and see us. Have a beer."

"Oh. Sure. Thanks." *Us*, he'd said. Yep, married.

She shot a last look at the house over his shoulder, thinking she might even be willing to marry a guy like that for such a great house. Oh well. Maybe she and his wife would become friends.

A friend. That might be nice.

When she got back to the porch, something had changed. Was the gap in the curtains a little wider? Was it possible the woman had witnessed her panic attack? Strike one against Uma if she had.

The lawn mower started up again somewhere behind the house.

Uma took a deep breath in, blew it out hard, made a fist, and pounded.

2

"WHO'S THAT?" UMA RECOGNIZED THE WOMAN'S VOICE from their telephone interview, although then it had seemed warm, a lifeline. They'd spoken only for a few minutes, but the woman—Ms. Lloyd—had sounded relieved, even excited, that Uma could start that day. Nothing weird had happened during that call, making Uma wonder what the ad was all about. Now, the voice was shrill, unwelcoming, through the thick wood of the door.

"It's Jane Smith, Ms. Lloyd," she yelled.

"Let's see your ID."

Uma hesitated. "You said I wouldn't need to fill out a W-4 or give you my social security card or anything."

"I said we were doing this off the books, honey. I didn't say I'd let some random stranger into my home without at least getting a look at who she is."

Right. Okay. Right. The woman had a point. Uma fumbled out her wallet and managed to pull her Virginia driver's license from the sleeve. "Where do you want—"

"Under the door."

Before squatting, she did a quick, paranoid scan of the road behind her. A dead-end street...good and bad. Isolated—good. This little town where doctors apparently treated people for free wouldn't even be on Joey's radar. The lawn mower sputtered angrily over a rock in the distance, reminding her of who'd been driving it. Random strange men as neighbors—bad. Very bad.

She shoved the ID under the door and waited, crouched down, eyes flicking from the road to the house and back. Looking for Joey. Always looking for Joey.

Abruptly, the door swung open, and Uma found herself on the floor, sprawled gracelessly at the slippered feet of her new employer.

"Jane Smith, hmm?"

"Actually, I go by Crane. It's, uh, Uma Crane."

"No kidding. Well, don't just lie there. Come inside before you let all the heat out." *The heat?* It must've been eighty degrees outside.

Uma took her first good look at her new employer. Even from her vantage point on the floor, it was obvious that the woman was short, almost perfectly round, as wide as she was tall, and Uma was willing to bet she couldn't fit through a doorway straight on. Coke-bottle lenses gave her dark eyes an owlish quality, which, when fixed on Uma, was rather disconcerting. An extreme case of helmet hair—round, glossy, and black—and a dark wooden cane completed the look. Uma had the distinct impression that she'd fallen straight into a spider's web.

> Old hag in need of live-in helper to abuse. Nothing kinky.

I won't let her hurt me, she decided in that moment. *No way will she walk all over me.*

"It looks like I'm your new live-in helper." She forced a goofy smile. "I guess that makes you the old hag."

The woman's eyes opened even wider, then narrowed to slits. "If you want your purse, you'd best take it now, else it'll stay outside." Uma rose and barely managed to snag her bag before the woman slammed the door and locked it with a definitive series of *thunk-clicks*. Four times she locked it, followed by a belated fifth.

Uma was inside. It should have been comforting, the knowledge that she was locked away, safely hidden. So why did she feel as though she'd jumped from the fire right back into the frying pan?

∿

Ms. Lloyd's house was like the Land Where Time Had Stopped. It owed its decor almost entirely to Laura Ashley, circa 1986. It was okay, if a little…still. As though nothing could move within its confines. Stale, close air where not even the dust dared to fly.

Someone had clearly cared about decorating once upon a time but lacked either the desire or the resources to keep it up-to-date. The result was like one of those time capsules. The furniture looked cared for but worn and had no doubt been the height of middle-class fashion in its day. The tables were dark wood, and the carpeting must once have been white or cream. Today it was the color of a tan Band-Aid. The only new thing in the place was the television. A ridiculously wide flat-screen dominated the living room, managing, through its sleek simplicity, to look almost like a piece of modern art.

As she took it all in, breathing the musty smell of a house long kept closed, the woman's big, black eyes followed her. "You look older than twenty-six." Charming. Her voice was high, girlish. It didn't match her dark looks. "And you're late, Irma."

"It's Uma."

"You're late."

"Yes, I'm sorry." Uma took a breath, determined not to let her new boss cow her. "You must not have heard me knock the first time. I went around to see if you were in back."

"Is that what they call it nowadays?"

"I'm sorry?"

"Flirtin'. I saw you over there with my neighbor," she said, her gaze swiping up and down Uma's body one time. "I know your type."

Her *type*? On this unseasonably sticky October day, Uma must have been the only person for miles whose body was covered from head to toe. She wore jeans and a dark, long-sleeved, cotton shirt, a scarf tied around her neck. In fact, the only person she'd seen showing less skin was standing in front of her.

Their outfits were embarrassingly similar.

"What can I do to get started?" Uma asked, choosing to ignore the woman's vitriol. *I'm stronger than you*, she thought, hoping it was true.

"You can start by making me dinner. I've been half-starved here waitin' for you. As I told you on the phone: you cook, you clean, you shop, you run my errands. I pay you every week the first month, then every other week after that. If I decide to keep you on." Ms. Lloyd pursed her lips and squinted at Uma as if she found the notion highly unlikely. "No phone calls, no men. No back talk."

Silently, Uma followed the woman's slow limp into the kitchen, where dishes overflowed the double sink and big, brown stains spread across the white linoleum floor.

"You talk, right?"

"Yes, ma'am."

"Do you understand the rules, or do I need to write them down for you?" She enunciated carefully, as if speaking to a slow child.

"I understand."

"I take my dinner at five, sharp. Early-bird hour." *More like geriatric hour*, Uma thought, the little bit of meanness giving her a semblance of power. "I won't stand for missing any of my stories, so you'd best hurry. Might want to clean first, though." Ms. Lloyd sank into a chair at the kitchen table and turned the full intensity of her dark eyes onto Uma.

This is it, Uma thought, taking in the stinking mess. *My life. This is my fucking life.*

She picked up the sponge, dark and shriveled, hard as rock, and ran it under water that took ages to heat. Breath coming fast, her heart fluttered with panic. All she wanted was to run.

I can do this. This is nothing. She's an old woman. She can't hurt me. This was about her future, about getting back some kind of life—a prospect that had seemed utterly impossible until she'd heard the interview that brought her here: a doctor offering free tattoo removal.

If anything, she needed to look at this job as a mental exercise. Physical activity to take her mind off everything else. *Besides, fighting makes you stronger, right?*

"You're getting your sleeves wet," Ms. Lloyd's voice cut in, pointing out the obvious—and the one thing Uma had hoped she wouldn't notice.

"I'm fine like this," Uma responded, sounding silly and small, despite all efforts at strength. "I don't mind getting wet."

Uma attacked the dishes with energy, if not gusto. Crusted bits came off slowly under liberal applications of soap and elbow grease, and all the while, she endured the woman's stare. Eventually, the dishes in the rack outnumbered the ones in the sink, and finally, the sink was empty.

"The menu du jour is soup and grilled cheese. Easy peasy. If you cook as good as you clean, we just might get along."

Easy peasy was right. It took only a few minutes before she plopped two plates and bowls down on the tiny kitchen table and moved to sit across from her new employer, stomach growling in anticipation.

From somewhere close by, a bell rang. It was an old-fashioned rotary-phone sound that the woman ignored.

"Need me to get that?" Uma asked.

"Nope. Got a bathroom upstairs needs cleaning." The woman's words stopped her before Uma could pick up her spoon.

"You want me to clean before I eat?" Uma asked, poised above the seat, the smell of food teasing her taste buds with a rush of saliva.

A raised eyebrow was the woman's only response, and Uma shut her eyes against the hunger. Work first, eat later. She could do this.

"Fine," she said, straightening. Strong. "Where's the bathroom?"

"Upstairs hall. Second door on the left. Supplies are down here. Your room's the last one on the right. Don't dawdle, and don't open the other doors. It's private." As if Uma cared what the woman kept in her house.

She squatted in front of the cupboard and rummaged around, the smells of bleach and melted Velveeta mingling in her empty stomach to make her gag. If the state of the kitchen was any indication, conditions upstairs were likely dire.

She stood, arms filled with containers of products so viscous they'd need to be chipped out.

Ms. Lloyd sniffed, her voice following Uma out. "It's not the worst grilled cheese I ever ate."

Limbs heavy, Uma stomped slowly up the stairs, fairly certain that the comment was her new boss's idea of a compliment.

～⌒～

An hour later, Uma stopped in the hallway on her way downstairs. There was nothing personal in this house, nothing human. The walls were decorated with crying-clown prints and bird lithographs. All signs pointed to Ms. Lloyd being a lonely, lonely woman.

She looked at each frame she passed until… Oh. Uma set down the bucket of cleaning supplies and leaned in to peer at the picture. A wedding photograph, man and woman both smiling happily. It looked informal, like a town hall affair, maybe taken sometime in the seventies. The woman was a thinner, happier, pretty Ms. Lloyd. There was something about the photo—the hope, the excitement, the infinite possibilities alive in their eyes.

Uma swallowed the lump in her throat and picked up the bucket, walking away.

What kind of life was this? Meals, TV, bed…the same rituals day in and day out.

God, what if she became this woman further down the road? She might not even take that long to sink to such lonely ruination. Uma and Ms. Lloyd—bonded in loneliness. The thought repulsed her but also brought with it the strangest desire to better understand her boss.

Downstairs, the woman snored on her chintz sofa in front of *Wheel of Fortune*. Uma's eyes skimmed over the ugliest doily arm protectors she'd ever seen to where gnarled hands lay clasped in her lap. Out of nowhere came the weirdest urge to take one of those hands in hers. Would her fingers be cold, dry talons, or would they be warm and soft from sleep?

No. Not Uma's problem. Empathy was a luxury she could ill afford. Maybe someday, but her stock was currently depleted.

She tiptoed into the kitchen and wolfed down her meal. Cold.

Once she'd eaten and finished the dishes, she looked around. The rooster clock on the wall told her it was just after 7:00 p.m. The sun had set, and the air was finally cool. The prospect of the long, dark, lonely night stretching ahead had Uma searching the house for something else to occupy her time.

Her eyes fell on the cupboard beneath the sink. *Yuck.* Might as well start there.

Three hours later, she'd finished the kitchen, to the sounds of game shows, the news, and the strains of big voices singing pop songs she didn't recognize. Funny that Ms. Lloyd was probably more up on whatever the kids were watching today than she was. Uma couldn't remember the last time she'd sat down and watched TV. Other than the first week in the shelter, she hadn't had the luxury of a television in six months, and before that…before that, she'd been cajoled into watching shows. But that was different. Usually football or cop shows. Joey, "the expert," always talked through everything, criticizing the inconsistencies.

Only ten o'clock. Uma took another look around. Was it worth continuing on to the next room? The clean gleam was so satisfying, she would almost have liked to go on all night. Little grunts emerged from the sleeping form on the sofa, making her decision for her. She put the cleaning things away and turned off the television, then took a deep breath and gently shook the woman.

"Ms. Lloyd?" she said quietly. "Ma'am?"

"Huh? Wha—?" Her boss looked almost like a baby, blinking the sleep out of her huge eyes. A fat baby owl.

"It's ten o'clock, and you fell asleep." Uma's hand remained on the woman's arm, oddly protective.

"Of course I didn't." Ms. Lloyd pushed the hand away, an irritable, old-lady shove, and stood up on her own. "You been cleaning the bathroom this whole time?"

"No. I cleaned the kitchen too. Would you like some help getting upstairs?"

"Of cour… What's that stench?"

"Stench?"

"It smells like… Did you use *bleach*?" She ended on a shrill note, nearly a screech.

"Just in there."

"How in God's name am I supposed to get to sleep with that smell? What were you thinking, girl?"

Uma refrained from mentioning that the stench hadn't stopped her from snoring through hours of scintillating programming. "I could open some windows."

Ms. Lloyd gasped as if Uma had suggested killing her firstborn. "Are you insane? Anyone could get in! You make sure you check the windows and doors every night before bed. Go on. Do it!" Ms. Lloyd shuffled to the back door, unlocked and relocked it, throwing the dead bolt four times, with a belated fifth. Her eyes followed Uma as she moved to the windows and tested locks. "You missed one. Look again."

No. Uma hadn't missed any windows, but she did as requested. "Do it twice if you have to." Every window, every door was locked, relocked, bolted, and double-checked.

Again, Uma caught herself feeling sorry for Ms. Lloyd, finally understanding the extent to which she'd made herself a prisoner in her own home. She wondered what had happened to make the woman need this level of protection, this shell. At first, she'd doubted there was truly a need for live-in help, when a cook or a cleaner would do just as well. It had seemed like a bit of vanity: a minion to do the crappy jobs, someone to push around. But Uma saw how badly Ms. Lloyd needed someone. In exchange for food, a roof over her head, and a few hundred dollars a month, Uma very well might be providing Ms. Lloyd's sole connection to the outside world.

How very, very tragic to be stuck all alone in this frozen, desiccated place.

In the upstairs hall, Ms. Lloyd stopped in front of the

first door and said, "I need you awake tomorrow mornin' at five o'clock sharp. Any lateness will be docked from your pay. Now help me to bed."

~~~

Uma had always been very sensitive to place. Anything remotely off, and she'd lie stewing for hours. The house, with its crammed decorations, dust, and gaping holes where memories should be, was an overwhelming presence, like an overdecorated wedding cake left stale and hulking in a corner long after the big event was canceled. Nothing but a badge of shame to be hidden away.

Uma closed her eyes, trying to force her mind to still. She always envied people who found sleep easily. Joey had been like that. He'd lie down, clamp one arm tightly around Uma's waist, and immediately fall into a deep, perfectly civilized sleep. No tossing or turning for him. Nothing to stain his pristine conscience. For Uma, the quiet, still night was like a vacuum, waiting to be filled with every doubt and worry her brain could offer up.

Insomnia greeted her in that minuscule room, the same as it did anywhere else: racing around her own brain, replaying events, wondering how it all could have come out differently. The dark ate at her, stole her breath, poisoned her thoughts. She wondered if she might die there.

Uma practiced her breathing exercises, teeth clamped tightly onto the meaty part of her thumb, and forced her brain to seek out something good, something positive.

After what must have been hours, she arose from the single bed and pulled a straight-backed chair up to the window.

Although they weren't visible, the foothills of the Blue Ridge were just past the woods and the grassy field out back. This and the place next door were the last homes before the lush, green ground moved gently but inexorably up and up. Beyond the hills were the violet-crested mountains. Country songs and anthems of yore ran through her head as she stared out at the dark. Songs her parents had sung when they were still together. Loving John Denver was one of the few things they'd agreed on.

Her window looked out on the next-door neighbor's house. Ive. Ivan. Ivan the Terrible. Ivan Denisovich? What was that? Maybe something she'd read in high school. Or Ivanhoe. Thoughts of Russia and England ran circles through her brain: a bearded man grimacing and an old film her dad had let her watch, illicitly, while her mom was away on one of her retreats. There were vague images of jousting, aggression, and blood, which fit in nicely with the face she couldn't stop picturing.

It was good, thinking of him. So much better than the alternative.

She imagined the sound of his name in his oddly rough voice. It had crackled when he spoke, like spitting logs in a fire. Ive. Burl Ives and Christmas, children skating, and Norman Rockwell. She pictured the red tricycle in his driveway—something else she would probably never have. She huffed out an annoyed breath at herself.

What do I want anyway? A tricycle in front of a picture-perfect house? A big, scarred lumberjack man with intense eyes and a sweet dog to welcome me home at night?

Who the hell was she kidding? That wasn't even Uma's fantasy, anyway.

Her fantasy was… What was it?

It had been the big city once upon a time. Artists and galleries with her work on the walls. Now…she had no idea. Besides, people like her didn't have sweet babies and lovely houses with flowers and landscaped gardens, husbands who mowed lawns. No, people like Uma made bad decisions, loved the wrong men, and eventually had to run far away from them, only to end up working for sad, old hags.

They had quite a lot in common, Ms. Lloyd and Uma. The woman didn't go outside; that seemed pretty clear. And though Uma may not have been quite there yet, the way her boss had shut herself in, the frantic rituals of her life, were eerily familiar.

Her isolation may have been self-imposed, but that didn't seem to make it any easier to break free. And Uma… Well, she'd been in a prison of her own making. She'd chosen to stay with Joey, despite all signs that she should go.

If she could rip off her skin and start all over again, she would. Before she could become like Ms. Lloyd. Before she could be trapped.

A dull sound cut through the spiral of thoughts dragging Uma down. It was loud enough to distract her from feeling sorry for herself—always a good thing—and repetitive enough to pique her curiosity. The lock on the window turned easily when she twisted it, but sliding the sash up was another story. She pushed and pulled, wanting—no, needing—to breathe the fresh country air. The sound continued, a bright punctuation in the still night, but she didn't dare bang on the window to try to get it unstuck. She sat there instead, face pressed to the cool glass, and wondered.

Only a dim light shone from behind the white farmhouse next door—probably a porch light. In the house, there was no sign of life. But that repetitive noise, so industrious for this late at night, kept Uma on the edge of her seat, filled with curiosity, almost ready to throw on some pants and run out to find its source.

She didn't go anywhere. But she spent long minutes, maybe hours, listening and wondering and then imagining what it could be. What on earth was he up to over there? Chopping wood? Bodies? Strangely, after everything, that notion didn't scare her one bit.

❧

Ive opened up a fifth can of cat food and set it down on the stoop. It was a new flavor, and he wasn't sure how the animals would react, but he liked to mix it up every once in a while. Keep 'em guessing.

It rarely worked, now that he thought about it. They didn't like change any more than he did. But still, it couldn't be good for them to eat exactly the same thing every single day.

There were the five cats he fed on a daily basis. The big one, Ornery, wouldn't let anyone touch her. Even after seven years of Fancy Feast, Ive still couldn't get close. The chickens, the rooster. Then there was the baby skunk, Pepe, who'd recently joined the evening feeding fray. The cats didn't seem to mind the new species, and this one was especially fond of tuna-and-shrimp medley. Little guy fit right in, wanting the same old flavor day after day.

"Not like us, right, Squeak?" he said with a smile. Because Ive did eat the same thing every single day. Not because he didn't like other foods, but why bother changing something if it worked? And okay, so he didn't eat *exactly* the same stuff, but his selections were limited. It depended on what he'd hunted or grown, what the chickens had laid, or what some farmer had given him in trade.

He bent to grab Squeak's bowl, filled it with dry food, and emptied half a can of wet food into it, then topped it off with water from the pump.

Once everyone was fed and had water, his charges going to town with gusto, he thought back to the woman he'd met earlier. He hadn't stopped thinking about her.

Uma.

Ive mouthed the name, enjoying the shape of it on his lips and tongue. Strange name for a strange woman. An intriguing mix of "help me" and "fuck off."

He patted Squeak on the back, enjoying the way the dog leaned into his caress.

Help me up, the woman had ordered, brassy as hell. Trouble. He could smell it a mile away. *And not just the usual kind either*, he thought, although he didn't dwell on what he meant by that.

Trouble. Always trouble. Between the two of them, he and Squeak sure had a nose for it, didn't they? They didn't go looking for it exactly, but they certainly didn't shy away from strays, as was proved by the menagerie chowing down on the doorstep.

Yep, Squeak had a gift. She'd sniffed out Uma, hadn't she? Had known immediately that something was wrong and offered comfort the way only she knew how. Ive pictured how the woman had looked when he'd followed his dog around the side of the house—defeated, tired, scared. He recognized that look, had seen it a hundred times. Matter of fact, that was the exact expression Squeak had worn when he'd taken her from Old Man Huber's place. Son of a bitch had beaten her so bad that Ive had had to carry her straight to Dr. Campbell's clinic. And Squeak was just a puppy.

He closed the door and loped up the drive to his house, needing to release his built-up aggression. It happened every time he got himself a new, injured stray— this anger. Rage so strong, so painful, he had to take care of it the only way he knew how.

Better than doing what he'd done to Huber. Only a tiny bit of guilt marred Ive's conscience over that one. He'd been so good. Hadn't hit anyone outside a ring in more than eight years when he'd heard a puppy's yelps over the fence. It had been bad, though. *Fucking awful.* Squeak and the cats and that other dog—the one Dr. Campbell hadn't been able to save. Jesus. How could you *not* hit a guy like that?

But he hadn't touched anyone in anger since. Steve—the sheriff, of all people—had taught him how to hold back. "You can be as pissed off as you want," he'd told him. "Just gotta learn not to hurt anyone. It'll only get you in trouble. Again." He'd taught Ive to box, then gotten him hooked on Brazilian Jiu-Jitsu. Ive was big, and he'd done some wrestling in high school before he dropped out, which came in handy in the ring.

Like pounding metal, fighting had saved his life.

An hour later, Ive leaned into his heavy bag, stilling it with his full body. He was slick with sweat, and the minute he stopped moving, the chill crept in. He hardly noticed it. Muscles loose, rubbery from exhaustion, his temper still simmered too close to the surface.

He couldn't blame the woman for his feelings. It wasn't Uma's fault what she did to him. She couldn't help that the sight of her, looking so defeated, had ratcheted all his repressed rage up to a boil.

He hated how scared she'd been of him, hated making her shy away. But when she'd held her hand out to him, had lifted her head defiantly despite her obvious fear, something different had entered the mix: admiration. Man, how could you not respect the balls it took for that little, frightened woman to face a big, scary-looking monster like him?

So, yes, he admired her guts. But it was more than that.

That little *Help me up?* was repeating in his mind. And when he thought of her in that moment, it scared the shit out of him. He'd never encountered this particular combination of sensations. She needed help, and he wanted to help her. He already knew that. He'd known it the second he'd seen her crouched down by Ms. Lloyd's house. It was like crack—that certain brand of trouble he'd never been able to resist: a victim of abuse.

What he wasn't comfortable with was the *other thing*. She'd stood up, head held high, chest out, nostrils flared in defiance, and he'd liked *her*. Her warm brown eyes were the kind that looked like they'd get melty in firelight. Even under her baggy clothes, he'd been able to tell she was the kind of round he got off on—more than a handful of tits and ass.

Don't go there.

He pushed off the bag, grabbed his shirt, and mopped under his pits before heading down the steps and back up the drive to his forge. He was conscious, as he walked beside Ms. Lloyd's house, of which window would likely be Uma's. It was dark, which was a relief, because he couldn't think about her up there, awake, maybe watching him. He didn't want to imagine how she'd look in whatever she wore to bed. For some reason, he pictured one of those long, old-fashioned, cotton night-gowns. White, with little, pink flowers. *When did I turn into such a fucking creep?*

Only then did it occur to him that not for one moment, through all of this, had he worried about Ms. Lloyd. The old woman had accepted a new stranger into her home, and he'd taken it for granted that *Uma* would be the victim here, not the other way around. Well, with the way Ms. Lloyd lorded over people, it was probably true. But it gave him a sense of...rightness, somehow, that he'd had a hand in bringing Uma to them. Binx had screwed things up royally with that ad, something he'd never forgive her for, but still, it had worked out.

The clock read midnight when he closed his door. Back in the day, he would have called Steve, challenged him to a late-night sparring session, but the man was getting older and tired more easily.

Oh well. He put on a clean shirt and his apron, stoked the fire, and decided to get to work. Much healthier than heading out into the night for a fight or a fuck.

It sucked, though, because there was something about pounding flesh rather than metal that satisfied Ive's rage better than anything else in the world.

3

UMA AWOKE WITH A START TO YELLING AND THE SOUND OF A cane knocking on wood.

For the first few moments, she was buried alive by panic, fear, and frantic breaths, arms and legs trapped by the weight of unfamiliar wool blankets. When sensation finally coalesced into thought, she managed to claw her way out of sleep and eventually out of bed.

"You open this door now, missy!" the voice yelled, sounding frantic. Ms. Floyd. No, Lloyd. Ms. Lloyd. Her boss.

She stumbled to the door and put her hand up to unlock it before her bleary mind realized what it was seeing—blue, black, and green words marring white arms, the sight still enough to make her sick.

I will not throw up. I will not throw up.

Last night came back in a flash. So hot with the windows painted shut. Claustrophobic. Itchy. In the dark, stripping down to her tank top and underwear, with plans to dress under the blankets in the morning.

Oh God. Breathe. Breathe.

She focused. First, on pushing sound through her tight throat. Miraculously, "Be right there" emerged. Or maybe "Sorry." Whatever she said, it must have been English, because it got a response.

"I will not be kept out of rooms in my own home," Ms. Lloyd screamed. "I won't have it!"

"Coming!" Uma called, tripping her way back to her bed, then rummaging around on the floor for yesterday's clothing.

"Open this door!"

Shirt inside out, jeans unbuttoned, but at least Uma was covered by the time she got the door unlocked.

Ms. Lloyd opened her mouth to speak, no doubt some scathing remark, but then closed it again as, from downstairs, the phone started ringing—a shrill, insistent sound. Ms. Lloyd ignored it.

Big eyes pulled her apart, sweeping top to bottom, seeing more than was comfortable. Uma forced herself to meet the woman's gaze.

After what seemed like ages of birdlike scrutiny, her boss delivered her prognosis. "You look awful."

Something about the insult—perhaps the way it was delivered, or maybe the fact that she'd noticed—was a teeny, tiny thawing on Ms. Lloyd's part.

Predictably, she ruined the moment by saying, "Get properly dressed and help me with my bath."

◈

It took less than twenty-four hours to get into the swing of the new job—for better or worse. It was amazing how quickly you could adjust to a new life, especially one as sedentary as Ms. Lloyd's, where everything that could possibly interrupt the flow of the day had been cut out. There was no room for variation. No excitement, no surprises. No air.

After their breakfast of oatmeal and a single cup of tasteless, gas-station-grade coffee came the morning television marathon. News shows, accompanied by Ms. Lloyd's laments on the stupidity of today's youth, of which Uma was apparently an excellent representative.

The woman was set in her ways and painfully frugal, whether by desire or necessity. Could she afford the few hundred she had agreed to pay Uma every month? Uma suspected it was a stretch to her already strained finances, but you never knew with old people. They'd live their whole lives like paupers and then, after they died, you'd find they'd squirreled away a fortune under the mattress.

A few times that first full day, Uma caught Ms. Lloyd eyeing her, but besides the morning's kerfuffle, there was surprisingly little conflict, as if Uma had undergone her trial by fire and could now rest easy. She didn't quite trust that notion.

She busied herself at work. It was laundry day, thankfully, since the clothes on Uma's back had been worn and worn again. But how to wash her single pair of jeans while still covering herself provided a brief conundrum. She eventually opted for a big towel around her waist— which would have worked out fine if they hadn't gotten a visitor.

When she first walked down the rickety wooden stairs to the basement, arms filled with the overflowing laundry basket and head full of overly specific directions on what not to wash with what, Uma had two thoughts:

How on earth did Ms. Lloyd manage these stairs in her condition? And more importantly, how did the stairs survive the woman's considerable weight?

The basement was weird, paneled in dark wood with a bar at the far end of the room. It smelled of old, moldy carpeting and stale smoke. Buck heads, probably hunting trophies, adorned the far wall. She hardly dared look at the glassy eyes staring at her in blank, creepy vigilance. It was dirty and dank, with an underlying nastiness that had Uma running back up as soon as she'd gotten the load in, towel clutched around her hips, back itching with the sensation that someone or something followed close behind.

At the top of the stairs, Uma hesitated at the door. There were voices on the other side.

"It's fine. She'll do," Ms. Lloyd hissed, and Uma leaned on the basement door, straining her ears.

"You sure? You know you don't have to do this. If you need me to, I can—"

What? Do what, exactly? She pushed her ear hard against the door, and it swung out with a crash, interrupting the conversation and sending blood rushing to Uma's cheeks.

"Oh, well, look at that! Here she is!" Ms. Lloyd chirped.

Uma's heart hitched up to warp speed when she saw the enormous silhouette standing in the front door. *Oh no. This is it. He's here. Joey, here to drag—*

The figure shifted, and perception caught up to reality. It wasn't him...not even close. Joey'd never been so tall or wide or calmly imposing. Self-consciously charming and perpetually wired about summed up Joey, not like this...this...monolith. Calm. Steady. A rock.

Her mental camera snapped a reluctant picture, wanting to memorialize this man's tranquility and bottle it, an antidote to her own messed-up life.

As she focused on the shift in reality, Ms. Lloyd and Ivan focused on *her*: curious, waiting for something—apparently a response to some question.

"I've came to see you, *dear*. Aren't you going to say hello?" What? To see her? And where the hell had that *dear* come from?

"Um. Hello, Ivan."

"You can call me Ive." God, she'd forgotten how intimidating he was. Not just his size, but his presence.

"Sorry. Ive."

"'S okay. Just came by to see how you'd settled in."

Uma had also forgotten how slow and deep his voice sounded.

She responded, oddly mesmerized. "Great. Yeah, good. Everything's just perfect." She snuck a look at his face to catch his eyes riveted to the worn floral terry knotted at her waist.

"New trend?" he asked.

"Laundry day."

"Ah."

Ms. Lloyd wore a little pursed-lipped expression that managed to look both satisfied at Uma's predicament and irritated that she'd taken to wearing her bath towels.

"Well, don't just stand there, Ive, honey. Come inside." Ms. Lloyd pulled him in and locked the door, four and then five times. Always five. "Did you bring the *Gazette*?"

"Oh, darn it," Ivan responded, sounding wooden. His gaze slid to Uma, then back. "They were all out again."

"Hmph. I might have to call old Shady Grady myself and ask him to hold back a copy for me next time. Couldn't possibly be selling out, since the darn thing's a rag, anyway. Not a real journalist in the bunch. And they never did seem to get my ad right."

"Yep. Always somethin', isn't it?" Ivan looked decidedly shifty. "So, you settled in all right, Uma?"

"Yes. Great. Thanks for checking in." The towel around Uma's waist made a bid for freedom. She barely managed to snag it before her shamefully threadbare granny panties became fodder for Ms. Lloyd's ridicule.

"Pleasure." Ivan's eyes rose to the TV bolted to the living room wall, only touching on Uma's struggle briefly before skittering away again. "How's the TV workin' out?"

"Oh, Ive, honey, it's changed my life! I can't begin to thank you enough." Ms. Lloyd was effusive, as lively as Uma had ever seen her.

"Just sittin' there in the house, goin' to waste. No use for it." He shrugged and glanced at Uma again, his cheeks slightly pink. "Least someone's enjoyin' it now."

"I wish you would let me pay you something for it!"

"No, ma'am." He shook his head stubbornly, his eyes returning to Uma's and staying there a beat, then another. The silence lengthened, until Uma's face started to heat, no doubt matching his.

A glance at her boss showed the woman's dark eyes darting between them, full of questions and a barely suppressed glee. Oh, lovely. They were the entertainment: reality TV right there in the entryway.

"Come on in, honey. Have a seat. Irma here can whip us up a fresh pitcher of tea." Uma didn't bother correcting her—her boss knew exactly what her name was. "Unless you want coffee? She can make a fresh pot."

"That's all right. I'm sure Uma's got better things to do." His eyes flicked to Uma then away again. "I gotta take off. Just wanted to…" His voice fizzled to leave a silence that he filled with an open-handed gesture, a hundred times more eloquent than his words. Clearly he was a man comfortable in his body, not his speech.

"Thanks again for checking in," Uma said as brightly as she could. Her voice sounded fake and uncomfortable…a professional voice. The way she used to talk to brides—before. In the kitchen, the phone rang, and with relief, Uma turned to get it.

"Don't touch it!" the older woman snapped.

"Not answerin', Ms. Lloyd?"

"Prank callers again."

Uma opened her mouth. "I could—"

"Leave it be," Ms. Lloyd said over the last steady, sonorous *dring*. "Not calling the police out for this, and no way I'm letting some prank caller bully me into changing a number I've had for thirty years."

"Let me—"

"No thank you, Ive. You've done enough."

"Okay then." Brows raised, he put a hand on the door and tried pulling it open before he remembered it was locked. "I'm right next door if you need anything." He turned to Uma. "If the boss lady here ever gives you time off, come on by for a visit."

"Sure."

"All right." He cleared his throat, stepped onto the porch, and waved. "Take care, Ms. Lloyd. Call if you need anything."

Uma watched briefly from the open doorway as he loped off, taking the porch stairs three at a time. His dog appeared from around the side of the house and fell into step beside him, tail wagging furiously.

As soon as the door was closed and locked behind him, Uma turned to find her boss crowding her, leaning heavily on her cane. "You *did* flirt with him, didn't you? Did you invite him to come over and see you? I won't have it. Men coming and going with you half-naked at the door."

Uma squeezed by her, *truly* angry at the woman for the first time. It was a more solid, honest emotion than she had experienced in days, maybe longer. It was good, clean. Real.

"I didn't invite him over. I barely said *anything* to him." The thought that she'd want to bring men into her life when she was running herself into the ground trying to escape one would have been laughable if it didn't make her so angry.

Ms. Lloyd stared at her with all the power of those wide, disconcerting eyes.

"Frankly, I wouldn't flirt with *any man*, all right? Especially not a married one," Uma went on. "That's not the type of person I am."

"You think—" Ms. Lloyd cut herself off midsentence. "As long as we understand each other. I won't have a home-wrecker living under my roof."

Whatever. The woman had no idea who Uma was or what she'd been through. No idea, damn it. "I'm not a *home-wrecker*." Uma gathered up as much dignity as she could and stalked off toward the kitchen, towel swishing dramatically about her knees.

"And make me lunch, Irma. I'm hungry," Ms. Lloyd called after her.

⤜∾⤛

Ms. Lloyd was not a particularly nice person. By the end of Uma's first full day, that was apparent. But, despite being a pain in the ass of epic proportions, the woman wasn't nearly as threatening as her ad had insinuated. World's bitchiest agoraphobe, maybe, but abusive hag? Not so far. Something didn't quite jibe, and waiting for the other shoe to drop kept Uma on constant tenterhooks.

On tenterhooks was a perfect description of her life since Joey. Long months spent running, always on the lookout, constantly wary. Utterly exhausted.

But for once, she wasn't running or looking over her shoulder, and that letdown, that release—along with the stress of dealing with Ms. Lloyd—turned Uma into a complete wreck by nightfall.

Another night. Already.

And then, worst of all, shower time—by far the hardest part of the evening.

In the bathroom, she set her towel by the shower and took in the lay of the land—memorized it—before turning off the light.

Okay. Pants off first…the easy part. As they did most every night, her hands clenched themselves into tight fists when she reached for her shirt, her body as unwilling as her brain. But, God, she couldn't stay dirty forever.

Painfully unclenching before forcing her fingers to claw at the cotton, then tearing so hard at it the neck scraped back her ears, and she didn't care. What was physical pain when the sight of your own body pulverized your soul? Just its shadow in the dark.

Through the invading moonlight, she took the two steps to the bathtub, blindly scrabbling to turn on the water, then inside, not even waiting for the temperature to adjust, because who gave a shit about something so inconsequential as comfort? Shampoo first—the easy part—then soap, with eyes squeezed shut. But even her eyelids couldn't obliterate the words. She knew they were there. Knew their intricacies intimately, despite never looking. MINE on her wrist. BITCH on both arms. One version misspelled and crossed out, and the rest... more. So much more. All of it burning, burning, burning.

Soon. Soon they'd be gone. It was why she was here, after all.

Water off, she dried herself as quickly as possible and yanked her clothes on over damp skin.

Done. Breathing hard, she went back to her room.

How could the same house, the same room, the same air, all shift so drastically with the setting of the sun? God, why, in the thick of these lonely hours, was she reduced to hashing and rehashing events that she'd never be able to change?

Once the light was out and Uma could hardly see her hand in front of her face, she stripped down to her top and underwear. It was definitely time to invest in some real pajamas—with pants and long sleeves.

Rather than get into bed, she went straight to the window. Because, as darkness fell, her priorities morphed, alongside her fears. The safety of locked doors and stuck windows warred with her desire to escape, to breathe real, fresh air. At those moments, the fear of what lay outside was nothing compared to the torture within her own brain. She wasn't convinced that she'd ever feel true freedom again.

And then the never-ending debate: to sleep or not to sleep. Sleeping meant dreaming. But staying awake meant dwelling on a dire past, a pathetic present, and a hopeless future.

Whatever. In the end, it didn't matter whether she went for option *A* or *B*—nights were hell either way.

The only thing that had staved off her panic the night before had been a certain rhythmic clanging, an echo in the night. Tonight, face pressed to the chilly window, she listened, waiting for its music to begin.

Nothing.

A deep breath in, and her mind started wandering— into safe territory this time: her father. Pops had been steady, regular. He might have been a hippy in the seventies, but somehow, over the years, his beliefs had morphed into something old-fashioned rather than New-Agey. Her mother, on the other hand, had favored more mystical spirituality, based loosely on ancient beliefs.

If she were here, she'd advise that Uma meditate. "It disperses the shadows of doubt," her mom liked to say. Uma knew it wouldn't work, but she tried anyway. She'd try anything right about now.

It was when she sank into the night, let it envelop her in a way that channeled both parents, that she eventually noticed the shadow moving in the dark yard below. She reared back briefly, panic flaring hot and tight in her throat, teeth already sunk deep into her hand, before recognizing the shape for what it was: the dog, Squeak. Sniffing in the grass. The animal squatted before disappearing into the hedge, from which she eventually emerged, head cocked to the side. Uma caught the glimmer of an eye, a pinprick in the night, and then noticed, with a hint of discomfort, that the dog was looking up, right at her window. Her first instinct was to duck down and hide.

She stilled. *It's just a dog.* Besides, she couldn't possibly be visible in the pitch-black room. Could she?

And then, from somewhere behind the house, the sound started, steady, regular…deliberate. A lifeline. A companion. Another soul alive in the dead of night. She sighed, a long, thin, pent-up stream of relief. Eyes floating shut, lungs finally functioning without effort, brain loose, just the tiniest bit comfortable. Little by little, her shoulders relaxed and her head dropped forward again, to lay against the blissfully cool glass.

Bang. A breath in. Bang. Breath out. Bang. Breath in… Bang… Out… For minutes…hours…forever, maybe, she rode the rhythm, thinking of absolutely nothing under the oddly comforting gaze of the neighbor's dog, lulled by the metronome of… What? What was Ivan doing back there? Whatever was behind that sound, she had no idea. Curiosity burned her with its need to know, yet somehow it didn't matter. All that mattered was that steady, metallic drone.

Later, she jolted awake, shocked to find that she'd finally, miraculously succumbed to sleep, face flattened awkwardly against the glass.

Uma's brain rattled with echoes of a disjointed dream—pinpricks of pain, screams, arms caught in a fisherman's net.

Outside was complete silence.

There was a thin line of drool smeared across the window, and beyond the window—

Uma's eyes refocused past the glass and landed on *that man* out there, seated on the steps of his front porch, lit from above, dog at his feet. He was doing something with his hands. Her attention caught on those deftly moving arms. Big and capable. Whittling? No, unwrapping something. Or wrapping. She watched with bated breath as he stood and went up the stairs, then disappeared into the shadows of his front porch.

There followed another sound, duller this time, but as repetitive as the metallic clang. Funny how the deep country quiet shortened the distance between neighbors. *Thunk, creak. Thunk, creak, thunk, creak.* Like a soldier falling into line, Uma's erratic heart once again took to the rhythm he set, needing its regularity, craving it like her lungs craved air.

Part of her wondered what the hell he was up to—but mostly, she didn't care. She just knew she needed that steady beat to get her through the night.

4

UMA'S FIRST EXCURSION INTO THE LITTLE TOWN OF Blackwood was a bittersweet affair. On the one hand, it felt good to be outside, driving with the wind blowing through her hair—an illusion of freedom.

On the other hand, her instinct for survival screamed at her to turn around the moment she left the claustrophobic confines of Ms. Lloyd's house. Out here, Joey was everywhere, hiding in corners, waiting for her to make one wrong move.

But the place was lovely, more village than town. Bank, churches, post office. It was all old and sweet. It came pretty darned close to fulfilling those Perfect American Life fantasies she couldn't claim as her own, and yet…they felt so familiar. The place was small and charming, with railroad tracks and a tiny library in the renovated train station. A small grocery store, a newish coffee shop, and an old diner. What looked like a slightly upscale restaurant, a pizza place, and a bar. She scouted out the thrift shop and admired the tiny city hall and its adjacent park.

If you've got to disappear somewhere, she thought, *it might as well be here.*

The homes she drove past ran the gamut from large and beautiful to quaint to dilapidated trailers forever grounded on cinder blocks. Chipmunk-cheeked, tobacco-chewing men and muumuu-wearing women loitered out front with children, enjoying the last of the warmth before true autumn set in.

It was the perfect fall day, the kind of day that Uma used to live for. She loved the fall, the scent of leaves on crisp, cool air tinged with the smell of wood smoke. It was a masochistic love, since the change in weather always brought a wave of introspection and melancholy. She couldn't stave it off any more than the trees could hold on to their leaves.

This year would be different. This year, it would be much, much worse. Her life had sunk to greater depths, making everything so much stronger and so much harder to bear.

But she'd come to Blackwood for a reason, and with all her boss's errands done, she decided to at least locate the place that had brought her here. Down Main Street, past the post office and a bar, and—

There. There it was: CLEAR SKIN BLACKWOOD. Her breath quickened at the sight of the unassuming sign, and she pulled into a spot a block farther along the road before getting out to double back on foot. Once she arrived in front, it felt weird to loiter in front of the mirrored plateglass window. Besides, Ms. Lloyd would have a fit if she didn't head back soon.

With a shaky breath, she turned back to the car but hesitated in front of the coffee shop. Good coffee and the

chance to mingle with normal people would be just the
thing before returning to Ms. Lloyd's. She had enough
cash for a couple of cups. She'd bring one to her boss,
maybe give her a taste of all she was missing, give her a
good reason to leave her house.

As Uma walked across the small lot, she noticed the
place right next door. MMA SCHOOL, it said, which didn't
mean a thing to her. As she drew nearer, she noticed
a small placard on the door: SELF-DEFENSE CLASSES FOR
WOMEN—INQUIRE WITHIN.

Should she go inside?

Yes.

She walked to the door and pulled. Locked. Damn.
For once, she'd worked up the courage to take a stance,
and the fates were against her. Oh well. It was probably
not meant to be.

The smell of fresh-brewed coffee and pastries washed
over her as she entered the coffee shop. It was big, with
exposed brick walls, huge windows, and lots of glass-
fronted display cases. The girls behind the counter were
skinny and pierced and painfully nonchalant. She ordered
a couple of lattes and turned to check out the crowd while
the baristas brewed and foamed and slouched.

Uma's eyes found him immediately. Ivan—no, Ive—
seated in a corner, his back to the wall, nodding at something a little boy said. The kid was adorable. Dark hair,
like Ivan's, and dimples so deep you'd lose a penny in
them. The boy's eyes weren't visible from where she
stood, but she wondered briefly if they were golden or
blue, or maybe one of each.

When she looked back at Ivan, the humor was
gone from his face. He'd seen her. Even from across

the room, she could feel the weight of his gaze, that stern intensity. He lifted his chin in greeting, and Uma raised her hand shyly in return. There was a third chair at their table—empty, maybe waiting for someone to join them.

At his wave to come over, Uma shook her head and pointed at the door, pasting a smile on her face and hoping fervently that those coffees would come up soon. A close-knit family like that didn't need some awkward, messed-up stranger butting into their lives and dragging them down.

She'd spent an unnatural amount of time thinking about Ivan the night before, and the one before that. Listening to the sounds he made, she'd pictured herself living in that big, lovely house and wondered what it would be like to be with a guy like that—someone so raw, with none of his edges smoothed out. Someone so the opposite of Joey.

When he waved again, Uma gritted her teeth through a strained smile and turned away, wishing she'd never come in here. Wishing that Blackwood weren't such a small town. Maybe also wishing she could, for a second or two, relax enough to walk past everyone and sit down next to Ivan, as if she belonged there.

I want to belong.

"Two lattes for Uma," a voice called. *Phew.*

With relief, she grabbed the coffees and headed for the door, nearly crashing headlong into a gorgeous brunette. The woman held it open for her with a smile before sailing inside. As she escaped, the kid yelled, and Uma turned to see him throw himself into the woman's arms. It was her, *the wife*. A beauty for the beast.

Something shriveled in Uma's chest. She flushed. This woman wasn't at all what Uma'd pictured. Ive's wife was sleek and confident. Modern in a way that didn't quite fit the man. Her tank top and easy white skirt were perfect for the sticky weather. In contrast, Uma felt overdressed. Like she was hiding something. A woman like that—a work of easy perfection—would take one look at her and decide that she was a charity case in need of fixing. The idea pissed her off, getting her so worked up that she whispered, "I'm nobody's project, damn it."

As she reached the car, someone called from behind her. "Hey, wait."

With a sigh, Uma turned to face him. A fresh cut on his forehead, to go with the bruise on his cheek, made him look even more like a thug than she'd remembered. The man wore cuts and bruises like his wife wore jewelry.

"You doin' okay?"

She nodded. He'd followed her out here. Why not send his wife instead? He was clearly not comfortable talking, and yet he'd made the effort. *Why?*

A wild thought splintered off. *I wonder what they talk about at night, in bed.*

"Ms. Lloyd treatin' you right?"

She nodded again and looked away from his messed-up eyes—too intense, too weirdly beautiful out here in the bright fall sunlight, where anyone could see.

Maybe he and his wife don't talk at all, the rogue notion went on.

He hesitated before finally saying, "Good."

Maybe they spend all their time fucking like bunnies. Where had that come from? *Enough.*

He looked like he had something else to say, but Uma stopped him. "I'll let you get back to your family."

"Oh. Right. You want to—"

"I'd better go." She nearly wrenched her arm closing the car door, then took off, getting as far from him as she could. Far from those eyes and those thoughts she couldn't seem to control.

Yet as Uma drove off, watching him shrink in her rearview mirror, rather than give a sigh of relief, her body slumped with something resembling disappointment.

～∾～

"Who's that, Ivey?" Ive's sister, Jessie, swung her hair over her shoulder in that way she had.

"New neighbor."

"What's her story?" Her eyes were bright with curiosity.

"Not sure."

"Why'd she run away from you like that?" Gabe chimed in, as usual, pinpointing the one thing that had bothered Ive the most.

Why *had* she run from him? They were in public, after all. It's not like he was planning on hunting her down and dragging her back to his lair. He'd been with Jessie and Gabe, for Christ's sake. She had to have noticed Gabe, at least.

"Guess I'm kinda scary lookin'."

Jessie said, teasingly snide, "You can say that again."

"You see me enterin' any beauty contests lately?"

"No, but you *could* make more of an effort."

"What? I'm in shape."

"You're in shape, Ivey, the way cavemen are. A

big, hairy bag of muscles. Not exactly what I'd call comforting."

He shrugged. The way he looked had never bothered him before. Didn't seem to matter in Blackwood. People knew him here, knew his story, where he came from, what he did.

What he'd done.

Nobody bothered him. And he liked it that way. But this time, he frowned.

"Like that. Right there." Jessie pointed. "You make faces like that, and people think you're out to kick butt. No wonder she ran away when you tried to talk to her."

"Look, are we done with this? I got work to do."

"Hey, I know how hard it is for you to stop working long enough to pay us a visit, but the least you can do is sit here for a few minutes and talk. Pretend you're civilized." Jessie placed a placating hand on his forearm, and he forced himself to relax.

It was that woman. *Again.* All four times he'd seen her, he'd gotten antsy. Last night, when he'd glanced up at Ms. Lloyd's place, he'd spotted her leaning against one of the upstairs windows, looking like a ghost. Or a prisoner. He'd wanted… What? What the hell did he want? To storm the battlements? Save her? Maybe beat the shit out of whoever made her so scared all the time?

Yeah. Probably that. Definitely that.

He was ready to bite Jessie's head off for pointing out the truth. There was no doubt she'd bite him right back. And the last thing he wanted to do was stir up family trouble. Not here. Not in front of Gabe. Not ever.

Still. He couldn't get Uma's haunted, hunted eyes out of his head.

"Somethin's happened to her," said Ive. "I can tell."

"Maybe we can help her."

"Yeah!" Gabe chimed in. "We'll fix her!"

Ive looked at them both and couldn't help but feel warm. He didn't have many friends, didn't trust many people, but these two—his family—he would trust with his life. They'd do anything for him, and vice versa.

"Not sure she's got the kind of trouble you can just fix," he said, giving Jessie a look.

"No," she agreed. "But maybe you can be there when she's ready to fix herself."

He nodded, staring out the window and wondering, for the millionth time, what had been done to Uma to make her so damn scared.

5

"PIGGY, PIGGY, YOU'RE A PIG, PIG, PIG." MS. LLOYD SNORTED in Uma's face, proving yet again that she wasn't so much an old hag as a twelve-year-old. Especially when it came to playing games. The Black Widow did not like to lose.

"Why am I only a pig when I'm winning?" Uma asked.

"Because I'm your boss." The woman managed to sound simultaneously reasonable and demented. "When I win, you're just a dumb-ass."

Uma threw down her last card, again victorious.

"Oh *hell*. Another hundred for me."

Playing for stakes had been Ms. Lloyd's idea, but playing for time off was Uma's. "That's two half days off," she said as nonchalantly as she could. Best not to get her boss worked up. The woman was a sore, sore loser, and Uma really needed time away if she ever wanted to get inside that clinic—her whole reason for being here.

"Oh, no, you little cheater. I want a rematch." The woman was insatiable. It made sense. What the hell else did she have to look forward to? They played again and again, but Uma still finished a couple days up. Ms. Lloyd was not happy.

After lunch, Uma waited until the older woman had settled in front of the TV before springing it on her. "Can I get you anything from town?"

"You're not going anywhere, missy."

"If you'll recall, I earned a full day away from here."

"You can't just—"

"I'm cashing in a half day as of right now."

"You can't go. The grout needs cleaning."

"The grout? Are you kidding me?"

"Don't sass me, missy. That tub's been—"

"The grout'll hold another twenty-four hours, Ms. Lloyd. I'm going."

"No, you—"

"Care to join me?"

"Don't be ridiculous, Irma. What would I do out there?" Indeed. What could a person possibly need outside these four walls? "Well, just know, if you're too late, you're not getting in here."

"What's too late?"

"This door doesn't open after dark. Ever."

A long look confirmed that Ms. Lloyd was serious.

Great, she thought while driving to the skin clinic. As if this outing weren't nerve-wracking enough, she had the threat of being locked out hanging over her head.

When she entered Clear Skin Blackwood, the waiting room was empty. It was comfortable, an oasis done in tones of blue and green. Calming colors. The decor was doctor's office chic, the receptionist friendly and eager to help.

"Hi there. Do you have an appointment?"

"Yes." She cleared her throat, unexpectedly emotional now that she had reached her final destination. "I mean, I called, and I was told I didn't need to make an appointment. You, or someone, said I should walk in. I heard Dr. Hadley on the radio. Her interview about the free care for people who've suffered from..." Uma didn't even know how to describe what had been done to her. She'd only ever spoken of it in euphemisms. She'd never said it aloud. Not to anyone. "I called, and you confirmed that you'd see me. Or someone did. Said I could come in and ask for, um, Dr. Hadley. That she would help me."

"Oh. Oh, of course." The receptionist's eyes got huge. They clearly didn't get a lot of people like Uma in here. "Please, have a seat, ma'am. I'll go speak with the doctor. I'm sure she'll want to talk to you."

Uma sat, overwhelmed by exhaustion. She'd made it to the end of her voyage. Then why did this feel like the beginning? She waited, at once too tired and too jacked up to distract herself with a magazine. *Ma'am*, she thought. *She called me ma'am.* It made her feel old.

The receptionist returned to the sitting room. She looked flustered, excited curiosity brightening her eyes. Mixed with pity, maybe? *Am I the reason she looks so keyed up?* The thought made Uma feel like a freak.

"Here you are, ma'am." She pressed a warm cup into Uma's hand. "Ginger tea. It's what we drink here."

Here? Like in the offices? Or like in Blackwood?

The receptionist hesitated for a moment, fiddling with magazines and flapping around, looking like she wanted to sit down, maybe have a chat.

"Hear about the cold snap down from the north?" the receptionist asked.

"Uh, no," Uma said, and with no more conversation forthcoming, the woman headed back to her cubby, disappearing behind the desk. While she waited, Uma imagined eyes on her, the woman wondering.

A couple of people entered, signed in, were called to the back. About fifty times, she thought about leaving, and fifty times, she talked herself down. This was it, why she'd risked coming back to Virginia, so close to Joey, why she'd agreed to wait hand and foot on Ms. Lloyd.

After an anxious half hour in the waiting room, watching the sun set outside, the inner door opened, and a woman in scrubs came out. She glanced around before her eyes settled on Uma.

"Would you like to come on back?"

She concentrated on the woman's narrow back and dark hair as they walked. Self-imposed tunnel vision.

So much hinged on this visit, possibly on this initial conversation. Again, she felt the urge to leave, to rush back to Ms. Lloyd's and hide. Never come back.

Too late for that. She followed the woman's scrub-clad form into the back, adrenaline making her buzzy and strange. Scared of what they'd say but floating on a weak surge of hope. If this worked, Uma might become a normal person again. She couldn't imagine the possibility.

"Come on in and have a seat, Miss..." The woman looked at Uma expectantly.

"Smith," she lied.

The woman's nod confirmed she'd accept whatever she was told. There was no appointment on the books, and they'd ask few questions. Curiosity, but no pressure.

These women, this place, they were trying to help people like Uma. She *hated* that she needed their help.

"I'm Purnima."

Sanskrit name, Uma thought, unsurprised. The woman was beautiful, gentle looking. She'd known a Purnima growing up—a good friend of her mother's once upon a time. What had become of her?

"The doctor will be right in," she said. "Can I get you anything while you wait?"

Uma shook her head and tried to smile.

Another short wait. Uma tried to distract herself by studying the room. In a half-assed effort at camouflaging the medical feel, the walls showed photos of the earth from space. There was a basket of sunblock samples, and she was tempted to take one, even though she couldn't imagine baring herself enough to need it. She couldn't even look at herself. How could she possibly ask anyone else to do so?

Oh, shut up.

She grabbed a couple anyway. Might as well protect her face. It was her only remaining commodity, after all.

On the wall behind her was a poster comparing different types of melanoma. Uma turned away from that. No need to see more blemishes.

The door opened after a brisk knock, showing a woman much younger than she'd imagined. Too young to be the doctor, surely. Uma had to reevaluate the mental image the doctor's voice had conjured on the radio the week before. She'd pictured a wise, older woman, not someone close to her own age.

Sunny and blond. She didn't look like her story. This

woman looked too innocent, too wholesome to have been hurt, marked, branded like cattle.

Panic streaked a cold swathe through Uma. Was it all a complex lie? A ploy to get women like her in here and then back to where they belonged? Back to the men who'd abused them?

Dr. Hadley must have seen something in her face, because she waited before speaking. She seemed to understand that Uma required time to evaluate, adapt, and adjust—or whatever the hell other touchy-feely shit she'd need to do to get through this. Did they teach people in med school how to deal with cases like her? The ones who were so fucked up they were more like stray cats than humans? Desperately in need of help, but no damn good at accepting it?

The doctor sat and put down her pen and pad, pausing briefly before pulling off her lab coat, unbuttoning her cuff, and rolling up her sleeve.

"Mine was right here," she said, jumping right into it. "You can see a tiny bit of scarring, but it's pretty much gone." She watched Uma closely. "I had another that I won't show you, but it's even better than this. On my belly. I can wear a bikini now. Not that I do, but…" She smiled gently. Her skin looked immaculate. White and beautiful, with the faintest shadow of some ugly memory she'd chosen to erase. "You're breathing a bit fast. Do you need a paper bag?"

Uma shook her head.

"More tea?"

She hesitated and then nodded. Maybe a moment alone would help.

The doctor got up and left the room, reappearing

moments later with two mugs. Real ceramic this time instead of the flimsy paper the receptionist had used. Uma's had a stick figure doing a happy dance, with the words *I pooped today* scrawled across it. She let out a huff of laughter.

Dr. Hadley smiled, showing perfect white teeth, and then cut to the chase. "Want to tell me about it? Or show me? We can talk as little or as much as you like."

Uma started breathing fast again. Embarrassed, but incapable of tamping down the panic. One hand flew to her mouth, and she bit down, vaguely aware of how crazy it must look.

"Or you can take my card and call me when you're ready."

Uma nodded. The doctor mirrored the movement and sipped calmly at her tea. Some part of Uma's brain—the part that could think clearly through the panic—wondered if this woman had already been a doctor when it had happened to her, or maybe she'd become a dermatologist because of it.

"I…" Uma's lungs struggled to suck in a thin stream of air, two, three. She shut her eyes. "I can't even look at myself. In a mirror. Or…definitely not in person. I'm *disgusting*," she finished on a whisper.

With an effort, she pried her eyes open, enough to see a bit of blue peeping out from under her massive watch. Turning away, she pulled the watch off and held her wrist up to the doctor. Baring four ugly block letters: MINE.

Uma didn't look—couldn't. She knew what was there, knew how stark it appeared against her pallor. Dark, violent streaks embedded into her. One word of many.

Every time she caught a glimpse, she relived that specific moment, that particular punishing hour. A piece of her past stolen, along with her body.

For Uma, more than most, her skin held her history. A part of it she would never be allowed to forget. Other scars faded, but not these—they were a constant reminder of how messed up her life was.

She heard her breath shaking as if from far off. Then there was the other woman's hand cool and firm against her skin. Compassionate but still assessing.

Strange how her brain flew to the last person who'd touched that skin. The neighbor. Ivan. Uma liked the name Ivan for him. Ive seemed too…incomplete, like an unfinished thought. And he was the opposite of that—the man seemed so utterly whole.

Dr. Hadley's touch was soft and comforting but lacked the calming power of Ivan's bigger, rougher hand. For the briefest of moments, she wondered how it would feel to bare her skin to that enormous, frightening-looking monster. Get him to hold her, maybe let her disappear into the steady beating of his heart, the way she lost herself in his nighttime percussion.

Would her body shock him?

No.

He looked like nothing would surprise him. A supremely comforting thought.

The doctor ran her fingers over the letters, stroked them with none of the clinical coldness Uma had expected from this encounter.

"We can do this," she said, placing Uma's hand back gently in her lap. "Any others?"

Uma swallowed with a wet click, accompanied by the

loud crinkle of paper on the examination table beneath her. The sound was jarring in the silence.

With clammy hands, Uma grabbed at her sleeve.

"Would you like a gown?"

"No."

If the doctor left the room to get a gown, Uma would lose every last shred of courage she'd built up. It was now or never. She dragged the thick cotton sleeves up to reveal both arms. The breath the doctor sucked in could be felt more than heard.

Oh God. I can't do this, Uma thought, flinching away, focusing on the ceiling, the floor, the earth poster on the wall—anywhere but at the mess of jagged lines her body had become.

"May I?"

"Okay," whispered Uma.

Dr. Hadley's fingers trailed over nearly every inch of Uma's arms, mapping the pain scrawled there. The woman exuded empathy, a gentle balm, as she catalogued the wrongs done. "This looks fairly recent."

Uma nodded slightly, swallowed hard on the emotion filling up her throat, and responded, "Six months."

"All of them?"

"Yes. They were all done on the same night. Except for one."

For all that time, Uma had avoided them. Months without seeing herself. Months of denial. They looked new in this blinding, white light. Raw. She was nothing but a gaping wound. Her skin festered out in the open.

"Oh no—" She gagged and lurched off the table. A trash can was pressed into her hands, and that day's green bean casserole made a painful reappearance, scraping against her throat, pushing tears out through her eyes. Funny that the only time she'd managed to cry during the six worst months of her life, it wasn't even real tears.

The hand on her back was soft and smooth. It tightened on her shoulder, then disappeared before reappearing with a box of tissues.

"I'm so sorry," Uma managed to say through lips that were stiff with embarrassment.

"Don't be. Please." Dr. Hadley's warm, solid hand held her naked arm—the ugliest skin the woman had probably ever seen. "Please."

Uma looked in her eyes and cringed at the sheen of tears there. *She can cry for me. So why can't I?*

"Have you reported this? Called the police?"

"No. I can't." It came out louder than intended.

Rather than argue, Dr. Hadley nodded, then took back the trash can. "Can I put this outside?"

"Thanks." The moment was mortifying on so many levels.

"Do you have a safe place to stay?"

Uma nodded.

"Are there more?"

"Yes." She swallowed again. "Yes. A couple more. My belly, my legs, and my…" She waved her hand in front of her chest vaguely, too ashamed to admit to what hid under her bra.

"It's going to be a long process. Newer tattoos can be a bit more intensive. But we'll take care of you."

She nodded, again overwhelmed at the emotion piercing through the embarrassment.

"We'll need several sessions. Lots of factors are

involved, such as how old they are and the color of the ink. Because most of them are new…" She looked a question at Uma, who pointed at her upper back.

"The professional one on my back is older."

"Okay. Well, this is going to take months. Can you do that? Do you have a place to stay for the next few months?"

Months. *Months* hiding out with Ms. Lloyd, enduring her quirks, her bitchiness. "I—Yes… Yes."

At Uma's expression, the other woman hurried on. "The treatment is no charge. We'll take care of you. Could you maybe come evenings? Weekends?"

"Yes. Whenever you can fit me in."

The doctor pulled down Uma's sleeves so Uma didn't have to. Would she ever be able to face her own body?

"And I don't have money now, but I'd like to pay for—"

"Please don't worry about that. I am so sorry this happened to you." Dr. Hadley took Uma's cold hand in her warm one. Like a lump on the hard vinyl of the examination table, Uma sat, shoulders bowed beneath the weighty legacy of all that ink.

But she'd bared herself to this woman, if only partially, and damn it, she'd survived. To have that person be sympathetic to her plight, to understand at least some of what she'd suffered, without pitying her… It was deeply comforting. She shut her eyes and imagined tears rolling down her face, sobs filling the void.

"I'm glad to meet you, Miss Smith."

"It's Uma. Uma Crane."

"I'm glad you came to us, Uma. I'm George. We're going to take good care of you here."

Uma believed her. This woman would take care of her skin, of that she had no doubt.

It was the rest that she worried about—the small, shriveled heart of her, deep down inside. Because that, she knew, was what she'd become. Just a shriveled little raisin of a heart. Despite this woman's kindness and the relief her promises of help brought, at her very core, Uma suspected that the pain would never really go away.

~∾~

Night had fallen, and the lights were on at the place next door when Uma emerged, still shaky, from the doctor's office.

Great. Unless she'd been bluffing, Ms. Lloyd wouldn't let her back into the house. She must have been kidding, though, right?

Uma took a couple of steps along the sidewalk, dazed and a little lost. What would she do if her boss didn't let her back in?

Sleep in my car.

It wouldn't be the first time—and it probably wouldn't be the last. Resigned to the idea, Uma moved forward, only to encounter the door to the martial arts place, propped open in invitation.

Should she do it?

Yes, she thought. *Do it.*

The idea appealed. It would be something to help distract from the pain of digging up all the horror of her life. Something to make her forget it all before facing the long, dark hours of night—whether in a tiny room or a car. She'd just endured one of the hardest hours of her life. She could do this. She could do anything.

This is it. Do it.

Uma walked inside, greeted by a gust of warm, gym-tainted air. It was a universal scent. She'd never been to a gym that didn't smell of rubber, socks, and sweat. There was no camouflaging it.

The woman at the front desk looked familiar, although Uma couldn't imagine where she'd seen her, having been in town less than a week.

"You here for the self-defense class?"

"Um, just to get some information, please."

"You're in luck! Come on in and take a class with us. I teach it. I'm Jessie."

"I can't do it today." What she really meant was *I can't afford it*, but she wasn't about to admit to that.

"First session's free. Come on, try it out. Starts in"—Jessie glanced at the clock on the wall behind her, and Uma's eye noticed her earring, a small, tasteful diamond—"about fifteen minutes."

Uma's hand went automatically to her own naked lobe, and she thought of everything she'd left behind: *my entire life*. As far as possessions were concerned, Uma was only a few garments from being naked. She'd arrived in Blackwood devoid of possessions. Like being reborn. She almost liked that thought.

"I don't have workout clothes."

"You can wear what you've got on. Next time, if you decide to come back, maybe some yoga pants and a T-shirt, but you're fine for tonight."

"Do you have a brochure or something? I've really got to go."

The woman handed her a card, and Uma left.

Minutes later, she stood on Ms. Lloyd's front porch,

pounding on the door, with cold feet and a strong sense of déjà vu. A glance at her watch told her it was after six. Definitely past dinnertime, according to her boss's rigid schedule, and the woman had left the porch light off. A sure sign of the kind of night Uma was in for.

"Go away!" the voice called through the door.

"It's cold out here, Ms. Lloyd."

"Yeah, well, you should have thought of that before you went gallivanting off and left me here to fend for myself, shouldn't you?"

"Please let me in."

"You can come back tomorrow."

"I've got no place to sleep."

"That's not my problem."

Uma dropped her head to the door. "Please. It's freezing out here!"

"You wanted the evening off—well, you got the whole night. You should feel lucky. It'll give you something to think about next time you try to skip out on your job."

"Would you mind throwing me my things? Please?" A perfectly good jacket hung in Uma's closet.

"Nuh-uh. How else can I guarantee that you won't go running off on me? No. You can get your stuff in the morning. Now git!"

Through the door, Uma listened to the *thump thump* of her cane as the woman shuffled away, followed by the exuberant trumpet call of the evening news. Should she continue knocking, just to drive her crazy? Probably not. She wouldn't put it past Ms. Lloyd to call the cops on her.

When did it get so cold? she wondered, shivering as she turned to eye the darkness beyond, hating to leave the porch and the slight shelter it provided. Her thoughts landed, for a millisecond, on the house next door, where she imagined Ive having dinner with his wife and kid, but even from here, she could see it was dark.

Not that she would have had the courage to knock anyway.

6

WITH FEW OPTIONS, UMA DROVE BACK DOWNTOWN. SHE tried the door of the skin clinic. Closed. A glance next door showed the martial arts school still wide open.

No more excuses, then. She walked inside.

"You're back!" said Jessie before handing her a form to fill out.

She put her name as Uma Smith, using Ms. Lloyd's address, removed her shoes, and moved into the room, where a couple of men fought on a mat.

The place was cavernous, larger than you'd guess from the street, and sparse. A male space if she'd ever seen one. Floor-length punching bags hung in a corner of the room, along with a few sets of heavy-looking weights and benches. Toys for boys.

Her eyes moved back to the pair fighting.

The one whose back was to the room was huge. They apparently grew them big around here. Both men wore padded head protectors, which covered their ears and left only their faces open. The little one did something with his leg, whipping it out in a surprisingly quick kick, and they both ended up on the mat. Uma stepped back with a start.

They went from kicking and punching to what looked like complicated wrestling, legs everywhere, bodies wrapped tightly around each other. It was almost tender before it got violent again.

They rolled, then got stuck in a complex knot of straining limbs and grunts. The smaller guy fought hard but was quickly overwhelmed, faceup on the floor, with the big guy above, covering him. *Wow.* Uma forced her breath to slow, through a blend of fear and something different—exciting and titillating and almost…erotic.

"Awesome, isn't it?" Jessie said from beside her. Uma barely spared her a glance. "They're clearly not the same weight class, but it's slim pickin's around here for training partners. These guys have been fighting each other for years."

Uma nodded to be polite but kept her eyes glued to the action.

"We cover some of this stuff in class."

The smaller guy pushed up hard into the other one's chin, then wrapped his legs around him, catching his head in a painful-looking choke hold.

"Oh Christ," Uma said aloud, repulsed by the violence but entranced by the image they presented.

"Well," the woman chuckled, "variations on this."

She finally looked at Jessie. "I wouldn't mind learning how to do that." Her voice came out a tad breathless.

"You've come to the right place, then." She moved up to the edge of the mat and stomped hard on the floor, twice. "Okay, guys! I got ladies lining up here, chompin' at the bit to get started. And it's not to look at your ugly mugs."

Uma glanced back toward the door and was surprised to see that several women had indeed arrived. They were taking off shoes, shooting the breeze, stretching on another mat. The stragglers shivered as they entered, and all everyone seemed to want to talk about was the cold snap. The idea of having to interact with them made her regret the impulse that had brought her in here. At the same time, she knew she wouldn't leave. Not with the way her heart raced, not with this messy mix of anticipation, fear...excitement. Besides, where the hell was she supposed to go? With the coming cold, the best thing she could do was stay inside.

The men high-fived into a hug. Then the big one turned and...

It was that man again. Ivan.

He pulled off his headgear as he approached, followed by Jessie and the other guy. His face changed when he spotted Uma. From relaxed and smiling to serious. He stopped a few steps away.

"Hey, Uma. Good to see you again," he said.

"Hi."

"You doin' self-defense with Jessie?" Ivan reached back and grabbed the woman behind her shoulders in a squeeze that looked slightly too tight. Not waiting for a response, he went on, "This is Jessie. Jessie, I told you about Uma."

It all came back to Uma then: the coffee shop, the kid, this woman walking in. *Of course.* She watched as Jessie wended her hands around Ivan's arm and twisted so she ended up outside his hold, rather than inside it.

On tiptoes, she threw her arm around his neck in a choke hold of her own.

"Don't ever let 'em get the better of you, Uma," Jessie said with a wink before pushing away to the center of the room. "All right, ladies, let's get started. Line up on the mat, please. We're going to begin with a little warm-up and then go into some simple evasion techniques."

Uma inserted herself into the back row, unable to stop her gaze from returning to Ivan. He left the mat, catching her eye before disappearing into a back room. She looked away a second too late, embarrassed to have been caught staring.

When Ivan and the other guy reemerged a half hour later, his messy hair was damp, curling around his face and the nape of his neck. He looked freshly showered and healthy, dressed in a tight T-shirt, with sweatpants that must have been a couple of decades old. Uma tried to ignore him, but the man was true north to her wandering eyes.

Like a car crash, she thought wryly. *I don't want to watch him, but I can't look away.*

"It looks like it's that time again, ladies. Our guys are back. Let's put our moves into situations we might encounter with real-life attackers." Jessie turned to the men. "Get your bottoms over here, boys."

Oh hell no. No, no, nonono. Uma barely caught herself before saying it aloud. She'd done okay with the other women, but this was touching men and pretending and—

No. No way.

"Ladies, as you know, here we have Ive and Steve, our handy man-puppets for the evening. They look mean and ugly—especially the big one—but it's nothing we can't handle, right?"

The women responded with a few raucous catcalls as the two men walked toward them. Uma's eyes caught Ivan's for a moment and shifted away.

Chicken. She faked bravado, forcing herself to look back. *A strong woman. That's what I am. Fearless.*

Their gazes met and held until her face must have turned the same shade of fuchsia as her sparring partner's shirt. The color looked fabulous on the other woman. Not so sure about her face.

"Okay, we're going to get out of a wrist grab. Let's show these guys what we've learned. Monica, you go with Ive, and Anne C., head over to Steve." They all moved to the center of the room and started in on their new moves. Everything was different—heightened—now that the men were back here. Uma kept her eyes riveted on Anne and Steve, avoiding the sight of Ivan's muscles shifting beneath his absurdly tight shirt.

"Great. Now, Penny! Get up there and show us what you got. Anne Riley? Why don't you try it?"

Jessie was working her way down the line, with Uma at the end. The wait was agony. *I can't do it. I can't. I won't.*

Penny and Anne finished up, and the next two went. Binx and somebody else. Uma stopped remembering their names and concentrated instead on preparing.

Okay, okay. She could do this. She could let a man touch her. In fact, this wouldn't be any different from when Ivan had held her hand. She wouldn't be intimidated by him.

That wasn't his goal though, was it? Intimidation.

That part was all in her head. The man might look scary, but so far, all he'd done was act inviting and friendly.

"Uma?" Jessie's voice broke through her thoughts. "You feel ready to try it out?"

No. "Sure," she said, the image of nonchalance. Maybe. She glanced at Ivan and looked immediately away.

"All right, let's partner you up with Steve. Ive, you and Monica can start."

Steve? Not Ivan? What a relief. *Right?*

And then the *real* fear kicked in.

Oh, Steve was nice about it, but Uma's hesitation was obvious. He didn't push, didn't pressure. But the first time he moved, she lurched back and bleated, like some pathetic barnyard animal. He was small compared to Ivan, and older, but he looked strong.

A man like him could hold her down, force her face into the floor, grind the imprint of the cold mat into her cheek. He'd cover her windpipe with his soft Italian leather loafer and show her with a twist of the heel how easy it was to crush the life out of a woman. With one hand, he could yank—

"I got this, Steve." Ivan broke through the flashback and muscled it aside, the tendrils of his deep, dark voice oozing around the images and pulling them apart. Behind Uma, he was real and robust enough to chase the memories away. "Need a break?" he asked, close but not overwhelming. She couldn't be sure whether she nodded or not.

Somehow she ended up at the back of the room, listening to the water dispenser *glug* in a way that was oddly reminiscent of how his words churned out—slow and solid and one rounded syllable at a time. His hand held a paper cup to her mouth, and water trickled into her parched throat. He was the third person to shove liquids at her that evening. She must have looked thirsty.

She was sitting on the floor beside him, his hand a cool, reassuring weight on the back of her neck, the innocuous view of the mat between her bent legs. There was a worn spot, where threads peeped through. Uma worried at it with numb fingers, pulling at the threads until one broke off, and it occurred to her that she was thoughtlessly destroying property.

He released her neck, and a waft of air reached her, fresh from his body. She smelled something woodsy mixed with sweat. *Man soap*, she thought. She hated herself for how weak she'd become. This was all wrong—not at all how her new life was supposed to be. She was supposed to be fearless and strong.

"I'm sorry."

He grunted.

"I can't believe I did that. It's just…" Uma cleared the tightness out of her throat and grasped at the paper cup shoved into her hand. After a sip, she mumbled, "Embarrassing. Sorry."

"Quit that," he rumbled softly.

"Sorry."

He sighed, sounded like he'd say something else, then settled for a second grunt.

"I guess I'll go." She set the cup aside and pushed up to standing, then stopped when his hand landed lightly on her calf. She looked down, met his eyes, and the room tilted. His hand tightened, but he didn't stand.

"Stay."

"Oh, no, I—"

"I'll help you. Come on." He got up and moved a few feet farther onto the mat, and she followed, like a sleepwalker.

Ivan led her through it again, attacking without touching or any hint of aggression. The movements were purely mechanical—a lean in, a counter. She swept her wrists in, up, and out, and he stepped away. It couldn't possibly be that easy in real life, but it was progress.

She didn't dare look at the rest of the class, didn't want to see the pity on their faces.

Jessie's voice rang out, telling the other ladies to move on to the second move. She and Steve were acting as attackers. Uma looked up to meet the curious gaze of one woman, Binx, whose eyes flicked between her and Ivan.

"Ignore 'em."

The second round involved a different kind of move altogether—what Jessie called an arm bar. A hand to the shoulder, countered by the brutal twisting back of the attacker's arm. There would be more invasion of personal space this time, inevitably, their closeness underlining what a sweaty mess she'd become in her long-sleeved shirt and jeans.

"Ready?" he asked. She nodded once and waited for him to step straight in, less than an arm's length away.

His hand landed gently on Uma's shoulder, but it might as well have been on her breast for the effect it had. Electrified by the contact, she grabbed and twisted.

"Follow through, Uma," Jessie called out, bringing her back into the class, back to reality. "He's a lot bigger than you."

No shit.

"Remember, ladies, you need all the momentum you can get with an attacker this much larger than you. Try it again, and put your body into it this time."

His hand was too low, too real. Uma wanted to shrug it off. Instead, she grabbed and twisted, followed through with her other hand and then her body, pressed into his. She ended with her face along his side, under one arm, in a place too intimate and warm for a room this bright, an audience this big—including *his wife*.

She could smell him again, that man-smelling soap, augmented by a light hint of sweat and a smoky metallic twang. Uma stumbled and leaned further into his body, grazing her chest against his elbow.

He stood her upright and muttered, "Good," but his eyes weren't on her face. She followed them to her arm, where a cuff had slid back to reveal the dark lines of a tattoo. Uma moved it behind her back and yanked the sleeve down.

She couldn't even look at him then, didn't want to see the disgust or the horror on his face. On everyone's faces. The pressure of tears prickled behind her eyes.

Great. My body decides to break its crying strike in front of a room full of people. She shoved the emotion down and stepped away.

"You good?" he finally asked.

"Yeah. I'll just…be right back." She escaped to the restroom.

After five minutes of internal debate, Uma managed to convince herself that it didn't matter what he or anyone else may have seen. They were tattoos. Just tattoos. There were tattoos all over the place. These people wouldn't have any idea how they'd gotten there or what they signified.

When Uma returned, no one paid attention to her. Except for Ivan, whose eyes followed her to the mat.

Again, she was hyperaware of him. Wherever he was, whatever he was doing, she could feel him. After a while, Jessie finally let the guys go and finished things up with a series of stretches. As soon as class was over, Uma grabbed her shoes and slid into them without untying them, ready to go.

Around her, the women chattered about class, then other things, like children and husbands, work, and plans for a quick drink at a local bar. Uma shook her head at their invitation, ignored the curious looks, ducked her head, and made a beeline for the exit.

They seemed nice. Jessie in particular. Her humor, her strength, the way she clearly didn't take crap from anyone, especially not her beast of a husband. That thought brought with it an odd little pang, which Uma promptly shoved aside.

Maybe I'll take the class again, she thought, more to fool herself than because she really believed it. *And then maybe I'll join the other women for a drink.*

Yeah, right.

As she approached the door, Jessie caught up with her.

"Uma, you got a sec?"

"I'd better go." What a complete lie. She had absolutely nowhere to be.

"Hey, so Ive said you just got into town."

"Yes."

"Well, I'm glad you made it here tonight." Jessie

smiled and waved at the last two women as they walked by on their way out, their glances lingering on Uma. "Did you enjoy class?"

Uma forced a smile. "I did."

"Is there anything—" Jessie must have seen something prickly on her face. She quickly changed tacks. "You think you'll come back next week?"

"I'm not sure."

"Just come back, okay? Please? If money's the issue, we'll waive the fees. No problem."

First the clinic and now here. People giving things away for free. What was with this place? No way would this have happened back in Northern Virginia.

Uma gulped back emotion again, nodding as nonchalantly as she could. "Thanks."

"I know you're over at Ms. Lloyd's place. She's a little…strange. But I get it, you know? She's had it rough."

Uma's curiosity piqued at that. "She has?"

Jessie grabbed her hand and squeezed it, ignoring the question. Suddenly, Uma couldn't find the energy to pull away.

"Let us know if you need help. Me or Ive. All right? Just ask."

"Look, I'm not a—" She took a deep breath and forced a tight smile. *Charity case*, she'd almost said. But saying it would have been confirmation. "Thank you."

"Of course."

The air had changed outside, was significantly colder than when she'd arrived.

Bad timing.

Back in the car, Uma rubbed her hands together in front of the vent and watched Jessie tidy up and turn off lights through the fogged-up front window of the gym. She seemed nice. A potential friend. That thought made her feel guilty, because there was something truly messed up about the way Uma looked at the woman's husband—that weird attraction she couldn't seem to control.

7

RATHER THAN SLEEP PARKED IN THE ROAD, UMA PULLED the car up the drive that divided Ms. Lloyd's property from Ivan and Jessie's. Set between the houses, the driveway disappeared into a forest, which seemed a tiny bit safer than sleeping out where anybody driving by could see. Luckily, she had a scraggly wool plaid in the backseat, but she hadn't a thing left to eat or a red cent to her name.

The gas gauge was almost on empty, which didn't bode well, but Uma would make do. She had to.

She left the car off, wrapped up in her threadbare blanket, and closed her eyes against the inky nothingness beyond. Of all nights to sleep out here, tonight took the cake—the unseasonal heat wave had come to an abrupt end, and not even a sliver of moon was left to keep her company.

She should go up to the house and knock again, bang on the door hard enough to *force* Ms. Lloyd to open up. Who in their right mind left a person to spend the night out in the cold like this? *Someone who's deathly afraid of the outside, that's who.*

After the initial heat of anger wore off, Uma felt a little bit sorry for herself—which was dangerous. Self-pity hadn't brought her a darn thing thus far. Whenever she let it overtake her, things took a swing for the worse.

Like the time, shortly after she'd left Joey, when she'd turned on her phone to call her mom. She'd been living in a women's shelter, the first of many, and all she'd wanted was to hear a familiar voice, maybe tell her that she missed her, maybe let out a whiny little "mommy" in the hopes that she'd drop whatever chant she was doing and fly home to take care of her daughter, give her a hug.

It had taken nearly ten minutes for them to find her mother, no doubt at the other end of the ashram, and when she'd finally gotten on the line, Uma had instantly regretted the impulse that had led her to slide the battery back in the phone and call.

"Oh my God, Uma, there you are. Where on earth have you been? How could you let us worry like this?"

"I'm fine, Mom. I had to get someplace safe."

"Safe? What do you mean, safe? You left home. You took off with no indication of where you'd gone! He said *you hurt him*! He's had the police out looking for you, Uma Crane!"

"I'm sorry you worried. I'm fine, though, so please ask him to call off the cops."

"I'm not the one you should apologize to, am I?" Her mom's voice got higher as she carried on. "You need to hang up right now and call Joey. Call that boy right away. Are you crazy, leaving him like that?"

"No, I'm not going to call Joey." Uma took a deep breath. "He *hurt* me, Mom. If anyone should be apologizing, it's him."

"Oh, honey, he's sorry for the fighting. He wants to make it up to you!"

Uma's mild irritation curdled into something harsher. Why wouldn't her mother listen? She never listened.

"You should really take a step back and think about this." The voice crackled through the line. "You're messing up the best thing you've got going on."

It was all so familiar, she couldn't even respond, couldn't tell her own mother what Joey had done to her and then have her minimize her pain. Mom, the peace-loving hippy, was also Mom, the lover of men—except for her father, that is, at the end. No matter what happened between Uma and Joey, it would always be Uma's fault.

Her mom's voice softened. "Do you need anything?" She did care, after all, in her own fashion.

"No. I'm fine. I'll be fine."

"Where are you, honey?"

"I can't tell you that. He'll come and—"

"Joey's a good man, Uma. You should give him a call. You can't leave the poor boy hanging, waiting for you like this. It's cruel."

"I'm not calling him, Mom. He hurt me. Badly. I need help."

"Oh, Uma, there you go again, exaggerating things. Don't you see that you won't get what you want this way? Listen, darling, Joey and I talked yesterday. You're lucky, because he says he'll still take you back. He's not angry about how you just up and left like that." Her voice had lowered into the *best friends* register she'd always tried to use. "He's hurting, sweetie. He's really hurting." Uma could imagine her expression: eyebrows up, tight little smile. Her *empathetic* face. People loved it. She could draw you in with that, make you feel like she'd do just about anything for you. "Tell me where you are, and he can come get you."

That was the thing about her mom. She'd help anyone in need, and she'd reach out, lend them her last five bucks or invite them over for dinner. She'd barbecued tofu for more strangers than Uma could count growing up. She was good that way.

Why the hell wouldn't she take the time to pay attention to her own daughter?

Uma had taken air in and let out a shaky, nearly crying breath. Easier, in the end, to let it go. "I just wanted you to know that I'm okay, Mom. I'll be fine."

"Oh, Uma. You've…" Her mom paused, maybe searching out the right words for an apology. Maybe she'd offer to fly her daughter to India, have her join her there for healing meditation and yoga. Maybe that wouldn't be so bad. "You've had us in quite a state" was all her mother said.

Every part of Uma had sunk with disappointment. She shouldn't have let her hopes get up, but she had. She always did. "Yep. Well, I'd better go," she finally bit out between stiff lips.

"Tranquility, Uma, my sweet child." She said it fondly, but Uma was still resentful.

"Yes. Right. *Hari Om*, Mom."

"Blessings."

After hanging up, Uma had sat there in the shelter

bedroom, waiting for the knot in her chest to unravel. The single bed beneath her had been threadbare but neatly made, like the others. She'd shared the room with two other women, all victims of domestic abuse.

No, not victims: survivors. *I'm a survivor*, she remembered thinking, although she hadn't felt like one. Because this was what life had come to. *This*.

Her mom and Joey teamed up against her. They made quite the pair, the two of them. Master manipulators, both, doling out enough guilt to last a lifetime. Uma's breath had started coming faster, and she'd gotten that tunnel vision, squeezy-eye thing that told her a panic attack was not far behind.

At some point, one of her roommates—Carla—had come in and found her rolled into a ball on the floor, clutching her phone in one hand, her other hand a bloody mass of tooth marks. She'd called one of the shelter volunteers, and they'd calmed Uma down.

When the police car pulled up in front of the shelter that evening, it hadn't even occurred to Uma to be scared. At the time, she'd had no idea to what lengths Joey would go to get her back—or to get back at her. She'd been sitting in the den with a few of the women, staring blindly at the TV, when Carla had come in, grabbed her arm, and drawn her quickly through the kitchen to the back door.

"Cops are here," Carla had whispered, out on the stoop. "You gotta go."

"What?"

"You said your ex works with the law?"

Uma had nodded.

"Well, girl, you gotta go. He knows where you at."

Uma still hadn't budged when the woman hung her purse over her arm, then nudged her toward the back gate with a final, hissed "Go!"

Uma had gone without thinking, following the orders of someone who'd been running from abuse for a lot longer than she had. Finally, at the gate, she'd looked back at the house, seen the blue lights of the police car reflected off the neighbor's siding, and realized that there really was no choice: she had to get in her car and run faster, harder, farther.

Curled up in that same car, the closest thing Uma had to an actual home, the oppressive weight of Joey's presence was everywhere. At one point, she'd considered stealing a new license plate, but she'd never been much of a rebel, and the idea of getting caught had been too scary. In New York, she'd been lucky to meet a fellow survivor who'd given her a place to hide.

God, she wished she were back there, warm in Benny's tiny bunk instead of freezing in her car.

I can't do this, she thought before taking a deep breath to quiet the screaming in her brain. She reached for something else, some other emotion than fear and anxiety and hopelessness to brighten her outlook.

And then, as if by magic, the sound started—that nocturnal, metallic clanging. In the perfectly dark car, it echoed like some kind of prayer bell chased by the smell of smoke on the chill air. Something about the sound, the smell, the rhythm, within the perfect, moonless vacuum, brought an aura of peace.

It cleared her head of those fuzzy, messy emotions, until something new emerged—a sensation so unfamiliar that it took Uma a while to identify it.

When it finally coalesced, she recognized it for what it was: anger.

Good, clean anger, sublimating weak and wretched into strong and firm. Without clear intention or thought, she wrenched up her sleeve and ran cold fingers over the lines scrawled there. She couldn't see them in the dark, but the words were there. A part of her now.

"Fuck you," she whispered. She'd never said that aloud. Not to her mother or to Joey or to the woman she worked for, who wouldn't even provide shelter for the night. It felt so good that Uma had to say it again before turning the key and revving the engine. "Fuck you all."

~∾~

The sound of an engine idling in his driveway set Ive off. He didn't mind hunters on his land—there were a few guys who asked him for permission every year. Poor guys living in trailers who needed the meat to survive, to keep their families alive. That was something he understood firsthand. He'd started shooting squirrels for dinner before he hit puberty. That was what you did around here when you were dirt poor and had no other choice. The guys who hunted on his land bagged enough venison to last them all year. Ive was glad to help.

But it was too early in the season for most hunters and too late at night. Not to mention, he had NO TRESPASSING signs posted every few feet. The only assholes out this late at night were drinking and shooting. Or fucking. And he wasn't interested in dealing with either on his land.

Grabbing his shotgun from beside the door, he headed out into the night. It was dark and cold. Truly, a stupid night to be out, whatever your reasons. As he walked down the drive, the adrenaline rushed through his veins, gearing him up for a confrontation. It was good, just what he needed—someone to yell at, maybe a little brawl to get the aggression off his chest.

He caught sight of the car—not a hunter. *Her* car.

All the fight went out of him, but if possible, the adrenaline buzz got even louder. What the hell was she doing out in her car on a night like this? The engine shut off.

He leaned his gun on a nearby tree and, without thinking it through, rapped his knuckles on the passenger window, hard. Immediately, he recognized his mistake. He thought he'd frightened her before? Jesus, what an idiot. The last thing he wanted to do was scare her, but the vague shape in the car looked like that painting of a scream. White face, gaping mouth, hands thrown in front of her as if to ward him off. He stepped back from the car, willing himself smaller.

"It's Ive, Uma. The neighbor."

She stayed against the opposite door but slowly lowered her arms.

"You okay?" he called, yelling to be heard and trying his damnedest not to sound scary. How the hell was he supposed to do that? "Need somethin'?"

The white hands fluttered like birds and her voice came through the window, sounding strangled. "I'm fine, thanks! Good!"

Fine? No, she looked scared and cold and in a real bad way. He pictured himself coming out here in the morning and finding her frozen in her car.

"You want to come on over to my place and warm up, Uma?"

"I...I'll stay here."

Shit. He couldn't very well force her, could he?

"Would you let me in?"

"I'd rather not."

This time, he could hear the trembling in her voice. Just scared? Or cold too? Damn, it must be thirty fucking degrees outside. No way she'd survive a night out here.

"Go away!" she yelled, and he almost smiled. Man, he liked her spirit. It was the same thing that had made her get back up and fight in self-defense class. Only, on a night like tonight, that spirit wasn't necessarily a good thing.

"You can't stay out here, Uma. It's fuckin' freezin'."

"'S fine," she said, her voice thin and high. She didn't sound fine at all.

"Come on. You gotta turn on the car or get out."

She shook her blurry head at him. "No gas!"

"Hang on," he said, then grabbed his shotgun and took off for his truck. He left the gun there and returned a couple of minutes later with his gas can.

"Uma," he called, rather than knock on the window again. Didn't want to freak her out any more than he had to. "Pull the lever," he said.

"What?"

"For the gas. Pull it." Once she did, he poured the gas in, closed the cap, then called, "Okay, start it up," and made his way to the passenger door, where he knocked on the window again. Gently. Maybe, just maybe, she'd let him in and then, if he played his cards right, he could get her out of the goddamn car and in front of the fire. "Can you please unlock this?" He bent down, purposely making his silhouette shorter, less intimidating, and bringing his face closer to the window.

She finally hit the unlock switch, and he slid inside, briefly blinded by the overhead. Her car was small. A Honda. He'd noticed it parked out front the past few days. It hadn't really fit into the local landscape. Around here, upper-class folks drove nice Hondas, SUVs, and hybrids, while the crappy ones went to meth-heads. Everyone else drove American.

It was a tight fit. He was like one of those origami swans folded in the front seat. The woman watched him through squinty eyes as he fiddled beneath it and slid all the way back, but even then, he felt like a giant. Probably not great on the scary-guy scale. A glance at her gas gauge showed that she was at an eighth of a tank.

"You didn't have to do that," she said, sounding slightly peeved. Why did he like that so much?

When he asked "Where's your coat?" she didn't answer, so he went on. "You're gonna spend the night out here in nothing but that? No way. Hell no. It's thirty degrees outside."

"What do you care?"

"Can't have you dyin' on my land, now, can I?" The words were gruff, he knew that, but he loved her attitude. Loved the way she wouldn't just give in.

"This is your land?"

He nodded, then turned to look out his window. "Can't see for shit tonight. Bad night to spend out here."

"Yeah, well, it wasn't my choice." She shivered visibly, despite the tepid air finally blowing through the vents.

"Here, give me your hands," he said. She complied,

and he gently closed his fingers over them. "Ah, hell, you're freezin'. We gotta get you outta here." Before she could react, he grabbed her keys from the ignition, hating himself for making her do things she didn't want to do. But he couldn't exactly let her freeze, could he? "Let's go."

He put on his big man's voice—the firm one that brooked no argument but was gentle when focused on a skittish animal. She stiffened by his side, clearly infuriated, but he hadn't left her with much of a choice.

Oops. Maybe not the best idea.

Fuck it. This was about her safety. He'd deal with the rest later.

That thought made him nervous. In a good way. Besides, he'd rather see her mad than scared.

By the time he walked around to the driver's side door, she'd opened it and seemed to be having trouble getting out.

"How long you been out here?"

"Since I got back from self-defense class."

"You jokin'?" He'd been kidding about her dying on his land, but a couple of degrees cooler, and a person could expire in less time than she'd sat out in this goddamn tin can. Ive went from worried to almost crazy, but he forced his movements to slow.

"Come on," he said, his voice as calm as he could manage. "Let's get you out."

"I'm fine, Ivan. I'll be—"

As she managed to stand, Uma started to collapse.

He caught her just in time and swung her up into his arms, frantic, but still careful. She was shivering hard.

He held her tight against him, wishing he could take

on some of that cold, and made his way up the drive, back toward the forge, excited and anxious and completely uncertain about what the hell he thought he was doing.

8

WHERE THE HELL WAS HE TAKING HER? HIS FEET CRUNCHED over gravel, going Lord only knew where. Images of hatchets and shallow graves flashed in Uma's brain, only slightly counterbalancing the comfort of his arms. *No way. Not this guy*, said Uma's heart. *This is one of the good ones.*

Right, the sarcastic voice in her head cut in, *because you're such a good judge of men.*

"Your house is up there," she muttered into his chest. "Where are we going?"

"Got to get you warm, okay?" His voice, so sure and solid, reminded her of his eyes earlier that evening. How patient he'd been with her in self-defense class. Surprisingly, the fear dissipated.

A few more steps, accompanied by the swish of grass and eventually the scrape of flagstone. The jingle of the dog's collar shepherded them to wherever they were going. How could he see? Neither animal nor master seemed bothered by the dark.

Werewolves, thought Uma with an edge of hysteria.

Finally, the swaying of his steps stopped, and the creak of a door sounded. His foot bumped something metal on the threshold. A trickle of light from the doorway illuminated several food bowls on the stoop.

He stepped in, and Uma squinted her eyes against the glare.

"Sit here."

He sat her in a chair in front of a merrily roaring fire. *Merrily*, she thought. *Why would fires be merry? Happy fires?*

"Stay." Uma barely had time to settle in before rough hands plunked something heavy over her. A quilt. He went outside with a hefty cast-iron kettle, only to return and plop it atop the woodstove. The fire was beautiful, alive. It had every right to feel pleased with itself. She got lost in the flames, then in the steam curling from the kettle's black spout.

Sometime later, his hand reentered her scope of vision, poured the water into a cup, and held it in front of her. It was thick, brown china, chipped. She liked cups like that—old-fashioned and durable. It suited the palm gripping it.

"Take this."

Uma stared at the cup until he squatted and put it to her lips. "Drink."

Oh. Of course. The first sip scorched her tongue. She didn't mind. On the other hand, the burn as it made its way down her throat was not pleasant. Not pleasant at all. She sputtered, coughed, and pushed the mug back into his hands.

"What is that?"

"Hot moonshine. Heat you up."

"It's disgusting."

"Well, I'm plumb out of champagne. This's what we got."

Uma reached up and wrapped her clammy hands around the too-hot mug.

The second sip wasn't as bad, and it did help. She wasn't quite normal yet, but she did feel…more. Her hands and feet prickled with the flow of returning blood.

Slowly, Uma emerged from her hypothermic stupor enough to allow curiosity to take over. She took in the space. It looked old. If Ms. Lloyd's house was a three-decade rewind, this place kicked her back centuries.

She took another sip, testing the drink against her tongue. It still seared her insides but was no longer uncomfortable, just unfamiliar—and perfectly suited to the venue.

Ivan's big hands scooted her chair back, scraping the wooden legs along the stone floor. He bent in front of the stove, opened the door—letting out a fresh wave of warmth—and fed a couple of logs into the fire.

"Figured you were a hunter out there at first. We get a lot up here. Drunk assholes shootin' in my woods. I thought you—" He huffed out something that might have been a chuckle. "Ain't never seen a hunter in a Honda Civic, though. Sorry I scared you."

"'S okay." Uma's lips were coming back to life, but they were still like rubber.

"Ms. Lloyd kicked you out, huh?"

"Yeah. I got back too late. She wouldn't let me in."

"Yeah. She won't open her door at night. Scares the shit outta her. She know where you'd be spendin' the night?"

She shook her head. It was loose on her neck.

"Didn't think of maybe gettin' a hotel room or somethin'?"

Uma ignored him and looked around. The building was made of stone. It was a large workshop, one side taken up by wooden barn doors. They were closed right now, but her photographer's mind could picture them thrown open during the day, no doubt a magnificent view of fields and forest and mountains beyond.

She turned in the chair to see that a massive worktable and anvil dominated the space. Large cast-iron gates leaned against a wall, and pieces of dark metal—rings, poles, curved shapes, and arrows—were strewn everywhere. There were railings, enormous gates, and what appeared to be brackets. Hanging along the walls and covering every possible surface were tools that looked old, polished by time and use. Leather, wood, and metal. She could smell it. She could taste it.

I'm in a daguerreotype, Uma thought. Sepia, cluttered with the paraphernalia of a bygone era, leached of color, soft around the edges. So much lovelier than reality.

"Here," Ivan said, pulling the quilt off her. "This seat's better." He coaxed her out of the chair and nudged her toward the far end of the room, where he'd cleared off an enormous overstuffed armchair.

An unmade bed looked incongruous in the corner beyond that. It made her nervous enough to turn away as she sank deeply into the seat. Ivan placed the quilt back over her, and the dog curled onto her foot with a sigh, going to sleep instantly. Lucky bitch.

"You're a...metalworker?"

"Blacksmith."

"Oh."

"Here." He grabbed her mug and went to a shelf to refill it, adding a dash of hot water from the pot on the stove.

"Thanks." Her voice came out a little slurred from the heat, the booze, the unexpected time travel.

She watched him surreptitiously as he turned over a big wooden crate and sat on it. The thing didn't look like it could take his weight, but after an initial screech of protest, it held. He was close enough to feel intimate, but far enough so she wasn't hemmed in.

He tapped a bottle of Coors Light against her cup in a toast. Their eyes met only to skitter away.

In between curious glances at him, Uma continued her perusal of the place. It was utterly manly, though not Joey's sterile version of masculinity: stark, cold, and modern. No, this space was a hodgepodge of things, utilitarian but nonetheless decorative. The curved iron candleholder beside them held a quirky metal shade. The quilt wrapped around her was made up of bits and pieces that had undoubtedly been around the block a few times. No Pottery Barn faux-tiques here.

It was hard to keep her eyes off the man and his odd brand of magnetism. What was it about him? It was impossible to define. She would have called it charisma if he'd been more charming, had smiled or laughed. If he hadn't had a wool blanket covering half his face.

"Where's Jessie?" she asked instead of wasting time trying to understand his allure.

"Jessie?"

"She mind you being out here in the middle of the night?"

"Uh, I think she's okay with it."

"Wow. That's nice of her."

"What're you *talkin'* about?" He screwed up his face. It was the most expressive thing she'd seen him do.

"I wouldn't want my husband out in a shack in the woods with some strange woman in the middle of the night."

"You wouldn't?"

"No. I'd want him right in bed next to me, where he belonged."

"Hmm." He nodded, his pursed lips barely peeking out from his beard. "Well, I got a bed right here. If a wife wanted to sleep with me, she'd know where to find me."

"You stay here?" Uma couldn't even look at the bed. The idea of it lurking so close behind them, messy and exposed without its quilt, made her flush.

"Yup."

"What about the house?"

"What about it?"

"You rent it out or something?"

"Nobody stays in my house. I work late. This is easy."

Uma *hmphed* and turned away from the bed they'd both ended up staring at before realizing what he'd said. "If no one stays in your house, then where's Jessie?"

"At her house'd be my guess, although I can't vouch for that. She's a big girl."

Oh. She cringed. "She's not your wife, is she?"

"Nope. Sister."

"What about the tricycle in the driveway?"

"Saved it from the landfill. Fixed it up for Jessie's boy, Gabe. Rides a real bike now, so I'm savin' it for..." He trailed off, then picked up a small, black metal ring from the table beside him, slowly spinning it in his hand. It gave Uma something to look at besides his face. "Nobody comes here. Ever. Besides Squeak and the girls outside, you're the only one."

"The girls outside?"

"Cats."

"Ah. Are they all girls?"

"Nah. Couple of males. But the ladies cause all the trouble." He suppressed a yawn, then threw her a look that on anyone else would have been pouty. "I gotta bone to pick with you."

Uh-oh, here it was. "What?"

"You called my workplace a shack. I'll have you know that this is a *forge*."

"Oh, well, *sorry*." Uma sounded snarky, but she couldn't help it. Nor could she help the tiny smile that came with it.

"And don't worry—wife position's still open."

"Oh. No, I mean… I'm not…" Uma sputtered, feeling like an idiot. He winked, and she had to glance away.

When she finally worked up the courage to look him in the face again, he was smiling. A real one. Wide mouth and big white teeth.

And just like that, it was back—that image of Ivan the warrior, fueled by bloodlust, his mouth open in a battle cry. Her pulse ratcheted up a notch.

"Where you from, Uma?" His words emerged slowly, rolling like so much lava down the rocky face of a volcano. Slow as they were, their heat snuck up on her, made her want to respond just to keep him talking.

She kept her answer vague. "Up north."

He nodded. "Don't want to talk about it," he rumbled, more to himself than to her.

"Not really."

He made a slightly impatient sound. It was an odd contrast: impatience from such a slow, careful man. He seemed to have a whole different concept of time. It reminded her of those big tree creatures in *The Lord of the Rings*. The Ents.

She took a swig of her drink, enjoying the burn from throat to belly.

Again, neither of them said a thing for a stretch, lost in a companionable quiet. He finally broke it. "What's someone like you doin' in Blackwood?"

"Someone like me?" The question jarred her out of her comfort, raised her hackles.

"Yeah, you know…" He hesitated, and color rose to his cheeks, two burning flags outlining the sharp bones below his eyes. "City girl like you."

"Hey!" Uma wasn't quite sure why it felt like an insult, but it did. "Why would you say that?"

"Don't worry. Ain't your fault where you're from." Another smile. It softened his words.

She couldn't help but smile in return. "Yeah, right. What about you? Did you grow up around here?"

"Yep. Born and bred."

"Nice place. Blackwood, I mean."

"Has its moments, I guess. So, what brings you here, princess?"

"I don't really want to talk about it, okay?"

"Sure. Got it."

"And don't…call me a princess."

"'Course not. Didn't mean a thing by it." Ivan's voice was gentle, and Uma had a realization. Despite the warrior image his size conjured, she suddenly saw him as he probably was: a big, shy man with confusing eyes, an unruly beard, and a ridiculously named leg warmer of a dog.

"I don't really like to talk about myself."

"Okay," he said, nearly smiling again. "So, what do you want to talk about?"

She huffed out a tiny laugh. "Hell if I know."

"Big conversationalist, huh?"

She shrugged and sipped at her drink, arms crossed protectively in front of her chest.

"Yeah, me too," he said. "So, you want to start over again?"

She nodded, but still they sank back into silence. Ivan bent down and nudged at Squeak until she turned and gave him her belly. He tickled her, big fingers softly mussing her fur.

It occurred to Uma that she didn't have a story ready. She'd never imagined herself having to explain why she'd come to Blackwood. She'd always assumed that she wouldn't meet anyone, wouldn't make friends.

With Joey, her friends had been picked off, one by one, deemed unfit for their company. By the end, she'd been entirely cut off from nearly everyone. He'd isolated her, left her with no one to turn to but him. His tactics seemed obvious in hindsight, but at the time…

"I'm sorry I was so short. I just… I recently got out of a really…a relationship." There, she'd told him. Sort of.

"Nothin' to be sorry about."

"So, you have a big family around here?" she asked, the only thing she could think of to say.

"Jessie, who you know. And her son, Gabe."

"Right."

"That's it. You got family?"

"My mom's in India. She lives on an ashram, does yoga and stuff."

"Oh. Interesting. That it?"

"Pretty much. My, uh…my dad died when I was in high school." Why was she telling him all this?

"Hmm."

"You got parents?"

"Not really. Never knew my dad. And Mom…she's gone too. Long time ago."

"I'm sorry."

He shrugged, then seemed to hesitate for a moment before leaning forward to say quietly, "Look, you need someone to talk to him for you?" His body tensed, oozing menace, and she wondered what kind of a *talking-to* he meant.

Uma shivered, a not unpleasant sensation. "Who?"

"Asshole you're runnin' from. One's got you shittin' your pants anytime a guy gets within spittin' distance of you."

"No," she responded, although a small, craven part of her imagined him pummeling Joey's face into the ground. His thick knuckles looked like they'd crunched their fair share of cartilage and bone. At the gym, she'd seen the potential damage he could do with that body. She had the feeling that if she said the word, he'd do it.

But no. Poor guy was probably some peaceful animal lover, minding his own business, and here she was, yet again, fantasizing him into the role of gladiator. "I don't need help. I'm fine." A statement so blatantly untrue, she could hardly expect him to believe it. "Besides, I'm learning self-defense."

"That's right. Good." He nodded with a smile. "I could teach you more, if you want."

"Oh, sure. Yeah. Thanks." Uma pictured the two of them going over those same moves, but someplace private, like right here in his overcrowded forge. She couldn't quite manage it, though, because every time she imagined their bodies coming together, it was on the bed, and the choreography much more illicit.

She snuck another look at him, his plaid shirt opened over a dark-colored T-shirt. His jeans looked filthy, but she figured that came with the territory. Blacksmithing didn't seem like a neat occupation. The denim curved around his thighs like a glove, tighter than most guys around here seemed to wear. She wondered if he had a hard time finding pants that fit him. Slim waist paired with thick legs. Tall enough to make you do a double take. She'd be safe with a man like that standing guard. The memory of being carried by him, face pressed to his chest, was so visceral, so real, she could almost feel it still.

"Thanks for letting me warm up, Ivan." She'd let the warm fire, booze, and the sight of those hypnotic hands caressing the peacefully snoring dog all work together to lull her into a false sense of safety, of belonging. It was time to go before she started believing it.

When she handed him her empty mug, their fingers touched briefly, and something flared, so ephemeral that she wanted to reach out and touch him again, just to see.

"So, you want to go out sometime?" His words stopped the glow, made it real and not something she'd imagined.

Go out? No. No, Uma couldn't go out with him, even

though he didn't scare her anymore. She couldn't get embroiled with another man.

No rebounds for Uma. Not here, not anywhere. She couldn't rebound after a relationship like the one she'd just left. She couldn't *anything* after her relationship with Joey. It had been the relationship to end all relationships.

This body might never succumb to a man's touch again, and that would be fine.

Except that last thought felt a little like a lie. Some small part of her might be the tiniest bit curious about doing *things* with Ivan, might even welcome it if she were a different girl in a different life. Images of pure, wonderfully disgusting animal sex came to mind until she pushed them firmly away. No, certainly not that.

Wining and dining and first dates and stuff? *Oh God.* Even worse. She didn't even know what that looked like anymore. The thought alone was enough to make her sweat. Dates meant intimacy and relationships and the possibility of love. None of which she could fathom.

So, no. Uma couldn't go out with Ivan.

Above all, she had a feeling that this was a nice guy she was dealing with. And she was decidedly *not* a nice girl. She'd lost the chance at being just another nice girl the day Joey Chisholm had flashed his baby blues at her and wended his way so firmly under her skin that she feared she would never get him out.

"You don't want to go out with me, Ivan."

He looked ready to argue for a moment and then nodded, slow, like everything else about him. He didn't look defeated, just calm, maybe a tiny bit determined.

Uma wondered if he was a stubborn sort of person. She thought he might be.

For some reason, she didn't mind the idea that he might try again. As a matter of fact, a contrary, selfish little piece of her hoped he *would*, in case she decided to change her mind.

"Where you goin' to stay tonight?"

"I'll figure something out."

"Got a bed right here."

Her body clenched unexpectedly at the idea. She couldn't tell if it was a good clench or a bad one. "Oh, no, I couldn't."

"Don't mind."

Uma waited to feel frightened at the idea of sleeping in this man's bed. Nothing.

Actually, that wasn't entirely true. She trembled. An image of their bodies entwined on the bed rose from her thoughts, so close she could reach out and touch it.

"Not lettin' you sleep in that car."

"I can't take your bed from you."

"We got another option," he said, voice smoky and full of promise.

～∽～

Shit. He hadn't meant to say that. Frankly, he hadn't meant to do any of it. The flirting, the teasing, the easy conversation. It had all come as one enormous surprise to Ive. Like one second he was saving a damsel in distress, and the next he wanted to rip her clothes off. With his teeth.

Ah, hell. He really shouldn't have invited her back here. He should have given her money, made her get a hotel room. Anything but this…this…temptation. Because this woman was clearly not in any place to be ravaged.

But, instead of responding the way she should have, the way she was supposed to, all shocked and offended— a new voice, warmer and darker, said, "Yeah?"

To which he couldn't help but respond, "Could share."

The silence lasted a moment too long, landing them for the first time in awkward territory. The fire popped, pulling them out of it, and Squeak let out a massive, satisfied doggy sigh before flopping her head back onto the floor.

Uma started to shake her head and then stopped. Ive was amazed at how much he could read in her eyes. Even though he'd never been overly perceptive when it came to women, this one was an open book. Not good. She needed more protection against…well, against guys like him.

"I'm kiddin', Uma. Place is all yours, princess." He said that last bit to annoy her. To protect her from him. He threw in a wink to seal the deal.

Was that disappointment he saw or—no. Just wishful thinking on his part.

"Where will you sleep?" she asked, and he liked that she worried about him.

"Don't you worry about me. I got plenty of options." He smirked, lacing the words with innuendo. "Bed's all yours."

"What? Oh, no, I couldn't—"

"I insist. Stay. Please. Else we'll have to get you a hotel room." He went to the fire, loaded it up with logs, and headed to the door, Squeak slow to follow—the traitor.

"Thanks, Ivan," she whispered, and he was glad.

"Anytime, princess." He smiled at her annoyed little breath.

Before heading out, he paused. "You want breakfast in the mornin'? Girls are still layin', so I got fresh eggs."

"Oh, no. No, I've got to get back to Ms. Lloyd's place."

"Lock this door, okay?" He waited until she nodded, then turned before adding, "Sweet dreams."

"Thanks, Ivan. You too."

He pulled the door closed behind him and waited. A few beats later, the lock *thunked*, followed by the sound of a chair sliding up behind it. Good on her. Looking out for herself.

Ive walked to his big house, went inside, and brushed his teeth, peed, then turned to look at the stairs heading up to the second floor. He kept the place just above freezing, so the pipes wouldn't burst, but it was barely warmer than outside. Why bother heating an empty house?

No beds, no blankets. Only the one threadbare towel and about five slivers of soap smashed together on the side of the bathtub.

He considered taking his towel into the kitchen, firing up the stove, and trying to make the place his own. But it was no use. He'd tried before. He'd even brought his entire bed in here once, in a bid to make it a real home.

At this point, he should probably just sell the house. This place wasn't him. It was too good for him. Too nice.

But he needed to finish fixing it up. The banister and then the porch. That windowsill upstairs looked like it might be rotting out a bit and—yeah. There was a ton to do still. He'd move in once he finished. Or sell it.

On that thought, he pulled the front door shut behind him and went to his truck, where he and Squeak would spend the night snuggled under a sleeping bag. He didn't usually mind being out in the great outdoors, even in weather like this. Only tonight, for the first time in for-ever, there was a woman in his bed, and the thought of her wrapped up in his sheets would be enough to keep him from getting any sleep at all.

9

UMA KNOCKED ON MS. LLOYD'S DOOR THE NEXT MORNING, feeling more rested than she had in months. Ivan's bed had been the warmest, coziest nest she could imagine. She'd spent long minutes this morning, half-asleep, with her face pressed into his pillow, shamelessly breathing him in. It was one of those tricks of chemistry or genetics or whatever that made his particular smell *exactly* what her body craved.

When she rounded the drive, and his house had come into view, she'd been oddly relieved to see his truck parked there, rather than in front of some random booty call's place. Silly, so, so silly, to care about that.

As expected, Ms. Lloyd kept her waiting on the porch. Uma was freezing again by the time her boss limped to the door, opened it, and grudgingly allowed her back inside.

"You stink," the woman said over her shoulder as she walked away.

"I didn't get a shower last night, did I?"

"You smell like smoke. Been over there again with that married man?"

"He told me the truth about that."

Uma followed her boss into the kitchen, watching the woman's shoulders shake with laughter.

"Yeah, you sure got me there, boss."

"You still managed to worm your way into his bed, didn't you?"

"For your information, I slept *alone* in his bed." Uma kept her voice as hoity-toity as possible. "Not that it's any of your—*oh my God.*"

They hung on the threshold of the kitchen, looking in. Uma swallowed hard.

Good. Lord.

It looked like a crime scene, a robbery gone bad. A frat house hit by a hurricane. The room had been destroyed. There was junk everywhere—dirty dishes in the sink, broken china strewn about, a dish towel dripping some viscous yellow fluid, something too red to be blood sprayed up the side of a cabinet, and about a centimeter of water covering the floor.

"Don't just stand there, girl. Place ain't gonna clean itself." With that, the woman turned and sashayed out to the living room.

This is a means to an end. That's all this is, thought Uma. *I'm big and strong and soon I'll be brand-new. I'll get through this.*

For some reason, this time, she almost believed it.

Nothing Ms. Lloyd did at this point could burst the bubble of a good night's sleep, she told herself. That, and the prospect of her first laser appointment in three days. Yes, darn it. Things were looking up.

She had a timeline now, and a haven away from this place. A self-defense class, a doctor to help her, and a strong man's bed to sleep in. *Yeah, right.* Nix that last thought.

Oh, but Ms. Lloyd had made her point. Uma would be punished if she disobeyed. It took all day to clean the kitchen—a mess that had probably taken only a few minutes to make. As she worked, Uma tried to imagine Ms. Lloyd doing the damage, but she couldn't quite picture it. Had it been done gleefully or in anger? Both images were creepy.

Something had to change.

～⁂～

The day passed painfully slowly, which had the dubious benefit of giving Uma time to think.

She thought of Ivan and his delightful strangeness. He appeared rough and mean, and if you didn't scratch the surface, that was all you got. But given the opportunity to delve a tiny bit further, the man wasn't an ogre at all. Far from it. He was… She wasn't sure what he was.

Sweet? Not quite. *Gentle?* Almost. But there was too much underlying violence there for that to be right. *Good?* Was that it? Was he a good person? Maybe. Yeah, just maybe.

She also thought of her boss and how very messed up she was. It was all a play for power, Uma knew that. Every little thing the woman did at this point was a test, to see how far she could push her new employee. And that meant one thing: if Uma was to have any chance at surviving this long-term, she had to counter with a play of her own. At least until something better came along.

That night, after dinner, Ms. Lloyd roped Uma into washing her hair, although she was fully capable of doing it on her own.

Uma managed to fit a single wooden chair into the house's only cramped bathroom, flush to the sink.

Rubbing the old woman's head was an oddly intimate activity, considering. It also, she quickly learned, put her at a distinct physical advantage.

"How did you wash your hair before I got here?" she asked.

The older woman's eyes were closed. She looked like she was enjoying this. A wisp of a memory floated to the surface—something Uma had heard about how spiders liked getting their bellies rubbed. Without her glasses, Ms. Lloyd looked young, naive. She looked like someone who needed protection. The way her hair flattened to her skull left her looking small, like one of those dogs that shrink to half their size once you get their fur wet.

"With great difficulty."

"Yeah, right. I'll bet you roped someone else in to doing it for you."

"Now why would you say that?"

"I can't imagine you doing something for yourself if you can get some sucker to take care of it."

Ms. Lloyd cackled at that. "You saying you're a sucker?"

"Absolutely."

"What if I told you I had your boyfriend over here sudsing me up like this?"

The thought made Uma laugh. "You mean Ivan?"

"Oh, so it's *Ivan*, is it? Not Ive? You don't like the way the rest of us say it? You just waltz into town, all secretive and big city, and use your hoity-toity voice to—"

Uma took a breath. She couldn't do this anymore if she didn't take a stand. Not another frickin' second.

"Ms. Lloyd, I need you to listen to me." Her hands stilled on the woman's head. "I have regular doctor's appointments. That's why I came to Blackwood. If I can't go to those, then I might as well go back to where I was before."

"You want me to pay you to take off whenever you want?"

"No, I want you to pay me to do my job and let me leave your home when I need to."

"Well, I need you here *all the time*."

"You don't."

"I do."

"No, you—" Damn it, this wasn't working. She sucked in a Pert-scented breath and tried again. "I'm sorry, but I have to leave sometimes. I'll try to keep it to the evenings—that way you'll hardly notice I'm gone."

"No. We can't open the door after dark."

Uma tried her best to sound calm and reasonable. "I'm not your prisoner, Ms. Lloyd. If you don't let me leave, it's like…slavery."

"You're fired."

She should have known this would happen. "Fine." Uma turned to go.

"What do you think you're doing?"

"I'm going. You're firing me, so I'm leaving."

"You can't do that!"

"Oh, I think I can."

"Think you'll find another job with your...secrets and fake name? Go on and try it. There're girls like you all over the place. New one every week. But jobs? Around here, they're hard to find." The woman's bravado was admirable.

"Right." *Calm. Stay calm.* This was a gamble, nothing but a gamble, and the odds were in her favor. "You know what, Ms. Lloyd? We both know you're fully capable of rinsing your damn hair. You're on your own." The sound of the door closing behind her was so final, she came close to turning back. But if she did that...she'd get nothing from the woman. No time off, no respect. Decisive, she started down the hall.

"Don't you dare leave, Irma. Don't you... Wait! Wait! Irma!" It was hard, but she kept going. "Irma! Get back here! Come back! We can make this work." A pause. "*Please.*"

God, this was harder than she'd imagined. Uma knew—they both knew, though Ms. Lloyd wouldn't admit it—that this wasn't about leaving her without someone to wash her hair or cook or clean up her crap. Those were simply the excuses she'd devised. The big ploy, the cover-up for what her real job was... No, the *reality* was, if Uma left, Ms. Lloyd would be alone. Utterly alone in this stale box of a place. And that was why this gamble would pay off, even if it made her feel cruel to exploit the other woman's fear. Uma couldn't imagine anyone had ever stuck around Ms. Lloyd for long. *She* would stay—so long as she could have just enough freedom to actually feel free.

Standing in the hall with that wedding picture staring her in the face, Uma waited a second, then two. "I'll go back in there and help you, Ms. Lloyd—I'll *stay*—but first, we need to agree on new terms."

The woman's breathing was audible through the door. She wasn't suffering from a heart attack or something, was she? Impossible. Her kind of mean outlived everyone—like a postapocalyptic cockroach.

"Fine. Fine. What do you want?"

Uma opened the door but kept to the hallway. "First of all, I will fulfill my duties to you. I'll help you out, but I am in no way your prisoner. You understand that, right?"

"Never said you were."

"Yeah, well, this way, we've got everything out in the open. So you understand, that crap you pulled with the kitchen? You do that again, and I'm gone. No questions asked."

"I didn't mean it, Irma. Keep your job. And evenings. Evenings are fine."

"Thank you." Here it was: the power of standing up for herself, but also, unexpectedly, the soft thrill of being needed. She hardened herself before going on. "Next time you make a mess like that, you'll wallow in it, because I'm not cleaning up that kind of mess again. Got it?"

"Yes, yes, I get it. Fine. Just…" Ms. Lloyd paused, clearly hating this. "My eyes are stinging. Could we wrap this up?"

"Could we wrap this up, *please*."

"Oh, you—" Ms. Lloyd stopped, breathing hard, her eyes staring at Uma with a strange mix of angry, pathetic, and proud. Apparently her need for companionship won out over her stubborn temper, because she gave in with a quietly whispered, "*Please*."

"And my name's Uma."

"Yeah, yeah."

"Say it."

"Oooma. Okay? You happy now?"

Right. Thrilled.

Without answering, Uma allowed herself the tiniest of smiles as she turned on the faucet and tested the temperature before rinsing her boss's hair.

Happy? No. Not even close. But satisfied? Certainly. And maybe a little bit hopeful that things could get better.

She'd just have to wait to see how it played out.

10

AFTER WHAT UMA CAME TO THINK OF AS "THE STANDOFF,"
Ms. Lloyd was surprisingly agreeable. In fact, she was
in superfine fettle the next day. Probably because Uma
let her win at cards. Their truce was friendly, and after
all was said and done, she might one day grow to like
the old bird. Stranger things had happened.

After a morning spent shopping, Uma went to the
kitchen to prepare what she had dubbed their "Leftover
Lunch." Today, it was tuna melts, using what remained
from last night's tuna casserole. At the store, she'd realized that her culinary upbringing may have had more of
an influence on her than she liked to admit, prompting
her to make slight changes to the menu.

From her bag, she pulled ingredients probably fresher
than anything this kitchen had ever seen and got to
prepping.

"What's that you're washing?" Ms. Lloyd asked dis-
trustfully from a spot close behind her. Her large breast
nudged Uma's elbow in a way that felt oddly familiar,
strangely comforting, almost maternal.

Of course the woman wouldn't recognize lettuce if it wasn't iceberg. "Lettuce. I thought I'd make a salad today with our sandwiches."

"And that. What's that?" She pointed.

"That?" *For the love of God.* "It's bread."

"Bread? Doesn't look like it. What kind of bread is that?"

"Whole grain, I think. I got it at the bakery in town this morning." Uma kept her voice light.

"Where's my Wonder?" Ms. Lloyd whined.

"This is healthier."

"Well, I won't eat it. Looks like cardboard."

"Dr. Oz says we have to eat grains. And greens too. You heard him."

"White bread's a grain."

"White bread is sugar. Just try it. One time, and if you don't like it, I'll leave it alone."

Ms. Lloyd was quiet for a moment, then came out with a grumpy "hmph," a sound perfected through years of overuse.

After setting the table, Uma ran out back and picked a few big branches of rosemary from the herb garden beside Ivan's house. It might not be floral, but it smelled good. She placed them on the table in the only vase she could find that didn't already contain a dried flower arrangement. Porcelain, with a crying clown, diamonds on its tights. She turned its face to the wall.

The table looked as nice as it was going to. Her photographer's eye enjoyed the bright greens dotted with red splashes of radicchio, tuna, and crusty bread topped with white cheddar instead of the artificial yellow cheese her boss favored. Overall, it was an enormous improvement upon every other meal they'd shared.

The women sat and ate quietly. Well, Uma ate quietly—the Black Widow huffed and puffed and whined, poking at her food, but eventually ended up eating every single crumb on her plate. Uma held back a smile of satisfaction.

"So," she said, clearing the dishes from the table, "did you enjoy your lunch?"

"Disgusting. Next time I ask for groceries, you'd better get me *my* groceries, or I'm docking your pay. Oooma." She moved off to the living room to watch her stories.

Uma smiled.

～∽೦ఌ～

That evening, Uma was washing up after dinner when someone knocked at the door.

Oh God. He found me.

Six months of running sent her heart into hyperdrive, and her already wet hands went cold and shaky. She turned off the water and went to hover behind the open kitchen door.

"Oooma, get the door!" Ms. Lloyd called.

She didn't move.

Breath held in tight lungs, Uma strained to hear above the sounds of *Jeopardy!*…and knew suddenly who it was. The air whooshed out, and she sagged against the wall in relief. Even if she hadn't recognized him, her boss's tittering would have clued Uma in to the fact that the visitor was a friendly male rather than a stranger from Northern Virginia, come to fetch her.

"That you, boy?"

"Yes, ma'am."

"Well, it's certainly an improvement. Hardly recognized you."

"Figured it was time for a change."

"Hmph."

"You giving Uma any time off, Ms. L? Or you back to your slave-driving ways?"

"Oh please, she's spoiled rotten. Free food, warm bed. Cash every week. She's gettin' a deal, if you ask me!"

Just as Uma was about to move through the kitchen door, he said, "She around right now?" Oh. He'd come to see her. Something about that idea made her hesitate, unsure what to feel. Good, bad, guilty? What did he expect from her? Had she led him on? Did she want to?

"You want to talk to her?"

"Yes, ma'am."

Was he there to ask her out again?

"Well, she's not currently available."

She stayed still and waited, stifling a gasp of outrage.

"Her car's here, so I thought—"

"She's very busy and doesn't want to be disturbed."

He paused then, longer than you'd expect. "Could you please mention that I stopped by?"

"'Course I will."

Steps sounded on the porch and then stopped.

"So, I take it the ad worked, then? You like her?"

"She's a bit mouthy. 'Course, it's only been a week. We'll just have to wait and see, won't we?"

"Guess so."

"What'd it say, anyway?" asked Ms. Lloyd. "Did they get it right? I never got to see it in print."

His voice faded in and out as he responded. "…nice… older person…live-in helper."

"Well, I guess it worked all right. Go on now, boy, and don't come back unless you've got those doughnut holes I like. And a copy of the *Gazette*."

Uma didn't hear his response, but she didn't really need to.

Why was Ms. Lloyd asking Ivan about the ad? With the distance between them transforming things, she'd probably misunderstood, but it sure sounded like—

Holy shit. Had *he* done that? Placed that ad?

A moment came back to her—that first meeting with Ms. Lloyd, when she'd called her an old hag. What if…

She covered her mouth to stifle an "oh" of embarrassed surprise and sagged back against the counter, stuck there until the woman came into the kitchen.

"What's got you?" asked Ms. Lloyd, looking the slightest bit guilty.

"Remember what I called you when we first met?"

The older woman frowned, eyes narrowed. "Indeed I do. You're lucky I didn't throw you out right then and there."

"Do you know why?"

"Why what?"

"Why I called you that?"

"Because you're a vulgar hussy, that's why!"

"There is that, but… Hang on." Uma stood up straight. "I'll be right back." She took off up the stairs and into her room, where she found the ad crumpled on the dresser, next to a stale, twenty-year-old bowl of potpourri.

In the dark hall, before heading back down, she hesitated again. Should she even show this to Ms. Lloyd? It would hurt her feelings, wouldn't it? Remembering the look on the woman's face when she'd called her a hag, though, clinched it. She deserved to know the truth.

Back in the living room, she pressed the paper into Ms. Lloyd's hand.

The woman read aloud, "'Old hag in need of…'" She looked up and blinked. "What is this?"

"The ad I answered for this job. From the *Gazette*. See? That's your number, right there."

"You mean…" Her voice trailed off as her owl eyes met Uma's. Despite her concern, it was shocking to see pain there, quickly stifled. "That sonovabitch."

"Is Ivan the one who placed this for you?"

"Yes."

"So, he wrote it?"

"Oh my—" Ms. Lloyd moved across the room and sank onto her pink floral nightmare of a sofa, looking small and defeated.

"Why would he do this?" Uma asked.

"I have no idea."

Damn it, why *had* he done it? Was it all some sick game? She thought back to the way he'd taken care of her, asked her out on a date, even offered his bed. That level of kindness didn't make sense. None of it did. And what about his relationship with Ms. Lloyd? Was he pretending to care about her? One day, Uma would be long gone from their lives, but they'd still be neighbors. He was the only outside contact she seemed to have. Her only friend. But what kind of friend did this?

"No wonder," said Ms. Lloyd, coming slightly out of her daze.

"No wonder what?"

"The calls. You've heard 'em. The damn calls."

"Because of the ad?"

"That'd be my guess. Pranks. When you called me a hag, you were… Let's just say you weren't the first."

"Am I the first serious response you've gotten through this ad?"

Ms. Lloyd shrugged. "Had a few before. Seven or eight. From previous ads. He always did 'em for me, no problem. I read 'em in the paper—every one but this one. He always said the *Gazette* was sold out so I didn't see it this time." She sounded listless, nothing like the woman Uma had grown to tolerate, if not completely like.

"Have you been advertising for a while?"

"Few years now. Maybe five?" *Whoa.* That was a long time. "Ive always does it for me. Always. Such a nice boy."

"You've had eight different people here in five years? How long did they last?"

"Couple of days. One of 'em lasted fifteen minutes." After a pause, the old widow reared her head. "And good riddance too. Darn girl couldn't even speak English right. Sounded like she'd been brought up by retarded pigs."

And there it was. The woman had a knack. In one fell swoop, sympathy gone, although the anger still lingered.

Ms. Lloyd swiveled to face the TV and turned the volume up, a clear indication that the conversation was over.

The rest of the evening was quieter than usual.

Uma found that she almost missed her boss's constant commentary.

∽൦

Later, in bed, it was harder to forget. What the hell was that ad about? Why would Ivan do something so cruel? It didn't fit. Rolling, she turned her pillow over and smacked it before laying her head back down. Uma closed her eyes. Drew in a breath. Opened them again to glare up at the ceiling.

He must have had a reason for placing that ad. Right? She twisted and flopped in the silence.

And why the hell wasn't he working? It was too darned quiet.

God, her head. She couldn't take another minute of this silence and doubt, wondering… She should go over there and ask. He wouldn't betray Ms. Lloyd like that for no reason, would he? And why did it feel like he'd betrayed *her* too when she'd answered it?

Because I like him.

Oh God, there it was. She liked him, and she'd turned down his request for a date, and here she was, alone in this crappy bed, again, and he was off…somewhere. Not working in his forge, in any case. Not keeping her company in that roundabout way, and somehow, the quiet was lonelier now than it had ever been before.

It felt like she'd been here in bed forever with nothing but questions and irritation and doubts, and damn it, where was he? If she went over there and asked him… No. Stupid idea. Besides, he wasn't even home, he was—

Clang.

There it was. The breath left her body, relief pressing her into her bed. He was there. Another bang, and another, and soon, without effort, her heart fell into step with his rhythm.

Nothing, *nobody* had the power to relax her like this,

to take everything else away. Rather than fight the urge, Uma went with it. She got up and dressed in the dark, grabbed that stupid ad and stuffed it into her pocket, and then tiptoed past her boss's door, down the stairs, and out the kitchen door—headed straight for Ivan.

As she walked, the clanging rang out, louder with each step she took. The thought that she'd finally get to witness Ivan the blacksmith excited her—and almost made her forget everything else.

The door stood open, leaking warmth like an oven. The place must get incredibly hot in the summer.

He was bent low over the anvil, hammering a piece of bright-red, burning metal with a mallet. Sparks flew like some kind of crazy fairy dust. He looked magical and mythical and so very…*right*. Powerful back and arms and hands worked in concert to hammer order into iron, and an errant thought escaped: images of him working her over the same way. Shaping and molding her into something strong and lasting. She trembled.

It took Squeak's wet nose to shake Uma out of her reverie. The dog met her in the doorway with what could only be described as a series of squeaks.

When Uma glanced up, Ivan was watching her. Only he no longer looked like the same man. This Ivan was a whole new creature, transformed. Intimidating in an entirely different way. He looked pleased to see Uma, but insecure, awaiting a verdict.

"Oh," she stammered out. "Wow, you're… Just wow."

And what a verdict it was. Gone was the beast she'd had a grudging connection with two nights before. This man was breathtakingly handsome.

"You shaved. And you cut your hair and… It's…

Wow. Amazing." The shock of the change was solid in the pit of her stomach. *Attraction*, she thought, skittering away from the notion.

Ivan got a pleased, self-conscious look on his face. A kid given a compliment he didn't know what to do with. It was adorable.

"Come on in and have a seat," he said a little too loudly, like maybe the beard had muffled his voice as well as his looks. As Uma walked past him, he leaned over his table, grabbed an earmuff-like thing off a hook, and handed it to her. "Put this on. I just need to finish up."

She pulled the ear protectors over her head and moved to her armchair in the corner while he returned to his hammering.

He worked and she watched, transfixed. Each strike of cold metal to hot was precisely aimed. The vibrations hummed through every cell of her body—the same rhythm she'd come to depend on nightly. Only this time, she felt it from the inside out.

Sparks blossomed in showers of bright gold, a halo for Ivan's body. He was an alchemist, a god creating worlds.

And his face. Oh, the man's face. Dark brows drawn low over eyes half-closed against the light, mouth tight, chin and jaw rigid, clamped in stern concentration. Uma couldn't help but imagine that expression focused on her, that hard body thrumming with excitement above hers. She crossed her legs to alleviate the pressure growing between them.

Why, oh why, did he have to shave it off? She'd been okay before. Puzzled at the faint stirrings of attraction, yes, but willing to put it down to the feelings of coziness and safety he engendered in her.

And then, there was how different he was from Joey. *That* was it. It rang truest. Back to faulty instincts again. They'd failed Uma so miserably when it came to Joey that she'd wanted to ignore them when it came to this man. She'd wanted to stay away, despite how easy it'd been. He'd gone from scary to trustworthy in less than a week—who was she kidding? *In less than a day.*

So, maybe her instincts weren't broken after all, merely slow. Like an arrow on a gauge, they needed time to swerve before settling on a final reading.

"You got more of that moonshine?" she asked, too antsy to just sit there staring.

He didn't look up when he said, "Yep. Right over on that shelf. You'll have to rinse your mug from the other night. Pump's outside. Sorry. No runnin' water out here." No running water? Uma's eyebrows rose at that, but she shrugged. "Got beers in the cooler too, if you'd rather."

Instead of going for the beer—the easy option—in kind of a show-offy move, which she'd surely regret, she went for the moonshine. As if to show how little she cared about germs and stuff, Uma filled her mug without rinsing it. "You want some?"

"Hell no." He shook his shoulders in a kind of exaggerated shudder of disgust. "Can't stand the stuff."

"Hey!" she laughingly yelled, her voice shakier than she expected.

"I'd take a beer, though."

She found the cooler and pulled out a bottle but couldn't find anything to open it with.

"Leave it there. I'll get it when I'm done."

With a shrug, Uma left it on the shelf and took her mug back to the armchair, where she curled up and spent several moments trying to relax, looking everywhere but at him. A nearly impossible feat, when he was so big, so very *there*. She finally gave up and let herself watch the show, imagining throwing open those big, wooden doors and taking shots of him while he worked, day or night. Light or dark. Hot or cold. Opposites, just like those funky eyes of his. She wanted to capture it all.

It was easy to let the ambiance he created form a surreal cushion around her, calming her and nearly wiping the stupid ad from her mind. She dipped her lips in the drink and kept her eyes on him, sinking heavily into it, the clanging of metal syncopating with her heartbeat, insulating them from the world outside. It was warm and dark, the light orange and intimate.

She was no longer in modern-day Blackwood, shying from the horrors of her life, but caught in some alternate reality, some other time, some place medieval. She pictured him half-naked, chest gleaming in the firelight, muscles bunching with each slam of the hammer, his skin beaded with sweat, pebbled with goose bumps.

Uma came out of her trance to find his hammer still, his eyes on her. Their intensity was palpable even from across the room.

He hung the piece he'd finished working on and untied his apron, making her wish fervently that he wouldn't stop there. She downed more of the moonshine, craving its intoxication. *Unbutton your shirt*, she thought, staring hard. Ivan apparently wasn't a mind reader.

He picked up his beer, popped the top on the edge of

a worktable, and came toward her, his nearness strumming her nerves. The crate creaked under his weight just like the last time she'd been there, and she flashed back to that moment, thinking how much could change in so little time. She took another sip and let it relax her further, remembering how she'd been wrung out when he'd rescued her from her car. He, the scary, untouchable next-door neighbor, inviting her in for a slightly weird midnight drink.

Tonight, now…he was a timeless magician whose body bent iron and sparked fire. Or was that the moonshine talking? She swore he was the handsomest man she'd ever seen: hard and sweet looking at the same time.

Tonight, although he'd unveiled another piece of his puzzle, he sat before her a mystery she desperately wanted to solve.

11

"CAN'T SLEEP AGAIN?" IVE ASKED.

Uma replied, "Didn't even try," then seemed to remember something, her features tightening. She stood, pulled a wadded-up piece of paper from her pocket, and gave it to him. "Here. Take a look." More carefully, she sat back down in her chair, and he glanced at the paper.

"What is... Oh." Understanding dawned as he read it.

"You write that?"

He hesitated before shaking his head.

"What the hell?" she asked.

He looked away, feeling his cheeks heat with embarrassment.

"You do this for shits and giggles? Trying to torture a poor old lady?"

"No way," he growled, seriously offended before tamping it down. It wasn't her fault. He'd be pissed too in her shoes. With a groan, he rubbed a hand over his nape, slugged back half his beer, and told her, "I gave it to a friend. Had too much shit goin' on and didn't have time to deal with placin' the ad again. She was headed to the *Gazette* anyway, said she'd ask 'em to run it again, but the stupid paper misplaced the old version, and when Binx went to—"

"Wait, Binx? From self-defense class?"

Shit. Hadn't meant to let that out. "Yeah." He sighed. "Don't think she meant any harm by it; she just does stupid crap, y'know? Without thinking."

Uma made a disbelieving little sound in her throat. "Why didn't you have them pull it when you found out?"

"I did! 'Course I did, Uma." The words came out defensive, so he pulled himself back. "Switched the ad as soon as I could. But the kid responsible for the ads kept screwing up and keepin' the old one. Maybe he thought it was funny, maybe he had his hands full and kept forgettin'—whichever it was, took a few days before they finally got it right. Hell." He looked at her. "I've been helpin' Ms. Lloyd for years now, you know? She's all alone. Can't find anyone. The people she does get take advantage of her, steal shit. Not like she has anything worth taking, but... They treat her like shit, and she's there all by herself, and one day, I'm gonna head over there and find her on the floor half-dead. And then I'll have to go out and hunt down the fucker who did that to her. I wouldn't want to put somethin' out there that'd attract people who'd want to hurt her. I'd never do a fuckin' thing like that."

Uma leaned forward in her seat. "You could have told her, at least. Warned her about it."

"No point hurtin' her over something' neither of us could change. And then you showed up, and I figured I didn't need to."

"Congratulations to Binx. You can tell her she managed to get half the loonies in the county calling Ms. Lloyd."

"What?"

"Yeah. She hasn't mentioned all the calls?"

"No."

"Well, good job looking out for her." She shifted back and drained her cup, leaving them in silence.

"I'm so damned sorry, Uma. If I'd a known…"

She eyed him a second before turning away, her features less angry if not entirely settled. "The ad got me here, didn't it? At least for now. And I have no intention of hurting Ms. Lloyd, so…I guess it worked out for everybody. In the end."

"True. Who'd have thought anybody'd be crazy enough to answer an ad like that?"

Her smile was a little bit sad. "Yeah, well, here I am."

He pictured himself leaning forward to kiss it right off her face. "I'm sorry."

With a toss of her hair, she puffed out a hard breath that changed the air in the room. "Guess I'm the only person *crazy* enough to answer that stupid ad." There was a challenge in those words.

"Yeah." He looked down at the paper in his hand and smirked. "Which part was it that sold you on the job? *Kinky*? Or maybe you're into the *old hag* thing."

"Oh please. Whatever."

"No, seriously. What'd you think when you read it?"

"What did I think? Seriously? Hmm, let's see. *Why not? Love a good challenge.*"

"Yeah?" he asked, not believing her but enjoying the back and forth.

"Yeah."

Oh, he liked this Uma. A little pissed off and sarcastic, maybe flirty underneath. He narrowed his eyes and leaned in, head tilted at an angle, focus divided between her eyes and her lips. "So, princess, just how *crazy* are you?"

Why did that come out sounding like a challenge?

She must have felt it too, judging from the way she responded, her eyes darting over his face, assessing him openly before she responded. "Crazy as a shithouse rat. Still interested?" She imitated his tone, was better at it. "How about you, *Ivan*? How crazy are you?"

"Baby, you have no idea."

Uma lifted her brows. "Did you call me *baby*?"

He stilled. Had he gone too far? Probably. He always did. But a closer look showed a new light in her eyes, bright and a little wild.

"Might have."

Her chest rose and fell once, twice. She broke her gaze away from his, put her cup to her mouth, and took a gulp.

"Better than princess, I guess," she said grudgingly but with a sharp stab of humor that he hadn't realized was there. In that moment, Ive knew he was toast. He'd do whatever she wanted.

Whatever she needed.

He caught himself staring and had to turn away before she ran, screaming what everyone in Blackwood knew about him anyway—that he was a psychotic freak.

She surprised him again when she abruptly shifted gears. "So, the beard. How's it feel without it?"

"Pretty good," he managed to say, rubbing his palm

over his chin, assessing. "Weird, actually. Been a few years."

"Yeah? How long?"

"Um, maybe six or so?"

"You're kidding."

"Nope. My nephew, Gabe? He's never seen me without it."

"Wow... *Wow*."

She looked at him so hard he had to look away again. What was it about this woman that made him feel exactly like a teenager?

❧

Uma couldn't help but stare at his gorgeous face and wonder what would make a man as handsome as this one hide for so long. Mid-perusal, her eyes came to a stuttering halt.

Freckles. A sweet smattering of them danced across the bridge of his nose. Funny how she hadn't noticed them when he'd had the beard. Shaving it off had uncovered more than his jaw. Layers of camouflage had peeled away to reveal a mass of contradictions. Freckles vs. scars. Soft, lush lips vs. hard, mean jaw.

Jesus, she wanted to see him in black and white, with such high contrast that the blue eye would be white and the freckles would pop like flecks of fairy dust. The other eye... Uma couldn't picture how that whiskey color would photograph.

He must have caught something in her gaze, because he sort of squinted at her, shyly flirtatious. Like dipping your toe into hot water after years without a bath; everything south of her belly button went sloshy.

Crap, what was this? She looked away first, relieved to see him get up, grab her mug, and move to fetch a new round of drinks.

"You been married?" he asked from across the room.

She shook her head. Something about the way he asked made her counter, "You?"

"Nah." He hesitated. "Came pretty close once, but—" He stopped short, and she could feel the story there.

Back on his crate, he handed her the cup and then reached his bottle out for a toast. "Here's to being crazy, right?"

They clinked, the sound reminiscent of a million toasts before.

Toasts her pops had shared with friends who stopped by for a drink after closing. Other toasts too: her mother and stepdad celebrating over mugs of whatever home-brew he'd made, before invariably spitting it out and lighting up a doobie.

There'd been toasts in college, with kids whose parents had no idea they were getting wasted on Mommy and Daddy's dime. At least their folks would have cared. Uma's mother didn't give a shit what she did to her body, as long as she did yoga and ate organic.

And then the toasts with Joey. Uma's mind wanted to shy away, but she forced it back.

New Uma faces the good and the bad, remember?

There'd been toasts in nice restaurants where he'd shown her off to his friends. Intimate dinners at his place, before it became *their* place. They'd toasted the future, kids, life together, *love*.

Toasted their tattoos. Together. Sure, he'd pressured her into it, but it had seemed fun, sweet. He'd gotten a massive UMA carved into his shoulder and insisted that she do the same. The JOEY on Uma's back seemed so innocuous now, compared to the rest. A scrolling beacon of perfection lost among the barely legible scribbles that Joey had eventually drowned her in.

Uma's mind skittered away from the *forgive-me* dinners she'd sat through. The nights she'd watched the food cool after slaving over it for hours, nights he'd stayed out with no explanation, times he'd come home drunk and coerced her into having sex with him. Those had been the worst. The feelings of confusion, distrust, even guilt, listening to him blame her for his bad behavior, his absences. She'd stopped forgiving him eventually and had, finally, tried to get away. That hadn't gone over so well.

"So." Ivan picked up the ad and shook it, yanking her back to the present. "Guess we got you here under false pretenses. Sorry about that."

Uma blinked at him through the haze of memories. Something about this place had her disappearing into her head more than usual.

He didn't look sorry, she noticed.

"I wouldn't call it false pretenses. I'd say the description was pretty accurate. Besides, you don't need to apologize to me," she said, sounding snippier than she'd intended, "but you might want to say something to Ms. Lloyd."

"Yeah. She know about it?"

"What do you think?"

"Damn. You tell her?"

"Of course I told her! I had to! You know what I called her? The day I got here?"

"What?"

"I called her an old hag."

He sputtered midsip. "You're shittin' me!" There was laughter in his voice, lighting him from inside, and suddenly those sweet freckles made sense on that stern face.

Uma couldn't help but smile along.

"Not shitting you at all. I called my boss an old hag. On my very first day of work."

"Oh man. Wish I coulda seen her face."

"It was like this." Uma pursed her lips, made big eyes, and Ivan laughed—a round, delicious, velvety sound.

A thin veil of happiness skimmed over the ache inside her, shimmering between them.

Their eyes met, snagged, held, until Uma's shied away, reaching for something, anything, to distract her from the palpable presence in the room—this unwelcome attraction. Her gaze settled on the bed, unmade, sheets a mess.

"Thanks for letting me sleep out here the other night."

"Anytime, babe. Or should I go back to calling you princess?"

She made an irritated *pfff* sound that she didn't really mean. Her brain was sluggish, slower than her mouth, which went ahead and asked questions she hadn't even thought about yet. Silly things like "So, why *don't* you have a wife, Ive?"

His eyebrows popped up into one of those sly, full-of-themselves looks guys sometimes had. "Why, you interested?"

Uma flushed again, hoping he couldn't read how quickly her mind slotted herself neatly into the big, white house behind them.

"Nooo." She drew it out, sounding petulant rather than cool. "You just… You're a good-looking guy. Aren't there women around here?"

"Haven't met the right one, is all." His eyes were still warm when they focused fully on Uma, making her nervy with expectation. "Wouldn't mind a family one day, though."

She went for a joke, way too uncomfortable with the whole conversation. "Well, you've got that house up there. The tricycle. You've practically got a little sign that says 'Insert wife here.'" When no response came, she got fidgety under his gaze and eventually looked away. "This place is great, though. Really great."

Ivan nodded. Uma nodded. It was like a fucking bobblehead convention.

"How old are you?" she asked, thinking he looked a little old to only now be thinking about starting a family.

"Thirty-two."

"Oh."

He raised his eyebrows. "I look older?"

"Not really. Without the beard, you look about twelve, but before…not so much old as impossible to tell. And then there're those bruises, the…" She let the words trail off as she indicated his scar. Some people didn't want their scars pointed out to them—herself included.

His smile said he wasn't easily offended. At least, not about his looks. "One of the perks of my job, I guess." He indicated the anvil behind him. It did seem pretty dangerous—literally playing with fire. "There's also the fightin'."

"Yeah. So I saw. Do you get hurt a lot?"

Uma remembered his limbs entwined with his opponent's, the sound of a hard tussle, and that *smell*.

Oh man. If she ever got ahold of a camera again, that would be her first stop—back to the gym to capture it all. There was nothing like the challenge of communicating those indescribable elements through a photo: the sounds, the smells, the adrenaline, and, above all, this man, the way nature surely meant for him to be. Uma wanted that so badly, she could feel the camera's absence prickle her hand like a phantom limb.

Fuck Joey. Just fuck him. For destroying my equipment, for taking my soul away from me.

"Yeah. Keeps me outta trouble."

"So, you make a living doing this?"

"Yep."

Feeling fidgety, she stood and crossed to the long wall that held the enormous set of gates she'd admired before, intricate and beautiful and masculine. "You're an artist."

"Nah. I just pound metal."

Her fingers lit on a piece of the gate, following it from the top to halfway down. It ran smooth and shiny black, graceful and strong, coming together with the other pieces in waves, without any of the scrolling curlicues you might associate with the medium.

"This is amazing."

"It's for out front."

"Here?"

He nodded, and she could see those gates framing the end of the driveway, facing the street, keeping out intruders. A strong statement.

She took a turn around the room, admiring other

bits of ironwork and random things that had nothing to do with metal. An African-looking wooden statue of a pregnant woman, her large breasts brazenly nude and not remotely sexual. A pair of mercury glass hurricane lamps, the melted candles inside saying they'd seen lots of use. A dog bed in the corner, with a big black cat snoozing comfortably. Funny that the animal had gone completely unnoticed. She squatted and ran a hand over its sleek fur. No response—just the slow, steady breathing of deep, unworried sleep.

Wouldn't that be nice?

"Is this cat alive?" When she looked up, Ivan's eyes were on her, warm and familiar.

"Gertie? Yeah. Doesn't move much."

"Is she old?"

He shrugged. "Had the vet out here to check on my animals. Said she's geriatric."

"I saw all the food bowls. How many animals do you have?"

"Well, got Squeak. And a few cats. There's a wild pony—call him Marley, 'cause of the dreads. The chickens…they're just the girls. Rooster, skunk, you know… Whoever shows up lookin' for chow."

"That's quite a menagerie."

"Somebody's gotta feed 'em."

"And pay for medical care."

"Vet gives me a break. I made him a railing for his new house. And a fence. Few other things."

She smiled, then stood and moved back to the armchair, feeling his eyes on her. "You barter with the vet."

"It's the country, princess."

"Guess I'm not in Kansas anymore."

Their eyes met and held, the warmth in his evident. Uma wondered if he could tell how much she liked him—not just as a man, but as a person.

He leaned in and asked, "So, how long you plannin' on stickin' around?"

"I'm not. I've got…something to do, and then I'm gone." Even as she said it, she hated the thought. Leaving this place. It sounded awful.

His expression hardened. "I don't know what happened with the asshole you're runnin' from, Uma, but I can tell it wasn't good." He canted even closer. "I know I'm big an' ugly, but I don't hurt women. You got that? *Ever*," he said fervently. "I will tear some shit up in a fight. I mean, I've been stupid as hell in my life, but never with a woman. *Never.*"

"Okay," she mumbled, oddly emotional about this outburst.

"Not sayin' it to make you feel bad. I'm just…" She could see him searching for words. "I don't want you scared of me."

"I get it."

He nodded and relaxed onto his crate. Uma sank back into the armchair, letting go of muscles that must have bunched during his tirade. What had happened in his life to rile him up like this?

"I'm not. Scared of you, I mean."

"Good."

After a moment, he leaned forward again, intensity suddenly full force—she absolutely *should* have been scared of that crazy light in his eyes, but she wasn't. She wasn't.

"You may be runnin' from some bad shit, but you

still got attitude. I respect that about you, Uma. Always liked that in a woman. But I'll tell you somethin'. I see a look you get in your eyes sometimes. I recognize that look. Seen it on Squeak's face after I took her from the guy who had her chained up in his yard. Used to beat the shit outta her. I seen it on…" He trailed off, obviously holding back. That was okay. He didn't owe her anything. And maybe she didn't want to hear what else he'd seen. "But I find out who your man is? What he did to you? I see him sniffin' around here lookin' for you? I will tear him apart, Uma."

Oh. She could imagine the scene clearly—Ivan taking Joey down neatly with a surgical punch to the nose, then holding him for her while she worked his skin with his own stupid tattoo machine. Vengeance like she'd never imagined. She wasn't sure she liked the idea of needing a big man to help her exact it, but the possibility was heady. There was no way to take to the courts for revenge. No, the law was Joey's domain, but this…

Absolutely not. Uma stopped her thoughts cold, feeling like a psychopath.

"No. You're not beating anyone up for me." She softened the words with a smile and met his eyes, where bloodlust still shone, perhaps even reflected in hers. "But thank you."

It took all the courage Uma had to reach out then and place her clammy hand over his warm one.

It was her undoing, that contact. Or maybe it had been his tirade—the idea that this man who hardly knew her, this stranger, was willing to defend her. Or perhaps the sight of his heartbreakingly beautiful face, lovely and bare. Either way, Uma crossed a line with that touch.

Like in a movie, when the shot pans around the room, flip-flopping the perspective, she'd changed the rules, broken the barrier, dragging them into unknown territory.

They both stared at her hand for a beat or two before their heads lifted and their eyes met.

He moved first, flipping his hand so their palms came together. That touch was so much more intimate than it should have been, like lying belly to belly, naked. Their skin rasped gently as his thumb rode the bumps of Uma's knuckles.

Ivan's lids looked heavy, and when she glanced at his mouth, it was no longer stern but lush and ripe and hungry. Her eyes fled the invitation there and skittered back to the safety of their hands, but that was ten times worse. Because watching that rough, callused thumb— capable of so much violence—barely skate across the surface of her hand, more gently than she'd ever been touched in her life… That was too much. Like hand porn.

Which obviously wasn't a thing.

Although, maybe it *was* a thing, and if it wasn't, damn it, it should have been. She could imagine the Tumblr feeds, ogled by closeted pervs like herself. She pictured herself hunting down shots of scarred, manly, thick-knuckled hands toying with pathetic, unsuspecting, small ones.

But then, in a moment of clarity, she knew, without fully understanding it, that what really turned her crank here wasn't him dominating her. Oh no. It was the other way around. Her own tiny hand lording it over his big one. *She* had the power here—or at least the illusion of it. And it was heady.

"C'm'ere." He sounded gruff when he tugged Uma

toward him. She resisted briefly, but not out of worry or fear. No, she resisted for the stupid regular reasons: Would she make a fool out of herself? Did her breath stink?

She gave in and allowed him to pull her closer, to the edge of the armchair, and met him halfway.

Their noses were first to meet, hesitant and intimate. Brushing lightly.

"Can I get a kiss?" His hot breath shuddered the question against her, and she could feel his anticipation, nearly as strong as her own.

Without letting herself think too much about it, she did as he asked. It was so easy to brush her mouth to his. A dry touch, with none of the messiness his lush lower lip promised, but enough spark to make her want more.

The second was a real kiss, the kind that makes a noise, lips pursed. Another like that, chaste and neat, but ridiculously exciting in its simplicity. They tilted their heads in easy, mirrored unison, lined up for a deeper one.

And then his tongue, the tip against her lip, sweet and soft, requesting permission. Permission was granted, and he slipped in, sipped at her. Not a perfect kiss, because there were still teeth in the way and noses and such, but with such synchronicity and heat that it was by far the best she'd ever had. Massive hands stroked her cheeks, her ears, her shoulders, making her feel tiny and cherished. Fragile, in a good way, but still whole.

It was so right, and he was so patient, that something pushed her to ramp it up a notch, bite his bottom lip— probably a little harder than she should have—pull it taut, then dive back in. He made a little noise when she did that, a sort of surprised grunt, which made the whole thing even hotter. Uma grabbed hold of his hair and positioned his head right where she wanted it, then wiggled against her seat.

That's when he started to lose it.

His big hands tightened on Uma's face, then moved to her shoulders, and finally her waist. He pulled at her, though not forcefully—more a suggestion, coaxing, like *Why don't you come over here and get on my lap? But only if you want to.* Uma wanted to. She did. But—

"No, don't. Don't, don't." She pulled back, gulping air. It was too much, too soon. "I can't. I'm sorry."

"Okay. It's okay."

Uma's face burned, her body finally alive, but she couldn't do it.

A glance at his face showed his cheek and jaw muscles bunched, his brow furrowed, and his eyes glued to her mouth. His face was stern and hard and a little bit flushed when he looked up and caught her eyes.

"'S okay," he said, then leaned back, purposefully giving her space.

"I'm sorry," Uma whispered.

"What're you sorry for?"

"For freaking out like that."

"You call that freakin' out?" He smiled ruefully. "I'm the one who's sorry."

"Why are *you* sorry?"

"I shouldn't have pushed you." His next words brought another wave of heat to her face. "You're so fuckin' hot, Uma. Got kinda carried away."

Really? Hot? Me? No, she'd been called pretty or pleasant, but never hot. *You clean up well,* Joey had said. Like, if she wore the right clothes and got the right haircut and put on the right makeup, she was acceptable for mixed company. But definitely not the type of girl to make a guy crazy. To make *this* guy look so helplessly lost.

"Thanks." Pleased but suddenly shy, she turned away, embarrassed by her own skittishness, wondering if she'd ever feel normal again.

"We don't have to do anything that scares you. Don't have to do anything at all. Unless you want to, of course. I wouldn't say no, if you asked." He shot a shy smile in Uma's direction before continuing. "We can do whatever you want. *Anything* you want."

12

ONCE THE WORDS WERE OUT, IVE COULDN'T TAKE THEM back. But as he watched her face go from surprise to something that looked like interest, he decided he didn't want to. Good. It'd give her something to think on.

The pause before she spoke wasn't so much awkward as it was full...of promise, maybe. He hoped.

She finally broke it. "I better get back."

He stood and stretched, whistled for Squeak, and made his way to the door. "Come on. I'll walk you."

When she went to grab her empty mug, he stopped her. "Leave that. I'll get it."

Outside, the air was bright, their breath visible, their footsteps on gravel the only sounds but for a lone owl and something skittering deep in the woods.

"Thanks for caring," he said, finally breaking their silence.

"Caring about what?"

"Ms. Lloyd. Not sure most people would give a damn the way you do. About the ad."

"Yeah. Well, she's not always nice, but she's…
lonely." She shrugged. "I guess I can relate."

He huffed out a tiny sound of humor and agreement
and glanced up at the stars, so bright above them. When
they rounded the bend and the dark house came into
sight, Ive had a moment of panic, like he'd regret it if he
didn't touch her again.

So he reached out a hand, and instead of grabbing
hers like he wanted, he rubbed the back of his knuckles
against hers. It was probably a reflex that had her turning her hand and stretching out her fingers for his, but
he took it, loving the feel of her skin against his, the way
she held on as if she liked it.

They didn't kiss good-bye or anything, but he kept
her hand until the last possible second, only loosening
when they reached the foot of the kitchen stairs.

She responded to his whispered, "Night," with a
smile, then turned and jogged up to the door.

He stood outside Ms. Lloyd's house and waited until
the lights turned off. Kitchen, hall, followed by a couple
upstairs switching on, then off. After a while, he started
back up the drive toward the forge, a jumble of things
inside him, too mixed up to unravel.

Ive wasn't the most sensitive guy in the world. He'd
always thought of himself as having two basic settings:
On and Off. Normal and Angry. Sane and Crazy.

What Uma did to him, though, blew that theory out
of the water. Nothing with her fit into any of his usual
categories. Nothing with her was simple.

As a rule, he paid attention to what people did, not
what they said. He had a learning disability—he'd
finally found out in prison. It was one of those things

that had made everything difficult growing up. He'd never learned how to deal with the constant frustration. It had always translated into anger. His grandma had yelled; his teachers had scolded. Eventually, the only thing to make a lick of difference had been Uncle Gus taking him out to this very workshop—a woodshop back then—and showing him how to use his hands. Even so, he'd spent his life feeling like he was shouting through a wall of glass.

Everything was different with Uma.

First of all, when she spoke, he actually heard her. That wasn't something he had much experience with. Usually, words rolled off him. Sounds were meaningless unless backed up by actions.

She'd called him an artist, said what he did was amazing. Her compliment had meant more to him than any he'd ever gotten. People had *oohed* and *aahed* over his work before, but their praise had been just words: worthless.

What she said was different. It held meaning, weight. Ive actually *heard* her. Like English dubbing on a foreign film. But, more than that, he felt like he knew her— knew what she meant without her having to say a thing.

He'd do anything with her, he'd said. But it was more than that. He'd do almost anything *for* her too. Anything at all to help her heal. When he'd seen her happy, he'd wanted to laugh himself; when she was scared, he'd wanted to die or—no. Not die.

Kill. He'd kill to protect her.

Some small part of him knew this wasn't normal. It wasn't what he was supposed to feel, but he couldn't help it. This was who he was. She'd been here a week, but it was like they'd been together forever. She belonged here.

He pulled open the door to his forge, took a deep breath, and drew in what he thought might be her smell, still lingering on the air. It was familiar, elemental.

His.

The knowledge was fierce and primal. It would have scared him if it hadn't been so right.

❧

Anything you want. Those words kept repeating—a flashing neon or a ticker tape in her mind. All the way down the drive, with Ivan by her side, up the back steps under his watchful gaze, closing the dead bolt behind her in the kitchen, up the stairs, quietly, and finally, in the lonely safety of her room, those three words echoed through her mind.

Under the safety of darkness, Uma stripped down to her shirt and underwear before getting into bed, the frigid air lovely against her overheated skin. She could almost hear the sizzle as she slid between the sheets.

It was like being a network of nerve endings, made sensitive by just that one amazing kiss. She couldn't remember ever feeling like this—so alive, on fire, awake in a way she hadn't been in years.

Tonight, Uma didn't want to go to sleep, although for once, she might have been able to without much trouble. Apparently, two moonshines and the protection of a strong man did that to a girl. It had been so long since she'd had that wash of girlish excitement—the crackle of new attraction. She wanted to revel in the sensation.

Anything you want.

After Ivan's offer, she'd been too shaky to stay without making more of an ass of herself. The walk down the drive had been excruciating—in a good way—filled with an awareness of him and the sort of anticipation that comes with knowing a guy likes you, but not giving in to the attraction.

And that kiss... If she *had* succumbed, oh wow. What came next would have been amazing. There was no doubt. She'd never been kissed like that. Had never reacted so strongly.

Would he try again? Probably. Did she want him to? Maybe.

Oh, who was she kidding? *Yes, hell yes.*

But she shouldn't. She wasn't hanging around Blackwood, after all. She'd be leaving once the tattoos were gone, and the last thing she needed was something to keep her here.

Uma breathed in, remembering Ivan's smell, reveling in the recollection. That first slow moment, faces barely touching, getting to know him with her nose before letting her mouth or teeth or tongue get involved. The moment had been distilled to nothing but those senses. She'd never been so turned on in her life.

They were so different, though. He was a man made to inhabit his body; everything in his life centered around his hands, his arms, his muscles, all working together. He was carnality itself, and Uma was—

She was a mess. And so, so tired of inhabiting this useless shell of a body. It had let her down when she'd needed it the most, left her vulnerable, pinned to the floor. Weak. Nothing but a pitiful, *weak* woman.

We can do whatever you want. The memory made

Uma shudder. God, how could someone who'd seemed like such a brute be that way? Would he really let her do whatever she wanted to him? Without trying to force anything on her?

No. No, she was leaving.

But then again, he was a man. And men *wanted* temporary, right? Lots of them did, so maybe—

Uma's eyes drifted closed as she remembered how carried away she'd been. She regretted not paying more attention to the feel of him under her mouth and hands.

Oh, why hadn't she touched more of him? What were his arms like? Those firm biceps, or the long slope of thigh she'd ogled as he worked. His face. Her breath caught at that. She wanted to touch his lips, to test their springy plushness with her hands.

She pressed her thumb to her mouth, wondering how much harder his would be under her fingers. Her imagination skittered on, over the stubble sprouting along his jaw. She wanted it rough, abrasive like sandpaper.

An image intruded: Joey's smooth, perfectly shaved chin. It was a cold shower to Uma's budding libido. She gritted her teeth at the memory of him pinning her shoulder with that chin while his hands held her arms and his deceptively heavy legs covered hers. Every part of him had incapacitated every single inch of *her* that night. She'd been helpless. Utterly.

No. This wasn't what Uma wanted to think about. She wanted to thrill at images of Ivan, thick and strong and raw. And yet so gentle. The antidote to everything Joey.

Joey. Would he ever leave her alone? As surely as he was out there somewhere, looking for her, he was with

Uma, every second of every day, dogging her footsteps. Haunting her life.

Fucking Joey. Regret fisted her innards, making her queasy as she thought of him. Maybe she needed to let them come, those images. Maybe she needed to let him back into her brain to exorcise him completely from her life.

Thinking about him took courage. Almost as much as it would take to finally work up the balls to look herself in the mirror, at the obscene evidence he'd left all over her body.

Okay, if this is what it takes. Uma opened her eyes, needing to be wide awake to face the memories.

∽◌∾

Uma was a goner the first time she met him. It had been a wedding, some cousin of Joey's marrying her longtime fiancé. Uma'd been there as the photographer. Considering her free-love upbringing, Uma had been a pretty inexperienced twenty-four-year-old—a couple of boyfriends under her belt, and a single, stupid one-night stand in college. Nothing that could have prepared her for Joey's laser-sharp attention.

He'd been lovely to look at: tall and wiry, almost slender, with piercing blue eyes that drew a girl in fast. Too fast. He'd had the same appeal Frank Sinatra must have had in his heyday: easy to look at, smooth voice, and pure sex oozing from every pore. Panty-dropping eyes to go with his silver tongue. A deadly combination.

Uma would never forget the moment she'd first laid eyes—or rather, lens—on Joey. She'd taken the photo, knowing it was a good one, and then realized, with a strange jolt of awareness, that its subject had been look-ing directly at her. He'd gazed right through the camera and literally set his sights on her. Out of all the perfect, well-dressed women there, how strange that he'd noticed the invisible one—the woman behind the scenes.

Uma had never considered herself particularly attrac-tive, but that evening, Joey had made her beautiful. He'd convinced her to dance, to kiss. She'd never done anything so unprofessional in her career, but he'd been pretty darn convincing. So convincing, in fact, that she'd had sex with him later that night.

That first night had set the rhythm for their entire relationship. Everything moved so quickly between them. Uma always wondered if he knew he didn't have much time before everything changed. Before he messed things up.

Within two months, she'd moved into his place, gone on the pill. By the end of the year, most of her friends had given up on her. Oddly, Mom remained the one person Joey hadn't minded sharing her with. Uma never understood how he knew from the get-go that he'd found an ally in her mother. He'd always had the strongest, oddest instincts when it came to how best to hurt her.

At the same time, Joey had taken such good care of Uma, given her everything he'd thought she wanted. He'd tried so hard to get her to stop working, telling her that this was also part of spoiling her rotten. It was the only point on which she'd staunchly refused to give in. Not working, she knew, would never make her happy.

Eventually, in a roundabout way, he'd ended up win-ning, even on that front.

After more than a year of refusing to admit that there might be trouble in paradise, Joey had cheated on her. It was a strange move from someone so seemingly obsessed. Why on earth would he cheat after making her the center of his world?

That's when she'd realized what he'd really done. He hadn't, in fact, made Uma the center of his world, but had rather made himself the center of hers.

She'd found out about his cheating when the woman called their home. She'd spilled the story, every detail so clearly *Joey* that they had to be real. Uma's hurt and embarrassment were terrible, but after suffering through Joey's apologetic self-flagellation, it finally sank in that she didn't care that much. A dangerous thought to have about someone so obsessed.

From there, things steadily grew worse until the day she left him. He started by accusing her of cheating, convinced she'd done it to get back at him. In all the time they'd been together, the only thing Uma had ever hidden from Joey was the money she'd put away to purchase her own car. A consummate liar himself, he had a sixth sense for when people tried to pull one over on him. Accusations led to yelling, then pushing, and eventually, a slap across the face, leaving an angry red welt in its wake. At the time, that slap had been the worst thing anyone had ever done to her.

She'd had no idea how bad things could get.

13

TATTOO REMOVAL SUCKS.

Uma had known it would—had spent a good chunk of the last six months researching it online. But it still surprised her how very bad it was. It hurt, *God it hurt*, but she would have withstood ten times the pain to get all of the poison out of her.

Motivation, it turned out, was quite the painkiller.

When she got to Dr. Hadley's office, only eight days after arriving in Blackwood, the lights were dim and the receptionist gone for the day. At Uma's knock, the doctor came to the door herself, a skeleton crew of one.

"Come on back, and we'll get started." She sounded friendly, capable, which was good, considering how raw Uma's nerves were. "I think we should take it slow and begin with one arm today. The treatment downtime is often the worst, so I want to see how you do and then work from there. That sound good?"

"Sure."

"Any preference on what we do first?"

Uma's eyes flicked down to her left arm. She'd had

the debate back at the house: most visible or most offensive? She'd finally opted for visible.

She lifted her left arm. "This one, I think. But I used the cream you gave me on both."

"Excellent. That should help numb you. Let's get your shirt off and ice this as best we can. Then we can get started."

Let's get your shirt off. It sounded so easy, a quick move: grab fabric, swing it up and over the head. Nothing to it. Only it wasn't like that. Her shirt, for one thing, felt stuck in place, impossible to move. Not heavy like a winter coat, but tight like a straitjacket, her arms trapped by…by what? *Nothing. Just take the damn thing off.*

It took strength to finally peel it away, and rather than clutch at it like a security blanket, she threw it to the side before lying back on the table to stare at the ceiling while the doctor covered her arm with ice packs. Her stomach roiled, but settled again after a few minutes.

The process sounded pretty simple: certain laser strengths worked for blue, others for black, green, and so on. Unfortunately, Joey hadn't stopped that night when one color was gone. No, when the bottle of black was empty, he'd moved on to blue, then green, and finally red. *Not your color*, he'd said with his brand of regret. Not her color, but he'd been obliged to go on anyway, hadn't he? Carrying on with his grisly work until every single bottle was empty.

"This is the laser; this is the chiller. I run the cool air over it first, which helps with the pain. You ready?"

Uma nodded.

"Okay. Let's begin. I'll start down here. Let me know if you need a break, all right?"

"Okay. Thanks, Doctor."

"Call me George."

"Oh, right. Thank you, George."

Dr. Hadley grabbed Uma's hand and squeezed it for a moment, handed her dark glasses, and put on her own before snapping on a pair of rubber gloves. At the push of a couple of buttons, a machine rumbled to life.

The thing was loud—shockingly so, at first. Uma could imagine how this might set off a soldier's PTSD. As it worked, the laser sounded like sharp bursts of automatic fire and looked like tiny, bright explosions burning white into her skin, like splatters of hot oil…but the burn lingered longer than bacon grease would have.

Pain is relative.

Getting the first tattoo had hardly hurt at all. She and Joey had been drinking, and they'd been happy. So stupidly in love. It had been his idea initially, although, being Joey, he'd changed history to suit himself and had given Uma the credit. There'd been a slight hesitation on her part. Yes, she'd loved him—or, at least, she'd thought she had—but she'd also known how people could change, known they could disappear from your life for one reason or another. She'd seen the impermanence of her mother's relationships and worried about putting something so indelible on her body. But Joey had prodded and cajoled her through that moment of sanity, making her feel bad for not believing in *them* as strongly as he had.

Since Joey had gotten tattoos in the past, he'd gone first. UMA. For some reason, even at the time, seeing those three letters scrolling over his upper back hadn't given her the feeling of security she'd been looking for.

And then Uma's turn. The four letters in JOEY took up more space than her paltry three, and on her back, they'd looked massive, as if already he owned more of her than she did of him.

Afterward, the tattoo guy—she could still remember his name, Zap—had rolled back his chair, giving her room to get up and look. "What d'ya think?" he'd asked around the toothpick in his mouth.

Uma had stood, staring over her shoulder in the mirror and feeling two distinct, warring sensations.

First, there was some pride. Her eyes caught Joey's, and she'd recognized it in his face. It only occurred to her later that it had been pride of belonging, while his had been pride of ownership. Not the same thing at all, as it turned out.

The second thing she'd felt upon seeing those dark, dark letters stamped on her skin was a sharp twinge of regret.

It was that feeling that came back to haunt Uma every time she caught even the faintest glimpse of Joey's legacy, the same weight that made sleep so elusive at night. *This is it.* The words had floated through her brain as she'd stared past her reflection into the mirror that night. *It's permanent. There's no turning back now.*

Feeling the doctor's zapper work its way over the thick black M embedded in her wrist, then the I, the N, and E, brought something new trickling in. It was the first time it had appeared in months, a tiny grain of a notion so foreign, it wasn't even clear whether it would stick around long enough to be identified. It dug down into Uma's heart, lodged itself there, and nearly choked her with its newness. As the ink dissolved slowly—oh so slowly—the sensation, whatever it was, dug in deeper, mingling with her flesh, melding with her blood.

After twenty minutes or so, Dr. Hadley—no, *George*—leaned back to switch the machine off. The absence of sound left the room feeling empty and so very still. She pushed her dark glasses up onto her head and smiled.

"That's it for today, Uma."

A reluctant glance at her arm told Uma that it was pretty bad. A whitish cloud over the tattoos, dotted with minute specks of blood, but the ink was still there.

"I'll put some petroleum jelly on it. It's best to leave it uncovered, if you can. Or wear loose clothing. Cotton. Not this tight thing you've got here. Can you do that?"

"Oh. I don't know. I—"

A wave of nausea rose up. Not again. She wouldn't throw up here again, damn it.

"I can't wear my shirt?"

"You can wear something loose, but it's best to leave it out if you can. And you'll need to reapply the petroleum jelly to keep from scarring. I usually recommend buying a pack of cotton shirts you can throw on."

"Okay. Yeah, okay."

Cotton shirts and petroleum jelly. At least today was payday.

"You okay?" The doctor looked worried.

Uma considered her question. *Am I okay?*

Practical matters aside, she actually thought she might be.

"I think so."

"The first session's hard. I know." Dr. Hadley grabbed Uma's hand again and squeezed. "You'll get through this. I promise. All right?"

"Yeah." Uma squeezed back. "Thank you."

It was true, she realized. She was going to be okay.
One less layer of ink to pull out. One day closer to
becoming a clean slate.

Hope was a tiny grain lodged in her heart. Like a
speck of dirt in an oyster shell, she had a sudden notion
that the minuscule particle would pester her, gathering layer upon layer of protective grit until it built into
something big enough to hold on to.

For the first time, there was light at the end of the
tunnel.

I can do this, she thought. And, for once, she knew,
without a doubt, that it was true.

∽૦৩∾

With no other options for now, Uma slipped back into
her shirt before driving back to Ms. Lloyd's place. As
she drew near the house, she came close to releasing
the brake and letting the car glide those few extra feet
down the road to Ivan's. The fantasy of disappearing
into his workshop and his bed to heal was unbearably
appealing.

She pretended, for the handful of seconds it took to
walk to Ms. Lloyd's front porch, that her arm didn't
burn and her heart wasn't tight in her chest.

The door, of course, was locked. Faced with the prospect of walking her scarred, aching body to Ivan's or
facing the she-devil inside, she'd opt for the latter.

"Please, please, please, open up," she begged Ms.
Lloyd—or God or providence—as she shoved uselessly
at the front door. She started banging, more frantic than
the occasion probably warranted. But standing there

made her feel naked, the pain of her arm bringing her
back to the night she'd worked so hard to forget. She
wouldn't look down, wouldn't acknowledge that it hurt,
wouldn't give these wounds another moment of attention. Blinders on, head in the sand.

Don't see it. Don't feel it.

"Ms. Lloyd! Let me in, please!" Her voice came out
thin, frantic. Her hands scrabbled at the knob again, and
she twisted, twisted, pushed.

Locked.

Uma's head turned woozy, eyeballs constricted.

Stress, she thought. *This is stress. Breathe. In. Out.
In. Out.*

The door suddenly swung open, and she fell in
behind it, jostling her boss in the process. After pulling the door from the woman's grasp and slamming it
shut, she leaned back on it, bent double from the waist,
gasping. It was like that first day here, against the side
of the house, and—

A ghostly whisper of Ivan's warm hand. Just a
memory, but tangible enough to calm her. She glanced
up and caught Ms. Lloyd's horrified expression.

"What the hell is that?" the woman snarled, pointing
at Uma's arm. Her sleeve was stained dark with grease
and dotted with blood.

"Nothing." She tried to move to the stairs, but before
Uma understood her intention, Ms. Lloyd blocked her
way, grabbed hold of the fabric, and yanked it up, baring
half her left arm.

It hurt. Oh, it hurt.

"You call that nothing? What is wrong with you?
This what you've been doin' in town? Gettin' these

filthy things put on?" Ms. Lloyd's accent got thicker when she was riled up. More country and less genteel.

"No," Uma muttered. Her vision, dark at the edges, narrowed on Ms. Lloyd's face, the focus too close: an eyebrow, a hair.

"You just did those."

She swallowed. "I didn't."

"Don't lie to me, girl. You think I'm blind? It's all red."

A tiny, snide little voice inside Uma almost pushed her to laugh. At Ms. Lloyd's innocence, maybe. The fact that she had no idea what a new tattoo looked like. It was weirdly liberating. Because what did it matter anyway, if she knew? "I'm getting them *removed*."

A pause. "What?"

She forced herself to watch the woman's face as understanding dawned.

Yeah, that's it, lady. Look at the freak show you hired.

Those enormous black eyes took in the story, read the words scrawled across Uma's skin, no doubt shoring it up as ammunition to drag out at some later date. The messy Js and Os, Es and Ys, veering off into skid marks when Uma had gotten a kick in. Other things too, marking Uma as devalued property, like where he'd forgotten the T in BITCH and scratched the whole word out. What she couldn't see was that he'd moved to the other side to start afresh. Mostly, though, what Ms. Lloyd stared at was a road map to the single worst night of Uma's life—a series of jagged, unintelligible inscriptions, documenting Joey's descent into jealousy-fueled madness.

"Who did this to you?"

"My ex." With a sigh of relief, Uma pulled the sleeve back down.

"I'm callin' the sheriff."

"No!" She stopped Ms. Lloyd with a hand to the wrist—bird thin and brittle.

"You sayin' you wanted this?"

"Of course not."

How could Uma explain what Joey had done? How he'd chased her to the door, yanked at her hair, pulling it out by the roots, and dragged her back by the ankle? Crushed her like a bug and trussed her up like a pig. Held her down and hurt her, over and over and over.

How could she possibly tell this woman about the humiliation, the degradation, the *foreverness* of it? How she'd begged and cried and tried to fight him off. But in the end, she'd endured it, hadn't she? Fucking weak, pathetic thing that she was, Uma had lain there and let it happen.

She wouldn't do that today. No cringing, no flinching, no giving in. Today, she'd—

"Well, honey, we've got to do somethin' about this, then."

"What?"

An evil glint shone in Ms. Lloyd's eye, and for once, it wasn't directed at Uma.

"We can't. He's… I can't go after him."

"Why not?"

"He's…he's powerful, Ms. Lloyd."

"He ain't powerful enough to get away with something like that."

"Oh, he is." Uma briefly shut her eyes, swallowed.

"Ridiculous." Ms. Lloyd's mouth worked for a while,

searching for an argument, a way to push Uma into doing something. "I'm gonna—"

"Listen to me, please," Uma broke in quietly, looking the woman dead in the eye. "You can't call the cops. You can't tell anyone about this. He's a prosecutor. In Northern Virginia. Big time." Ms. Lloyd opened her mouth to argue again, and Uma stopped her. "You want to stay in this house forever, hidden away from the real world? That's your prerogative. I'll do your shopping, I'll cook your meals and clean up after you, as long as I'm in town, but I won't ever try to make you go outside. Never." Her voice came out in a harsh whisper, surprising in its strength. "You can lord it over me and treat me like crap, but remember that it's because I *say* you can. Don't you think for *one second* that you get to decide anything for me. I make my own choices now. Nobody else gets to decide for me. Not you or anybody else. Got it?"

In the moment that followed, Ms. Lloyd stared at Uma with her big, unblinking owl eyes. The ticking of the rooster clock in the other room counted down the seconds. Finally, instead of the irritation Uma had expected, understanding dawned—perhaps even a jot of respect.

"*Got it?*" she repeated.

Ms. Lloyd reached out and grabbed Uma's hand, hard and quick, before letting it go and turning around to thump her way into the kitchen.

"Don't snipe at me, Irma," regular, mean-ass Old Lady Lloyd spat over her shoulder. "You gonna cover yourself up, or do I have to look at those nasty things all night?"

"I need to buy a couple of shirts, but…" Uma's voice trailed off. She'd apparently used up her store of courage for the day.

"What? Spit it out."

"I've been here a week. It's payday."

"Oh, for heaven's sake," Ms. Lloyd muttered, veering off toward the musty, rarely used dining room. "Always wanting somethin', aren't they?"

She waited in the entryway while her boss rustled around in the other room and returned to press a wad into Uma's hand.

"Thank you."

"Tomorrow, you go buy yourself something decent to wear. It'll be a relief to see you looking nice, for once."

After the other woman walked off, Uma looked at the money in her hand. It wasn't nearly enough to live off in the real world, but it felt like a fortune.

Amazing how fast perspective could change. A few months ago, she'd pulled in a cool four thousand on a wedding—just one day of shooting and another half day processing before getting it to the client. All that money sitting in the bank, but she couldn't touch it. Not with Joey looking for her. One wrong move, and it'd be all over.

But today, she was rich off a couple hundred bucks, a boss whose contempt had only slightly diminished, and an inappropriate attraction to a man she should be avoiding like the plague. What could possibly go wrong?

14

WITH HER NEWFOUND RICHES, UMA BOUGHT JEANS, A PAIR
of ankle boots, and a few cotton tops, plus a bright-green,
summery tunic from the sale rack and a navy cardigan
dripping with sequins. Fully aware that her choices were
completely impractical—ostentatious even, considering her finances—she bought them anyway. Maybe
she could feel like a woman again. Slight progress, but
nonetheless worth celebrating, right?

Joey would have hated her purchases. The thought
made her smile. Weird to think that the things he claimed
to like about her in the beginning—her easy laugh, dark
humor, quiet vivacity—were the first to go.

She'd never been the show-offy type, but there was
nothing wrong with a little attention every now and then.
Uma thought that she might even have been fun, once.
By the time she left him, Joey had leeched every ounce
of color from her life, cloaking her in a sad spectrum of
grays. Ironic in contrast to the ties and shirts he favored:
pinks and purples and bright, bright blue, like his eyes.
He was such a peacock when it came to his wardrobe;

he must not have been interested in competition from his girlfriend.

Driving back to the house with her new purchases, Uma wondered which one she'd wear to go see Ivan later.

The idle thought brought her up short. *I'm an idiot.* Acting like he was expecting her when she hadn't seen or heard from him in two days.

After dinner, Ms. Lloyd watched Uma come downstairs in the green shirt and said, "You look nice." They both stopped moving at those three words, blinked, and waited for the other shoe to drop. Uma half expected her to finish the sentence with something like "for a sideshow freak." Surprisingly, Ms. Lloyd didn't temper the compliment with an insult. Of course, she couldn't hold back her curiosity. "Where you headed looking like that?"

Uma held up a six-pack of beer she'd picked up with her precious few dollars. "Thought I'd go see Ivan and take him this."

"Is that what young ladies do nowadays? Visit men with bottles of booze?"

"Yep."

"Not very subtle, is it?"

"Maybe I'm not a subtle person, Ms. Lloyd."

"Well, you tell him I'm still mad at him."

"About the ad?"

"Yes," she sniffed, glancing at an enormous bouquet she'd received that morning. "He'll have to do a whole lot better than flowers if he wants to make it up to me."

"I'm sure you'll figure something out." Uma moved toward the door. "You have a key I can use to get back in later?"

"Not after dark. I won't—"

"Do you have a key? Yes or no?"

After a brief hesitation and a huff that might have been for show, Ms. Lloyd pulled a key on a chain from around her neck and unlocked the bureau in her dining room. She rifled around for a bit, found a key, and pushed it hard into Uma's palm, keeping her hand there as she spoke.

"You lose this, I will never let you back into this house. *Ever.* Understand?"

"Yes, ma'am."

The look she gave next was pure Black Widow, lips pursed in disapproval, one eyebrow higher than the other, eyes wide, unblinking. It was her judgmental, *don't try to play me for a fool* face.

"Oh, stop it," said Uma, before walking out the front door and locking it behind her—five times.

She could tell Ms. Lloyd had a million things she was dying to say, but she wouldn't give her the chance. There would always be time later on for insults. Over a game of rummy, perhaps, or during one of their contentiously healthy meals.

The new-Uma, new-shirt high carried her halfway down Ivan's drive before she realized he wasn't home. The little cottage-like structure, up until then always blazing with light and heat, was cold and dark; no Squeak to greet her either. She stood in front of his empty workshop, deflated. Her left arm throbbed hot and tight beneath the sparkly cardigan, even in the cool night air.

He'd apparently gone out for the evening. Probably publicly unveiling his gorgeous face, sharing it with the world. She pictured him in some bar, surrounded by women, neck deep in cleavage. It pissed her off. He'd shaved for *her*, damn it. Then she'd gone and skipped a night at his place—one night.

Absurd though it was, for a moment she was convinced he'd taken off to punish her. *Maybe I'm overreacting*, she thought. *Maybe not every man punishes you for perceived injustices.*

The walk back up the porch steps was a sad death march compared to the twinkle toes she'd pranced out on.

"What, d'you get stood up?" Her boss's voice was perkier than ever before.

"Nope." Uma smiled tightly and made her way to the kitchen.

"I found it odd, actually, that young Ive would be home on a Saturday."

"Why's that?"

"He's never around on Saturdays. Has a standing date, I believe."

No way would she take the bait. Uma swallowed the oily ball of jealousy that rose up to clog her throat, glanced down at the six-pack in her hand, and considered her options. It was too cold to sit out on the porch, drinking alone, and Ms. Lloyd was already being insufferable. She could imagine her saying "There goes the neighborhood" in that irritating, singsong Scarlett O'Hara voice she put on.

And Uma wanted to show off her new clothes, damn it.

That decided it.

She ran up to her room for her purse and car key, ignoring Ms. Lloyd's pointed stare from her perch on the sofa.

"Change of plans. Headed out for drinks instead." Uma purposely kept it vague. The woman didn't need to know that those drinks would be solo.

Sounding smug, Ms. Lloyd called, "Don't stay out too late!" before the door slammed.

She'd known that Ivan was never there on a Saturday and yet had let Uma waltz over there anyway, all full of hope and excitement.

Uma took a moment to seethe on the front porch before shaking it off.

"Jerk," she whispered and tromped down the steps to her car.

❧

Blackwood's one and only bar was noisy and dark on a Saturday night. Uma could have driven all the way into Charlottesville with its bigger, classier places, but she liked the idea of getting to know her new town.

My new town, she thought before tamping down the possessive edge to that phrase. Blackwood was just a pit stop. She kept forgetting that important fact.

Despite what the name implied, there was nothing particularly cozy about the Nook. Had it not been for the low lighting and the warm bodies filling it, it would have had all the atmosphere of a walk-in freezer. Uma didn't have tons of experience with places like this—a country dive.

Everything, from the neon High Life sign buzzing in the window to the oddly assorted mix of people crowding the single room—even the general air of frenetic debauchery—was all new and wonderful. The unfamiliar rush of sidling up to a bar on her own, without

Joey's heavy hand pressed to her lower back, made her light-headed.

She looked forward to sitting and having a drink. Like an adult. Like a *person*, for God's sake. She pushed through that stupid fear of seeing Joey everywhere and forced herself to be strong, independence a steel rod in her spine.

The bartender acknowledged her immediately, another sign that things were going her way. He seemed efficient, so she didn't take the attention personally, although a tiny part of her was flattered that he'd noticed her at all.

"What'll it be, dahlin'?" he asked, British accent completely out of place in the wilds of central Virginia. Was this a put-on?

"Whatever's easy."

"You're in a bar in the arsehole of the world on a Saturday night, love. Nothing's easy. But I'm in the mood for a challenge."

"Surprise me," she said, in part to find out what kind of beverage a British bartender would sling and partly because she had no idea what to order.

As he headed off to mix her drink, a shoulder bumped hers, and her breath caught in her throat when she saw it wasn't Joey—not even close, but still, the stress made her jumpy.

A few minutes later, the bartender set a tall glass in front of her. "Pimm's Cup," he said with a flourish. It looked like a fruit salad, so spiked with garnish and decorations, there was no easy way to approach it.

"Fancy," she said as her heartbeat slowed to a normal rhythm.

"It's good to have someone to fob all me fancy

umbrellas off on. So don't go anywhere, all right, love? This one's on me." He winked.

Uma forced a smile, wishing she could take a quick snapshot of the cocktail and another of the bartender, who was handsome in a blond hustler kind of way. Maybe a third shot of the couple, grinding inappropriately on the dance floor. All sweat and tongues.

Next week. Next week, she'd spend her last fifty bucks on a cheap point and shoot. Hell, she'd get a disposable camera if she had to. She needed something to filter all the newness that made up this updated version of her. *My new me.*

The bartender came back and pointed at her glass. "What'd you reckon?"

"It's delicious."

"What's your name, love?"

"Uma."

"Rory." He held out a hand, and she hesitated only a few seconds before giving him a firm shake. She liked him. Confident, kind, no bullshit. "You meeting someone?"

"No, I'm not. I'm on my own." She took a breath, ignoring the itch in the middle of her back that insisted Joey was somewhere close behind her. "New in town."

"That so? You've come to the right place then."

"What about you? Lived in Blackwood long?"

"Few years now."

That was a surprise. You'd need a knife to cut through that accent.

"You look about bowled over. Don't reckon I blend into good old Virgin-i-ay?"

Despite her nerves, she laughed at his atrocious faux southern drawl. "Hmm. Stick with the Brit thing."

"You don't need to tell me, love. The girls fancy it." Another wink and a shrug before slapping his hand on the bar, close to where hers lay, and pushing off in the direction of other customers more in need of booze than Uma.

But I sure could use the company, she thought as the anxiety trickled back in.

He's not here, she worked to convince herself. And to prove it, she swiveled and did a slow turn to scope out the rest of the bar, secretly hoping she'd see Ivan. He would obliterate this fear of Joey. He'd take it and bash it to bits.

This was quite a hookup place, bodies bumping and humping in time to music that was as out of place as the barman—some kind of clubby dance music, electronic and hip-hop. Nothing she'd recognize.

The tiny dance floor was crowded with people— girls in a group, a few guys apparently trying to push their way in, unsuccessfully, and some couples going at it. Around the dancers were arranged a scattering of two-tops, with a few booths against the fogged-up front window. Every table was occupied.

All these people crowded into a relatively small space made it sweltering inside. Sticky. Uma had the weirdest awareness of breathing in their air. Hot, moist, full of booze and maybe sex. Most people had stripped down to tank tops and T-shirts, and she stood out for her overdressed state and the skittishness she couldn't quite hide.

She looked around again, in search of something she could be a part of, and *boom*: she felt a wave of jealousy at the sight of a tall man dancing with a woman.

He's mine, her brain spat unreasonably. A split second later, she saw it wasn't Ivan. Not even close. Jesus. When had she become completely obsessed with her next-door neighbor?

To clear those ridiculous thoughts, Uma did another quick scan of the dance floor. Her gaze kept going back to that same couple, whose torrid moves made her insides a little heavy. She was like an intruder who couldn't look away.

What would Ivan dance like? No matter how she tried, she couldn't quite picture it.

She came to with a start when her sweaty glass was plucked from her hand, to be instantly replaced by a fresh one.

"Watch out. This one packs a *punch*."

"Mmm!" she said with a thumbs-up to Rory. "What is it?"

"Regent's *Punch*. Get it?" She groaned and went back to watching her couple.

Rory's voice was suddenly close to her ear. "Like to watch, do you, Uma?"

She turned to find him leaning across the bar, a knowing little smile on his face.

"What?" she asked, then followed his eyes as he nodded toward the couple. "Oh. I'm, uh… I'm a photographer."

He looked interested. "That so? Well then, I reckon you *are* a voyeur."

Although she blushed, Uma bit back the denial. She'd decided to stop lying, at least to herself.

"A professional voyeur, no less. Getting paid for your fetish. *Lucky girl.*" He pushed off and left her to think about that. Uma watched him go. Straight back, wide shoulders, thin hips…rangy. And yet, she couldn't have been less interested. A burst of cool air whooshed in to suck away some of the room's stifling heat, and Uma glanced toward the door, unconsciously hopeful she'd see her handsome neighbor.

No luck, but the extra jolt of excitement remained, mixing with the booze in her veins. Lord, was she in trouble.

A little off-kilter from the booze, she spotted him. *Joey.* Blood rushed to her face, and she almost fell off her stool in fear when he turned and—

Not him. Thank God. Not him. Her heart continued to pound a rough beat in her chest. Too big, too much.

A few seconds later, there he was again, in the mirror behind the bar. For a long, suspended moment, she could see her pulse pumping darkly behind her eyes, could hear its *thwump* deep in her head.

In another heartbeat, the man shifted, morphed into someone completely different. Not him. And neither was the woman near the door, whose short hair was the only possible resemblance. Shaking so hard it must have been obvious to the people around her, she pushed her tunnel vision back and forced herself to focus.

Enough was enough. Fueled by Pimm's and British punch, with a good dose of anger thrown into the mix, Uma made a decision. Joey didn't get to show up in her life anymore. He didn't get to be a ghost in her mind or smother her skin. This had to stop. Now. She got up, made a dash through a break in the crowd toward the restroom, locked herself inside with relief, and stared in the dingy mirror.

This is it. She grabbed hold of one sleeve. Her breath

picked up, tight in a chest that had suddenly grown too small to contain it. Inch by inch, her right hand revealed a decorated left arm. And all the while, her eyes remained fixed on her face, defying her. She pulled the green fabric to bunch at the elbow and waited for her gaze to catch up.

A knock on the door broke up her internal duel, and she released the sleeve, relieved in a cowardly way, but also weighed down by so much disappointment.

That fantasy of the dancers? Of Ivan touching her, just wanting to touch her? How could any of that be possible if she couldn't even look at herself?

At a second knock, she called, "Be right out!" and washed her hands, looking herself in the eye, hard and straight.

She couldn't look tonight. Fine. That was fine, but she was done letting Joey decide her fate. No more jumping at shadows or hiding in restrooms.

Rory's smile when she made it to her seat helped ground her when he asked, "So, what do you photograph?"

She blinked at the question, so mundane in a world falling apart at her feet. So practical and regular and… calming. "Weddings, mostly," she forced through lips that were still numb.

"Right. You ever do anything more…I dunno… artsy?"

"I, uh… I used to, but recently, it hasn't been… possible."

"Well, if you do, let me know. We're nothing special, but we do show art at *Le Nook* from time to time." He wiped the bar in front of her with a rag and leaned down to rest on folded arms. "That wall, and that one over there." He pointed. "We could put up some lighting, you know. Make it a bit posher for you."

"Oh, I couldn't…" Uma stopped, made herself examine his face, open and friendly. *Don't mess this up*, she thought. *Don't let Joey come in here and fuck up a real opportunity.*

Okay, so she was missing a few essential things, but she had to start somewhere, right? There was no one here to keep her from doing what she wanted. Joey was at the other end of the state. Maybe farther, for all she knew.

And *fuck* Joey. Just fuck him for marking her like that. Fuck him for showing up here tonight. Again and again and again, if only in her brain.

So, sure. Why not show some pictures? "Yeah, that sounds nice. I'd like that. I just, uh, don't have access to a camera right now, so—"

"No worries. Bring your work in when you can, and I'll take a look. I could even put out some nibbles for the opening. Make it like a real gallery."

The idea was exhilarating, the possibilities endless.

"Where are you staying, Uma?" Rory added.

"Saint George, next to the big, white farmhouse."

"The house beside Ive Shifflett's place?"

"Yeah."

"Cell Block Eight."

"What?"

"You with the old biddy next door? One who never goes outside?"

"Yep." Uma's lips compressed a bit at that description, honest though it was. She was oddly protective of her boss. "Why'd you call it that?"

"It's that cul-de-sac. Only two houses on it, and they're both…you know."

"No, what?"

"Never mind. Not my story to tell. Anyway, I've got one more fabulous cocktail for you to taste."

"Oh no, I can't." She probably wouldn't be able to afford two cocktails.

"It's on me, love."

She considered Rory's tempting, mysterious smile and thought of the trip home. Could she do it? Walk down the street, all by herself, out in the open, where anyone could follow her? Could she put herself out there like that? She'd have to return the next day, in broad daylight, to get her car.

"I'll take it." Her voice sounded stronger than her insides. Was that all it took to be strong? Booze and bravado? And the hope of seeing a big, burly blacksmith at the end of the road? "I'll walk home," she said, her voice strong and sure.

He reached under the bar for a glass and *tinked* it against hers, a knowing gleam in his eye. "Cheers, Uma."

"Cheers, Rory."

"Welcome to Blackwood."

∽◌∾

The walk back was quick and full of fancy. In her imaginings, Blackwood became not just a pit stop for Uma, but a real home. She'd find a lovely little cottage to rent, work weddings on the weekends, and the rest of the time, shoot photo after photo of everything. Those pictures would be shown in Rory's bar but also elsewhere.

She was so caught up in the infinite possibilities of

her new, beautiful life that she hardly noticed where she was going. She'd made it halfway to Ivan's workshop before realizing she'd bypassed her boss's place altogether. Fueled on pipe dreams and instinct alone, her subconscious had led her not to her temporary residence but straight to the neighbor's. Okay, so she might have had a crush. She'd admit that. But the man probably had girls all over town.

Uma decided then and there that she couldn't care less. Rather than hesitation and self-doubt—which was pretty much her constant MO—she made the firm, albeit tipsy decision to forge ahead.

Which was how she found herself, at crazy o'clock on a Sunday morning, doing the most spontaneous thing she'd ever done: knocking at a near-stranger's door.

A dim light shone through the workshop window, and she might have imagined the warmth of the wood beneath her knuckles. After a few seconds, the door swung in, and Uma took an involuntary step back.

It was too late to run, too late to turn around. With a certainty she hadn't known in months, maybe years, she knew what she wanted was right there, in the flesh.

15

HE WAS BEAUTIFUL.

Still big, still intimidating, but half-naked and sleepy, Ivan looked soft, approachable. His groggy face was hard to read, one squinty eye open, the other crinkled shut.

"Hey, Uma. What're you doin'?" His voice was beyond gravelly, into some deeper key that wouldn't have been audible more than a couple of feet away.

"I came to see you."

"Yeah?"

"You weren't here earlier."

"Got a standin' date Saturday night—with my nephew."

"Oh." That was a relief. All that jealousy for nothing. "Can I come in?"

It was almost insulting how long it took him to decide, but he eventually turned and preceded her into the room, pulling up the form-fitting boxer briefs that had ridden low on his haunches. Squeak, asleep in front of the fire, barely lifted her head in acknowledgment of the new arrival. It smelled different tonight. No longer a workshop, it had that slightly musky, sleeping-man scent. The one you don't notice when you wake up to it but have to air out if you reenter a bedroom. It softened the usual fire and brimstone of the place.

Uma's eyes scanned his shadowed shape, and the word *voyeur* popped into her head. Rory was right. It made so much sense. She'd always spent time with people who had to be the center of attention—her mother growing up, then all those drama department friends in school whose friendships hadn't withstood Joey, and then Joey himself. It was a rare moment of insight to realize what a parasitic relationship she'd had with those people. All of them. No, not parasitic—symbiotic. They'd craved the attention, and she'd thrived off giving it to them.

This man, self-sufficient to the extreme, didn't want anything from her. Or at least nothing complicated.

"You need a bed to crash?"

"Did you mean it when you said you'd do whatever I wanted you to do?"

A brief hesitation, then a slightly breathless, "Yeah." Another pause. "You drunk?"

She shook her head, and it was as clear as a bell. Clear and calm and supremely focused. "I drank enough to give me courage, but the walk home sobered me up."

"Where'd you walk from?"

"The Nook," she answered, recalling Rory's words about this little section of town. *Cell Block Eight.* "You went to prison." It was more of a question than an accusation.

He tensed up at that but didn't deny it.

"Why? What'd you do?"

"Beat someone up."

"What for?"

"Had my reasons."

"Were they good? Your reasons?"

"Thought so at the time." In the middle of the room, he looked away and turned back to her. Ivan rubbed a hand over his eyes and spoke wearily, "What can I do for you, Uma?"

Something came over her. That inner voyeur, once identified, had taken on a life of its own. Here, with a half-naked Ivan, its pull was strong, deep in her bones.

I want to see you.

She wondered what it would take to get him to pull his underwear off.

"Take off your shorts."

Uma thought the words and then they were out, charging the air between them. Positively zipping with energy. A barometer in that room would have swung wildly in both directions, unsure whether to settle on *Stormy* or *Electric*. Either would have suited her fine.

She was fierce, wide awake, as she watched first surprise, then awareness overtake Ivan's features. His chest rose and fell, the sounds coming from him grown harsh.

He was measuring her, she could tell, trying to figure her out. She saw the exact moment he decided to give up.

Smart man. It was a lost cause.

"Come closer," he said. So Uma could see him better? So he could get a clearer look at her? So he could touch her? She wasn't sure she could take him touching her, but she gave him three small steps.

Still a ways from the rumpled bed in the corner, he stood beside his anvil, shirtless in the half-light. She wished he'd pick up the hammer and make the sparks fly again. She wished for bared teeth to go with the dark smattering of fur across his chest and arrowing down into his waistband. Uma wanted him feral, a beast she could tame. Would he bite her if she let him?

Her gaze slid down his body, taking in the long lines marred by gentle whorls of dark hair and the occasional scar. Thick thigh muscles wrapped in white, white skin. Their heft excited her. Her nostrils flared with some strange, animalistic desire to bite *him*.

Oh, *that*. *That* notion was right.

"Will you take your shirt off?" he asked.

She shook her head. "No." It didn't even sound like her voice—harder, surer.

A strangled little half sigh escaped his mouth, and Uma felt for him; she really did. Only she wanted so badly to see him that she couldn't let him off the hook. So she waited.

And then he did it. Throwing his head back to look down his nose at her in that defiant way that big men have—professional athletes in the stadium, soldiers on the battlefield—he curled his fingers around the elastic clinging to his hips.

Without blinking, Uma stared, panting lightly. Nothing could have pulled her away.

For once, she wasn't the self-conscious one. For once, she was in the position of power, the watcher instead of the watched. Was it wrong to enjoy it? Probably. She nearly put her hand out to stop him. She shouldn't demean him like this.

He smiled. A strange hybrid of a smile—a perfect mix, much like the man. The kind of smile a gentle monster would give. Half-sweet and half utterly wicked.

Uma fell into the moment headfirst, drunk off stronger things than booze. She squinted and bit her lip in concentration.

She'd done strip shows for Joey—pathetic seductions after a few drinks on a Friday night. He'd enjoyed her embarrassment, probably more than the nudity itself. The bastard had gotten off on her powerlessness.

This was different.

Uma commanded, and Ivan complied. He could overpower her at any moment but *chose* not to. She was drunk off his acquiescence.

The shorts made a sound as they dragged over his skin, a slight rasping against hair, followed by the creaking of bones as he bent to tug them off. None of it was particularly graceful—his grace was reserved for the anvil—but it was lovely. Perhaps even lovelier for the lack of finesse.

And his body. Lord, his body. From the irresistible blend of uncertainty and cockiness in his eyes to the hard curves of his chest and the sleek line of his flank, he was beautiful. Below the waist, his penis—no, his *cock*—rose, half-hard, from a dark thatch of hair.

An answering weight settled in Uma's belly, making her panties uncomfortably wet. She liked that he was already aroused, the fact that *this situation* made him hot.

"You like me telling you what to do," she said in a voice clogged with desire. It wasn't a question.

He licked his lips before speaking, glancing down at his erection and letting out a tiny, strained laugh. "Guess so."

She couldn't laugh with him or even smile. This beautiful man, stark naked in front of her, was no laughing matter.

"Good." She stepped closer to him, with a first, brief pang of uncertainty, wishing, yet again, for something to filter the intensity of the moment. To protect her. "Don't move."

She waited for a beat, testing whether or not he'd do as she asked, giving him time to defy her. But he was still, utterly still, breath bated, waiting. For what came next. For her.

She circled him, and the view from behind was just as satisfying. He was massive, with muscles that should have intimidated but only turned her on. She reached a hand out, tentatively at first, to curve over one hard hip, and mumbled, "You're so warm."

He shuddered in response.

A patch of freckles congregated on his right shoulder blade, a sweet constellation. Stretched up on tiptoes, Uma managed to press her lips to the center of the cluster. He smelled perfect, like his bed—warm and clean and manly and sleepy, with a burnt metallic undertone. Her tongue painted a wet stripe across the dots, confirming that his taste matched his smell: elemental and delicious.

Standing behind him, she laid a trembling hand on his other hip and hesitated before leaning fully into his body, her head settling on his back with a sigh. She swayed against him, a strange, sexy slow dance that finally swung her back around to his front.

He reached for her, and she almost stepped back, loathe to give up control. But when he bent to touch his mouth to hers, it didn't matter who was leading. The sparks between them had a life of their own. He kissed her long and slow until she was too breathless and had to break away. The noise of protest he made was gratifying, and Uma loved this feeling of being in charge. She tugged at his hips, pulling him closer to the bed. She sat, and he slid onto his knees between her legs.

Another kiss, hotter than the last—deeper and needier—had her clutching his hair and him holding her still and everything so close to combustion that she stopped it. She had to now, or it would be too late.

Catching her breath, she urged him back to standing, bringing his cock right there, fully hard and straining in her direction, and this was right. Ivan naked and Uma clothed, calling the shots.

Funny how it felt so scripted, all of this, like a choreographed dance she'd plotted out ahead of time, like she knew exactly what she was doing. And yet, from one moment to the next, she had absolutely no idea what was coming.

You're a voyeur. The words echoed through her brain. They were both at the mercy of Uma's long-denied, never-acknowledged, messed-up desires. Desires that pushed her to take hold of him and cant her face forward to rub against his erection.

Ivan's entire body tightened at the contact, and his breathing grew loud and ragged above her. His hands stayed suspended by his sides, however, wanting but not daring to touch. The skin of his cock was soft against her cheek, softer still when it pulsed against her hot, dry lips. It occurred to her that this may be the first time she'd ever held a man like this, admired his body without the pressure of what was expected of her.

Ivan was letting her give rather than demanding anything of her.

Another shuddering breath from Ivan led her eyes inexorably up, up, up over miles of craggy terrain, to his face. He was crushingly handsome. The most beautiful man she'd ever seen, especially with that particular look. Lost, hungry, and close to losing control. His fingers, white at the knuckles, dug into his thighs.

It made Uma feel like pushing him further, to get a glimpse of the wild animal poised to emerge. Without moving her gaze from his, she bent again and ran her tongue down his length, leaving a wet path in her wake. His low, breathy moan spurred her to continue, wetting his entire cock from root to tip. She imagined how all that saliva would help her slide onto him. Not that she'd need it. Her underwear was drenched.

"Uma," he whispered, "please."

She smiled and shook her head, instead using the moisture to stroke her hand up and down, up and down. Every pull at him bumped the head against her lips and waiting tongue and brought him closer to the bed, so his knees were finally trapped between Uma's.

This is power, she realized. From underdog to top dog in the blink of an eye. Having this big man at her mercy made her feel wicked and alive. He could break her with one hand, if he chose, and yet—

How easy would it be to pull Ivan atop her and let him take over? He'd yank her clothes off and see what lay beneath.

She stiffened at the possibility. Could he stand to look at her if she let him do that? What would he think, seeing another man's ownership scrawled so blatantly across her skin?

What Joey had done, forcing her the way he had…

He may have bested her physically, but he would never know this kind of power. *Never.*

Rather than dwell on the past, Uma pulled away.

"Touch yourself," she ordered and was gratified when he lifted his hand. Slowly, he clasped himself, almost tentatively at first, which seemed so wrong for a big man like him.

"Tighter," Uma scraped out over a throat that was raw with want. "Squeeze yourself tighter."

Being in charge apparently changed her, made her into a tyrant.

"I want you so bad, Uma."

She admired how big he was, his hand, his cock, his thighs.

"Use both hands, Ivan. Pretend you're fucking me."

"Feels so good." His molasses voice slid over her, dark and sweet, and she nearly lost it. They were the three sexiest words she'd ever heard. She wanted to take them and bottle them and spread them all over herself, writhe in the sensation they gave. His loss of control was a drug.

"It looks good, Ivan." This couldn't be Uma talking. She was no femme fatale. "You're beautiful." His head jolted up at her words, with a little scoffing sound. "You *are.*"

She leaned back on his bed, raking her eyes down to her own filthy peep show, then back up, dying to see his face when he came. Ivan the Viking warrior, above her, pretending to take her, using himself. The rhythm took over, and Uma imagined his ass hardening with each thrust. Her own hips writhed slightly, trying without success to gain some sort of friction on the bed. She could have reached down, but touching herself could wait until she was alone in bed. She wanted to be present for this. Every detail needed to be imprinted on her brain, available for playback at her leisure.

She startled them both by moaning. His eyes popped open to meet hers. It wasn't clear which did it, Uma's moan or meeting her eyes, but something in him snapped. His hand moved faster, gripping himself so tightly that it had to hurt. That sound of skin on skin, with the occasional slick, sliding noise, was absolutely filthy.

"Oh, fuck, Uma."

Her eyes darted, face to cock and back, taking in every detail of this man losing it for her. His hands forgot to do the little twist at the top; his muscles bunched almost painfully; veins protruded along his thick forearms. He looked surprised when he came, on a quiet moan, eyes half-closed but still burning into hers. She looked away long enough to watch three long spurts fill his cupped palm.

There came a moment of stillness, rife with what they'd done. A harsh breath escaped when Uma finally remembered to let it out, and she croaked, "Come here."

After wiping his hand on his discarded shorts, Ivan flopped onto the bed and lined himself up beside her and pulled her into a tangle of limbs, his naked and hers fully clothed. There was something almost sad about the contrast. She didn't dare picture it with her clothes off—his pristine skin still looking naked beside hers, littered with ink.

He leaned over her, a sweet smile on his face, and said, "I want to kiss you again." Asking permission, taking care in that way he had.

Uma couldn't help but smile back at him, just a little.

His lips were full and soft, his kiss so sweet. And so intense. It started slow, then lost control. Even with a couple of jarring tooth clashes, it was the most passionate kiss Uma had ever had, deeper tonight with their new knowledge of one another.

Twice, he reached for the button on her jeans, and twice, she pushed him away.

They made out like that, mouths and hands and writhing bodies, for what seemed like forever, learning each other. First hungry, then deep and sweet, tapering off to gentle caresses, until she settled into his neck, and he eventually relaxed and fell asleep, half on top of her.

For a while, Uma enjoyed his weight and the silence. The fire had died down, leaving the workshop dark and cold, full of unfamiliar shapes.

Finally, she fretted. Again, that nasty habit: the worrying at night in bed. She'd managed to sleep in this bed before. She could do it again. Any reasonable person would pull the blanket up to her chin and snuggle in with the gorgeous man she'd made out with.

But not Uma. She had to tear it apart, piece by piece, worry at it and make it into something bad.

"What you doin'?" Ivan's groggy voice broke in to interrupt her insane musings.

After a brief hesitation, she decided to be honest. "Fighting with myself."

"What about?"

"Whether or not I should leave."

He grunted and pushed up on an elbow, a dark shape above her. "Who's winning?"

She smiled briefly. "Guilt. I shouldn't have even come here tonight."

"Why not?"

"It's just not a good idea. I'm too…raw. You know?"

He didn't answer right away, and Uma wondered if she'd hurt him a little. It never feels good when someone regrets what they've done with you, especially if they're still right there in your bed.

"Well, you may think guilt's winnin', but from where I'm sittin', you're still here, lyin' in my bed." He flopped back down and pulled her with him, tucking her head onto his chest. "Only regret is that you won't let me into those pants so I can return the favor."

She laughed and pushed at the hand touching her waistband.

"What is it? You don't like to be touched? 'S that it? Or's there something you don't want me to see?" Uma stiffened. "'S dark in here, Uma. You don't even have to take 'em off. We'll keep the jeans on, okay? Lights off, covers on?"

She didn't say no, which was like a resounding yes. She could almost pretend not to notice what he was doing. Slowly, so slowly, he tugged open the button and pulled down the zipper. The jagged sound was muffled by the blankets. His hand slid into her pants, one inch at a time, giving her time to push him away.

It was quiet with her breath tightly reined. She didn't hear him breathing either, but she could have sworn she heard the lazy, measured beating of his heart. They were waiting, listening to each other. Every tiny, wet, embarrassingly sloppy noise was loud in the vacuum created by their held breaths.

The thought of how long it had been since she'd bothered to shave down there gave Uma a brief moment of embarrassment, but then his rough fingers slipped through her curls and down, and he didn't seem to notice, or mind, the hair there. His middle finger descended farther. She jerked when it glanced over her clit on its way to part her lips.

That finger continued its tortuous downward trip, gently penetrated her, giving her a brief moment of satisfaction, and returned to her clit. Uma curled up on herself again, on a burst of expelled breath, and Ivan breathed out and in, the sound restrained.

It was too much, too close, too quiet, too intimate, breathing his air, his smell. He dipped down again and pressed farther this time, his finger huge inside her, but nowhere near fulfilling this craving her body had suddenly developed.

"You like this?" he whispered.

Uma couldn't respond. She needed air to respond.

"You're so fuckin' wet."

Oh, that was embarrassing. Why did he have to go and point it out?

She managed a little sound of protest, and he stopped entirely.

"You want me to stop?"

Did she?

She hesitated, then finally shook her head, and after a beat, he chuckled gently and started up again, faster, finger pressing into her, thumb rubbing quick circles over her clit.

"I wanna make you come so hard. Like you did for me. That okay? Will you do that for me?"

No way could Uma respond. Besides, she didn't want to tell him that making her come was more of a marathon and less of a sprint. That, if she was honest, she didn't really come when someone else was involved. She couldn't. Oh, she knew how to do it on her own, but no guy had ever gotten it right. She'd pretended for Joey, of course. Otherwise, he'd have punished her for it, pouted for ages afterward.

"I'll bet if I fucked you right now, I'd slide right in. You're so wet. Nothin' to stop me at all, is there?"

Whoa. Those words ratcheted things up a notch. And Ivan apparently didn't expect a response, which was good, since listening to him talk was its own sweet torture. A little mortifying, but so goddamned hot.

He leaned in and pressed his face into her neck, ran his nose into the hollow behind her ear, and followed it with his mouth. Before Uma could prepare for the shock, his teeth were on her, nipping their way to her earlobe, and then biting, just how she'd imagined.

More than the touching and the talking, it was the mental image of those big, strong teeth tearing her apart that did it. Uma moaned, an animal sound that would make her blush when she thought of it later, and a groan that she was incapable of containing. Her next utterance was closer to a scream, but Ivan took it from her, sliding his lips over hers to consume her shouts.

And…*oh fuck*…there it was. That elusive orgasm. The one she'd heard about but never quite been able to achieve. The kind that takes you somewhere else, outside yourself, away from all the pain. She couldn't say how her body felt, only that it blew her mind and left her completely spent.

"Good girl," he muttered, and she didn't even bother to correct him.

"Oh, shit."

Her words, when she finally spoke, were graceless, but he laughed gently into the side of her face and swooped down for another mind-numbing kiss before settling them back onto the bed in a cozy nest.

⤳⤳

She fell asleep almost immediately, pressed to Ive's side. Fully clothed. He, on the other hand, didn't fall asleep for ages.

He wanted to get her naked so fucking badly, and he was hard again just thinking about it. Why wouldn't she get naked? He remembered the way she'd hidden the tat on her arm in self-defense class. He thought that might be it. Was she embarrassed by it, or was he completely off base?

In any case, she wasn't scared of him. Not with the way she'd ordered him around tonight. Ive smiled at the memory of Bossy Uma. Man, she'd been sexy. He pulled her tighter against him, loving the feel of her curves, all soft and warm, even through the layers of fabric.

He ran a hand down her side, along the dip in her waist, and farther, over her hip, where he squeezed—just a little bit. This was the kind of woman you wanted to take big handfuls of. Grab on and ride. Or, in the case of this one, maybe let her ride you.

He wasn't used to that—women on top. All his life, he'd been big and ugly and mean, and women assumed he'd be the one calling the shots. Not that he minded either way.

Sure, Ive liked getting a little pushy every now and then, but he didn't want to hurt them. Hurting women was—he didn't even like to think about it, especially not here, with Uma right there in his arms. He pushed the thought from his mind and smoothed his hand down her bent leg, to the cuff of her jeans.

Gently, very gently, he slid his fingertips underneath, up above her socks, to her skin. Gently, so gently, almost like air, the way he'd touch a fawn or a barn kitten, he stroked her there. Not even stroking really, more just a soft settling. But it was enough. She was what he wanted. Not smooth, but stubbled over with lady hairs, a texture more feminine than anything he could imagine. Better than smooth, really.

She shifted slightly, snuffling adorably, and he pulled away, not wanting to get caught in this forbidden foray. Man, even that little touch had been sexy. He thought about trying the same thing elsewhere, getting a tiny feel of her belly or her breasts. But that would be going too far, and he knew it.

A betrayal of trust. The worst possible thing you could do to someone. No, he wouldn't betray the trust she'd shown him thus far. He'd rather die.

～⌒～

Waking up fully clothed, wrapped up in the hottest potato of a man ever, with a dog nose wet against her face, was not exactly the most pleasant experience ever. Add to that Uma's burning desire to pee, and she was pretty darned miserable. But opening her eyes to Squeak's smile helped, followed by a glimpse of a naked Ivan, curled around her like an enormous vine.

She kicked away the comforter and smiled at the John and Yoko portrait they made.

Uma's breath puffed visibly in front of her, confirming that it was absolutely freezing. Squeak pushed at her again, and she extricated herself fully from the big man's hold, making sure to cover him up again. She speed-walked to the door to let the mutt out and cast a fruitless glance around, maybe hoping a bathroom had sprouted overnight. It was a brief struggle to locate shoes under the bed and a near-hysterical moment spent thinking she'd left her purse at the bar, keys and all. She finally found it sitting on Ivan's anvil, in plain sight.

Once she got herself as together as was possible, Uma went to open the door again, unsure whether to leave Squeak out or not. The dog answered that question by pushing her way back in, followed by two black cats, and running to Ivan's bed, where she rooted her way back under the covers.

Uma smiled at the sight of them there, awash in a wave of premature, bittersweet nostalgia. This could—and probably would—be the only time she'd get intimate with this man. If he ever saw what was hiding under her clothes, he'd run as far as possible.

Without letting herself think about what she was doing, Uma reached into her purse and pushed the battery into her old phone—a relic from her other life. As it powered up, Ivan snuggled farther under his comforter and wrapped a thick arm around his dog. Maybe he thought he was still snugged up to Uma. She smirked.

The photo would be perfect: lovely, warm man, smelling like sleep, his big body no longer an instrument of intimidation, but one of pure, sweet pleasure. Ivan's hair was a dark, tousled mess that Uma wanted to run her fingers through. There were so many things she hadn't gotten to do, to touch and smell...and taste.

Two legs peeked out from beneath the blanket—one human and one canine. Uma pressed the button, and the stupid, electronic shutter-click sound was like coming home. She glanced at the screen, memorized the image, and quietly pulled the door closed behind her.

The music started, just as her finger moved to power off the phone. It was immediately recognizable and entirely chilling.

Joey's ringtone.

She'd know it anywhere. A glance at the screen showed his photo, the one she'd taken of him singing karaoke one night in a bar with a bunch of his colleagues. He'd done "My Way" in a near-perfect Frank Sinatra imitation. And there it was, "My Way," ringing out as if he'd been waiting for her all this time. As if he'd known the second she turned on her phone.

How? How had he done that? Did he know where she was? Could he trace her? Or was it some kind of auto redial?

Uma's shaking hands dropped the phone, and it landed with a dull thud in the grass. She bent and shut it down, frantically, before rushing back to Ms. Lloyd's house, happy glow utterly decimated.

16

AFTER THE PHONE CALL FROM JOEY, THINGS CHANGED FOR Uma. Everything was worse. Much worse. The fear was constant, and even the pain was back, her skin raw. Twice, her boss commented on the constant scratching. She must have looked like a smack addict coming down.

The worst part, though, when she really allowed herself to feel it, was how she'd lost all sense of hope. Again. That tiny spark she'd barely sensed a few days before was gone, leaving nothing but a brittle, hollow shell, her heart a dried bean rattling around inside—hot and parched and feverish with fear.

Joey was out there. Uma could swear she felt him closing in. And all because of that photo. She'd followed an honest impulse, and everyone could be punished for it. For a stupid picture. She regretted that impulse; she truly did. If Joey found her, she'd have to delete it—the only proof she had of what had happened with Ivan. The thought made Uma sadder than anything else.

But she couldn't involve Ivan in her sordid life. She wouldn't put him in the crosshairs like that. The biggest favor she could do for him would be to stay out of his way. If Joey ever found out about him, he'd obliterate him.

So, Uma avoided Ivan all day Sunday—a difficult task.

She walked to the bar for her car, keeping an eye out for passing vehicles. She also went so far, later in the day, as to hide out in the kitchen when Ivan dropped by to see her. It killed her to pretend she wasn't there.

Because Ivan would do something crazy for her. He'd said so himself. He'd go after whoever hurt her and go back to prison and it would all be Uma's fault. She liked him too much to destroy him like that.

So, instead, she let Ms. Lloyd lie, straight to his face.

Sunday night was the worst she'd had since arriving in Blackwood—dark, agitated hours spent fighting the memories of Joey's hands on her. The hot prick of the needle in her skin, the electric buzzing of the machine in her ear, ink blossoming stark on the carpet beside her face. She eventually succumbed to sleep only to dream of him killing Ivan.

When Monday finally dawned wet and nasty, Uma felt hungover, the pain physical.

The only spark was the thought of the self-defense class that night, until she realized she'd have to skip it. She couldn't risk going.

Her eyes closed against the memory of Ivan. His touch, his arms around her. For such a short time, he'd made her feel so alive, so real. No way would she risk going to class and running into him again. Finally, Uma pulled herself out of bed, heavy and exhausted.

Breakfast was a gray smudge on the day, the first

of many. Laundry, cleaning, lunch, all succeeded each other as occupations for her body, while her mind...her mind ached, alone, somewhere outside of herself.

"Girl, you'd best get your head out of your ass right now," Ms. Lloyd said when Uma burned dinner that night.

"Sorry, Ms. Lloyd."

"What the hell is wrong with you?"

"Nothing."

"Don't give me that crap, or I *will* fire you."

"It's none of your business, okay?"

The woman stared at Uma, clearly waiting for something more.

Another standoff, only this time, Uma didn't have the strength. She couldn't do it, couldn't lie to Ivan and stonewall Ms. Lloyd. Finally, on a harsh exhale, she let the words come out. "I'm scared."

"What you scared of?"

Uma didn't respond.

"Get out."

"What?"

"Just go."

"Are you kidding me?"

"No."

"You're firing me?"

"I'm not firing you, girl. I'm telling you to go outside and get some fresh air."

Uma turned to look out the window. "It's raining."

Ms. Lloyd blew out a grumpy sigh and pushed Uma toward the back door. "Go visit your boyfriend."

"Hey! He's not my—"

"Whatever." The woman shooed her outside and

closed the door, leaving her on the back stoop in the cold early evening.

Are you freaking kidding me?

Uma banged on the door, yelled "I need my jacket!" and waited as Ms. Lloyd shuffled toward the living room. After a couple of minutes, she returned with her fleece and purse. Left with no choice, Uma walked down the steps, through the soggy grass to her car. It looked like she'd be attending self-defense class that evening after all.

She was secretly glad.

∽◈◊◈∾

It was a relief and a disappointment to see that the back half of the gym was dark when Uma walked in a few minutes later. No men duked it out on the mats. Instead, a gaggle of women took off rain gear and spread out, stretching and chatting.

Class was good, easier than the first time, although Binx was there, which wasn't easy to stomach now that Uma knew about the ad.

They learned how to get out of a stranglehold from behind. A good skill, surely, but Uma couldn't help but wonder: Would things really have turned out differently if she'd known how to protect herself the night Joey had held the gun to her head?

"What if he's got a gun?" The question popped out of her mouth, mid-demonstration, louder than intended.

Her comment drew the attention of every woman in the class.

"The attacker?" Jessie asked.

"Yeah. What if…" Uma swallowed. *One in five*, she'd

read. *One in five women has been sexually assaulted at some point in their lives.* These women weren't judging her. Chances were, at least a couple of them had been hurt by a man. They were on her side. "What if your attacker has a gun?"

"You run."

"What if it's not an option? Like, maybe he's got that gun to your head?"

"If you want to stay alive, you do what your attacker wants." Jessie turned to the rest of the class, and Uma's body sank, just a little, with an odd sense of relief. "I can show you a couple of moves, but really, ladies, these are last-ditch choices. Weapons up the stakes. If someone approaches you with a gun, your best bet may be to talk yourself out of it." She caught Uma's eye, delivering this message right to her. "If all else fails, *do what he wants.* There's no shame in doing whatever it takes to stay alive."

Uma blinked and looked away.

Jessie called them all forward to teach them a disarm and paired them off to practice. Uma's awkward moment was quickly forgotten.

Beside Uma, Binx stage-whispered to her partner, "You guys see Ive yet?"

Uma stiffened.

"No. Why?"

"Oh man, he looks goood," she said, looking as lascivious as a five-foot-tall blond pixie could. "I might not fight back tonight. Might just let him jump me." She pushed Anne's hand away and twisted into the follow-through.

"Hey, Binx, that's my brother you're talkin' about,"

Jessie called from the center of the room where she was walking one of the women through a leg sweep. "Keep it clean."

"I know it, girl, but *great day*, that man is lookin' G-U-D good." Binx's eyes landed, for one long beat, on Uma. Was that a challenge?

"He is?" said Uma's partner, Monica, a cozy-looking woman with cats printed in pink across her sweatshirt.

"Mon, honey, you have no idea. Saw him at Southern States today. Thought I might faint right there next to the fertilizer."

"You sure it wasn't the fumes?"

"Shush, Anne," Monica broke in. "So, what happened? Why's he so hot all of a sudden?"

"Y'all are gonna have to see for yourselves. But he's mine, ladies. I got dibs."

Uma tamped down another wave of hostility toward the woman, this time not for the ad, but for talking about Ivan like that. Like a piece of meat. She didn't like that one bit, because he was hers, damn it.

Which was one hell of a thing, wasn't it? Wanting someone but knowing you had to stay away.

≈

When he saw Uma's car in the lot, all the air whooshed out of Ive's lungs. He pulled up beside it and sat for a few seconds, watching the women through the front window. There she was, looking so much taller than the first time he'd seen her. She smiled at something one of the women said, and he realized that was the first time he'd seen that expression on her face—relaxed, easy, happy. Man, she was *pretty*.

He moved to get out, then froze when she bent forward to grab her "attacker" around the waist, tackling the other woman to the ground. *Oh, fuck.* He couldn't wait to get under her.

She made to get up but hesitated on all fours in a perfect reenactment of the fantasy he'd gotten off on the night before. That thought stopped him cold, and he sat back, giving himself a moment to tamp down his eagerness.

Uma was avoiding him. He was almost positive she'd been hiding in the kitchen when he'd gone by to see her. He just couldn't figure out why. The night they'd spent together hadn't been awkward. It had been perfect. The only issue he'd had was with her taking off like that without waking him up. He planned to confront her about that, but…was that it? Did she think he'd be mad about that? Was that why she'd avoided him for two days? No way. He'd been nothing but gentle with her. She knew he wouldn't hurt her.

Or did she?

It took more than one night of intimacy to gain the trust of someone who'd suffered at the hands of others. He knew that. Knew it well. He'd seen it with his dog, and he'd seen it in people.

She stood again and moved off to the side of the room, away from where the other women stood, deep in conversation. Okay, so maybe she wasn't a hundred percent confident yet. But she looked like she was getting there.

And Ive intended to do whatever it took to help her.

17

MID-MENTAL ARGUMENT, THE DOOR JANGLED, AND TEN pairs of eyes locked on to the man entering. He came inside and stopped, self-consciously brushing his chin. Uma could see him get pink from fifteen feet away.

His "What, I got somethin' on my face?" was met with laughter by everyone but her, and looking around, she could tell the other ladies were as floored at his loveliness as she'd been.

They swarmed around the man, the older ones flapping excitedly, while Binx and one of the Annes sidled up to him with flirty eyes.

"What made you decide to shave it off?" Monica asked.

He shrugged, and his eyes met Uma's before he got even redder and looked away. "Needed a change, I guess."

"Come on, let's get back to work, ladies." Jessie clapped and pulled everyone back to the mat. "Look at Uma. She's the only serious one here tonight. You ladies are pathetic."

Ivan caught her gaze briefly before she turned to concentrate on Jessie.

The practical part of the class was a nightmare, of course. When Steve arrived and the women all lined up against the men, Uma's skin immediately went up in such a fierce, prickly blush, her discomfort must have been obvious. With half the class's eyes on her, she faced off against Ivan and was satisfied to see that he looked as awkward as she did.

Head bent in preparation for the breakaway, he whispered, "You okay?"

She nodded.

"Just took off," he said through a shy, little smile.

It was adorable. How the hell was she supposed to resist this man? "Had to get to work," she whispered.

He touched her, and rather than shove her attacker away, Uma spent an inappropriate moment leaning into him. Finally, he nudged her shoulder, and she went through the motions, pushing, twisting, and following through. But, oh, she didn't want to. Despite her decision to avoid him—for his own good, she reminded herself—she wanted nothing more than to let him wrap her in his arms again, to sink into his strength and heat.

It was the curiosity shining in Binx's eyes that finally woke Uma up to how she must look: like one of his damn cats trying to get a good rub in.

After a couple of times through, Ivan moved on to his next victim. He got back around to her right after, cutting in before she could be paired up with Steve. This time, *he* lingered inappropriately, and it was all she could do to push out of his stranglehold.

For the rest of class, she ignored him, looking everywhere but at that beautiful face.

"I think Ive's face needs celebratin'," Binx called after Jessie had wrapped up.

Uma hung back while the women crowded excitedly around Ivan yet again. "Anyone wanna head over to the Nookie?"

"You don't seem impressed," Jessie said, indicating the rabid swarm around her brother.

"It was just a beard," Uma said with as little inflection as possible. Unfortunately, Ivan chose that moment to look up at her over the women's heads. Their eyes met, and she shivered.

A glance at Jessie showed her eyes flicking curiously between them.

"Hmm" was all the woman said before pulling on her coat and heading to the desk to grab something. Uma made a run for the door.

"You goin', Uma?" Ivan's voice stopped her.

"Where?"

"Over to the Nook for a cold one before headin' home."

"Oh, no, I don't—"

Jessie came up beside her. "Come on. I'll buy you a drink." She put an arm around Uma's shoulders and steered her out the door. "Get a move on, ladies. You can molest my brother outside or at the Nook, but you can't do it here. Out!"

The women spilled out onto the sidewalk and meandered down the block to the Nook. Once inside, Jessie leaned close and asked, "What's your poison?"

"Whatever you're having's fine."

The other woman swaggered confidently to the bar, drawing the eyes of nearly every guy there. Jessie was tall, loose-limbed...confident. Her perfection highlighted Uma's deficiencies.

And the woman could defend herself. That was maybe the most attractive thing about her. She had an "I'm gonna kick your ass, and you're gonna love it" kind of thing going—a Quentin Tarantino heroine, ready to fend off hordes of attackers beautifully. She'd even look good in a yellow jumpsuit.

The bartender, Rory, said something to Jessie, and her back stiffened. *What's going on there?*

Rory smiled, despite Jessie's obvious hostility. He glanced Uma's way, caught her looking, and gave a friendly wave. She waved back.

She was acutely aware of Ivan as he gathered chairs for the group. When had she grown this extra set of antennae developed for the sole purpose of detecting his whereabouts?

She knew he was there, of course, before he squatted beside her.

"Tried to visit you yesterday," he whispered.

"Yeah. I was out." Uma ignored the question in his eyes.

He touched her, just on the shoulder, but she had to pull away. If she didn't, she'd end up in his lap, and that wasn't allowed to happen.

"You need a drink?"

"Jessie's got it. Thanks."

With a nod, he stood and walked to the bar, his back tall and a little stiff.

"So, you live next to the big guy, right?" Binx

moved down into the next chair, and Uma stiffened. Not only had she placed that stupid ad, but she was also Uma's personal nightmare: petite, blond, pert, pretty, clearly into Ivan, and her eyes were bright and inquisitive on Uma's.

"Ivan?"

"Uh, *Ive*. Yeah," she said in a *duh* tone of voice. "Looks like you guys know each other."

"Sure. He's a nice guy."

"Really? Hmm. Never thought of him that way before." Her eyes slid from Ivan's ass to Uma, a feline grin on her face. "You know he's a *beast* in bed." She made a half-moan, half-roar, sex-kitten sound, and Uma couldn't help but hate her, just a little bit.

Did she know that firsthand? Uma had a sharp pang of jealousy.

Binx seemed to expect a response. The best Uma could come up with was "Have you known him long?"

"Since elementary school. We graduated high school together."

Oh? "What was he like?"

She looked at him, considering. "Different. Not quite as big. Angry streak a mile wide. Always gettin' into fights. Kickin' ass and takin' names. Fuckin' and fightin'. Pissed off at the world." She leaned in, warming to her subject. "You hear about Gabe's dad? You know, Jessie's boy?"

Uma shook her head as casually as she could.

Binx leaned in farther, obviously enjoying the honor of divulging the gruesome details. "Ive bit the guy's ear off."

"*What?*" Uma was horrified and...something else.

Scared? Titillated? Maybe somewhere in between. It was *disgusting*, but she could see it in her mind's eye, in perfect, lurid detail.

Savage.

"Huge fight. Few years after high school. I was in college, so I only heard about it through my sister, but…" The woman lowered her voice and continued. "He went to prison for it. Almost killed the guy." She whispered the last bit, full of drama, clearly enjoying herself. Uma was slightly queasy.

"Why?"

"They say Frank was beatin' Jessie, and— How long you plannin' on stayin' with us, Uma?"

"Oh, um. I'm just here to… I mean, not long." Uma looked up to see Jessie lower herself into the chair beside her.

"This is for you, from *Rory*." Jessie set a ridiculously froufrou pink cocktail on the table, so crowded with umbrellas and fruit that it took Uma a minute to find the straw.

"What is it?"

"Singapore Sling. He says you'll like it, even though it's not *strictly* British."

"Well, thank you."

"Don't thank me. It's on the house. So's mine." She lifted a tall drink. A clean orange column, devoid of decoration. It seemed oddly significant.

"What's yours?"

Through tight lips, Jessie said, "It's a Slow, Comfortable Screw Against the Wall."

Binx hooted with laughter and slapped her thigh. "The dawg! What is up with you two?"

"The guy is a complete asshole. I ordered a beer, and he handed me this instead. Then he wouldn't let me pay for it 'cause it would make him *feel dirty* to take money from me."

Binx laughed harder before saying, "You mean in exchange for sex? Too bad it ain't the real thing. When was the last time you got laid?"

"None of your business."

"Oh, please, sugar. Everything's my business."

"If you haven't heard anything, it's 'cause there's nothing to tell. So cool it, Binx."

"I believe I've hit a sore spot." Binx looked at the bar, caught Rory's eye, and gave him a girly, four-fingered wave. "Never did get why you hate him so much. The man is scrumptious."

"He's a man whore. It's disgusting."

"Ain't nothin' wrong with a horndog, sugar. 'Specially if you're in a period of extreme drought. Tall drink of water like that… Wonder why I never did him." Binx's eyes narrowed on Jessie, moved to Uma, and then swung to Ivan, who sat at the other end of the table, looking ill at ease surrounded by the other women.

"Ive, on the other hand." She cleared her throat. "If you'll excuse me, girls, my arid regions need a little waterin'."

"Jesus, Binx," Jessie groaned. "That's my brother you're talking about."

"Well, you know how it is. Me and Ive. When I'm dry, I wet my whistle at the f—"

"Shut up!" Jessie screeched.

The little blond waltzed over to Ivan, who looked,

if anything, more pained than ever when she plopped onto his lap.

Uma turned away.

"Don't worry about Binx."

"What do you mean?"

When Uma looked at her, Jessie indicated Binx and Ivan. "I take it you know my brother."

"We've hung out," Uma said carefully.

Jessie had that curious look on her face again. "This is the very first time he's agreed to come out with us after class. Ive doesn't go out. *Ever.* And he made sure you were coming before committing."

"Oh?"

"Yep. You like him."

"I don't—"

"He and Binx have been doing their thing off and on for years. It's not serious, though. It's okay. I can tell he likes you too."

Uma swallowed and raised her eyebrows.

"Never seen him like this."

"Like what?"

"Can't keep his eyes off you."

"Oh."

"He's a good guy, you know. Despite how he comes off."

"I know that."

"You do?" she said skeptically.

"I owe him a lot."

"How so?"

"He's been...generous, that's all."

"That's exactly it. Ivey's the most generous person I know. To a fault. He'd do anything for the people he loves. Me and Gabe…well, we'd never have made it without him." She paused, then turned her full attention on Uma. "What's your plan here, Uma?"

"My plan?"

"I don't want to say 'What are your intentions toward my brother?' but, you know… Are you plannin' on stickin' around, or is this a pit stop for you?"

Uma could hear the regret in her own voice when she responded. "I'm not staying. After I finish what I came here to do…I'm gone."

"You need to disappear." It was a statement, not a question. "You're runnin' from someone."

"Yeah."

"You considered stickin' around?"

"It's too close. To my ex. He's a prosecutor in Northern Virginia." *Oh crap.* Why had she said that? What was it about Jessie that made her want to spill everything?

"You're kidding."

"Please don't tell anyone."

Jessie nodded. After a moment's thought, she leaned in. "Don't get Ive involved in your problems. Please. He can't afford to get embroiled. He'll just get into trouble. Again. He can't help himself."

Oh, this wasn't good. The conversation was putting Uma on the defensive. The thing was, she'd have liked to tell Jessie to mind her own business, but the woman was right to be careful. You couldn't fault her for meddling. She admired how brother and sister seemed to take care of each other.

"There's nothing for him to get involved in. I'm here to get something done, and then I'm gone. That's it."

Jessie looked at Uma hard, searching, before nodding

and finally letting her expression soften slightly. "Look, I don't want you to th—"

"Oy, ladies. How are the two loveliest birds in Blackwood doing tonight? Enjoying your drinks?" Rory knelt between their chairs, charm flowing off him in waves.

"This is delicious," Uma replied, glad for the interruption.

"Singapore, 1897, a colony of the Crown, which made it British enough, I suppose. The Raffles Hotel, where this fine concoction was invented, was where most of the Yanks holed up. This delightful mixture of gin, cherry brandy, and juices was referred to as the 'pink sling for pale people.'" He leaned back with his lazy, wicked grin and looked Uma up and down. "And you, *dahling*, are beyond the pale. Quite literally." He winked.

"What does that even *mean*, Rory?" Jessie said, mouth tight and eyes squinty.

Rory turned his blue eyes to Jessie. "It's too subtle for you, love. I'm afraid you wouldn't understand it." He was cold, all trace of smooth-talking flirt gone.

"Oh, please. Subtle? You're the one who gave me a Slow, Comfortable Screw Aga—"

"Fuck," he interrupted. "It's a Slow, Comfortable *Fuck* Against the Wall. Thought you could use one, love."

Jessie turned red and sputtered.

Uma's eyebrows rose in surprise. Where was the suave tale spinner? This guy was kind of an asshole. She looked from one to the other, wondering what kind of sordid history led two friendly people to be so rude to each other.

"Uma, love, I brought something for you." Rory held out a hand. From it hung...a camera.

It was like gold. No, better than that—a security blanket, or a long-lost love. She almost moaned at the weight of it.

"What's this for?"

"It's for you."

"Oh, but I can't."

"You'll be doing me a favor, trust me."

"How so?"

"After you left the other night, I dug it out from the storeroom, charged it up for you. Somebody left it here perhaps three years ago—charger, case, and all. I reckon they're not coming back for it. Sounded as though you could use one. I'm not certain of the quality, but it should tide you over for a time, right?"

"Oh, wow," Uma breathed as she shifted it into her right hand, let her grip slip into place, the pads of her fingers tingling. It was a crappy point and shoot, but she didn't care. It was beautiful. Perfect.

Her heart picked up speed. This must be what drug addicts felt with their next fix in hand.

"Wow, this is…" She looked at Rory and would have cried if the tears would come. "Thank you."

"No worries, love." He winked, rose to standing, looked down the length of the table, and raised his voice. "Got your hands full, haven't you, Ive, mate?"

Uma pressed the On button, wound a hand through the strap, and lifted it to her eye. As if by magic, he was there, more real than before. Ivan, saying something to Rory, making everyone at the table laugh. Looking through the lens took the edge off seeing Binx perched on his lap. She snapped a picture, turned the camera, snapped another. Zoomed in. *Click, click.* Ivan didn't look exactly comfortable, but he didn't appear unhappy either, surrounded by women.

Oh, but this was good. Her armor. A relief. Protection.

In her element, Uma stood and took two steps back. Even those steps were right. She never stumbled while she worked, never. It was her superpower: unerring confidence when looking through a lens. Her anti-kryptonite. That's how Joey had eventually gotten the best of her—he'd broken her equipment, left her defenseless.

Someone settled a hand on her shoulder, bringing her back to the room.

"Glad to see you like it, love," Rory said. He clapped her once on the back, then headed to the bar.

"You seem pretty excited about that thing," Jessie said, her voice reaching Uma from a different plane. She could hardly hear her.

"You have no idea."

"Guess he's not an asshole with everybody, then."

"You mean Rory? He's been nice to me. Just like everyone else here."

"Probably wants to get in your pants," Jessie said, sounding snide.

Uma looked at the man behind the bar, snapped two photos of him and a close-up of Jessie. And she was photogenic on top of everything else. Did the woman have no faults? "No. He doesn't."

Jessie snorted in response. "I gotta go. Sitter needs to be cut loose." She stood and pulled on her coat. It was one of those sporty, silver puffer things that only thin women can wear. "See you next week, ladies! Ive, don't forget I need you tomorrow."

The group dispersed. Monica said something about hurrying home to Kevin before he managed to kill their sons. Uma hadn't finished her drink, but the sight of Binx cozying up to Ivan was nauseating. Her hand on his chest and his clasped over it, a half smile on his face as he shook his head at something she'd said. Probably something sexy and cute and clever. He bent and chuckled at whatever it was, and Uma knew: she'd been delusional about him. He'd never looked at her like that, all lazy and smiley. Not once.

I'm an idiot. He'd been nice to her, letting her sleep in his bed, kissing her and the other stuff, but she realized it was all out of pity. Jessie had been wrong. Ivan didn't like Uma; he felt sorry for her.

She buttoned up and waved vaguely before heading out.

18

THE CAR WOULDN'T START. OF COURSE IT WOULDN'T.

Of all the times and places, this might not have been the worst, but it was certainly the most infuriating. She turned the key in the ignition again and…nothing. *Shit!* She'd have to go back in and—

A knock on the car window brought her head up and memories flooding in. Déjà vu from her first week in Blackwood.

She opened the door.

"Trouble?"

"Yeah."

"Pop it. I'll take a look."

She popped the hood, and Ivan disappeared behind it. The tiniest sliver of a hand was visible, a sleeve moving around behind it. She wondered if he knew what he was doing. Of course he did. He was exactly the kind of man who could fix a car.

"Try it again."

She turned the key to an empty click.

"Battery's dead. Got cables?"

"No." Of course not. She wouldn't even know what to do with them if she did.

"You stay in there. I'll give you a jump."

Ivan drove his truck up beside the Honda and rummaged around under both hoods for a minute. Finally, he started his truck and asked her to do the same. Nothing. Not a solitary sound.

"Shit." Uma laid her head on the steering wheel. It had been an old car to begin with, and the most she'd done in as long as she could remember was fill the tank with gas, so it could be anything, really.

Ivan opened the door and crouched down. "Come on, I'll take care of it in the mornin'."

Without lifting her head from the wheel, she took a deep breath. "I owe you so much already."

"No you don't."

She sighed. "Sorry to ruin your night like this."

"What are you talkin' about?"

She finally turned to look at him. "You know. You and Binx."

His eyebrows lifted toward his hairline. "What about me and Binx?"

"You looked like you were having a good time. I'm sorry to ruin that."

"Binx is an old friend. Wasn't plannin' on doin' anything with her, though."

Because you like me? Uma's pathetic inner voice screamed. "No?"

Ivan shrugged and looked away. "Figured you might need a place to crash again tonight."

His words brought Uma's body humming back to life. Amazing how little it took to get her going nowadays.

Simmer down, she thought. *He's just offering a place to stay.* Besides, she was supposed to be avoiding him for his own good.

"It'd be great if you could drop me at Ms. Lloyd's. She's been behaving herself. Gave me a key and everything."

Gruffly, he said, "Suit yourself. Come on. I'll take you."

She got out of the car and locked it, pointlessly.

Despite the size of the cab and the growl of the engine, the inside of Ivan's truck was small and quiet, hemmed in. Uma heard his breathing and thought she might be able to smell him too—that woody fire scent that her body was already conditioned to respond to. In some offbeat version of Pavlov's dogs, she'd sniff him and go into heat.

"You been avoidin' me, Uma?" His voice sounded harder than before.

"No!" she said, breathless at the lie. "I told you. I've been very busy."

"Hmm." His mouth curved down.

He pulled up in front of Ms. Lloyd's and threw his truck into Park. A crack of blue light shone through the living room curtains—the television. Uma looked at the house for a moment. She had no desire to go in there. She wanted to go home with Ivan, to sink back into his bed and let him help her forget. Teach her how to feel real again. And why shouldn't she have that? Joey didn't know she was here, after all. He couldn't possibly, could he? The phone call was some automatic thing set up to scare her, but no way he'd traced her here...right?

"Okay. Thanks."

"I'll come get you in the mornin'. We can change the battery."

"Thank you." She made as if to open the door, dragging out the motions of getting out. And if she were really dishonest, she could blame Ivan for the look he gave her, the way it held her, forcing her to stay, despite all her misgivings. So light, but still a weight that anchored her there. She couldn't move. Didn't want to.

And enough with the paranoia. Joey wouldn't find her here. He'd never connect her with Ivan.

When her eyes got caught up in his, her breath snagged, tight in her throat, and she wondered, *Couldn't I kiss him again? Just once? Is it so bad to want one more?* Didn't she deserve this little bit of happiness before leaving this place forever?

"Change your mind?" he said, the smile already playing with his lips.

Uma answered after a sigh. "Yeah."

Blame it on the Singapore Sling.

❧

Ivan's workshop was dark and cold. Squeak was there to greet them, but the place had none of the golden, flame-drenched magic of Uma's previous visits. Ivan went to work providing light and warmth, but something about the space seemed almost sad now.

Why would he live here when he could be in that beautiful house? It occurred to Uma that this man might very well have as much wrong with him as she did.

He bit off someone's ear, for God's sake.

As he lit things, she took off her jacket but kept hold of the camera and looked around the room, snapping

pictures of everything, despite the lack of light: a rifle
hung on an iron rack above the door, a bow and arrow
beside it, a random, worm-eaten newel post and a pile
of books lay next to the bed on the floor—mostly big,
coffee-table-size hardbacks on wrought iron and land-
scaping, with a couple of ratty paperbacks thrown
into the mix. She read a spine—*Ender's Game*. Huh.
Impossible to imagine Ivan reading for relaxation. Her
eyes swung back up to the gun. It should have frightened
her but oddly didn't.

"You hunt?"

"Yep."

"What do people hunt around here?"

"Deer. Squirrel if you're dirt poor."

"And you?"

"Ate a whole lot of squirrel growin' up."

Uma shuddered at the thought. Squirrel and rabbits—
little bones.

"Today, mostly venison."

A straight-backed chair sat near the bed, almost invisible beneath a heap of clothing made up of jeans and
shirts, maybe boxers. Something sticking out from the
bottom caught her eye: a bright-blue tie, oddly out of
place here.

"You own a tie."

"Hmm?"

She dragged it from the precariously balanced pile
with a light hiss of slick fabric and let it dangle from
her fingertips.

"Think I can't spruce up?"

"I have a hard time picturing it." Uma tilted her head
and shut one eye. Nope, she couldn't wrap her mind

around the idea of him in a suit. She didn't mind, though. Joey had been a clotheshorse, made for designer duds. Ivan was made for something more elemental. Uma liked that about him.

"Let me take you to dinner, and I might show you." There was a challenge there.

"You asking me out again?"

"Maybe. You gonna change your mind if I do?"

She shrugged as nonchalantly as possible. "Just might."

"I'll think about it. One rejection's about all I can take in a week."

Uma set the camera on the bed and pulled the tie taut between her hands, enjoying its satiny feel. Somehow, she ended up behind Ivan, who knelt, stoking the steadily growing fire. She could see the top of his newly shorn hair, the blunt tips of his shoulders, the rounded, work-hewn muscles lining his arms.

Physically, this man could do whatever he wanted with her. The thought turned Uma on and scared her—the two sensations not mutually exclusive. She stepped closer, daring her fear into submission.

Ivan sat on his heels and let his back flatten against her legs. It was hot in front of the fire, but she stood her ground. God, she liked him there, kneeling at her feet.

The hair under her fingers was silkier than it looked: finer, sweeter, like him. She gave it a slight tug, tilting his head back and bringing his eyes in line with hers. She could almost hear the click as they connected, could feel it somewhere in her abdomen, the echoes skimming along her spine to her fingertips, where the tie in her hand immediately took on new meaning, a second life.

Purposefully, Uma stretched it out, showed it to him

before pulling it over his eyes and smoothing it over his battered nose. He didn't complain when she yanked hard, tying a fat knot at the back of his head.

In the silence, his breathing sped up to match hers.

What on earth am I doing? she thought. "Can you see anything?"

"No."

"You sure?"

"Nothing." Almost anxiously, he added, "I'll keep my eyes closed."

Uma nudged him so he turned toward her, but when he made to get up, she set a hand on his shoulder, kept him down—as much as she, or anyone, had the power to keep this man down. He hesitated, and Uma sensed the tight strength of him, restrained. The tension eased, and his lips parted.

He sat, head level, back straight.

He's waiting for me to tell him what to do, she realized.

It was warm beside the fire, but the air was still cool enough to make Uma's nipples pebble into hard little nubs. She reached forward and tweaked them, enjoying the feel of her own body for the first time in months.

"What are you doing?" His voice sounded pained, impatient, and so fucking turned-on. "Are you touching yourself?"

She nodded before realizing that she had to speak. "Yeah."

"Tell me."

"My nipples."

"What are you doing to them?"

"I'm kind of…pulling on them."

"Why're you doin' that?" Ivan sounded tormented.

Uma spoke, hardly recognizing the words as her own. "They're so hard they kind of hurt."

"Oh, shit." His breathing was frankly asthmatic, his excitement palpable. "Show me." As an afterthought, he added, "Please," and it sounded an awful lot like begging.

"You want to feel?" said the vixen wearing Uma's body.

"Yeah, yeah."

She dropped to her knees in front of him, bringing their chests together. He followed orders so well. The thrill of being in charge ran through her veins like electricity.

Uma's voice was a combination of eager and condescending as she said, "Go ahead, Ivan. You can touch them."

He surprised her, because although his hands shot up, rather than go straight for the prize, he clasped her arms, ran his fingers lightly up them, over her shoulders to her neck, then forward to her jaw. He clasped her gently, one hand cupping her ear and the other under her chin as he bent his head and dropped a kiss on her mouth. A wet swipe of lips and tongue across her cheek to her neck, and back to her face, her lips. He made a lost little noise before dropping his hands, one to clasp her waist, the other, finally, her breast.

His fingers pinched and she yelped. *Fuck.* He kept surprising her, this man, tender and harsh, playful and helpless. So different from Joey, whose need to control had turned sex into a performance—contrived, choreographed perfection. It had been good for a while, but quickly turned hollow.

Ivan was an animal first and a man second, and by

letting Uma lead, he was tamping down those natural instincts. But like a caged feline, he couldn't seem to help nipping every now and then.

Am I playing with fire? she wondered. *Mistaking a lion for a kitten?* Maybe, but it was too good to stop.

Ivan's palm settled over her, warm and rough and a little disorganized. It was so massive covering her breast that she felt small there for the first time ever.

"Oh, Christ, Uma. Christ," he breathed into her mouth just before she bit his lip. He jumped, and his hands spasmed against her body, clasping and tightening. "I gotta touch your skin. Not this." He pulled at her shirt. "You, Uma. I wanna feel *you*."

Ignoring her frightened inner voice, Uma grasped his hand and led it down, beneath her top, to place it on her breast, over her bra. He squeezed once, brought his other hand beside it, and before she fully understood what he planned, he'd pulled both cups down. Only her shirt kept her from full exposure.

She groaned his name before he put his mouth over hers again, swallowing her words and distracting her from what else he was doing.

He was tweaking her, taking those hard points and flicking them. He pulled away, bent down, and bit Uma through her shirt, right above the nipple, in a way that was so possessive she felt it, a clenching ache deep inside.

He moved his head down a couple of inches. "You're beautiful, you're so fucking beautiful," he rasped out and sucked hard, right through the fabric.

Uma fisted his hair in her hands and pulled him against her, letting her eyes fall closed with a quiet "ah." It was too much and not enough. Again and again he pulled, nuzzled, bit, and sucked, all the while peppering the air with little grunts that were out of control and sexy as hell. Finally, she urged him over to the other breast, and he went to work there.

Before she knew what she was doing, Uma tugged his head away and unbuttoned her pants. "Take off your shirt," she whispered, and he did, clumsy in his hurry. She shifted back to her knees and crawled forward until their chests were pressed lightly together, hot skin to damp cotton.

"Fuck, it's good," he groaned, and he was right. It was amazing. Too much. So close to being perfect.

He grabbed her hips, and Uma could feel his excitement when he pulled her harder to him. "I'm so fuckin' turned on with you, Uma. So fuckin' worked up. How'd you get me like this?"

"I don't know. This isn't...me."

He squeezed her hips, ground them together, and then reached out, found the opening in her jeans, worked his hand inside, and cupped her. "Oh, *fuck* yeah."

"Take off your pants, Ivan."

19

UMA HAD NEVER SEEN IVAN DO ANYTHING AS QUICKLY AS he whipped off those jeans.

He hadn't changed since she'd last seen him, but still, his body took her by surprise. It wasn't the muscles or the prettiness of all that pale skin that got to her. It was how *real* he was. As if Joey had existed on some other, more ethereal level, but Ivan was right there. With her, solid and true.

What am I doing? part of her wondered. And in the back of her mind, it was clear that she was an idiot, because no matter how hard she worked to convince herself otherwise, this couldn't be just about sex. She wasn't supposed to be liking a new guy. She was supposed to be avoiding men, not falling right back into bed with the first one to come along, especially not in this temporary town.

I can't stay. Can I?

"That bad, huh?" he said, kneeling again in front of Uma.

"What?"

"Get my pants off, and everything screeches to a halt. Guess you don't like what you see this time. Was hopin' I'd convince you to take yours off too." He grinned.

"Oh."

He touched the blindfold. "Got this on, after all."

She couldn't do it. Not because of what he might see, but because of what *she'd* see. Her arm against his skin would look filthy. Like shit on a Monet. Nothing would kill her desire or her *confidence* faster.

She collapsed in on herself, a bundle of stupid insecurity. Suddenly, she had to get out of this place, this town. It had sucked her in, made her feel like she could stay and be…what?

"Look, Ivan, you've been really nice, but I'm not…" She made as if to pull away, but Ivan's hand circled her calf, tight enough to remind her exactly who was top dog around here, if he chose. He could crush Uma like an ant. Not something she could afford to forget.

"Stay."

"I have to go."

"Stay here."

"Don't tell me what to do."

"Please."

"I'm not one of your strays, okay?" She tested her leg, tried to subtly pull away. His hand loosened.

"Strays?"

"Yeah, your dog. And all those cats outside. And all the others. You feed a damned skunk, for God's sake."

"It's a baby."

"Exactly! And there's Ms. Lloyd. You take care of every broken soul for miles around, me included."

"You're not broken. Don't you—"

"You think I'm not broken?" Her laugh came out harsh, humorless. "I'm a mess, Ivan. I'm a freak. A fucking freak! I don't want you to look at me. I can't even stand to see *myself*."

"Oh, baby." He reached out, and she shifted back.

"No. No pity. Please."

"I just want to make it better, Uma."

The prickle of tears pressed hard to her eyes, shockingly unfamiliar after so many dry months. "You can't, Ivan."

"At least let me try."

And she wanted to. She wanted him to make everything okay.

"You trust me, Uma?"

Yes.

She took a breath in. She'd known him, what, less than two weeks? But the answer was obvious.

"Yes," she whispered, releasing the air from her lungs. "Yes. I trust you."

"All right, then close your eyes."

"What?"

"Let me make you feel good, Uma. Trust me. Please."

With eyes squeezed shut, she waited while he got up, stumbled around the room, and returned to wind something around her head. The tie? Had he taken it off?

"See anything?"

"No." She reached up. Not the tie. This was thick and rough. Cotton.

"Good. Stand up."

She stood, disoriented and a little seasick and not at all sure she was ready to take orders rather than give them. He moved her back a few steps to the bed. She settled on top, cross-legged, listening to her own heart and the popping of the fire, breathing in smoke and metal. Waiting.

The mattress dipped under his weight, and he was there, close beside her.

Her hand reached out blindly to land on his forearm, stilling him. "Will you stop if I ask you to?" She sounded wretched. Scared and tiny.

"I'll do anything you ask me to. *Anything. Always.*"

Oh shit. Those words were like a spark to Uma's tinder. "Then come 'ere," she gasped, digging her fingers into his flesh and enjoying how he obeyed—instantly.

A shift of mattress and his breath. His nose found her cheek, lingered, skimmed along her skin to her ear, before trailing farther down to graze her neck and back up—a circuitous route to her mouth. Once he reached her lips, tongues twined, teeth clashed, and he wound around her.

"Ouch!" His knee sank into the back of her hand, and she pulled it away, holding it to her chest. "What are—"

"I've still got mine on. The blindfold."

"Are you serious?" Uma giggled when he moved in and jostled her again. She tilted precariously before he gripped her hand and brought her back against his body. Her giggles turned to squeals when his hands moved to her waist and poked her, just enough to tickle.

Her screeched "Stop that!" stilled him immediately.

"You want to stop?"

"No. I meant the tickling. Actually, I…I haven't laughed in a while." And she'd never laughed in bed with a man.

"If that's the case, then—"

Ivan's thick hands were surprisingly precise as they made their way up her body, manhandling her into a prone position, head on the pillows and legs curled in protectively. He explored her with half tickles, half caresses that gradually lost their sense of humor. She went from howling laughter to groans and finally quieted entirely.

Uma opened like a blossom under his attentions, limbs heavy and relaxed.

As her cries died down, other things took center stage: the rough rasp of his fingers against her skin as he slowly pulled down her pants, followed by the soft, soft slide of his lips against her belly. Perhaps sexiest of all was Ivan's breathing, surprisingly erratic and shaky, peppered with manly little grunts and groans. Animal sounds. Sounds of discovery…and satisfaction. Like an explorer happy to have his theories confirmed. *I did this to him*, she thought with a sense of pride she'd never thought she'd have in bed, of all places. *I made this big man shudder.*

Underwear followed pants. When he grasped her shirt, she stopped him. "I…I don't think I can do this."

"Here." He took her hand and held it to his face, showing her his blindfold. "I can't see you. I won't look."

She swallowed her anxiety down. "Okay. Okay, but—"

"Just say stop. That's all you've gotta do, baby."

Finally, with difficulty, her shirt was pulled up and over her head, careful not to disturb the blindfold.

For a few silent moments, Ivan settled beside Uma, trailing one hand, exploring her body by touch alone. Lightly, so lightly, mapping her shape.

"You're soft," Ivan whispered as his fingers found

surprisingly tender spots, like the round underside of her breast or the outside of her knee. Places she hadn't known were beautiful. For ages, he learned her, probably better than she'd been known by anyone, and yet…

"Stop, Ivan."

He stopped.

"I want to touch you now."

"I'm right here, baby."

Ivan's body was so different from hers. Not soft and pliant, but firm and rough. And unlike his lazy, reclining progress, she was all business, sitting up to reach the other side of him.

Uma's scars had been invisible beneath his touch, but his were textured, immediately obvious. She lingered on each one, enjoying the variations she found there. There and elsewhere: the rough patches at his knees and elbows, the crisp hair on his chest and farther south. His cock stood in her way. It lay stiff and hot against his belly, barring passage south and demanding further attention.

She grasped it in her hand, loving how heavy it was, how it needed more than one hand to do it justice. The desire to own him took over, and she threw one leg over his wide thighs, hefty with muscle and slightly scratchy beneath her.

"Ooh, yeah. So good," he groaned, arching off the bed into her hands. He was silky along the shaft and wet at the tip, like he'd been the first time she'd seen him. Only this was entirely different. Their bodies were more important than they'd been; touch was essential and smell elemental. When Uma dipped her head, she took in the scent of him, along with the taste on her tongue, and it overwhelmed her with desire.

"My breasts," she ordered. "Touch them."

It was so good how he obeyed like that. Rough hands flew to her breasts, palming them and rubbing them along his length, up and down, with her mouth at the tip.

"I'm gonna come like this, Uma. I want to make you come first."

"You'll come when I tell you to come, Ivan."

"Oh, fuck," he moaned, out of control. "Let me do you first. Please. Come on. Please, Uma, baby." And Jesus, did she like the sound of him begging.

"Say it again."

"What?"

"Beg me some more."

"Uma, you've got to let me touch. I want to taste you. Please."

Amazing how the blindfold made her hungrier. She let go of his cock and moved up to bury her nose in his neck. She bit and sucked, reached her hands up to grasp his head, and found the tie covering his eyes.

"I love that you kept this on. Now all we can do is feel." It was a strange sentiment from someone who'd used sight as a crutch for so long. A blind voyeur.

His palms landed hot on her breasts, his aim impressively precise.

"You done this blindfold thing before?" she asked, breathless.

He chuckled. "No. Just been thinkin' 'bout gettin' you naked. A lot."

He planted his hands on her ass and pulled them up to sitting, leaving her momentarily disoriented.

Soft, wet licks were followed by tight, intense pulls on her nipples.

"Your teeth," she said, almost grunting the words. "I want your teeth."

Immediately, he bit, thrilling her with the pain and the pleasure and the way he followed her orders.

She succumbed, lost in it as he nibbled and licked with endless patience. *What would he feel like down there?* she wondered.

"Kiss me," she whispered after what seemed like hours, nudging his jaw. But instead of moving to her mouth, as she'd expected, he kissed her right where he was, taking her demands literally, with a loud, slurpy, sexy french kiss right on her nipple. He took orders well. Too well.

It was heady and sweet and sexy as hell, being in charge. She could get used to this if he let her.

In that moment, she had so much tenderness for Ivan, treating her with such care. Slowly taming her. So calm, you could almost forget how strong and scary he was.

Maybe it wasn't so bad to be one of his strays.

I don't want to leave Blackwood. The thought rose up from nowhere, scaring the hell out of her. *I want to stay here, with this sexy, scary, sweet man.*

～◌◌～

Man, his woman was bossy. And he fucking loved it. The way her voice got meaner as things progressed.

First, it was her tits. They'd been perfect. Her nipples, like little cherries, answering one of the questions he'd been asking himself since the first time he'd seen her. He couldn't get enough of the way they felt in his mouth, against the new scruff on his cheek, pressing into his cock.

Then her belly, as he made his way down her body, all soft and pliant, the way a woman was supposed to be. He let his fingers continue to learn her, wanting to memorize the shapes and wondering if maybe he'd buy some clay and sculpt her. It was something he'd always wanted to take up, just never had a reason to before.

He wished he could see her. The skin under his fingers was perfectly smooth, and he wondered, for a brief second, what she could possibly be hiding from him.

"Fuck, you feel good."

She huffed out a skeptical sound, which would have made him smile if it didn't annoy him so much. She truly thought there was something wrong with her. What the hell had that stupid ex of hers done to make her so insecure? Maybe he'd called her names, told her she was ugly. He remembered the way Frank used to talk to Jessie and didn't doubt the power of words.

A sharp nudge from her hands, another command rather than a suggestion, brought him back to the room, and he moved farther down the bed, grasping her by the hips and settling her hard over his face.

"Oh!" The exclamation sounded like it was wrenched from Uma's lungs, and her hands clenched his head. For a second, he thought she intended to push him away, teetering on the brink of refusal above him. He waited, holding back with difficulty. He wanted this, so badly. Wanted her like he'd never wanted anyone in his life. Something about this woman made him more than horny—she made him…hungry. For her, for sex, for life.

Fuck it. He turned and nipped her along the crease of her thigh, then dove face-first into her.

〜∞〜

All the shit Uma had worried about disappeared with each swipe of his tongue, each rough, whiskery scrape of his jaw and slick slide of his nose between her lips. Ivan's hands were magic—sometimes keeping her firmly anchored to him, and at others, when it all got to be too much, fluttering over her, doling out touches of reassurance.

After a while, she lifted up slightly and pulled at his hair, yanking his head out from under her. It was hard to convince him to move. When he finally did, it was to say, "Come on, babe. Been dyin' to do this," before dipping down again to lick right up her center.

"You've got to stop," she whispered, letting her fingers slide over the blindfold. "I can't come this way."

"What do you need?"

"I don't…" Uma swallowed over the weird bout of panic suddenly trying to push its way out. "I don't know. The other night was good."

With a gentle grunt, he pulled away from her hands, moved his enormous shoulder up to spread her thighs wider, and slipped a finger into her. It was big, and from the dark confines of the blindfold, the sensation was overwhelming.

Another finger added to the first, to plunge in hard and tight and a third slid in, bringing with it a twinge of pain. The pain was good, though. It made it all feel real.

"Is this good?" After a moment, he went on. "I can't see you. You gotta tell me."

It felt good, yes, but… Could she tell him? Should she dare? Joey would have—

Fuck Joey. Just fucking fuck *him.*

"I need you to touch my…my clitoris. My clit."

His thumb pressed her there, giving her a little jolt, but—

"Can you lick me again? Like before, except with your fingers inside too?"

He groaned a pained sounding "*fuuuck*" in the best way, before shimmying back down and carrying on.

"It's good. It's so… Wait, wait, I'm—"

She twisted above him, tried nudging his head away with a palm. Nothing, no reaction. He just pulled tighter against her and continued to fuck her with his hand, licking her harder with his tongue.

The fingers and the tongue and the steely arm around her thigh were too much and yet so very right. Not too tender or nice, which was exactly what she wanted. Uma didn't fucking deserve to be coddled or loved. She deserved pulled hair, bruises, and harsh orgasms forced from her body.

She deserved it. Oh God, she'd deserved everything that had happened to her. Everything. The pain, the shame. *Fuck, oh fuck.* The tattoos, even. She deserved to drown in all that ink.

She clawed and pulled, unclear on whether she wanted to get away or if she needed him to hurt her. Maybe both. Twisting and pushing, digging her toes into his side, tugging at his hair, none of it made him turn on her the way Joey would have. It only served to make him work harder. The man was an evil genius, giving her what she didn't think she deserved.

His fingers bent and prodded, tweaking her just right, even as she yanked hard enough to sting his scalp.

With a moan, he stopped, and she could imagine his expression—the one that she wanted to see there: wet mouth, flushed cheeks, his eyes buzzing with want. For several seconds they paused like that, her fist holding him up by the hair, suspended. It had to hurt, but he was either too out of it or too *into* it to care.

The hand disappeared from around her leg. Slicing through the silence came the sound of skin rubbing skin, and with a start, she realized he was touching himself. Masturbating. Right there, beneath her.

"Go on," he said, sounding even needier than she felt, "do it. Use me. Come on me."

Oh God, he likes it.

Picturing how it must look, his fist pumping himself with short, tight, violent pulls, made her clumsy and desperate. She was hurting him, and he liked it. So fucking wrong. Weird and wrong and shameless, but it flipped a switch in her, and she lost it completely. The image obliterated her tenuous control, and she shoved his face back at her body with more force than she would ever have dared with a weaker man. *He can take it.* She knew, with absolute certainty. *He can take whatever I give him.*

Her hands pressed his face to her body, drowning him, and all the while, he groaned and muttered things against her flesh, pulling so hard at himself that he rocked beneath her. It had to hurt.

Oh, the noises the man made: these harsh, hungry little grunts, wild and uncontrollable and absolutely the sexiest thing she'd ever heard in her life. The best part was the words, a diatribe she'd never imagined would be sexy like this. He muttered things that made no sense: *Make me* and *Fuck you, baby*. Words that should have made her cringe. Nonsensical filth that had her digging her nails into him.

Telling her he was hers. *All hers.*

Somehow, the orgasm snuck up on Uma. She tightened around his fingers, to his surprised grunt. All the straining and clenching brought it on too fast. One minute she was listening to him, tense with the fury or the want or *something*, and suddenly the nervy twinge blossomed at her clit, deeper tremors radiating out from the solid pressure of his penetration, and finally, through the almost palpable mirage of his hungry gaze on hers, she came.

Part of her wanted to rip off their blindfolds, but mostly she was glad for the barriers. The intimacy of meeting his eyes would have been unbearable.

As the last of it left her, Uma sank, boneless, onto the pillows, unsure if he'd come or not.

"You're so fucking hot," he said as he joined her high on the bed, voice all fast and frantic, wound up like his breathing. "I wanna fuck you, Uma."

She moaned, stretching back out and tugging at him, ready to let him in. He could do anything he wanted with her. "Oh God. Hold on. Just hold on," he said, placating, as he grasped her hip. "I want to fuck you," he began, "but…"

She stilled. Uh-oh. Here it was. He'd caught sight of her skin, and she repulsed him. Or maybe she'd been wrong. Maybe he'd been able to feel the tattoos somehow. Maybe he—

"I don't have a condom."

She paused. "You don't—"

"I'm a fuckin' idiot."

"Don't you ever—"

"They're in my truck."

"What about—"

"Never had a woman out here before."

"Oh." He climbed over her, one calf between her thighs, knee pressed against her wet core, and leaned his forehead into hers. His face smelled like sex, and she had a flash of what it would have been like with the beard. *More. Better.*

"Here, spread your legs a bit farther," he said, pulling her down and framing her with his arms, sliding between her legs, thighs together.

"Ooh." Uma was powerless to hold back the moan when he pressed his shaft tight against her. He slid easily along her lips. Up and down. She tilted her head as if to look, meeting his forehead with hers.

"You tryin' to see it too?"

All she could do was grunt out a sound, as close to a laugh as she could get.

"Yeah. It's frustratin', but it's also... *Oh God.* I can smell you. Us. I hear you too. It's all so much more. And, Jesus, Uma, you feel so fuckin' good."

The smell *was* stronger here. Warm and musky in the space between their bodies. His voice was tight and urgent like she'd never heard it. And his body. Ah, she couldn't get enough of it. The skin beneath her hands was scalding. And he was right. Everything was unbelievably intense. He was slippery sweat and musky lips, liquid pleasure and dark pain. Wetter, harder, saltier, sweeter. *More.*

His hard, hot cock pressed to her body forced a gasped, "Oh God!" from Uma. Jesus. She bit her lip at the idea of trying to fit *that* inside her.

Ivan shifted above her, and one large hand slid down

her waist to her hips, anchoring them in place. Sure to leave five perfect round bruises on her skin. They were marks that would eventually fade and disappear, but they'd be *hers*. She owned those bruises, unlike every other mark on her body.

The bed lurched when Ivan moved again, this time straddling her thighs. His hand grabbed hers roughly, *roughly*, and wrapped it around his cock. It was stiff and insistent and soaking wet at the tip.

"Squeeze it and—" He rubbed her hand up and down over his shaft, clumsy and painfully tight. "*Please.*"

She followed his lead, not very good at it but excited to try and turned on by the gruff way he used her. Their roles had reversed again—but he seemed more desperate than she had—in charge, but only barely.

Ivan's hand left hers to reach up and palm a breast. It was a selfish move, not about giving her pleasure but about taking his own. He *wanted* to touch her like that, and suddenly she had her own selfish desire to watch him come. With her free hand, she reached between her legs and swiped some of her moisture, brought it up to lubricate him. Another shift, and she pulled him down between her tightly clasped legs. With that move, it all got easier, more obscene. The sound of her hand sliding wetly along his length and his ragged grunts having her groaning in turn.

Joey had never lost it like this man did. He'd never shaken with wanting Uma. Nor had *she* ever wanted him like this, her body aching and unbearably empty, her skin nothing but a sheet of raw nerve endings. She wanted to bite and slap and scratch. She wanted to *rut*. Like an animal.

Ivan said, "Fuck me, Uma. Fuck me with your fist. Slide it on you. Get it wet. You're so fucking wet."

He pulled back, pushed, pulled, pushed, dragging her into a mind-numbing rhythm. The tight hold that should have scared Uma. Made her instead let go. It was a heady powerlessness and reminded her of this ever-shifting balance between them.

"Jesus, girl," he muttered. "You always get this wet?"

She shook her head.

"Huh? Do you? You always beggin' for it like this? Tell me. I can't see you."

"No." In a moment of clarity, she understood what he was looking for. It was his turn to be the big, bad man. Only, unlike Joey, he didn't need to hurt Uma in order to get his rocks off.

Beg me, Joey had said. *Beg me, you stupid bitch.*

Ivan, on the other hand, wanted his ego stroked. *That* she could do. "No, Ivan. Just for you."

He groaned a shaky "ooh."

"It's true," she said, realizing how powerful this man made her. "I've never wanted a cock the way I want yours."

"You want me to fuck you. Say it."

"I...I don't know, Ivan. Your cock's big. I think it may be too big for me."

Oh, he liked that. He bucked against her. *Hard.*

"I'm gonna fuck you anyway, Uma. You'll take it. Say it."

"I'll take it. I'll take whatever you give me."

"Me too, Uma. I'll take whatever you want. Anything you give me."

His rhythm faltered, and she could feel the control

ebbing from him, flowing straight into her. She struggled until he released his hold slightly. Enough for her to line their bodies up. She reached a hand down to nudge him so the tip almost notched into her. Just an inch, a centimeter, not even that far, really, but enough for them both to stop, frozen. She had a moment of guilty desire. A tiny, reckless spark of *do it, slide him in.*

The beast took over, flipping them so she was on top, thrusting against her from below, exactly as she'd imagined. *Rutting.*

She pulled harder, interspersed with those risky slides against him for a couple more minutes, before he pushed her hand roughly aside, took hold of himself, and circled the head against her clit before jerking away.

Filthy, lewd images crowded her mind—a stranger's fantasies. Again, she wanted him inside and imagined how it would feel to take his hot come, to feel it fill her and drip out afterward, like her own little secret. She was back, full circle, to the fantasy where she had children, only this time in a dirty way, in a *get me pregnant, fuck me full of your come* kind of way.

When he finally came, it was with a sound of such helpless shock that she wondered if maybe she'd said those words aloud. *Had she?*

It didn't matter. Nothing mattered as this frightening, strong, beautiful man lost himself with her. She wrapped her hand over his impossibly tight fist as his shaft pumped three hot, thick spurts onto her thigh.

Mesmerized, she ran her finger through his come, blindly brought it to her mouth and tasted. Heedless of the stickiness between their bodies, Ivan bent and kissed her, long and hard.

∽৩৶৹

They were quiet as they walked back to Ms. Lloyd's. Uma couldn't stop thinking of Ivan's invitation. "Stay here," he'd said after their...what? Make-out session? Lovemaking?

"I can't," she'd responded, wondering whether he'd meant tonight, for a while, or forever.

Ivan hadn't argued.

The idea that he wanted her to stay seemed way too good to be true. Too easy after all the struggle.

As they approached the back door, Squeak ran up and dropped a stick at Ivan's feet. He gave her a good scratch behind the ear and threw the stick, smiling. *A couple of weeks ago, I couldn't even imagine this man smiling*, she thought. *And now...*

She kept her eyes on the dog, whose pleasure in the game was evident. *This is what I want*, she thought. *I want this dog and this life. This man.*

Dangerous thoughts for a woman busy running from her past. A woman with no intention of sticking around longer than it took to clear the writing from her skin. And then there was the danger. To Uma, to Ivan. If Joey found her here, he'd... For all she knew, he could already be on his way. And she'd let herself get sucked back in.

He'd asked her to spend the day with him tomorrow, and she wanted it. So badly it scared her. She couldn't say no, but she also couldn't ditch her boss, so she'd agreed to go see him that night instead. She shouldn't, of course, but he'd kissed her and—

"I'm not planning on sticking around, you know,"

she said, interrupting the silence. Someone had to put a stop to their madness.

"So you said."

"I've got to leave Virginia eventually. Go far away. Maybe out west."

"Hmm." Somehow, he managed to invest a lot of skepticism in that sound.

"He'll find me here, you know?" Uma hated how scared her voice came out. She met his eyes defiantly, expecting arguments. What she saw there instead made her itchy.

"Unless you stand up and fight. Let me take care of him, Uma."

"I can't do that. I can't."

"Bullshit."

"He works with the law, and he's powerful. You don't know him, Ivan. You don't know who he is."

"Well, he doesn't know me either."

She walked inside, leaving Ivan watching her— shivering at the thought—and made her way silently upstairs to the bathroom.

Things were different tonight as she turned out the light to undress and prepared to step into the shower. Strange how quickly things were changing in her life, in ways she never could have expected. For once, it wasn't the state of her body that she regretted the most as she squeezed her eyes shut and let the water sluice over her skin. It was the scent of Ivan disappearing down the drain, the imprint of his kisses on her lips and his hands on her body. Ephemeral elements that she had no way to capture.

It was silly, she knew, since she'd see him again

tomorrow, but still, while Joey's marks were indelible, Ivan's were too easily washed away.

Eyes still closed, she put her cheek to one naked shoulder and rubbed, the motion sensuous, lovely.

What if I showed him?

He'd be disgusted.

Pushing back the idea, she soaped herself up and got rid of all traces of what they'd done. Every last bit.

Somehow, as her hand ran over her breast and her nipple hardened at the contact, the hot water, the humidity, the way her body felt swollen and sultry and heavier than usual, all of it came together, and she remembered his voice. That fucking voice. *I'll take whatever you want. Anything you give me*, he'd said, and she wondered, *Would that include the truth?*

The thought of—*Oh God*—of his eyes on her. Not covered, but open, aware, there…seeing her. This…this thing that she'd become. This—

Me. He'd see me.

Would he kick her out of his place? Run screaming? Turn away with disgust? Probably. Possibly?

Or maybe not.

Once she shut off the water, Uma stood dripping in the shower, out of breath, with her flesh pebbled with goose bumps, not from the cold, but at the very dim prospect that Ivan would like what he saw.

20

PREPARING HIS HOME FOR A WOMAN WAS A NEW EXPERIENCE for Ive. He'd bought wine and fresh condoms—house condoms, as opposed to the traveling truck condoms that came with a history he didn't want anywhere near Uma. He washed his sheets and made up his bed, caught sight of the wine and realized he couldn't possibly serve it in his nasty mugs.

Back at the store, he remembered to pick up a cork-screw. Fancy glasses wouldn't do you a lick of good if you couldn't open the damn bottles. After clearing off a table and setting it all up there, he'd decided he might need something other than venison, eggs, or pickled beets to offer her and had gone back out to get more civilized snacks. Three trips to the store in a single day, and he'd spent more than he generally did in a week, but it was worth it. She was worth it.

He was prepping for the evening as if it were some kind of messed up senior prom. Nervous and itchy and so fucking horny he could hardly contain himself. Like a virgin.

And it was only three in the afternoon. He'd seen Uma parked out front of Ms. Lloyd's house, and every time he'd driven by, it was all he could do not to go up there and knock on the door. Just to see her face.

Later that afternoon, he went back out for the final purchase. It had come to him in a moment of inspiration. He ran the silky fabric through his fingers, a little bit hating how it caught on the rough edges of his skin. The women in the shop hadn't even looked at him strangely when he'd bought them, so he figured men buying women gifts like this was probably something they were used to. Weird. He hadn't gotten anything for a woman in years, and when he had, he'd basically been a kid.

A ring. That's what he'd bought for Angela. As big a diamond as he could afford on his factory worker's salary—which hadn't been all that big—but she'd still loved it. He couldn't remember ever getting her anything else. Of course, there was the house. He'd have given her that, if he'd had it then. He'd have given her the shirt off his back. But by the time he'd inherited the place from Uncle Gus, Angela had been long gone. She'd refused to visit him in prison, called him a psycho, told him she'd never speak to him again. Exactly like his mom, who'd screamed at him and baby Jessie, then taken off, leaving them with their grandmother.

Thinking about the frustration he'd felt with Angela and his mom, even Grandma, made him twitch with the need to hit something. Metal to metal always helped, but flesh on flesh was better.

He couldn't explain the feeling, but he understood the need. It was rage, they'd told him inside, and it needed to be *managed*.

Manage, he thought with a nasty, dry little chuckle. *What a stupid fucking word.* Management made him think of bosses and suits. Offices. As if you could some- how *organize* your anger, tell it what to do. *File it away. Yeah, right.* The only way he'd learned to deal with it had been when Steve, a cop, had started teaching classes at the prison. Ironic, wasn't it, how learning how to fight properly had helped him to control—or rather, refocus—his anger. Fighting had gotten him into prison, and fighting got him out. After that, there'd been the ironwork, also learned when he'd been locked up.

He glanced at the clock. Shit, she'd be here soon. No time to pound it out. The thought of her had him breath- ing more evenly. He paced around, wondering what it looked like through her eyes. He glanced at the fabric draped over the back of the one wooden chair in the room, wondering if they'd use either one. He could bend her over the chair, tie her hands with the scarf, or…she could tie *him* up, use him however she liked. Oh, man, that got him going again.

A tiny part of him cringed at how turned-on he got when she bossed him around. And why the hell not? She hadn't complained about him manhandling her every once in a while, and it clearly wasn't easy for her. He just liked it both ways, apparently, and—

A knock. Ivan wiped his sweaty palms on his pants and went to open it. "Down, girl." He nudged Squeak aside and pulled the door open.

"Hey."

"Hey."

Her eyes widened as she looked him up and down, and her lips curled up into a gentle smile. "You look nice."

"Oh. Thanks." He ran his hand through hair that he'd actually brushed. He'd had to buy one of them too. "You too. C'mon in."

"It's a beautiful night outside. The sky's insane. I don't think I've ever seen so many stars."

"Oh yeah? Maybe I'll take you for a walk later." Again, something he'd never done—walked with a woman. Angela would have rather gone straight to hell than spend time outside. "Go stargazing."

"I'd like that." She sounded like she meant it.

Uma squatted down to scratch Squeak behind the ear, and Ive had to stop himself from grabbing her. He had to give her time, not maul her as soon as she got inside. And seeing her down there, loving on his dog, was… He swallowed hard and turned away.

"The place looks amazing," she said, still squatting, like maybe she wasn't quite ready to come back up and get the evening started. He grabbed her hand and pulled her to standing, then led her to the table, feeling stupidly proud of his accomplishments.

"Oh, a tablecloth. Fancy! And wine? This is—" Her hand landed on the chair back, and the scarf scrunched between her slender, white fingers. "It's amazing, Ivan."

There it was again, his full name. He loved that. The way she wouldn't short him a syllable. He loved the smile too, how she blushed when he paid attention to her.

She took it all in, the meatballs, the cut veggies, the shrimp kebabs, the cheese. Red wine, white wine. Sliders and mini sausages. She laughed and turned to him. "Meat, meat, meat, and…cheese?"

"Hey, I cut some celery."

"You think we'll drink *two* bottles of wine?"

"I didn't know what you liked, so I got 'em both."

"You went way overboard."

He sort of nodded, embarrassed at being called out but still a little proud that he'd managed to impress this sophisticated city girl. "Burgers are venison."

"Did you hunt them yourself?"

"Them? No, I hunted *it*. They don't come as burgers, you know, princess," he teased.

"They don't?" Her voice was flirty and light, just like that smile. Women didn't flirt with him usually. No, usually he'd check a woman out in an obvious sort of way, and she'd either ignore him or let him know she was up for it. None of this sparkling eyes and flushed cheeks. More like dirty words and illicit touches. Then uncomfortable truck sex.

Uma looked happy, and still, her fingers fondled that scarf. He couldn't pull his eyes away. She caught him staring and looked down. "What's this?"

"Got you those too. In case…you know."

It was the green one. The same color as those little dots in her eyes. It was beautiful against her skin.

The change came over her. Like a switch. Uh-oh. Her expression was strange. Maybe he'd gone too far.

The first scarf wafted around her neck, and she picked up the second one. The thicker, wider black scarf that he thought of as his.

When her eyes met his this time, she looked positively wicked. Oh man, *this* was the woman he'd hoped to see again tonight.

What was it about this woman that made him feel so reckless?

∽✑∾

Uma's best laid plans would always go awry. It was a rule in life. But apparently life was telling her to stop trying to control everything.

She'd come to Ivan's place tonight with the full intention of baring her skin and giving him the chance to get out when he saw her as she was: someone else's leftovers.

Instead, this.

How could she possibly refuse his offering? They'd do it for real. Blindfolded again, because it was what he thought she wanted.

He'd given her everything. And for a split second, it scared the living hell out of her. Until she picked up the second scarf with its thicker weave.

"Come here so I can put this on you."

"Want a glass of wine first?"

Oh, right. That was what a civilized person did. You sat and had wine and snacks and *then* you ravished the beast who'd put himself out to please you.

"Okay, sure," she sighed.

Ivan smiled. "You don't, do you?"

Uma shook her head and smiled back at him.

"Good." He picked up the corkscrew. "'Cause I don't even know how to use one of these."

She said, "Come here," and he set the corkscrew down before obeying.

He caught her wrists as she moved to twine the black fabric around his head. "Can I get a kiss first?"

"Oh, right." Her eagerness was a little mortifying, but his smile told her it was okay. Gently, sweetly, he leaned in and put his lips to hers, giving just the right amount of pressure. Slowly, with impossible calm, he kissed her. When he pulled away, he left her barely able to stand on her own.

"Wow." She hadn't meant to say that out loud.

"Yeah."

"Now, can we…"

He smiled and grabbed a box of condoms before moving to the bed. "Yeah."

It was different this time. Every move felt set up, somehow. He pulled back the quilt, and they settled on the bare bedsheets before putting on the scarves. *Premeditated sex, with intent to shag*, she thought a little hysterically. Would he notice that she'd taken the time to shave? Probably. He'd spent enough time down there last night. He smoothed her blindfold on, and Uma muffled another nervous giggle.

She was quickly losing her cool. This wouldn't do. Jesus Christ. If she didn't have her cool, what the hell would she hang on to?

"Relax, baby."

"I'm okay," she protested too quickly.

"We don't have to do this, you know."

"I want to."

"You sure?"

"Yeah. Yes. Yes."

A pause. "What do you say if you want to stop?" Ivan asked.

"Um…stop?"

He laughed against the side of her face. "Yeah. You'll say it, right? If you want us to stop? Or if I do something you don't like?"

"Yeah. I'll say it."

"Good." Oh, there were those lips again, kissing her to distraction. And there went her sparkly cardigan, followed by her shirt and punctuated with a hot, wet ellipsis of kisses along the side of her neck. A nip at her shoulder coincided with the snap and zip of pants—his, not hers—and the sound of fabric sliding against skin. Her bra went next—oh God—and those perfectly coarse fingers deftly undoing her jeans. She shimmied out of them, nearly falling off the bed in the process. Ivan's grasp on her arm saved her at the last minute, and her gasp of panic turned to a huffed laugh-groan when he pulled her in and took her nipple in his mouth.

As Ivan slowly made his way over her body, taking her apart, piece by piece, and loving her back together again, odd things came into focus: the slight sting of woodsmoke in her sinuses, the scent of metal embedded in his hair, the gentle *tink-tink* of Squeak's collar as she shifted on her bed in front of the fire. Everything was made sharper, more poignant, by the blindfold.

Kisses along her belly, placed with the utmost care, interspersed with moments of complete abandon, grabbing hands melting into moaning mouths, and her slick wetness making noises she should be ashamed of. He tickled and licked and bit his way around her body until she couldn't stand it anymore. "Stop it!" she yelped.

"What?" he said, his voice sounding breathless.

"You're killing me, Ivan. I want us to do this." Why did this suddenly feel wrong? She swallowed back the doubt. "Now."

"I'm killin' *you*?"

She could hear the smile in his voice, clung to it. *This is Ivan. Good, kind, sweet Ivan.*

Forcing a playfulness she suddenly wasn't sure of, she slapped his arm and tried to pull away, more unsettled than she'd realized. In search of distraction from the shakiness in her limbs, she asked, "Can you the find the condom, or do I have to—"

"It's right here, baby."

She forced out a breath and made herself sink back against the pillows.

Okay. This was it. She was doing this. *They* were doing this. With a nod, she said, "Good. Now, put it on."

The crinkle of the wrapper, the snap of the rubber, the smell of it jarred her overripe senses. "Come here."

He was over her, poised. "You ready?" He was out of breath, shuddery.

And suddenly she wasn't ready. Not at all. She remembered the last time, with Joey, and what had felt like nerves turned to something else. She was shaking. "I don't know."

"Okay." He paused and pulled away, then after a moment settled at her side. "What's going on?"

"I... Oh God. I want to do this with you, but I'm..."

"Tell me."

"I want to look at you. When we do it. I want to see your eyes. I want to know it's *you*."

"Okay."

"But I don't think you'll...want to keep going. If you see *me*."

"Oh, baby, I—"

"No. You don't understand. It's bad. *It's so bad.*" Her voice got away from her as she did her best to hold back a sob.

"Tell me about it. Tell me what happened to you."

21

HE'D ASKED HER FOR THE STORY, BUT SUDDENLY, IVE didn't want to know. He was almost afraid to—afraid of the rage it'd stoke inside him. He'd take back the words if he could.

But he wouldn't, really. Of course not. Because the last thing he wanted to do was make her feel bad about herself.

"If I show you what he did to me, Ivan, you'll never be able to look at me again."

"That ain't true." He took a deep breath and pulled off the condom, grimacing at the pinch of rubber against his hard-on. "Don't have to show me. Start by tellin' me the story."

"I don't…I don't want you to feel sorry for me."

"I know, baby," he said. What did she need? What could he do for her? Maybe getting out into the dark, starry night would help. "Come on, let's go for that walk."

They managed, somehow, to get dressed, then pulled off the scarves and spent a few silly moments blinking at each other like squinty-eyed moles. That brought the smile back to her face.

He got an idea. "Grab the quilt, and I'll get this stuff, and we can have a picnic."

"In the dark?"

"Hell yeah. That's the way we roll in the country." He emptied a basket filled with iron odds and ends and repacked the food in its fancy wrappers, then stuffed everything inside. "Red or white?" he asked, arms suspended above the bottles.

"I..." She hesitated, eyes darting between the two bottles. "I don't—I have no idea."

"That's okay. We'll take 'em both."

"I should know that, though, shouldn't I?"

"What do you mean?"

"I should know what I like."

He shrugged. "Not if you don't drink wine. I don't."

"It's not that, it's... I hate this about myself. I hate it so much."

"What?"

"I let everybody else decide. Joey always ordered white wine for me. He never asked me what I wanted. Not once. And the thing was, I was used to that. I didn't want to decide."

"That's okay. I can pi—"

"No," she interrupted harshly, hand up and dominatrix expression in place. God, even that tiny little taste made his cock throb. He was one sick puppy. "I want red wine."

"Red it is. You ready?"

"Let's go."

Once outside, Ive remembered the corkscrew and

went back in, leaving her alone to gaze up at the starry sky. He found it on the table, then rooted around in a dresser drawer for a couple of thick sweaters. It was cold enough that they'd need them, along with the quilt.

From the door, he took a quick glance around and spotted the two scarves on the floor. Should he?

No. The blindfolds stayed here. Whatever happened between them out there tonight, they'd have their eyes wide open.

～∽∽

They got settled in the back of the truck. Tailgating, Ivan called it, although it seemed more like camping to Uma.

"Girl, this ain't nothin' like campin'. You want to see how we do it out here, I'll take you with me someday. Up there." He motioned to the mountains behind the trees. "Appalachian trail's just up over that first rise. Could do some hikin', have ourselves a campfire."

"Roast marshmallows?"

He chuckled. "Yeah. Make s'mores."

She said, "I'm in," and his chuckle morphed into a happy little sound.

After making her put on one of his enormous sweaters, he pulled the sleeping bag from the cab of the truck and spread it out for them like a blanket, then set everything up again. Uma liked it this way, just them under the stars.

Ivan served wine. This time, the sound of their two glasses clinking together in a toast didn't bring with it a flood of memories. Uma was right there, in the back of a truck, with this big, handsome man who'd gone out of his way to treat her like a princess.

Ivan leaned against the back of the cab and snuggled

her into the crook of his arm. The stars were even more incredible, leaning back like this.

"What kind of moon's that?" she asked.

"Almost a first quarter."

"How can you tell if it's coming or going? Lord, I should know that. My mom would kill me."

"Remember how dark it was the night you tried to sleep in your car?"

"Yeah."

"That was the new moon."

"Oh. So now it's waxing?"

"Yep." Ivan leaned forward to snag one of his little burgers, handed it to her, and made quick work of two of his own. "What do you think?"

"Delicious."

"Didn't even know what you liked to eat."

"My mom's a hippy. Tried to bring me up vegan."

"What's that?"

"Vegetarian, except without eggs or cheese or anything like that."

"Oh, so you—"

"I rebelled. Love meat and cheese and eggs. And"— she clinked her glass to his again—"red wine."

"Better than white?"

"Yeah, it's"—she took another sip and swished it around her mouth the way she'd seen Joey do in posher restaurants—"rich, and I don't know. Carnal or something."

"Carnal?"

"Or, um…meaty, maybe. No, that's not right. More like *earthy*, or of the flesh." She shivered. In fact, that was exactly how she would describe Ivan.

He took a slow sip in silhouette, eyes closed. Her gaze traveled along his neck to where his Adam's apple moved as he swallowed, then back up to catch the flash of his eyes on her.

"Seems all right to me, but my taste buds are burned out from too much Coors."

"I've never been a big drinker."

He smiled. "That's okay too."

"What else you got for me to taste?"

"Oh, this is a blue cheese. Lady at the store told me it's French. The mother of all blues, she called it. Here." He handed her a cracker and made up his own.

"Roquefort."

"You know this stuff?"

"Yeah." She didn't elaborate. Joey had enjoyed teaching her all about the finer things in life. Cheese and foie gras. She'd enjoyed the cheese but refused the goose liver. You could take the girl out of the commune, but you couldn't force her to eat tortured animals. She hadn't been completely deaf to her mother's teachings, after all.

They ate a little of everything. Sometimes he fed her and sometimes the other way around, but what she liked most was rediscovering it all with this man. Erasing the bad and replacing it with the good. She liked the way he offered without insisting. She liked the way he listened to her opinion.

Before she knew it, the bottle was gone, and they'd decimated the snacks.

"What'd you like best?"

"Your venison."

"Yeah? You just sayin' that?"

"No. It was good."

"You ever think about hunting?"

She jerked a little at the thought before letting it settle over her.

"No. Never. Do you use a gun?"

"Yeah, that and a tomahawk."

"Wha—Oh. Ha-ha." She snuggled farther into him, liking this. Liking *him* so much.

"We're out of red. Wanna try the white?"

"You brought it?"

"Girl, I brought *everything*."

"Everything?"

"Got the condoms."

"What about the scarves?"

He hesitated before saying, "No."

She let out a big breath. "Good."

"Come here," he said, pulling her to him and into a heady kiss, slow and sweet and deep. "Everything okay?"

"Yeah."

"Is this okay?"

He meant them, what they were doing. "Yeah."

"You go out with me now?"

"You mean like a date?"

"Yep."

"What's this?"

"No, I mean dinner, movie. Maybe get lucky?"

She hesitated. "Don't expect me to wear a dress."

"No dresses. Got it." He pulled her down and rolled them onto their sides, squeezing her close against his body so everything lined up. They fit perfectly under the quilt.

"When?"

"Um, how about tomorrow?"

"Aren't you sick of me yet?" she asked, teasing, but kind of worried that he was. She rolled to her back, facing the stars rather than him. His hand stayed at her waist, light, but definitely there.

"Hell no." He sounded a little surprised at the idea. "Kinda gettin' used to you hangin' around." Ivan cleared his throat. "Like I said. You could stay here. For a while, I mean. As long as you wanted. If you got sick of livin' next door."

"What, in your truck?" she joked, deflecting the thrill of hope that the invitation gave her. *Yes, yes, yes. Oh please, yes. Let me stay here, and you can keep me safe. Forever.*

"Yeah, right." He chuckled, but there was a tiny bit of insecurity in his voice. Oh crap. He meant it. He really wanted her to stay. "You could stay in the house. Pick a room. Get you a bed and stuff."

Uma closed her eyes against the hope swelling almost painfully in her chest. It would be so easy, wouldn't it? To let him take care of her.

"What's the deal with your house?" she deflected.

"No deal. Just fixin' it up." Ivan's hand moved from her belly to her hip, stroking her gently through her clothes.

"Do you have a kitchen there and working bathrooms?"

"Sure. Workin' on detail stuff now."

"But you don't live there."

"I gotta finish it before movin' in."

"You give tours?"

"Sure. Show you around tomorrow before our date."

"Oh, so you assumed I'd go on that date with you?"

"Nah, but I figured if I upped the ante and asked

you to move in with me, you'd have to say yes to the lesser commitment."

Uma smiled. The hand still stroking her tightened a fraction and skimmed up her waist to her breast. "So, how long have you had this place?" she asked.

"Six years."

"You've been working on it that long?"

He nodded, his nose nuzzling the side of her face and his hand running back down to slide under her shirt. "Yeah."

"Must be amazing inside."

"It's too nice for me."

Uma didn't like that. "What do you mean?"

"I don't need a big house like that, all that fancy scrollwork and trim and stuff. Grew up in a trailer."

"So, what are your plans for the house?"

"First, I thought maybe I'd—" He cleared his throat and shifted away, taking with him the heat of his hand. "You don't wanna hear this crap."

"No, I do."

"So, when my uncle left me the house, it was like I could change the future. Had plans for...stuff."

"Seems reasonable to think of the future."

"Well, it didn't pan out."

"I know how that goes." Something about his reticence made her want to spill her own story. That was why they'd come out here, after all. But still, she hesitated.

He must have sensed what she was thinking. "Why don't you tell me your story, Uma?" he asked gently.

She sighed. "I had plans before I met Joey."

Ivan went completely still, his breathing taking a backseat to his listening.

"Joey was…convincing. Lawyers are like that. And he's good at what he does. Got me to do things I didn't really want to do, you know?" She wasn't sure if he did, but he nodded anyway. "It all happened so fast between us, like he'd decided on me, and he wanted me, and he wanted me *now*. I kept thinking we'd talk about what I wanted later. And then later and then later and then…later never came." She closed her eyes and continued. "I used to have friends. I didn't notice they were gone until I looked around one day and it was just me. Well, me and Joey. But not even that, 'cause he worked all the time, came home late—dinners, drinks, schmoozing. All that political crap. And I had weddings on the weekends."

"Weddings?"

"I'm a photographer. Weddings are my bread and butter."

"Makes sense."

She shifted and craned her neck to look at him. "What makes sense?"

"The photographer thing. The way you were with that camera last night. And the stuff you do. How you look at things…at me. Like you're framing a shot in your mind."

"I do that?"

"Also, your hands." She clenched them unconsciously. "You're always doin' that. Squeezin' 'em, openin' 'em, like you're itchin' to pick somethin' up." He nudged her gently. "But go on. You were talkin'."

Uma took a huge breath in and continued. "I was in so much denial that it could have gone on for a while, I guess, but then he cheated on me. With a colleague.

They'd been working this case together—the first time he was lead prosecutor on something that major. That was his excuse, at least. How high stress it was, how they were thrown together, a tight-knit team, blah, blah, blah." The shifts in breathing beside her told her of Ivan's reactions, but he didn't interrupt. "It got so confusing. He apologized, so loving and so, so sorry." She huffed out a frustrated breath, trying to explain why, how she'd let it happen. "He convinced me to stay, but I felt different. Things had changed, and I think he knew it. We had an okay couple of months after that, although he still spent so much time at work. But when he was home, he was this perfect boyfriend. Like diamonds and flowers and spoiling me rotten and constant, constant attention." She shrugged. "I guess I kind of liked it. Even though I never entirely trusted it. But, frankly, it wasn't what I wanted."

She shifted a little, enjoying the arm that wrapped around her. Comforting, but not imprisoning.

"Then he lost the case. It was a big deal. In hindsight, he must have been on something even while they were trying it, to keep up with the workload and the media, all the pressure. When they lost, his boss made him take some time off. That was the last straw. He'd be sucking back the booze, probably popping pills, while I was trying to process photos in the next room, him constantly breathing down my neck. One night we fought, badly. And he hit me." Tears pricked at Uma's sinuses, not uncontrollable, but enough to let her know that the emotion was there. Clean and unfamiliar. "He apologized, said he couldn't help it. He was overtired... The whole fucking rigmarole you hear from battered women. I couldn't let myself keep falling for that. So, I decided to move out. Packed up, because I wouldn't stand for that kind of crap. Nobody gets to *abuse me*, you know? He acted normal. Probably too calm. He seemed resigned to it and…"

She swallowed, and his arm loosened a smidge, enough to let her know she could go whenever she needed to. She appreciated his subliminal support and wondered if he was even aware of it. "I was all ready to go when he broke *everything*. All my equipment. Every camera. Even my goddamned Nikon. He smashed every single thing that mattered to me. He was wasted, weird." Uma's throat clicked dryly as she remembered bits and pieces. "Earlier that week, he'd come home with a tattoo machine."

Machine, she thought, *not gun.* "Guns are for shooting, Uma. For hurting or killing," Joey had sneered. "Only white trash use the word *gun* for this." Ironic, of course, considering what he'd done in the end—the way he'd used the machine to torture her.

"He didn't say where he'd gotten it, but it didn't look new, and I wondered about…you know, cleanliness."

"Why did he have it?"

"For us, he said. To show our undying love. And, that night, I'd never seen him so amped. Pupils like black holes. I don't think he'd slept all week. I heard this buzzing in the bathroom, like a deranged doorbell or something. I slammed my way in, looking for my things as I packed everything up, furious, and there he was, sitting on the toilet seat, etching my initials inside a heart. In black, right on his own forearm. Like something you'd see scratched into a tree."

She paused, recalled Joey's words as he'd shown her the bloody, red mess he'd made of himself. "Proof of my undying love," he'd said. That was when she'd started shaking.

"It flipped a switch in me. One second I'm packing to leave him, and the next, I'm freaking out. Really freaked. But also still pissed and ready to… I don't know…"

What would she have done that night if he hadn't caught her and… Who could say? She might have cooled off and left. It wasn't worth thinking about what could have been.

"I was beyond reasonable. Screaming, scared. Just out of control. Before, I'd wanted to cut up his clothes, his precious Armani suits, you know, to hurt him. But by then I realized how far gone he was and… He disappeared into the spare room. I tried to turn, but he came back and he had a…" She choked on the words, the image—no, on the *feelings* it all brought up. Fear, absolute terror. And surprise. That prickling skin that signaled her fight-or-flight instinct kicking in.

The rush of adrenaline had made her feel strong that night.

What a joke.

"He had a gun. I'd never seen it before. He just… walked into the bathroom and put it hard against my head. The front. Right here. Like this." She put her finger to her head, no longer feeling Ivan's reactions against her, completely lost to the memories she'd worked to suppress these past few months: the cold sink against her cheek, the tiles under her shins as she sank to her knees.

"'I'll shoot your fucking brains out, you stupid bitch.'

That's what he said to me." She gulped past the lump in her throat. "I believed him."

Ivan's thick arm tightened, and she had to shrug it off. Too much, too tight, too warm. She sat up a bit, to breathe, and turned her face away, relieved that they were doing this outside where there was air. Cool and cleansing and a little painful in her throat.

"There's this moment…" Uma paused, not sure she could tell the rest of this. But she swallowed and made herself keep going. "When you have to decide whether you want to live or die. And I wanted to *live*, damn it. I'm not the type of person who just gives up…but after a while, I changed my mind. It wasn't the pain, so much. I'd stopped feeling how bad it hurt. It was the other stuff. There was this regret, like, *oh fuck, what have I done*? It was so permanent…that feeling that there's no going back now or…or *ever*. But the worst thing? Worse than anything else in my entire life? I was so fucking *helpless*. Trapped there, like a…a…bug pinned down. A butterfly in one of those frames. I couldn't move. He held me, and I was forced to…to take whatever he gave me. He wanted to mark me for life, to make me his, and fighting him just made it worse. I had to *take it*."

The buzzing of the machine, that dark, chemical smell, and Joey, yelling obscenities when he couldn't figure out how to change out a bent needle. Other things too, like the way he'd watched her face instead of his hand, not caring what he wrote on her skin, just eating up her hurt, getting off on it.

Ivan's voice rumbled out from the darkness, sharper than ever. "I'll kill him, Uma."

She shook her head.

"Where is he?"

"No, Ivan. You can't."

"I can."

"I know you *can*. But I don't *want* you to. Please." His breathing churned beside her, and Uma wondered what this kind of story did to this kind of man.

"Tell me who he is."

"No way."

22

HE'D FUCKING RIP THE GUY TO PIECES. SHE MIGHT NOT
think she wanted him to, but it didn't matter. Men like
this Joey guy didn't deserve the air they breathed. He'd
hunt him down and tear him apart like the—

"I've lost you, haven't I?"

"No."

"Liar. You're thinking about all the ways you're going
to hurt him." Uma sat up farther and leaned over him, her
head blocking out the stars, which he couldn't even see
anymore anyway—not through the cloud of rage.

She put her small hand in his hair and pulled, bringing
everything sharply back into focus. "You, Ivan, will not
do anything to Joey. I *will not* forgive you if you do."

The burn at the roots of his hair felt good. It shocked
him back to earth and forced him to listen. Forced the
rage to bank again.

"Kiss me, then."

"Not until you promise."

"Just fuckin' kiss me."

"Repeat after me. 'I, Ivan…' Ivan what?"

"Shifflett."

"'I, Ivan Shifflett…'"

"I, Ivan Shifflett…"

"'…do solemnly swear…'"

"…do solemnly swear…"

"'…not to go against the wishes of one Uma R. Crane.'"

"What's the *R* stand for?"

The hand in his hair tugged, harder this time. "Shut up and repeat after me."

"Shut up and—"

Another tug elicited a groan from him, and her face moved in toward his, as if to eat the sounds right out of his mouth.

"You will not go against my wishes," she whispered.

"I will not go against the wishes of the beautiful Uma R. Crane."

"I'm not beautiful."

"You're fuckin' gorgeous."

"I'm not."

"I can't get enough of you."

"Why? What's wrong with you, Ivan?"

"You got all night?"

"Yeah."

"Whatever. There's no way we're wastin' it talkin' 'bout me. Come 'ere." He reached for her, pulling her down atop him.

This kiss was different. Like every kiss they'd shared, it had its own place in Ive's mind, a catalogue of their time together. This one was almost unbearably tender. Gentle. He'd never been close like this with anyone. He'd been with women, and he'd even thought he was in love once—with Angela—so they must have shared something, but it had been nothing like this. How could you even feel shit like this from a kiss? And after only a couple of weeks of knowing each other.

The idea scared him suddenly. What the fuck was he doing, falling for a woman who'd leave him one day, just like the rest? The difference with this one, he figured, was she'd already warned him she had no plans to stay. At least she was honest. That was more than he could say about the others.

She'd leave him, eventually, but he didn't think she wanted to.

Above him, Uma shimmied slightly, and he forgot, momentarily, the anger and the panic.

∽∾

It happened amazingly fast between them. Every single time they touched, it was like a fuse igniting. A ridiculously short fuse. Only this time, there was something more there. She wasn't entirely sure, but she thought it might be her story.

It made it all the more intense, more real, and, at the same time, completely reckless. It was in her, and she sensed it from him. Ivan the Terrible completely, madly desperate. *For little ole me.*

Strange how his desperation gave her so much power. There was something truly messed up about that. Yet, the titillation was so strong that she couldn't even bring herself to feel bad. That's just the way it was.

She pulled his hair, ground their hips together, and let their mouths move from sipping to licking to devouring each other. At some point, her hands managed to unzip and open pants, yanking his down slightly, and with his help, pulling hers off entirely.

Her mouth moved, and "I want to fuck you" came out in a voice that belonged to someone she'd never met before. That woman gave orders and didn't wait to see if they were followed.

The little moan he let out in response was perfect, one of those sounds Uma could get addicted to if she wasn't careful. The challenge was to see how to get him to do it again. She shifted down his thighs to take hold of his stiff erection and squeezed, still awed by the thick heft of him. The weight was perfect. Even heavier than she remembered. After a few tight strokes, she let it smack back against him and moved off him to root around in the picnic basket. She found the strip of condoms and ripped one off with her teeth.

"Hey, you're not supposed to do it like that."

"Oh, yeah?" she taunted, using her teeth again to rip open the packet. "How am I supposed to do it?"

He didn't respond as she leaned back and rolled the rubber down his shaft. They shuddered together.

"You ready?" he asked, even though she was clearly in charge.

"Are you?" Who the hell was this woman? A woman who got on top of a man and undressed him just enough to guide him inside her. What had happened to the old Uma, who always let other people's personalities over-shadow her own?

"Yeah, come on." Ivan tugged at her waist, her ass, her hips, trying to move her without taking over. "I gotta fuck you, Uma." The man sounded frantic. He didn't wait for a response but pulled her back up, so their bodies lined up.

Her stupid brain went back to the first night she'd met Joey, how he'd cajoled her into having sex with him. It had been a true seduction, not *quite* against her will, but not entirely what she'd wanted either. In hindsight, Joey must've gotten off on the coercion, the surrender, the ambiguity of her consent. There'd been none of this urgency, none of this raw need—so honest, so *fucking* real.

Ivan's cock nudged her, seeking entry from below, and she came back to the present with a slight Joey hangover. Suddenly needing to know she really could stop this anytime she needed. "Stop!"

Ive stilled, sank back down. Not impatient or angry at all.

"I just…" She turned, swallowed, and blinked away the tears that suddenly threatened to fall. "Why're you so nice to me?"

"I like you."

Oh. Uma tried to pause her ever-racing mind.

That simple, huh? He liked her, so he showed it. No games, no denial, no manipulation, no bullshit. *He likes me*, she thought, barely comprehending the simplicity of it all. *He likes me.*

"I, um…I like you too, Ivan."

"Good." His boyish, excited smile was barely visible in the dark, but it brought a jolt of worry, shadowed by guilt. *I'm going to hurt this guy.*

"You're thinkin' too much, Uma."

He was right.

She was about to have sex in the back of a pickup, and instead of enjoying it, here she was, worrying—again.

Enough. It was time to let go and enjoy the moment. No Joey, no worries—nothing to get between her and this man so hell-bent on having her. She let herself feel, really feel, the point where their naked skin came together.

Planting her hands firmly on his chest, Uma leaned forward, filled with the anticipation of what she was about to do. She lifted up onto her knees and reached beneath her. There he was, hot and willing, and before she could think too hard about the last time she'd done this—

No, not the last time *she* had done this. Tonight had nothing to do with the last time she'd been penetrated. But she wouldn't think about that right now. She refused to remember it.

Instead, she took him firmly in hand, lined him up with her body, and worked him, slow and steady, inside her. Her breath hitched once when the fit was too tight, and she paused. They stopped—breathing, listening, waiting for the other to put a halt to everything. He didn't. She didn't. Somewhere close by, something hooted.

Ivan flexed.

"Don't move," she managed. "Give me a second? Just—"

He held himself utterly still inside her, his self-control palpable, and she loved him a little bit for that restraint.

Perhaps more than a little.

Suddenly, she remembered a time with Joey. It was a hotel room in Atlanta where he'd gone for a conference. She'd gone along for fun, and it *had* been fun. Good food and music. She'd taken a ton of photos there. But it was the sex that came back to her. Their hotel room had been equipped with a jumbo mirror, which, if you happened to have sex on the desk, provided quite a perspective. The thing was, Uma had only noticed the mirror halfway into it. She'd turned her head and taken in the way Joey's body had slammed into hers from behind, the quick, mechanical piston of his hips. She'd stared at where their bodies came together and gotten turned on.

Her eyes had wandered up his body, to his face. With a jolt, Uma had realized Joey wasn't staring at her body or their bodies together. He'd been mesmerized by himself. His own face, his own muscles. Like a scene straight out of *American Psycho*, the man she was having sex with was more interested in flexing for the mirror than sharing anything of consequence with her.

And here she was, thinking about that bastard—again.

It was time to stop. Now. Forever.

Uma shifted, squeezed her inner muscles, and Ivan moaned, tightening his hold on her.

"Good," she said.

I want to feel everything. To be here. With this man.

She didn't have to see his face properly to know the look he'd have: a little surprised, a little excited. He liked her in charge, enjoyed giving her power. And the thing was, it only made him seem stronger.

When she leaned back, he gasped, and the sound of it—the helpless, needy, uncontrolled sound—made her feel like a fucking *goddess*. Like she'd wrested control from him and taken exactly what she wanted, and *oh Lord*, that was good.

She licked her finger and reached down to touch herself, the circling of her clit her only outward movement.

But everything was so tightly clamped around him that she wondered how she'd last. This was… It was…

Uma had never quite believed her mother's claims about the tantric powers of sex. The notion that fucking was somehow a spiritual experience. She'd always thought it was another hippy excuse to run around and hump like bunnies.

But this—him pulsing inside of her and her body contracted in orgasm, pulling him in—this was more than just for procreation or even fun. This was something else entirely. Like reaching new heights of understanding or making magic. Touching those stars so far above them. As if this was bigger than them, it was—

Ivan's muttered "Jesus" told her that he felt it too.

She lay slumped on top of him after, staying that way as he softened. He reached down and held on to the condom while she pulled up and off him.

On her back, Uma opened her eyes as wide as they'd go and sighed, already mourning the loss of him inside her.

Air had never smelled so clean, night sounds so ethereal. The sky was absolutely majestic.

After he settled back in beside her and pulled the quilt over them, Uma sighed a second time and almost giggled, thinking of her mother in India, halfway around the world.

Sex outside in the cold autumn night. Yeah, Mom would be proud.

She snuggled into this beautiful man's side and let the giggle bubble out.

There you go, Mom. Om fucking Shanti.

23

As always, Squeak woke Ive at the crack of dawn, and, as always, he'd get up right away to attend to her needs. Well, to hers and to the dozen other creatures who depended on him.

This morning, though, it was a lot harder. It may have been the four hours of sleep he'd gotten. Or maybe the woman sprawled across his body. Yeah, that was probably it.

He was covered by so much of her that he was hot. Crazy, considering he could see his breath. But, man, she felt good, even fully clothed, against him. He loved the weight of her, the warmth of her breath on his collarbone, and the tickle of her hair against his chin.

A quick glance at the clock showed it was just after five. Still mostly dark outside, but definitely time to get a move on. He wondered what time Ms. Lloyd expected Uma back at her place. If he hazarded a guess, he'd say probably around now. Not because the woman needed help at the butt crack of dawn, but to be a pain in the ass, as was her way.

At his dog's insistent squeal, he slowly scooched out from under Uma, careful not to wake her. Better to move now, before the tail started thumping into overdrive and the whining turned to barks. Squeak had been obliged to pull him out of enough mornings-after to know exactly what it took to get Ive moving.

Boots first, then he grabbed his towel and soap and stumbled to the door to let her out. He pulled it closed behind him, knowing how much noise the animals would make while he fed them. He bent and filled the cat dishes with dry food, still buck naked and fucking *freezing*. Wet food was at night only, but you'd think the animals didn't know that, the way they looked at him accusingly, bum-rushing his calves, always pissed at the hollow ping of kibble rather than the hiss of cans opening.

Into the woods for a long morning piss, then back to the hand pump beside the workshop for a quick wash. It was too damn cold to be naked out here. He could go up to the big house, like a normal person, but why waste the time?

Teeth chattering and skin puckered into a million tiny goose bumps, he walked back inside and moved to relight the fire. Only once the flames began eating away at the logs did he stand up, preparing to reward himself by returning to bed, when Uma made a sound. A low, unearthly kind of noise like he'd heard only once or twice in his life.

❧

Joey was gouging Ivan's eyes out, and it was a million times worse than anything Uma had experienced. She was blind and naked and freezing cold—

Oh God, Joey was there, above her, and she could almost feel the needle burning into her flesh. There was a hand, rough on her arm, and she shrieked. Frantic, turning, flopping like a fish. Another hand, and Joey's hot breath had her yelling, keening.

Nothing worked. Writhing, straining, flailing, scratching, and searching for escape—a wild, rabid animal. A rat caught in a trap, a lizard brain. No, less than that: an amoeba without conscious thought, just an instinct to survive. All the pushing and pulling only served to land her on her rear, hard, until she scrabbled away—the last resort for a woman buried alive. She'd scrape her hands to the bone if need be.

It was his voice—that goddamned voice—that eventually got through to her. "Uma, baby. Uma. Uma, I got you. I got you. You're okay. I got you." A litany of slow, patient words spun like a finely woven web, one layer at a time. They slipped and slid over her and clung, wrapping her in their warmth before they finally got through.

Ivan. It was Ivan. She was on the floor, in his arms, big and warm and safe—her cocoon. "I'm here, baby. I'm here." He rocked, and she *was* a baby, a newborn in his grasp.

One hand moved to her face, comfortingly rough, while the other cupped her ear. So tender and sweet. How could all those hard edges feel so very soft?

He kissed her. Forehead, the corner of an eye, cheek, mouth. Gentler touches than a man his size should be capable of. His breath warm and familiar. She tasted toothpaste and salt on his wet lips, as though someone had been crying. Not him, surely?

"Come here," he said, pulling her into his lap, and

she wanted it so badly, that closeness. She wanted more of it.

His eyes were whiskey and ice. A stranger's eyes. His voice she knew intimately. She'd memorized the feel of his calluses against her soft places, the smell of him, but these remarkable eyes were still unfamiliar after the time they'd spent blindfolded and in the dark.

"I got you," he whispered again, and she let him take her weight.

After maybe ten minutes, Uma took a deep, shaky breath in and unstuck her face from the crook of his neck.

"Morning." She cleared her throat and tried again. "Morning."

"Mornin', baby," he said, his voice so gentle it almost broke her heart.

"Nightmare."

"Figured."

"I...um...I've got to pee."

With the tiniest huff of what might have been a laugh, he nodded, slow and unsure, before releasing her.

"Need company?" He managed to make it sound almost lascivious, which was a feat, given...well, everything. And she was so thankful for that. His humor, his seemingly endless support.

"No. Thank you. But I wouldn't mind something for my breath."

He stood and helped her up, handed her a tube of toothpaste, and sent her out.

She headed toward the shelter of the line of trees, ignoring where the drive curved back up to Ms. Lloyd's place. She'd have to head back there shortly, although she didn't want to. Didn't want to go to her next laser appointment, didn't want to do anything but stay here with Ivan. Even if peeing outside in the freezing cold wasn't exactly her idea of a good time. One reason for him to move into the big house, with its perfectly good kitchen and electricity and running water. Oh, and heat.

Then again, there was something about his cozy, little space that suited him to a T. Man at his most elemental. She picked her way toward the edge of the woods, the hangover of her dream disappearing into chilly practicality, and it occurred to her that he'd been completely naked when he'd held her: hale and hearty and shamelessly nude in the crisp winter morning. Whereas she had gone to sleep fully dressed. Even here, without a single witness, in the great outdoors, she squatted under an oak tree, *incapable* of glancing at her own body.

Because of Joey. All because of Joey.

She stood and pulled up her pants, let her eyes take in the landscape in a way she hadn't before. The big, white house, pointlessly empty. Farther along, the forge, with its chimney puffing out smoke like an industrious little train, so busy, so full of life with its mini herd of cats eating beside the door, and the man inside…flesh and bone and so much heart. And beyond it, past the fallow fields, loomed the Blue Ridge Mountains: timeless, beautiful. Permanent.

They'd be there forever, those mountains.

Forever. Unlike Joey and his stupid ink.

Not his. Mine. My ink. My skin.

He'd wanted to make his mark on her? Well, she was done letting him. Today. Right now. Done.

With a sure stride, she returned to the forge and

opened the door to a welcoming waft of heat. Always warm in here, always inviting. And there he was, Ivan, his eyes just as enveloping, only they offered so much more than heat.

She paused on the threshold and, at his smile, moved toward where he lay in the bed. Patiently waiting.

"You okay?" he asked, half sitting up.

"Yeah." He made as if to say something else or shift or stand up, and she stopped him with a hand, palm out. "Hold on. There's something…" She swallowed. Mouth dry, she tried again. "I need to show you something."

Ivan did nothing but blink, and she saw the worry there, tightly reined.

"You'll be disgusted." She held back a sob, breathed through it, and shut her eyes hard.

"I won't."

"Okay. *Okay.*" Breathing hard, like she'd run from the woods, though she hadn't, she reached for the hem of her shirt, started to pull up, and—

"Stop!"

She opened her eyes. God, when had she screwed them shut?

"Come 'ere," he said. Begging, almost begging.

"I need—"

"*Please.*"

She hesitated only for a second, then walked to the bed, where she stood for an awkward moment before he reached out and pulled her under the covers, into his warmth.

"Don't want you doin' this alone, baby."

That, after everything, was what sent the tears rolling. Quiet tears. *Her* tears.

And through those tears, with Ivan watching over her, Uma pulled off her shirt and took back her skin.

∽◌◠

Everything in Ive's body came to a standstill: his breath, his heartbeat, probably the blood in his veins. Last night's story had in no way prepared him for this. Nothing could have prepared him. It took less than a second for him to understand.

Ah, fuck.

Breathe.

In for ten counts, out for ten.

And now, focus. You're losing her. Focus.

Some functional part of his brain found it ironic that he was using those anger management techniques after all. Who knew?

He forced his gaze to her shoulder, her beautiful shoulder, destroyed by that...*motherfucking*... Jesus, *he* didn't know a word bad enough, strong enough to express how bad it was.

"I'm gonna find tha—"

"Don't." She stopped him. "Let me finish."

This kicked-in-the-gut feeling, breathless and nauseated, was exactly like his first day in prison. No, worse. Like the day Frank had hit Jessie. The worst day of his life. Until today.

Maybe it's not as bad as it looks, he thought. *Maybe she wanted this.* But the tattoos looked like nothing you'd choose—not even close to what the guys did to each other inside. This was disorganized, jittery, like the scratchings of a possessed child. Was that an M? He squinted at a series of letters on her wrist, shifted back.

and saw with a start what it said—MINE, the letters more faded than some of the others, but still there. The bastard had tried to claim her skin.

"He... *Joey* did this to you."

It wasn't really a question, but she nodded, drew another deep breath, and met his eyes.

She asked if he was okay. *She* asked *him*, and goddamn it, something broke in his chest.

He leaned in and kissed her, eyes wide open, pushing out the hatred and the rage as best he could, because he wouldn't lay that on her. Not after everything else she'd gone through.

But fuck if he'd let the dude off.

She pulled slightly away and put a hand to his chest, holding him back so she could move on to her pants. Quickly, efficiently, she undid them, pushed them down, and awaited his verdict in this nightmare of a striptease.

Parts of her were covered, absolutely coated, in ink. Multicolored streaks, masquerading as words, ran up and down both of her arms, her shoulders, over to the top of her back. Her breasts, those beautiful nipples... This was what people did to show ownership, to a gang or a person. She'd been *branded*. Like cattle, only worse, because he could see, here and there, where the fucker had run out of ink or lost control of the needle. There, where it petered out, he thought she must have fought back, and in one place, a big blotch so thick and dark, he wondered if the bastard had pierced a hole in her.

On her beautiful, soft, perfect skin, it was absolutely obscene.

He forced his eyes from her body back to her face. "What he did to you, he's gotta—"

"Shh." She put a hand over his mouth. "This is for me. Let me keep this."

This…? It took him a second to realize what she meant by *this*. This moment. Sharing her body with him, her pain. That's what she meant. And he was ruining it for her.

But fuck, never in a million years had Ive imagined the horror. He'd thought the guy had beat her, but not…

No wonder she couldn't look at herself. He could barely look at her without feeling… Oh God. So much shit, roiling inside.

Nausea. Horror. Pain. And then anger. No, not just anger, because he'd felt anger before, and this was so much more. Stronger than anything he'd ever known. Even compared to when Frank had beaten Jessie, this was way off the scale.

Because, back then, he'd been a stupid kid, his anger diluted from being constantly pissed off at the world.

Today, his rage was a sharp point, honed by years of containment. Years of calm.

He leaned back, needing to see everything, taking her all in at once, like ripping off a Band-Aid. He was deaf to whatever sounds she might have made, blind to everything but the obscenities etched into her skin. *His woman's* skin. *His woman*, defaced by some monster.

Oh shit, the rage was so right, whooshing through him, filling the hollow spaces, the cracks and crevices, overwhelming him, along with the knowledge of what he had to do.

Kill the fucker. Tear him apart, limb by limb. Destroy him.

It was fate. Everything about his life, every decision

he'd ever made, everything he'd ever done. It had all come to this one moment. This one person. This, *this* was what Ivan was made for.

Because Ivan loved Uma. And that's what you did for the people you loved.

24

"IVAN."

His gaze ran back up her body, over her arms, where the ink was positively virulent in the unforgiving light of day. Her stomach heaved, but he was looking, and so would she, damn it.

Finally, he ripped his attention from her skin and came back to her, his eyes taking a while to focus on hers, and when they did...

"I'm sorry, baby," he said, his features relaxing slightly. "So sorry he did this to you."

She'd thought she'd lost him there for second. But now that he was back in the room, his hand went to her face first—bless him—before stroking over her body, taking it in. Fingers trailed over her shoulders, down her arms.

His silence said it all. Uma had exposed her innards, and all he could do was stare. He couldn't tear his gaze away. *Of course* he couldn't. She'd torn herself open, exposed her aching, bloody heart, rent it still beating from her breast, and handed it to him on a fucking platter, and she couldn't even look at him for fear of what his expression might be.

Shock? Pity? Revulsion?

"See?" she said, voice raw, chest hollow and dry as a bone. "It's disgusting. Why would you want to look at me like this?"

"Shh." He bent to press his lips to her jaw. "You can't disappoint me. You know that, right?"

"Don't." She turned away, squeezing her eyes shut. "Don't fucking pity me, Ivan. I can't take that."

"I don't, Uma. Look at me."

"I can't."

He kissed her—a slow, sweet press of lips, a luxurious stroke of tongues, punctuated by the scrape of his jaw, the movements between them so tiny, so intimate, their sighs a secret shared. Her breath expelled hard, emitting something noxious she hadn't even realized had been blocking her throat, and he took it in.

"Look at me. Please."

It was an effort to open her eyes again. An actual physical effort. But she did it, for him.

Gently, so gently, his hand rested on Uma's shoulder and trailed down, a first stroke, followed by his eyes and then hers. For a second or two, she couldn't quite catch her breath as she let herself look. How strange for her body to be so unfamiliar, the skin not her own.

"'S it hurt?"

After a deep inhale, she looked away from herself and focused on him. "Only for a couple of days after a laser session. I'm getting them removed. That's why I'm here."

"What, they don't do that up in the big city?"

"The place here does it for free for…people like me. I heard the doctor who runs it talk about it on the radio." She shook her head. "At first, I couldn't believe it. I was convinced it was a trap."

"Joey's got connections, huh?"

"You have no idea."

After a brief hesitation, Ivan kissed her again, this time on the tip of her shoulder. She turned to watch his lips against her shame.

Not my shame, my life. My experience. Me. The affirmation was overwhelming, almost painful in its clarity: she owned these lines. Every one of them. She'd suffered for them, would suffer even more. They were hers, just as surely as anything she'd ever done or achieved, only these were greater because she'd *survived*. Like badges of courage, unfamiliar but without the slightest doubt hers. She'd earned them, after all.

Her next breath was clean, easy, the fear gone like a filter taken off, and she could *see* herself.

Above her, Ivan continued his sweet perusal, slow and thorough, and like a tourist in her own life, Uma followed along. He traced the circles around her nipples, then leaned down for the bees' nest of scribbles on her belly, back up and over to the B in BITCH—the one he'd spelled right. It took a while for Ivan to take the scenic route back to her face, and when he did, there was a change in him too, a smile on his mouth if not in his eyes.

She felt the air he forced into his lungs before he said, "The tats're kinda badass."

A joke. He was doing his best to adjust, and he was joking.

Her heart twisted up inside, so hard it hurt.

At her look, he met her gaze and said, "What?" It was a challenge, a show of admiration. "You think I'm kiddin'? *You* are a badass."

With a huff, she looked away, a little embarrassed at the attention or the compliment, and sore from too much emotion.

For several beats, they shared something. Trust, maybe. Understanding. Whatever it was, it hurt. He leaned in, pressed his forehead to hers, and whispered, "I got you, Uma."

She closed her eyes, swallowed back tears, and nodded, a tiny movement he had to be touching her to have felt.

The mood changed. He broke it again, just like that.

Pasting a grin on his face, he bent to lick a path from beneath her ear to her shoulder and palmed a breast. "The tats," he said between swipes of his tongue, "are *badass*."

She liked that he wasn't handling her with care right now, how he knew when to move on. And God, she liked how he weighed her in his hand—not too gently— before his fingers moved inexorably to her nipples and pinched. Only a light pressure, but enough to send a jolt through her.

"You…are…such…a guy," she managed through a series of gasps. Because, damn it, she didn't want to be coddled—she wanted the unreserved hunger that shone in his eyes. Maybe just a little of the mean and savage man she'd mistaken him for once upon a time.

"You're fucking beautiful, Uma." She still didn't entirely believe him, but the words felt good anyway.

"And this"—his hand skimmed her arm—"this is just history. It's who you are. Like this." He touched the scar on his face. She reached up too, and their fingers met where the angry red mark emerged from his hairline.

"How'd you get that?"

He hesitated. When his voice came out, it was tighter, less liquid. "Fight I mentioned."

"What happened?"

"My sister's ex and me got into it."

"Why?"

"Kind of a bad story. You really wanna know this?"

"You think I can't take it?"

His eyes slid to hers. "Oh, you can take it. I'm worried about me."

"You don't have to talk about it if you don't want to," she said, maybe a little hurt.

"I don't want to," he said defensively, "but I have to."

"No, you don't."

"I do. After everything you shared with me." He let a hand settle on her belly—where several jagged lines came together in an illegible scrawl. "Besides, it's kind of who I am, you know? Why I'm here."

"Oh."

Propped up on his side, head in his hand, he started. "Frank—that's Gabe's dad—beat Jessie up. Bad. So, when you told me about Joey, I thought that's what you meant."

"Oh, he hit me that night. But he also—" A flash of memory. Struggling, Joey holding her down, the fear that she'd never leave that room—not alive, at least. "Well, this happened."

"Yeah."

He leaned in and kissed her shoulder, that place where a crude heart had been etched and then crossed out in the space of a few short hours. Bile rose up as she remembered the pain of that heart, the pain of the lines over it even worse. She pushed the memory back.

Another kiss followed the first, this time on Joey's name, penned in block letters, skittering off on the Y when she'd bucked, hard. He'd run out of black ink halfway through that one. It had finally felt like the end—a reprieve—but he'd only disappeared for a minute before returning with more colors. The sight of all those bottles, brimming with ink, had about done Uma in. That was when she'd decided to let herself die.

She closed her eyes hard on the memory, shoving out the stench of ink and blood.

Ivan grasped her right hand and ran it across his abdomen to a white scar on his side. "Got this one in a car accident. I was such a fuckin' young asshole. Almost lost a kidney. This was before the fight. I'd just gotten out of high school."

"How old were you when the fight happened?"

"Twenty-two. But Frank was older than us. Son of a bitch got my sister knocked up while she was still in high school."

"Oh no."

"Yep. Then he beat her senseless, and I fuckin' lost it. Lost it all, I guess. My job, my place. My girlfriend. *Fiancée*, actually," he said with an exaggerated French accent.

"Oh." She shivered, prompting Ivan to yank the quilt up, wrapping them in it. Once they'd settled, she went on, hesitant to ask. "What happened with her?"

"Turned out she wasn't interested in bein' married to a felon. She left me before I was even convicted. Actually, she didn't officially break up with me. Just started sleepin' with everyone else, claimed I'd hurt her. That was kind of a sign."

"That doesn't sound very loyal."

"Nope. Loyal, she was not. Asked her to sell her engagement ring to help Jessie. Told her I'd get her another bigger, better one later, but she refused. Not even to buy food for a nursing mother."

"Whoa." Uma jerked back. "Jessie was *nursing* when he beat her up?"

Ivan's chest rose and fell a few times before he answered, voice strained. "Yeah. Did it in front of Gabe."

"His own kid?" He gave a brief nod before Uma grabbed his hand in solidarity. "Where is he now?"

"Lives a few miles over, in the valley."

"You ever see him?"

"Nah. He knows better than to come around here."

"What about Gabe?"

"Doesn't know his dad." Ivan's voice sounded full of challenge. "He's got me."

"He's a lucky boy."

"Remains to be seen."

"No." She tightened her fingers around his. "Anyone would be lucky to have you."

"Yeah? Anyone?"

"*Anyone.*" Now she'd gone and done it. Somehow, without saying the words, she'd let him know how she felt about him. Switching gears quickly, she said, "So, tell me about the fight."

"Fight was pretty one-sided. I had a lot of practice,

since I spent my first twenty-one years fightin' everyone who looked at me wrong. Been makin' up for it
ever since."

"Problem teenager?"

"You could say that. Pissed off at everything.
Thought the whole world had fucked me over. So, when
I had an actual reason to hurt somebody...man, I kicked
the shit out of him. I mean, I hurt him *real bad*."

"Do you regret it?"

"Hurting him? No. I'd have killed him if the cops
hadn't shown up. Steve was the first guy on the scene.
Guy who owns the martial arts school. He was already
sheriff back then."

"He owns it?"

"Yeah. You didn't know that?"

"No. I thought he was just a police officer."

"Well, sheriff."

"So, Steve showed up and—"

"He took me down." She could hear the admiration
in his voice. "Did some crazy, wrestling-type moves
on me before I could kill Frank. Good thing too.
Otherwise, Jessie would have been completely alone,
and Gabe would have had a dead dad and an uncle still
in prison."

"And now you're friends with Steve."

"Yeah. Funny how these things happen."

"Well, I'm glad you're here."

He took advantage of her position to kiss the top of
her back, right below her neck. That was the first one,
there. The tattoo she'd chosen. *Idiot*, she thought, a little
less angry with her old self.

"This one's different."

"Yeah. We got them done together. By a guy named Zap."

"Ooh. Never trust guys whose names come straight from comic books."

She chuckled and brought her hand back to his body, to another scar. This one invisible under the hair on his belly but clearly textured beneath her fingers. He shivered under her touch and tightened his arm around her.

"Appendix," he said, voice a little breathier than before. "Probably the only one I got that's not my own damn fault."

Continuing her exploration over one sharp hip bone and down, she let her fingers trail a hot path, enjoying the feel of soft, resilient skin that had seen so much, the muscles tensing as she went. "Oh, what's this one?"

"That?" His eyes, slightly glazed, took their time moving to an irregular spot above his knee, and rather than wait for his explanation, she shifted, stroking up and down, up and down. "No idea." Another stroke up brought her hand to graze his half-hard cock, and she left it there, tantalizingly close. "Honestly, baby, not sure I could tell you my name right now."

"No?" She smiled, sultry and powerful as she watched his Adam's apple bob when he swallowed. Their eyes met for a second before traveling down, together, to where she touched him. With a shaky breath in, she said, "Thank you, Ivan."

"For what?" he mumbled.

"Being here. Taking it in so easily. Still being... attracted to me?"

"You kiddin'?" He smiled and caressed her with his

eyes, then with his words. "Told you you're fuckin' beautiful."

She said, "I want to make you feel good," and let her finger stroke him, a slow discovery in that same up-and-down cadence.

Another swallow. "Yeah?" He cleared his throat, and their eyes stayed fixed on her hand—so pale on his thick, dark cock. "I'd like that."

Slowly, she lifted up and over him, admiring this body so alive and well lived-in, and planted her knees to lean down and kiss his belly before moving her mouth to his erection. He groaned when she kissed it gently, just the tip. The feel of it against her lips put her in charge again.

The tide shifted, with her taking control as he gave it. She rather liked that idea—a finite amount of power to be shared in infinite configurations—like a drop of mercury, separating and reshaping over and over again.

"Move back," Uma ordered.

The view from where she kneeled was amazing. Layered over his physical perfection were the scars, each with its own story. A mere mortal in the body of a god. She'd call this photo something like *The Beast Awaits*, or *Anticipation*, or maybe *Want*. She'd probably need to take a dozen shots to capture it fully—a hundred. The physical aspect of him leaning back on his hands, arms straight, abs pushed into stark relief by the position, along with the warring emotions on his face: the desire, the raw want, with something darker underneath.

Her eyes flicked to where she'd left the camera two nights before. How could she have forgotten all about it lying there?

Should she? *No. Enjoy the moment. This is too good, too real to filter.*

She took the mental picture and stored it away for another time before leaning in and giving him what he wanted.

She marveled again at how good he smelled up close—like soap and smoke and metal.

"Did you take a shower?"

"Of a sort." He chuckled, tilting his hips up so the head of his erection bumped her mouth.

She licked him. His taste was ambrosia—not the immediate satisfaction of a chocolate bar, but the subtler flavor of good, strong chemistry. It confirmed everything she'd ever heard about genetics and attraction. This was right; it was meant to be.

He let out a noise that would have been a whimper from a lesser man. Her mouth closed over his cock and pulled him deep.

They groaned in unison, a lascivious song of pleasure born deep in their bellies. Pleasuring him was heady, elemental. The only thing more satisfying would have been to sink herself onto him. She pulled and sucked and grazed with her teeth, tearing up and gagging when she accidentally took him in too far, but not minding for once. God, he was huge. Stiff and dark.

She lifted up and glanced at his face. Ivan was flushed and sleepy looking, but his eyes shone hungry and bright beneath heavy lids.

"It's so good, baby," he whispered. The approval was soothing, so wonderful that she continued to watch him as she moved to lick, teasing his head until he looked crazy. With another groan, he sank back onto one elbow and set a hand gently on her head. It was like a question.

"Suck me again. Please."

She thought about teasing him for a bit longer but wasn't quite sure how. *I'll have to work on my femme fatale routine.*

Instead, she did as he asked, letting him fill her mouth, then nudge her throat. Uma had never done this before, taken someone in that far of her own volition. But with Ivan, she wanted it. She wanted him to fill every crack, every tiny little crevice Joey had created. She relaxed, and he sank in another centimeter. Up and down, but this time with suction, the next just tongue, another time with teeth. She learned him, played him like an instrument.

Who knew giving a blow job could be so enjoyable? It was amazing, unbelievable, a *treat*. She was lost in it. The in and out, the taste, the smell, and those fucking *sounds* he made. Uma owned his pleasure.

Without thought, she reached down and gently weighed his balls. She heard the moment he changed. Harsh breaths peppered with groans were forced from his throat, and the hand on her head finally grasped her hair, giving her the rhythm he needed. One pull, two, faster than she would have done it on her own, three, and he tugged her up.

"Stop, stop, you gotta stop."

"No." She went back for more.

"I wanna fuck you again, Uma. I wanna look at your face when you come. Please. *Please.*"

What was it about the sound of Ivan begging? Who needed water or food or even air? God, she could live off that sound.

With a seesawing motion, she leaned back, pulling him with her until he was on top. He hovered over her, taking her in, memorizing her.

Why would he do that? Why would he want to? She nearly pushed him away or covered his eyes, but instead ignored the niggling doubt and accepted the perusal. Slowly, so slowly, he leaned into her and rubbed his chest against hers, nipple to nipple, and the crisp rasp of hair to skin, the rough brush of his thighs against hers. She shivered and pulled in a shaky breath.

"You want me to fuck you again?" he asked. She nodded. "Let me hear you say it."

"I want this."

"I like it when you tell me what you want."

"I already told you."

"Say it again. Use that bossy voice."

"You've got to fuck me, Ivan." He stayed there, watching her, so she grasped his ass and pulled him. "I want to feel you inside me again."

Rather than answer, he looked down between them to where their bodies nearly met. Slowly, painfully slowly, he dipped his hips until his cock settled against her. Another maddening pause before he dragged through all the wetness that had gathered there. She felt more than heard his gasp.

"So wet. Guess I'm doin' somethin' right, huh?" He chuckled, and she joined him.

She loved this: laughing during sex, like maybe it didn't have to be deadly serious all the time. His ass clenched beneath her hands, and his cock slipped down, glancing her clit with an electric twinge before coming back up again. Down, up. The gliding rhythm was perfect, almost stimulating enough to make her come.

"Put it in me."

"Can't."

She stilled. Clearly she wasn't bossy enough. "*Now*, Ivan."

"You got a condom?"

Oh. A tiny dose of reality seeped in. "Oh. Right. I completely forgot."

He smiled at that and held up a hand, a condom tucked between his fingers. "Some of us like to plan ahead."

Her heartbeat kicked back up a notch, and her pelvis lifted unconsciously toward him.

He skimmed his hand down her body to cup her between the legs. "You ready?"

"Yeah."

"Stay there. Don't move. Don't do anything. Let me take care of you." That didn't sound bad—quite good, in fact—except what if… "But if you want me to stop, it's like last night. Just say so, okay? And we're done."

She nodded. No longer surprised that he understood her so well.

As he pulled it on, the smell of latex, always unpleasant in her mind, floated on the air, mingled with the musky smell of their bodies, and took on a whole new dimension beside her newfound acceptance. The blankets shifted, rustling, and Ivan was back, warm skin pressed to her.

"Hold on a sec." Ivan clasped Uma's jaw firmly and swept his eyes down her body, skimming her skin before kissing her, long and slow and deep.

It was so different now, watching him move, drinking

in the emotions he wore so plainly, eyes wide open. The two of them truly bared for the first time. He thrust into her slowly at first, then all the way out, and sliding back in as if they had all the time in the world. For a second, the sight of him emerging from her body again, all shiny and slick from her, made her close her eyes and wish for the blindfold. It was too much, only not because of her ink.

"Look at me, baby," he ordered, and how on earth could she refuse him anything? He was deep inside her when their eyes met again and everything skittered to a halt.

"Don't go, Uma," he whispered.

"I'm not going anywhere," she promised without even meaning to.

"Stay with me. Here."

"I'm here. I'll stay."

With a groan, he closed his eyes and lost himself. Everything became grasping hands and pumping hips.

All it took was a few minutes before the first flutterings of orgasm stirred within her. She flew apart in a dark, sinful climax, the kind you get from digging too deep and uncovering things best left untouched.

"Ah, fuck," he grated out in a voice she'd never get enough of, "so fucking good. So good." He thrust a few times, messy movements that showed how far gone he was. Ivan's words had her pressing her fingers to herself, in search of an elusive second orgasm.

He said, "I wanna come inside you."

And she wanted that too. She wanted to spread her legs wider, to absorb everything he could possibly give her. "Yeah," she panted, rubbing herself hard. "Ivan."

"Yeah," he echoed, frantic with need, lost. "Ah, fuck yeah."

His hands, hard as vises on her, the filthy things he said led her straight into it—another climax. Different this time, weaker, more in her head than her body. She was aware of Ivan shouting as he came, thrusting another handful of times, tight and jerky, before collapsing onto her.

Their bodies cooled, and the craziness subsided, but their touches didn't stop. A gentle squeeze of her hip, a callused thumb to her face, his weight too much but so very perfect as he nuzzled her neck. As their breathing eased, he shifted off a bit and settled at her side, leaving her chilled, her with a shadow of regret for what she'd done.

She'd promised to stay here. Tied to a man. A new relationship? *What would Joey do if he found out? What would he do to Ivan?*

Who the fuck was this person she'd become? This wasn't her. Uma was reasonable. Never in a million years would she allow her libido to make decisions for her. Even that first time with Joey had been more about lack of confidence than sex. He'd pushed; she'd pulled; she'd lost.

This morning was nothing like that. Layers of her had been peeled away, pieces of her past flaking off like chips of paint.

Lovely. Remove my shell, and apparently I'm a fucking wildebeest. A complete sex fiend.

Ivan kissed her hard and rolled off, leaving her alone and cold on his bed. She looked away as he got rid of the condom, her mind snaking out to the cold reality of life beyond these four walls: dealing with Ms. Lloyd, her next appointment with the doctor.

"Hey, Uma." Ivan bent to pick something up, then came around, and it was a strange jolt of surprise to see the camera in his hands.

"What are you doing?"

"Let me take your picture, Uma. You're beautiful. I want you to see how beautiful you are. No matter what happens."

That same old fear reared up for a second, along with a moment of shock, but his words sank in, and the look on his face...

"You want a picture of me?"

For a second or two, his face tightened, and he lost the young, sweet look she'd gotten used to. "Want more than that," he finally said, and the words resonated deep in her chest.

With a big breath in, she capitulated, imagining the photo—more permanent suddenly than the ink on her skin. "Go ahead. Take it." Eyes screwed shut, she turned and waited for it to be over. Just when she thought he'd never snap the damn thing, she felt it—a shift, a realization. Whatever it was, it felt as real as the metal Ivan pounded with his hands. As real as the photo she was letting him take.

He wanted more.

She turned to him, opened her eyes to the camera and the man on the other side, and let him see all the things she might be willing to give.

With a flash and click, she was immortalized. Uma Crane, baring skin and soul.

She sighed as he kissed her, trembled a bit as he

dressed her, slow and sweet, and once he'd thrown on his clothes, they walked down the drive hand in hand before a long kiss good-bye beneath Ms. Lloyd's kitchen window, heedless of the woman's squinty stare.

And all the while, it grew on her, a realization, piercing and true: she was okay. The shame was gone. And so was the regret.

But there was something else there instead. What was that? Sadness for the loss of the girl she'd once been—the girl she'd lost that night. But something else. *Acceptance*, she thought. And as she stood in the kitchen window, watching Ivan's figure walk away, straight and strong, it felt an awful lot like love.

25

"I, IVAN SHIFFLETT"—*SMASH*—"DO SOLEMNLY SWEAR"—
punch, smash—"not to go against"—*smash*—"the
wishes of one *Uma R. Crane*."

Panting, Ivan rested his head against the heavy bag,
his breath like a damn racehorse rode hard, his fists
shaking. All of him shaking. No, not shaking—nothing
so controllable as that. More like an earthquake, rolling
and vibrating and tearing up the whole fucking world.

The problem was, these were the early tremors. The
quake had yet to hit. And when it did…

Pushing off the bag, he went in again, attacking with
a tight volley of punches that rocked it right back into
his crazy dance. Steam came off his body, visible in the
cold, clear light of day, but the rage…that festered deep
inside. A tumor, sick and dark, expanding by the second
and *begging* to be taken care of. Carved or…ripped out.

But *goddamn it* he'd promised.

*I will not go against the wishes of the beautiful Uma
R. Crane.*

He'd said those words to her, in the back of his truck,

and he'd meant them, but he hadn't fucking known. How could he have known what he was promising?

Oh God. His arms clung to the bag, and the sound that came out of his mouth…the sound was bad. He knew it when Squeak whined and moved away. But he didn't know how to stop. He couldn't stop.

If he didn't kill him—*Joey*—then the fucker'd get away with it. And Ive couldn't handle that. No justice. No fucking justice in this world.

"*No justice*," he said over and over as he pummeled the bag, wishing he could spew the poison, until his chest hurt and his hands were numb and there wasn't a dry spot on his body. But it wasn't working. It wouldn't work, and by the end, without his really noticing the change, his strikes took on the ring of his own brand of justice, and that felt infinitely better. Infinitely right.

Swallowing, he pushed himself off, noticed Squeak curled up in the opposite corner of the porch, as far from him as possible, and headed to his truck, still soaking, but what the fuck did it matter?

The gym. He'd go to the gym. Find Steve and maybe pummel his ass. That might do it: cut out the fury, burn it or cauterize it or…

No. No, first to the forge for some clothes. He couldn't show up looking like this, even at the gym. He grabbed a shower, changed, made a quick phone call, and, at the last minute, picked up the container of dog food by the door and threw it into the truck. Just in case.

First, he'd go by Jessie's, to look something up. No big deal. He needed to know. The man's full name, if nothing else. Just his name. As he steered toward his sister's, he didn't let his thoughts stray from the road itself—his hands on the wheel, his eyes hyperalert, his foot on the pedals. Motions that meant nothing. Just driving. Just going for a drive.

In front of Jessie's, he took stock. Breathing fine, pulse a little weird, but, hey, he'd beat the shit out of his bag for probably—a glance at his dash shocked him. *Three hours?* One spent in his forge, shaping hot iron, then another couple on the porch, pounding leather. Was that possible? The sun, high in the sky, confirmed it, and suddenly, what started as an idea became an urgent mission, a crusade, burning brighter than reason and promises or anything else.

For Uma. For justice.

～✦～

All day, Uma thought of Ivan. His hands on her, his cock inside her, his expression when he came. The night spent in his bed, safe and warm in his arms. And *sleep*— he'd given her real, honest-to-goodness sleep, like a miraculous gift. That alone would have been enough to make her fall for him. But then, there was the way he'd calmed her, taken on her troubles, how he took on everyone else's.

Her body was shaky and tired as she worked at Ms. Lloyd's, but it didn't matter. It was a good tired. Emotional and wrung out, but also…*thoroughly fucked*, she thought with a giggle. She'd heard him earlier, hammering and then pounding at his punching bag, which hadn't helped her oust him from her thoughts. Not that she wanted to, she thought with a secret smile. Even here in Ms. Lloyd's creepy basement, folding laundry, it was easy to bask in the bright glow of him.

Could she really *love* him? Was it even possible after so short a time?

Yes. I love him.

A noise from upstairs startled her out of her thoughts, flushed and excited and a little bit…lovesick.

It was no surprise that her mind went straight to Ivan when she heard it again and identified it as knocking. She was so convinced it was him—missing her, wanting to see her face, the way she wanted to see his—that it took her a moment to process his sister standing at the top of the stairs.

"You sure she's down here?" Jessie asked, peering into the dark basement.

"Got a visitor, Irma."

Even that stupid name couldn't bother her today.

"Right here!" she called from below.

"No need to walk me down, Ms. Lloyd. I just want a few words with Uma."

"Oh? What's she done now?"

"Nothin'. Didn't she tell you we're friends?"

Ms. Lloyd scoffed. "Never seen anyone make faster time in this town." Uma couldn't hear the rest as Ms. Lloyd walked away from the top of the stairs.

"Wow." Jessie sounded breathless as she came down the stairs. "This place. It's…"

"I'd invite you to sit, but it's…not very inviting."

"Yeah. Listen. I need to tell you something." Jessie's voice was low and urgent, her eyes a little frantic.

"Okay."

"Ivan made me promise not to, but…sometimes doing the right thing is thicker than blood, right?"

"What's going on?"

"Does the name Joseph Chisholm ring a bell?"

"What?" Uma's vision blurred, and her legs went liquid. She stumbled back onto the sofa. "Oh no."

"I thought so. Ive's gone after him."

"How'd he—?"

"He came over to use my computer. Actin' real strange. He asked me to keep Squeak for him and left a shit ton of dog food, talked about feedin' the other animals if I didn't see him come back tonight or in the mornin'. So, I went and looked at his history after he took off. Ive's a dumb-ass with computers. Doesn't know how to cover his tracks. Anyway. His Internet search? *Commonwealth Attorney Joseph Northern Virginia.*"

"Please God, no." Uma's whispered words overlapped Jessie's. She didn't need to hear the end. Didn't want to know any more.

"Turns out there are only two up there. So he cyberstalked the one named Chisholm before taking off. I remembered what you'd said about your ex being a prosecutor and—"

"Oh, no, no, no. *Fuck!*" A buzzing started in Uma's ears, louder than her words. Her head was shaking back and forth, side to side. It wouldn't stop. She couldn't stop it. Any of it. Anything.

"All right. So, Ive's gone up there to find him. You know he'll do somethin' stupid, right?" Jessie was louder, the frantic edge right there in the forefront.

"He promised," whispered Uma.

"What?"

"Oh God. When did he go?"

"Couple hours, at least. Didn't think to check the

computer until a little while ago. He's not answering his phone."

"Then it's already too late."

"Look, I called Steve and—"

"The cop? No! Oh please, no."

"Look. He's our friend. I had to tell him. He"—she lowered her voice—"said you were a *person of interest* in some case?" When Uma didn't respond, Jessie moved closer to squat at her feet. "What is goin' on? I want to help, but you've got to tell me. Let me help."

"You can't help if the cops are involved." The words came from deep in Uma's chest. A dead place. "They're on his side and…nobody can help." Something occurred to Uma. "I don't get it. How'd Ivan find out about Joey being a prosecutor?"

"I told him," came Ms. Lloyd's voice from the top of the stairs. "He called when you took out the trash."

"Wait. *Now* you decide to answer the phone?" Uma asked, disbelieving.

Ms. Lloyd shrugged. "Know about the ad now, don't I? Figure I'd give the caller a piece of my mind instead of being scared."

"I trusted you!" Uma shrieked, the betrayals like a knife to the chest—Ms. Lloyd's and Ivan's. "He's going to *kill* him, Ms. Lloyd. Don't you get it? Ivan'll go back to prison for this." Uma looked between the two women, frantic. "Joey works with cops, judges. He's been *hunting* me for six months. What do you think he'll do when Ivan shows up there? Oh God, I've got to go. I'm going. I'm going. I'll go and—"

"Hold on," said Ms. Lloyd. "No running off half-cocked. It'll only make things worse."

"What *fucking* choice do I have?"

Jessie said, "I don't think this is the time for—"

"Shut up, both of you, while I get a drink." Slowly, Ms. Lloyd made her way down the rickety steps. "You'll screw it all up. You hear?" Her voice was low enough to cut through the yelling and sharp enough to pierce the cloud of panic hanging in the air. Her eyes, when Uma's met them, were deep, dark anchors. "Welcome to Leon's man cave. Mr. Leon Lloyd. My *hus*band." The way she stressed the first syllable made it sound like a dirty word. She hobbled to the back wall and flipped a switch, lighting up the animal-head trophies hung high on the wall and shimmering over the dust motes floating on the air, then placed a glass on the bar with a decisive *thunk* and filled it with a golden liquid.

"Is he—" Uma began, briefly derailed from her panic by Ms. Lloyd's odd behavior.

"Dead? Yes. Dead as a doornail. Dead, dead, dead." The last was said in a singsong.

Uma mouthed a silent *oh*, exchanging a frantic look with Jessie before saying, "I'm sorry, Ms. Lloyd, but—"

"It's Cookie."

"Cookie?"

"My name. Cookie Lloyd. You can call me Cookie. Lloyd was *his* name."

"Cookie? Your name is *Cookie*?" A hysterical titter welled up inside Uma. Cookie? All this time, her evil nemesis's name was *Cookie*?

But she didn't have time for this—for hysteria or panic or… She stood. "Jesus Christ. I've got to get out of here, got to do something."

She'd made it halfway up the stairs, Jessie right

behind her, when Cookie said, "He died right here, you know."

"Oh shit," Jessie whispered. They stopped and turned despite themselves.

"Bastard already put me in the hospital twice. Last time, his buddy, the *sheriff*, dropped by to see him, told him he'd have to rein it in or people'd start asking questions. Cracked ribs he could hide, a black eye, but the broken ankle, now that raised eyebrows at the emergency room." She smiled and pointed at her leg, the one she limped on.

"Cooked, cleaned, sucked him off. Son of a bitch never was happy, no matter what I did. He *had* to hurt me. Said it was my fault. And my mama brought me up a lady. Taught me to grin and bear it. Wasn't till the miscarriage that things changed."

Uma gasped in a breath at that, shocked at the image of a young Cookie Lloyd in a family way.

"He killed my baby. *Killed her.*"

"I didn't know there was a baby," Jessie said, still quiet.

"A girl. Knew it in my bones." She nodded, eyes glazed over with a film of memories. "Bastard murdered my baby girl and put me in the hospital. Everything changed after that. I wouldn't take it again. *Never again.*"

Uma suddenly realized her breaths were coming in fast and sharp with more than just worry over Ivan. Cookie Lloyd's pain floated up the stairs, jagged little bits intermingled with the dust particles and the scent of thirty-year-old bourbon sludge.

They were wasting time down here. Uma was frantic, but she couldn't seem to stop the litany emerging as inevitably as a train wreck from the older woman's lips.

"Blackwood Sheriff arrested me the night I killed him. Leon, that son of a bitch. Three weeks after the miscarriage, and he tried to make me *do it*. Doc said to wait two months, but I didn't refuse 'cause of that. I told him no because I'd never *ever* let him get me pregnant again. No way I was bringing a sweet little baby into this foul, disgusting place." She slugged back her drink, slammed her glass on the bar, and meandered over toward the deer heads on the wall. Her veiny, wrinkled hand reached out to touch a shiny, black nose.

On the stairs, Uma stood, transfixed.

"See that space between the two heads?"

Cookie Lloyd couldn't see the other women nod, but that didn't seem to matter. She continued. "Always wished they'd let me keep his body after they embalmed him. I'd have dug him up myself, if they hadn't put me in prison for so long. Too rotten after eight years. I wanted to get a taxidermist to stuff Leon's head. I'd have stuck the stupid fool up there, right where he belonged."

Holy shit. That knocked the air out of Uma, the image of the man from the wedding photo, his glassy eyes staring blindly out from the wall.

"Men. Filthy, disgusting animals." Cookie turned to them with a sweet smile. "Lucky for me, I got my house back. Your uncle, Jessie, never touched a thing here. Let me move back in after I got out and left it to me when he died. Killing Leon could have ruined my life, but I was lucky. Not all of us are that lucky, though."

Her face sobered, and she moved quickly to the bottom of the stairs. "Old Gus and Ive are the best men I've ever met in my life. The best. You need to know that. That boy is one in a million, and what he's willing to do for you... Don't you stop him, Uma. Let *him* do it."

"Don't you regret what you did?" Uma asked, knowing the answer. Too shocked to deal with the rest.

"Not once. Not for one single second do I regret killing that man and putting us both out of our misery."

She didn't think she could do that, and she knew she couldn't let Ivan do it for her. "I've got to go, Ms. Lloyd. I can't stand here and—"

"Yeah? Well, if you don't let him take care of this problem, the problem'll still be out there, won't it? You might want to think long and hard about what you want for the rest of your life. You tired of running now? How you think you'll feel when you're my age?"

Justice. The word beat its rhythm in Ive's mind, his dead muscles, his aching heart. *Justice*, the letters screamed out from the statue right there, in front of the Fairfax County Courthouse.

What a joke.

He glanced, for the millionth time, at the paper crumpled in his fist. The picture he'd printed of the bastard he'd come here to kill. *Deputy Commonwealth Attorney Joseph Chisholm.* Just thinking the name sent another one of those furious tremors through his body, so strong it should have shaken his truck, should have unbalanced the statue's fucking scales.

Swallowing back another mouthful of bile, he sat in this parking spot and watched the comings and goings of every pathetic cog in the system. Finally, too taut to stay folded up in his seat a moment longer, he got out and slammed the door.

Fuck, he hated courthouses. Hated lawyers. Hated this goddamned joke of a justice system that let bad people get away with so much evil.

He hadn't eaten all day, but the hunger felt like strength—a fire in his gut mixed with the fury and this aching *need*.

He'd stay here, at the front of the building, where he was bound to see the fucker sooner or later. Unless he hadn't come to work. I've paced back and forth, up and down, eyes searching, skittering from one person to the next. The lulls were the worst, because there was nowhere to focus. Nowhere to put this…this…this fucking thing, this illness or whatever the fuck it was trying to tear itself free from his gut.

Jesus, what if he didn't come to work today?

Running a hand over his hot, sweaty brow, he turned to squint at the building's front door, then headed inside.

"'Scuse me," he rasped out to one of the guys at security.

"Can I help you?"

"Yeah." Fuck, his chest hurt. "Supposed to meet someone. Uh, Joseph Chisholm. He here today?"

The man looked at his colleague, his face squinted in a way that would have been comical if in a different situation—a different world. Slow, too slow. I've wanted to take him by the throat. To shake the memory out of the man's brain and into his mouth and—

"Hey, Sid. You seen Joey C. today?"

"Nope."

Fuck no.

"He have an office someplace or—"

"Wait, hold on. I'n't he on the Seilheimer trial? Judge Herndon? Yeah, they're in there. He musta got in early, before we came on." The man looked at his watch. "Should be out in a bit."

Ive wasn't sure if he managed a *thanks* before he turned and headed for the door. He was here. The man was *right here* in this building, and the anger was eating Ive up alive.

"You could sign in and wait right—"

He spun back, so fast his vision blurred, and he had to shake it clear again.

"There another way out of this place? Another exit?"

After a pause, the first man responded, "No, sir," and Ivan shoved back outside, where he'd try to breathe. If only he could get some fucking air.

This was it. Today. Joey Chisholm would die today.

Uma wouldn't need to spend another night afraid.

26

"Ivan's still not answering." Jessie ended the call again, phone clutched in her hand. They stood on Cookie's front porch with no idea what to do next.

"Shit. Shit! Okay, do it. Call the sheriff again. Call Steve. I'll turn myself in. Whatever I have to do."

"What if it's too late? If we don't get the cops involved, we can—" Jessie stopped, closed her eyes, and shook her head. "You're right. We have to call."

She started to make the call when Uma stopped her, suddenly calm. So completely calm.

"I'll call him."

"He's not answering."

"Not Ivan. I mean Joey. I'll call him and—"

"Oh, hell no. What are you—"

"I can talk to him, convince him to come here to…I don't know, get me. If I do it fast enough, Ivan can't get to him." The idea was nauseating, but it made sense.

"You think it could work?"

Emotion screwed up her face, made it tight with fear

and the memories of that day, but she had to. How could she not do this?

"It'll work. Come on. Give me the phone before I change my mind."

After only a brief hesitation, Jessie handed it over, and Uma started dialing. Nobody picked up, so she tried again and again. All the while, Jessie beside her, visibly anxious. Finally, third time was the charm.

"This is Joey Chisholm."

Oh fuck. His voice. Uma swallowed, choking on the memories. A hand landed on her arm, and she opened her eyes, hadn't even noticed they'd closed.

"Hello? Who is this? Listen, I don't have time to—"

"Joey?" *Inhale. He can't hurt me.* Jessie squeezed her arm, and Uma met her eyes and held them, steady. "It's me. I mean, Uma."

No sound. No sound at all. Not here, not on the other end of the line.

"I…" *Say it. Just say it.* Jessie nodded, biting her lip, looking nervous as hell. "How are you?"

"Oh…oh." He was all gaspy, surprised, and…happy? "Oh, I knew you'd come to your senses, sweetheart."

Trying her best to sound natural, she went on. "So, uh… How would you like to come get me?"

"That would be…Yes. Of course I'll come, Uma. You know I want to see you. I've been waiting for you to call."

"Can you come now?" she asked, feeling utterly unafraid somehow—calm, strong, and ready for whatever happened.

Jessie nodded encouragement.

"Where are you?"

"I'm in Blackwood, Virginia," she said, taking in the landscape around them before raising her eyes back to Jessie's and holding them. "How soon can you get here?"

∼⟋⟍∽

Back and forth, Ive paced the sidewalk, his eyes glued to that door, waiting. Every time it opened, he lost a breath and a heartbeat, and every time, it took him a while to get it back. A dude bumped him on his way out, clearly not happy and in a hurry, and with a look, Ive knew his story: he or someone in his family in trouble. Dealing with the courts, working shit out by the letter of the law, which was the worst fucking way possible. He could relate to that man. He *was* that man.

The thought brought him up short. His body stilled, and his eyes focused, for the first time, not on what lay past those dark glass doors or what would come out next, but on the person reflected in them: him.

The guy looking back at him in filthy jeans, ratty button-down plaid shirt, and scuffed work boots looked rough. He looked like a convict. Like he deserved to be here, getting his sentence handed to him on one the scales of justice.

A sudden curiosity drove him to edge closer to the glass and see what it revealed. It showed a face that was well worn, his experiences etched into his face like every other bad guy there. He looked like exactly what he was: an ex-convict up to no good.

He watched his brow wrinkle up with his first whisper of a doubt. So, what was the plan, anyway? Come up here and tear some shit up? Kill a guy? With what? He looked down. His bare hands?

Jesus. Had he truly evolved so little since his youth? Another glance in the glass showed lines carved into his cheekbones, circles under his eyes. He looked tired and worn. Like a guy who'd lived.

But have I? Have I really lived?

Immediately, his mind went back to that morning and everything that had happened between him and Uma in his workshop. Then back to last night, before he'd found out about her skin, when he'd just known the goodness of her, without all the bad shit.

He wanted to go back. To that perfect evening spent in the bed of his truck, beneath the stars.

He wanted a do-over. And not just for now, but for before too. For her: he wanted her not to have lived through hell. He wanted to meet a younger, happier Uma, whose life hadn't been destroyed by that son of a bitch. And for himself too. Who would he be if he turned back time to before prison, before the biggest mistake of his life?

Suddenly, he wished the woman he wanted could look at him like he was one of those normal, straight-backed citizens, rather than one of the losers slinking their way out of the courthouse.

In an unconscious gesture, he reached down, expecting warm fur and finding only air.

Shit. He was so used to having Squeak by his side. What the hell would she do if he went back to prison? Jessie'd take her, but what about everyone else? Ornery, the mean cat, and Gertie, the rug cat, and all the others. And what about Pepe, the baby skunk? Not to mention any animals that were bound to show up some day in the future, looking for help. *Ah hell.* He couldn't leave them.

Not only that, but he didn't want to.

He realized with a jolt that he *liked* the guy he'd become. This man whose experiences were etched into his face, the way Uma's were etched into her body. By that same token, he understood that what was between them—this intense, unexpected caring between two near strangers—would never have happened if they hadn't been *exactly* who they were today. They were united by their histories as much as their chemistry.

And he liked that fucked-up quality people got when they'd survived the shit life threw at them. They came through the other side stronger, maybe less whole, but with more grit. He liked Ms. Lloyd's crazy limp and the notch in Squeak's ear. He liked that Ornery was, well, *ornery*. And hell, he liked how Uma's sweet, soft core was covered in an exoskeleton of pure fucking titanium.

I promised not to do this. I solemnly swore. The thought rose up, like a vengeful phoenix from the ashes of his idiocy. *If I do it anyway, I'm betraying her just like Joey did.*

He had to go back. Now. Before it was too late, he had to go back and—

"Excuse me, sir?"

Ive blinked before turning to face a pair of police officers who'd approached him from the sidewalk. Behind them, a squad car sat quiet, its blue lights on.

"Yeah?"

"We'd like to ask you a few questions."

"Um, sure." He blinked again. Sweat, he realized, sweat in his eyes on this cold fucking day.

Beside him, the door to the building opened, and a man strutted out.

Holy shit. It's him.

He squinted at the loud blue shirt and tie beneath the guy's expensive-looking gray suit, then let his eyes move back to the face. *Joseph* fucking *Chisholm.*

Ive had no trouble recognizing him from his picture, even with the phone pressed to the man's ear. He stalled by the door, engrossed in his conversation.

One of the cops spoke, and Ive had to unglue his eyes from the man to focus on this new problem.

"Uh, sorry. What's that?"

"What's your business here today, sir?"

"I, um…" He swallowed, brain divided, eyes flicking from them to the man on the phone.

"I knew you'd come to your senses, sweetheart," Joey said, his voice slimy and pleased.

The cops again, talking, and Ive swung back, feeling weird. Wrong.

"Wait, wait, I need…"

"Of course I'll come. You know I want to see you. I've been waiting for you to call."

A hand clamped onto Ive's arm, and he almost shook it off before remembering where he was, who he was with. Just in time, he stopped, stilled, held his breath.

"Sir, we need you to come with us."

"Stop that man," he said, wanting to struggle. "He hurt a woman. That was her on the phone. He's—"

"Sir, you need to calm down. Now."

Fuck, he wanted to tear his arm away and roar, to tackle that fucking bastard to the ground, but he didn't. What stopped him was his own profile, reflected in the glass. What would it look like if he fucked this up? Was he willing to gamble it all away? Willing to waste more years and months and those precious lost hours?

It took more strength than he knew he possessed to relax his arms, calm his voice, and let the officers lead him aside while Joseph Chisholm drove happily toward the woman he loved.

He'd find a way to get to her first, before it was too late. He could love her, and protect her, and respect her enough to listen to her wishes—even if fear for her was rattling like mad in his chest, ticking like a bomb waiting to go off.

∽◌∾

Uma sat in Blackwood's coffee shop for an hour and a half before finally giving up. Joey wasn't coming. It was time to go. She didn't know whether to feel relieved or disappointed. A little of both, probably. Although the relief was currently winning.

Why hadn't he come? It didn't make sense.

She seesawed back to fear. Did Ivan get to him after all? After the phone call? No. No way. The sheriff would have heard it on his…thing by now. They'd know.

But, God…she thought of the call. How Joey'd surprised her by sounding eager. Through the fear, she'd had a flash of why she'd gone out with him to begin with. It was strange to be reminded that not everything had been bad. It made her feel like less of a loser for staying with the guy. It had also calmed her, grounded her, made her more decisive, sucked away some of her terror.

He'd sounded gleeful when they'd talked. Mentioned a surprise he had for her and said "I love you" before hanging up. How weird that she used to repeat those words back to him. Today, they left her cold.

And now he hadn't shown. She'd given him more than enough time to drive down from Northern Virginia and locate the coffee shop.

She pulled out Jessie's phone again and called. No answer. What was he playing at?

"Think it's a no go?" Steve said from the table beside hers, and she nodded.

She stood and stretched, eyeing the coffee shop's dark window. Something wasn't quite right.

Oh God, Ivan. Please, please, please don't have done anything stupid.

Steve and Jessie walked her to her car.

"Let me know if you hear from him, and we'll try this again. Keep the phone open so he can call you back. Speaker phone. Witnesses. Be safe."

She glanced at Jessie, who lifted a hand. "Keep the phone. It's yours."

"Okay. Thank you. Thank you both."

"No problem," said Steve. "Call my direct line or 911 if you need anything. Give 'em my name."

Jessie hugged Uma tightly and closed her car door once she was inside.

She turned the ignition and set off back home, hoping against hope that she'd see a big, white truck in the drive next door.

Instead, she saw Joey Chisholm's red Audi and felt it like an anvil to the chest.

This wasn't the plan. How'd he find the house? He'd known. He must have known.

Shaking, she pulled over and put the car into Park,

tugged on the emergency brake, and turned off the ignition—normal, everyday things, but it took all her concentration not to forget a step. She kept her eyes on his car, adjusting to the sight from the safety of her own, and once the shaking settled down, she dialed.

"This is Sheriff Steve Mullen."

"He's here."

"Lloyd place?"

"Yeah. What should I do?"

"Get out of there. Now."

Breathing hard, she shook her head, more for herself than for him. "Would a recording get him in court? If he admits to what he did?"

"Wouldn't hurt. But a witness'd probably do just as well. Come on now."

"Can you record this call?"

"Don't do that, Uma. Get out of there."

"What about 911 calls? They're *always* recorded, right?"

"Yeah, but—"

"All right. Thanks."

She ended the call and dialed before getting out and walking across the yard.

"Hey, sweetie pie. You miss us?"

Joey Chisholm stood on Ms. Lloyd's front porch, smiling that white-toothed grin and looking ten years older than the last time Uma had seen him.

Beside him stood her mother.

"You were supposed to meet me at the coffee shop."

"I like this better," he said, looking around. "All this rustic charm. It's so much more personal, don't you think?"

"You need to leave now."

"I don't think so, sweetie. You called *me*, remember? And here I am." He threw his arms out and lifted an eyebrow in a move that was pure Joey. His self-deprecating charmer shtick stolen directly from Frank Sinatra.

Forcing a deep breath, she looked at her mother as she went up the steps. "What are you doing here, Mom?"

"Uma, love." Uma let her mother hug her, but when Joey made to move, her hand went up. There would be no touching from him. Ever again.

"We stopped by to celebrate." Joey held up a massive bottle.

"I'll pass, thanks." She met his gaze when she spoke, forced herself to be strong, but kept her eyes moving. She wouldn't trust him for a second.

"Why don't you invite us in? It's real French Champagne—your favorite. Perfectly chilled."

"No." Fucking champagne. Always with the white wine and the champagne. Lady drinks. He'd never stopped grooming her to be a lady. Well, forget it. She was no lady, goddamn it.

She'd take moonshine over champagne any day.

She turned to her mother, her attention still focused on Joey. "When did you get back?"

"I flew into Dulles a couple of days ago, and I'm just barely over the jet lag. Such a crazy trip. Do you have any idea how exhausting it is? Delhi to Paris is fine. All the Hindis are so respectful, quiet. And the vegan menu's wonderful, but my goodness, the Paris to DC flight was just a mess. I—"

"What brings you back to the States?"

She blinked. "You, of course, sweetie! You! How could you—"

"I take it Joey called and asked you to come get me."

"He said you'd disappeared off the face of the earth, but he thought you might be close. He traced your phone to central Virginia. He was worr—"

"I'm fine, Mom. I'm fine now. You can go back to the ashram."

Her mom's eyebrows pulled down into that little-girl frown she did when puzzled. "I came all this way to see you!"

There were two ways of dealing with this: the easy way would be to thank her and pretend to want this.

Or she could tell her the truth, once and for all.

"I needed you six months ago, Mom. I told you that. I needed you and I asked for help and you didn't come."

"Well, I'm here now! We can—"

"No, we can't. You can go back to India, or you can stay in the States, but *we* are not doing anything. You're about five and a half months too late for that, Mother."

Mouth open, mouth shut, mouth open… It was strange to see her mom sputter. Strange and empowering.

"I need to talk to Joey now. You're welcome to listen, but you might not like what you're about to hear. You can stay or go. Your choice."

"I'm staying right here. With my baby girl." *Even if you don't appreciate me*, her look said. Whatever.

Uma turned to Joey, and it was obvious he was ready. Oh, the man liked a good challenge. She'd seen that side of him in the courtroom.

God, his eyes were blue. So transparent in the fading light that you'd think you could see him inside out. Only that was one of his tricks: looking guileless while keeping his sadism under wraps. It reminded her of Ted

Bundy, the handsome serial killer who'd pulled people in so easily only to cut them limb from limb.

"I called to tell you to let me go," Uma said, enunciating each word as if he were half-deaf.

"We could have discussed this at home, honey."

"Really? Because I remember the last time we discussed something in your home, and that's not an experience I'd like to repeat. Ever."

"I'm sorry about that, Umami sweetie." She hated that stupid nickname. "I'm sorry I hurt you."

"Are you?"

He leaned in, giving her the full intensity of his eyes "I regret the way we ended. I'm sorry you left me."

"Oh, *that*. Right. Do you regret doing this?" She ripped up one sleeve, then the other, and shoved her arms in his face, barely registering her mother's shocked gasp, and continued, choosing her words with care. "Do you regret forcing me down and marking me against my will, Joey? What about when you put the gun to my head and threatened to end me? You regret that? Do you?"

He didn't spare her arms a glance, and she realized he couldn't. He'd have to admit to what he'd done then, wouldn't he? Maybe he'd see her as damaged goods now. Honestly, that wouldn't be so bad.

"Look at me, Joey. Right now. Admit what you did." She leaned in, hand fisted white, arm pressed almost to his nose, lines standing out in stark relief to her white skin.

"I'm sorry I hurt you, Umami doll." He didn't look remotely sorry. He looked slightly irritated and embarrassed in a keep-your-voice-down kind of way. "You just…you were really *harsh*, you know? You went kind of crazy. And the things you were saying? I couldn't get you to understand." Joey leaned in to whisper, as if no one else could hear. "Why couldn't you just listen to me?"

"What do you want now, Joey? You've got half the cops in the state after me. My phone's being monitored." She made a big show of the phone held tight in her hand. "I can't access my bank account or use my credit card without raising red flags. What you're doing can't possibly be legal. Why are you harassing me like this?"

He swallowed, and the tightness around his mouth showed how irritated he was at her outburst. Clearly, this wasn't going the way he'd envisioned it. Well, tough shit, because this was Uma's show.

"You need to come home now. I get it. You're upset about the"—Joey waved at her arm—"misunderstanding, but…" He leaned in close, and she got a waft of those tiny mints he bought by the case. She nearly gagged when he stage-whispered, "You. Punched. Me." Each word came out harsh, punctuated by shallow breaths and a light shower of spittle. "You tricked me, tied me up, left me there, Uma. *For the cleaning lady to find!* How could you do that to me? Did you honestly think I'd let you go after that?"

Her mother shifted where she stood and opened her mouth to talk. Uma interrupted her.

"I tricked you?" She was loud now, and he *hated* that. He hated vulgarity. "You, Joseph Chisholm, hand-cuffed me for *seventeen hours*, beat me, and marked me. *Against my will.* You wrecked my skin with your insane chicken scratch, and…you…"

This was the hard part. The part she'd never said to

anyone. This was the bit she wasn't sure she'd be able to get out. But she did. She said it.

Uma swallowed hard, closed her eyes, remembered the feel of Ivan's lips against her skin, and found the courage. "You *raped me*, Joey. On the living room floor. You pushed my face into the carpet while I tried to scream at you to stop." Oh man, the tears were coming. Rolling down her cheeks in streams. And although she'd said everything quietly, the intensity in her voice had to have carried halfway across the state.

On a sob, her mother pushed away from Joey.

"Do you remember that part, Joey? Huh? Do you? I tried to say no, but how could I with my underwear stuffed in my mouth?"

Joey's lips opened, then closed into a hard, thin line.

"You know what cracks me up right now, though, after everything?" She pushed a laugh into her voice, watching as the rage suffused his perfectly formed features. He was mad, really pissed. And that was what she wanted from him. Experience had told her that when Joey was angry, he did stupid, stupid things. "You thought I wanted you back today? Remember? Look how you came running when I called! My God, how stupid can you be?"

"*You dumb bitch!* Of course you said no that night. But you didn't mean it. You always liked it rough." He grasped her arm, hard, and twisted, so the phone fell to the porch with a thud, and she saw the outline of a gun sticking out of his pants. "You're mine, remember? See this one?" He pointed at a tattoo halfway up her arm. "This one took the longest, right? Remember that, sweetie pie? JOEY'S BITCH, it says. And you loved it.

Every second of it. The sex that night? You fucking wanted it so bad. You could say no all you wanted, but really, you were dying for me to stick it in you."

From somewhere close by came the sound of an engine. The police. It had to be. "You liked hearing me scream, didn't you, Joey?"

He yanked her against him and slammed her against the wood of the door, thumping her head hard.

"D'you miss me, Umami? God, I missed you." His breath was hot and vile against the side of her face. One hand moved to her breast and squeezed. "I missed *this*."

"Joey. You need to let me go. Now."

"Oh no, honey. Seven months I've been looking for you, waiting for you to pop up someplace. No way I'm letting go now."

He squeezed harder and moved in for a kiss. Before she could think about what she was doing, Uma reared back and let her fist fly, punching him hard in the nose.

Stunned silence. The calm before the storm.

Joey went at her, hands tearing at her hair, her clothes. Reaching for his gun, he leveled it at Uma, and without even knowing quite how she did it, she moved, her body led by instinct and memory and an intense desire to live. It was that pattern she'd worked and reworked in self-defense class, just days before. She'd practiced it on Ivan, and apparently, it worked. Without thought, her arms swung up and out, the momentum powering her knee into Joey's crotch. His weapon went skidding to the floor, and he was left panting and clutching himself in soundless agony.

～∞～

When Ive spotted the bright-red Audi parked in front of Ms. Lloyd's place, his vision went dark for a second or two. And then he saw *them*. The man on the floor of the porch, Uma above him. He had a brief moment of pride before Joey attacked again. He was up and on her, and the other woman, whoever she was, did nothing but scream while Joey tackled Uma to the ground, swinging wild, ugly punches.

Oh fuck no.

Everything happened fast after that. He roared up— more on the lawn than not—and barely got it into Park before throwing himself out of the truck and into the fray. They were caught in the glow of his headlights, that fucker not even noticing Ive until it was too late.

And when he got his hands on him, what a relief. It was easy, with the fucker on top of Uma. He just grabbed him and threw. Down the porch steps, where the guy landed with a *thud*. But it wasn't enough.

He'd kill him. It was too late now. He really would kill him. He barely registered the shrill keening of that stranger's voice or the shriek of a siren not too far off or the metallic *cachunk* of a rifle, but as he moved to finish the job, his head turned in time to catch the door swinging open to reveal Ms. Lloyd, looking like some deranged Robert Rodriguez heroine, shotgun pumped and looking for a target.

"Don't do it, son," she said, barrel leveled straight down at Joey Chisholm but eyes on Ive. "Uma was right. Bastard ain't worth it." And although it took him a few seconds for the red to fade from his vision, when Ive's eyes landed on Uma, her inked-up arms bared to the world, he decided she might be right.

The cops arrived, the sheriff leading the charge, but Ive didn't pay a bit of attention. What mattered was that Uma was safe and whole and fucking *strong*. She handed her phone off to Steve and headed straight for Ive. He'd seen the way she'd taken that fucker down, and he was proud of her. His woman. He moved to pull her into his arms, but her outstretched hand held him off.

"Where have you been?" she asked, out of breath and hissing mad. Her pupils wide in her pale face.

He stilled, understanding the importance of this moment. "I had some thinkin' to do."

"Were you going to hurt him?"

Fuck. He couldn't lie to her. "No. I was gonna kill him."

"I told you I didn't want that."

"I know."

"But you left anyway."

"I left, but—"

Her hand came up again, and this time, she looked more than pissed. *Cold.*

"I had to call him to save *your* ass from getting into trouble."

"You didn't have to do that, baby. I was com—"

"I don't want to hear it." She stepped into his body, leaned up, and whispered close to his ear, "You promised, Ivan. *You swore to me.*" She looked at him, hard, and at the hippy woman on the porch. "Ivan, Mother. I need some space and some time to think right now. Come on, Cookie. Let's talk to the cops."

With that, she bent to scoop up the cell phone and walked to meet the sheriff.

27

WHEN UMA WOKE UP, SHE COULD HEAR HIM HAMMERING away. Only it wasn't just a sound or a rhythm; it was everything she had left of *him*. She closed her eyes, imagining his capable hands in her hair, his eyes devouring her body and—as she had every day in the week since everything blew apart—she got up, in nothing but a tank top and underwear, and sat by the window to listen. Each clang of his hammer was a punch to her stomach. To her heart. And though he'd come by a few times, had even thrown pebbles at her damn window one night, she couldn't do it. How could she ever trust him again?

Even with the leaves mostly off the trees, she couldn't see Ivan's workshop past the bend in the drive. And she'd tried.

From down the hall came the sound of Cookie getting up, her slow steps a little lighter for all the excitement. God, the woman was so happy about everything that had happened. Joey in jail, her mom making an effort—at least what felt like one. Jessie visiting in the evenings, her adorable son in tow. Cookie was in heaven with all the company.

So, why aren't I happy?

Stupid question.

When Cookie's wailing got too strident to ignore, Uma opened her door, still half-naked, and called down the hall, "Hold your horses, Cookie. I'll be right there."

"'Bout time. What is it I pay you the big bucks for, again?"

"Yeah, right." Uma smiled. She had access to her money again and didn't need Cookie anymore, but she wasn't ready to go. Soon, but not yet.

That evening, Jessie came to the house alone with beers in tow. The women sat out on the back steps, drinking together and watching the sunset.

"When's your next treatment?"

"Couple days."

"What's it like?"

"Hurts like crazy."

"Worse than getting 'em?"

"It's relative, I guess. Yes? No, because…" Uma's voice trailed off as she pressed her wrist to her face. MINE, it said. And it was.

"So, when're you moving out of this place?"

Uma shrugged, not quite willing to look at the other woman.

"Oh man. I can see it already. You and Cookie, old as the hills, deaf and blind, yelling at each other as always."

They shared a smile at the image and tilted their beers back to their mouths.

After a breath and a pause, Jessie asked, "So, you talked to him yet?"

Uma didn't need to see where Jessie was looking to know whom she meant. "No."

"You should."

"I plan to. I needed time to think."

"You done?"

"Pretty much."

"What d'you come up with?"

"I'm crazy about your brother. I just can't be with another man who makes decisions for me."

"Oh, girl, I get that. Trust me. But you know what happened with him, right?"

Uma raised her brows and looked at Jessie while she took another deep slug of the beer. Geez, she'd downed it fast. Yeah, well, she had an excuse.

"He came back."

"Okay."

"No, I mean, he decided not to do it. Before you called Joey. Before any of it. He realized that what you wanted meant more to him than some kind of macho reprisal. So he came back."

Something loosened in Uma's chest, something she hadn't even realized was tight. "What the hell took him so long?" she asked, sounding angrier than she'd intended.

Jessie chuckled and took another swig. "Oh man. So, get this. Apparently, he was a mess when he got to the courthouse. Like a big, sweaty, heart-attacky mess, just loitering. Can you imagine that? Ive all…hopped up and… Anyway, as he was about to head back here, he got stopped by a couple of cops. Searched him, searched the truck, asked him the kind of questions he gets asked all the time. Being an ex-con and everything."

"Wow" was the only word Uma could get out past the rushing in her ears.

"Yeah. So he wasn't thrilled."

"I can imagine." Suddenly, she needed a second beer. She grabbed it with one sweaty hand and twisted off the cap, took a sip, and pressed it to her face. "What's he up to over there? Spending a lot of time in the big house."

"What do you think?" A quick look at Jessie showed the woman's eyes focused on her, all humor gone. The expectation there was dizzying. "He's gettin' his place ready."

"For wh—" Realization hit Uma like a sledgehammer. "*For me?*"

"Now don't go running over there all pissed off that he's taking your ability to choose away and all that crap, 'cause he's not. He's giving you a choice. Another option."

For the first time in days, Uma felt the first tiny stirrings of hope and excitement. Of something to look forward to.

In the distance, Ivan went out to his truck for about the fiftieth time and grabbed something from the back. It looked like a rug, rolled up. As he turned back to the house, he caught sight of them and raised his head in greeting. He paused for a second, and she could feel the yearning from here. When she was about to lift a hand to wave back, he turned and slowly carried his load up to the house.

"So, what's happening with Joey?" Jessie's question drew her back to their conversation.

"Aggravated assault. And rape."

"Good." Jessie sputtered, "I mean, not good, but I'm glad they got what they needed to take that bastard to court."

"Don't worry." Uma shoulder-bumped her. "I know what you meant."

"So, what're you going to do now? I mean, you could probably get your own place and move back up to Northern Virginia, if you wanted, right?"

"Yeah, I could." Uma looked at Jessie again and back at the big house, remembering her first sight of that place and its owner. That first solid handshake, the most comforting thing she'd felt in forever. That was one thing that hadn't changed as she'd gotten to know him. Nothing felt better than Ivan's hands on her skin.

Maybe she'd had all the time she needed to think. Maybe she was ready to find out what came next. She smiled and finished her beer.

After a few more minutes of silence, she pulled two more beers out of the six-pack and stood up. "Mind if I steal these?"

"All yours."

She smiled her thanks. "Better check on Cookie."

Jessie stood and stopped her with a hand. "I got it."

"You sure?"

"Think I can't take what she can dish?"

"Yeah," said Uma. "You'll do just fine." But still she hesitated, more from nerves than anything else. *He came home. He changed his mind and came home. For me.*

"Go. Go on."

At Jessie's nudge, she set off toward Ivan's house without any sort of plan. "See you Monday?" Uma said over her shoulder.

"Not till Monday? Don't you want to come out for drinks with me and the girls this weekend?"

It felt *good* to have an actual friend again. "We'll see if I'm free this weekend," she answered with a smile.

～◎～

She looked taller than she had before as she approached, more in control. He wasn't sure if that was an entirely good sign—for him, at least. On the other hand, the two beers she held definitely were. A peace offering. Or more like a consolation prize? A *Sorry, dumb-ass, you lose, but how about a beer?*

By the time she rolled up and handed him the bottle, he'd worked himself into such a state, he slugged it down embarrassingly fast.

"Whoa. Guess you were thirsty," she said with that crooked smile he liked so much. "Working hard, I see." She sat on the step beside him, mirroring the position she'd had with his sister moments ago.

Jessie. He'd told her not to get involved, but the little brat couldn't keep her nose out of his business. Well, it had gotten Uma over here, so he could probably forgive her.

"Yeah. Tryin' to get the place ready."

"You finally moving into the big house?"

"Maybe. Depends." He couldn't possibly look at her. "Sort of waitin' to hear from a possible…tenant. Or roommate, I guess you could say."

"Oh yeah?" She smiled again, only this time her flirtatiousness came out a little more. He liked this side of Uma: a little flirty, a little bossy.

"Figured my proposal has a very slight chance of being accepted."

"Hmm." She stood up, filled with purpose, pushing the boss role a little bit further. "You owe me a tour. Show me around."

His answering grin felt good on his lips—God, days without talking, and he'd missed the hell out of her. "Yes, ma'am."

They went up the front steps, and he tried to see it through her eyes: perfectly finished, pristine paint job, not a fallen leaf or speck of dirt underfoot. He knew she'd notice the other details too, with her photographer's eyes: the wavy glass in the windows, original to the house; the perfectly fitted, working shutters; and copper gutters. The only thing out of place was the big punching bag hung where a porch swing should have been. Maybe they'd look for one of those together.

No. No point getting his hopes up. They hadn't talked it through yet. It could still go either way.

He opened the door, and she hesitated beside him, one foot suspended above the welcome mat. The mat looked too clean. He could see that. He'd just bought it, after all. Okay, he could fix that. To prove some weird point, he scuffed his boots all over the letters before stepping through.

Once inside, Uma's breath caught on a strangled gasp. *Oh no.* She hated it. Or even worse, she thought he was certifiable for having a place like this.

Because, let's face it, the house was a little sterile. Like Whoville licked clean by the Grinch. Not a stick of furniture, not a tchotchke or gewgaw in sight. The walls were painted a stark, glaring white.

Nothing else.

When her breathing went back to a normal sort of

rhythm, he dared to look at her, just a slide of the eyes, but long enough to catch her look.

"Oh, Ivan," she whispered, brown eyes glowing in the fading light. "It's beautiful."

Thank God.

Again, he squinted and tried to see it from her perspective, how it really was, without the layers of garbage he'd shoveled out, the paint he'd sanded off, all the hours of work he'd put into it.

The house was grand. Its ceiling floated high above their heads. Every breathtaking detail: trim, newel post, every stair tread polished to a shine. Crown molding that, like the window glass, was original to the house. And utterly still. So quiet you could hear a pin drop.

All that was missing was a little life.

Love.

He followed her into the first room on the right. The parlor.

After an initial, soundless *oh*, she started talking. Finally.

"Needs color. Something warm, maybe an earthy gold. And plantation blinds for privacy, but no curtains. You wouldn't want to cut out any of this amazing light." She moved to the center of the room, facing the fireplace, and he might have imagined something proprietary in her step.

"Oh, Squeak would love an area rug there, in front of the fire. And the cats. Cats love a good rug, so it would have to be big." Her eyes flicked to his, burning with excitement. "An armchair there, large enough for you, Ivan."

"What about you?"

"What *about* me?" Oh, there was the challenge he'd been expecting.

"You got the animals and me all accounted for. Although maybe not Pepe. Now, what about you, Uma? Where're you gonna sit?"

"Hmm." She slitted her eyes and took a slow turn around the room. "I imagine a dusty blue or turquoise chaise."

"A chaise?"

"Or a fainting couch. And lamps. If you think that overhead light's staying on all the time, you've got another think coming."

"Lamps," he repeated, allowing the tiniest bit of hope to well up in his chest. "Come on. I'll show you the rest in a minute, but you gotta see this first." He led the way back into the entryway and up the stairs, to the last door on the landing—the master bedroom.

He pushed the door open on the only furnished space in the house. He'd gotten a big bed—king size, just in case—and rugs to keep her feet warm in the morning when she got up. Bedside tables and a mirror and hangers in the closet. The quilt from his workshop was here, clean and folded across the foot of the bed. There were a few odds and ends, like the bookshelves and ratty armchair from out back. It didn't look completely done yet, but it was cozy. Almost like a home.

"This is yours, Uma. Your bedroom. Not mine, not ours. Yours."

"Wha—"

"Hang on. Let me explain." He rushed to stop her, touching her arm and wishing he could pull her into his body entirely. "What you decide to do is your choice. I get that. And the last thing I want to do is take that away from you. But I want you to understand…" Ive swallowed and looked away from those luminescent eyes. "Sometimes in life, you work hard for somethin' without knowin' quite why. *Now I know.* I've been workin' on this house all these years for you. For us."

"Ivan—"

"Wait. I'm not tryin' to force your hand. And we've only known each other a few weeks, so… This place, it's yours."

"The room is beautiful, bu—"

"Not the room. The house. The house is *yours*, Uma. For as long as you want. Forever. With or without me."

"That's… I can't take—"

"You can do your photography. And I'll keep doin' my thing. You can keep checkin' on the old bat next door, if you still feel the nee—"

"Stop."

He stopped. She moved forward and put one slender hand on his chest.

"Why did you decide not to go after Joey?"

"Aw, hell." He stepped back and thought about it. There were lots of reasons, some of them having to do with survival and self-awareness. But the most important was the realization that he'd taken her power away from her, by going against her will. Exactly the way Joey had when he'd tied her up and hurt her. Ivan would never do that again. "It's complicated."

"Try me."

"First of all, I had to go. I had to." Unconsciously, his hand went to rub his chest, hard. "Thought I was gonna die, Uma, when I saw what he did to you."

"I thought you didn't—"

"I couldn't live with it, you know? My body, my brain, it was like they'd seen you got hurt by him, and there was nothin' left but makin' him pay. No choice but to go. It's what I do when I love someone. I can't…" He shut his eyes tight, opened them, and met hers. "And then I got there, fuckin' crazy as hell, and I saw myself. I saw…who I coulda been and who you woulda been if he hadn't done that."

"Oh, Ivan. You shouldn't do that to yourself."

"No, but you know what I realized? It's gonna sound insane, but…if he hadn't hurt you, if I hadn't made all my stupid mistakes, if…if the ad hadn't run in the *Gazette* and… You wouldn't be here."

She gasped at his words—a tiny sound, but enough. Just enough for him to latch on to. "We wouldn't be here, baby, if we hadn't gone through all that shit. And I couldn't imagine not goin' home and seein' you again. Gettin' to know you." He leaned in, eyes down, and put his forehead to hers. "How could I find out everything there is to love about my woman if I break the first promise I ever made her?" He whispered the last bit.

Another sound, this time the shaky sound of Uma crying, and he cringed before starting to pull away. But she stopped him with a hand to the back of his head and a quick, wet kiss.

"I didn't think you'd listened," she whispered. "I thought you…didn't *care*."

"I can be a bit slow. Sometimes takes me a while to catch on. But I usually do, baby. Eventually."

She sighed. "Good." She stepped into him and put her cheek where her hand had been—right up against his heart. "This is good, Ivan."

"You like the place?"

"Yeah, but I don't mean just the place. I mean you, me…"

"Us," he finished for her, because it seemed so right.

"Yeah. Us."

His arms went around her and pulled her in tight—probably too tight, but Ive wasn't good at holding back. "I love you, baby."

She nodded against him and sniffled. "Me too. God, me too. When you…when you came back and pulled him off me, I thought…I thought you'd do it then, and I couldn't stand that you'd do something so awful. *For me.* But you didn't. You didn't lose yourself. We won." She shook her head. "God, yes. Yes, I'll move in. I love our room."

"Your room."

"It's our room, Ivan."

He ran a hand down her back, remembering the places that bastard had marked her. The beautiful Uma Crane. Something skittered through his brain, a question from the night he'd made the promise he'd almost broken.

"So, what's the *R* stand for?"

She pulled back with a question on her tear-stained face, the most gorgeous thing he'd ever seen.

"Huh?"

"Uma R. Crane you said. I made my vow to the beautiful Uma R. Crane. What's the *R* stand for?"

Oh, man, her smirk kicked him right in the gut, and he couldn't help but smile.

"Guess you'll have to wait and find out," she whispered, taking off of her shirt and yanking him back toward the bed with a smile.

**Read on for a sneak peek at the next book
in the Blank Canvas series.**

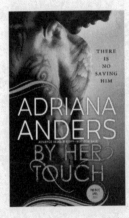

He Will Always Bear the Scars

Undercover cop Clay Navarro left the Sultans biker gang a changed man. Its ringleaders may be awaiting trial, but he wears the memory of every brutal act he had to commit tattooed across his skin. He doesn't have space in his messed-up life for anything gentle—not now, maybe not ever.

Dr. Georgette Hadley is drawn to the damaged stranger's pain, intimidated but intrigued by the warmth that lies beneath Clay's frightening exterior. But when the Sultans return looking for revenge, she finds herself drawn into the dirty underbelly of a life forged in violence…that not even her touch may be able to heal.

1

THE MOMENT APE'S HAND LANDED ON HIS SHOULDER, Clay Navarro knew the game was up.

It could have been the look in the asshole's eye that told him, or the way his fingers dug into Clay's muscle way too hard to be friendly. Probably, though, it was that other thing—that elusive animal intuition that told you your life was about to end.

He managed, somehow, to shrug off Ape's hand and veer off into the head, mumbling something about taking a piss. As soon as the door closed behind him, he leaned down and spoke into the button mic sewed onto his leather vest. He was frantic. God, was he having a heart attack? Wouldn't that be something, to have a heart attack on the day all the shit was supposed to go down?

"Shit's hitting the fan here. Whoever's listening, I need backup."

He glanced at the tiny window and considered trying to make a break for it, but there was no way he'd manage to squeeze through. But man, he couldn't risk the op at this crucial moment, even if it meant saving his skin. Not when they were so close to taking the sons of bitches down. There was no choice but for him to go out and face whatever Ape had in mind for him—try to stall him and bluster his way through. Whatever it was, they'd catch it on the wire.

Back in the hall, however, flanked by three of Clay's Sultans MC "brothers," he was pretty sure there'd be no bullshitting his way out of this. There was a sick sort of glee on Ape's face when he shoved Clay into the manky vinyl dentist's chair, brandished his tattoo gun, and said, "Thought you needed some new artwork, *bro*." After a pause, the man smiled and said, "How about your lids?"

"No fuckin' way, man." His heart rate spiked.

"Knuckles, then," said Ape, and Clay knew better than to argue. There was a chance he hadn't been made—that Ape was just being his usual sick self. Considering everything that was at stake, he had to ride out that hope for as long as he could, and if that meant letting the crazy bastard ink him up some more, then so be it. He forced his body to relax, forced a smirk onto his face.

But then one of the other bikers grabbed for him, and it was all Clay could do not to go down swinging. He submitted at the last moment, pulse flying, reminding himself that he just had to make it through a few hours before it was all over, one way or another. The biker grimly held him, head locked so he was staring straight ahead, unable to watch as Ape pressed the tattoo gun to his finger. He tightened his jaw through the inking—a quick, messy job, even for Ape—and broke the hold long enough to glance down at his knuckles.

DEAD MAN, they said in big, thick black caps. *Fuck.*
"What the—"

"Sit your ass down and stay put, or I'll pop your fuckin' eyeball," Ape said through gritted teeth. He brandished the tattoo gun at Clay's face.

Clay bolted up, but the two MC brothers were on him in a flash, grappling him back down. One had an arm locked around his neck, holding his head still for Ape and that *damned tattoo gun.* Clay flinched away, tried to push free, but there was no stopping that needle coming straight for his eyes.

He slammed his lids closed and prayed for a miracle.

"What the shit?" Clay managed to spit out before Ape went to work on his eyelids. The only thing worse than the pain was the fear. He breathed through it as best he could, waiting it out as Ape inked him. He didn't open his eyes until he was sure the needle was away—and even then he was left blinking and dazed, eyeballs stinging.

"What are—" Clay began, fighting to sound normal even after all this—until he spotted Ape pulling out that little *ax* he carried around with him everywhere. He stiffened, fought, expected to feel the deep slice of a blade in his skull, to see Ape's crazily grinning face through a film of blood, his brain matter scattered across the walls.

He should have known better. Ape might be a total lunatic, but he didn't do anything without Handles's approval. The only thing he carved at was Clay's shirt. With the sharpened ax blade. The fucker sure had a flair for the dramatic.

So maybe Handles didn't know yet. Maybe there was

still a chance he could ride this out until the end. Or at least until backup arrived.

Something occurred to Clay's crazed brain as Ape picked the tattoo gun back up and leaned in to etch something onto his chest. The asshole hadn't touched Clay's leather cut—the biker vest would have been the first thing to go if they knew for sure he was an undercover cop. Ape was killing time until Handles got back. Nothing more.

I'm not a dead man. Yet.

But if he wanted to convince his brothers he wasn't a cop, he needed to work a lot harder at being Jeremy "Indian" Greer instead of Clay Navarro. And, right now, Jeremy would be pissed as shit.

"The fuck, man?" he bellowed, elbowing one of the other men away, breaking free. The needle slid against his side, and Ape moved closer, pressed harder. He stank of stale booze and old sweat, piss, and blood.

"Think we don't know who you are?"

"Are you out of your mind, Ape?" Clay reached for his KA-BAR—of course Ape would have been cocky enough not to take the knife off him—his mind flying through the options. *Get the fuck out* was foremost among them. He threw a knee to Teller's groin, took a millisecond to enjoy the sick groan he got in response, and slid a hand into Ape's filthy hair before the other man could react. Jesus, it was so greasy, he almost couldn't get purchase. Finally, he managed and pulled the shithead into him.

"You got a death wish?" Clay snarled.

"Do you?" The man's breath was fetid, rotten, like his mouth had never seen the business end of a toothbrush. "We know who you are, you fucking traitor."

"Oh yeah?" He inhaled through his mouth, ignoring the sound of the others gathering, and set his blade beneath Ape's ear, right where the carotid would be in an actual human being. With Ape, who the fuck knew? The bastard probably had raw sewage running through his veins. "Why don't you tell me?"

Beside him, someone moved, and Clay pressed the knife in—just a couple of millimeters, but enough to make Ape gasp and throw up his hand. "No closer, man. He's gonna fuckin' kill me."

"You wanna tell me what's going on here, Ape?"

"Got a call."

Clay waited, the early fog of nerves giving way to the precise, clear-cut vision he got when adrenaline did its job. Energy and strength shimmered under the surface of his skin. God, he was born for this shit.

Clay asked, "Call from who?"

"You're hurtin' me, man," Ape moaned. Clay tightened his hold.

"Shut up," interrupted Clay. "What's this traitor bullshit?"

"Got an informant. Told us you're—"

Something hard and cold was pressed to his forehead. A gun.

"Put it down," said a voice right beside Clay's ear, dark and certain. Fuck. Of all the guys in the club, Jam was probably the deadliest. Ex-military, ex-con, and racist as fuck, Jam had wanted Clay's blood since the day he'd seen his too-dark skin. If Clay hadn't saved his life about a year ago, the psycho would never have voted him in. "Handles's on his way back. Told us to lock you up till he gets here."

"I'm not what you're thinkin', Jam."

"Not thinkin' a goddamned thing…*Brother*."

For a good five seconds, Clay waited, the barrel of Jam's gun burning a hole in his temple and the blade of his KA-BAR ready to slice into Ape. Five seconds during which he pictured doing it—ending this man's life in exchange for his. It was almost worth it. Almost.

Except a whole goddamned operation depended on Clay getting out alive and giving his testimony in federal court. It depended on Handles going through with the huge deal that was set to happen in less than an hour—was probably happening right now, in fact. The only way Clay could ensure it went down as planned was by releasing Ape, because if he held on, he was a dead man.

Finally, he opened his hand and let Ape go. The big dude came after him then, of course. All brawn and no smarts, as usual, but with Jam's weapon leveled on him, Clay was powerless to counter. A meaty fist to the jaw, another to the stomach, and Clay waited, doubled over, for his breath to return.

Fisting Clay's hair in a parody of his earlier move, Ape leaned down and whispered into his ear, "You're a dead man, Indian." He spat a fat, sticky wad onto Clay's face, wiped his own, and backed up a couple of steps.

"Grab his phone and his weapons. I'll lock him in his room till Handles gets back," Jam threw over his shoulder before leading him away.

"Not a traitor, man," Clay tried in the hall.

"Shut your face," was all the answer he got as Jam brought him to his room, where he pulled the key from the lock, shoved him in, and locked the door behind him.

Through the door, Clay heard him tell someone to shoot on sight.

Jesus, how the hell was he going to get out of this? He turned to look at the room and found it ransacked. Fine. They wouldn't have found anything incriminating anyway. Giving a hard exhale, he pulled out his phone and made the call.

"Speak to me," said Tyler.

"Wire not working? I asked for backup thirty minutes ago."

"We'll get someone in there soon as we can."

"They've got me in my room, under guard, while they wait for Handles. Did it happen? Did you guys get him?"

"No. He never showed."

"Fuck." Clay ran a hand over his face, surprised to see blood when he pulled it away.

"Bread there with you?" Tyler asked.

"Don't know where he is. Why?"

"If you were outed, stands to reason—"

Beyond the walls, something blew, rattling everything and sending bottles flying. The air in the room stilled for a millisecond in that strange vacuum of suspension that happened before everything exploded.

When the next wave of chaos came, it was in the form of shots fired outside the club walls, along with agonized screaming and shouts from all over. More gunfire in rapid bursts—club AK-47s, from the sound of it.

Clay put the phone back to his ear and yelled through the dense fog of noise, "The fuck's going on out there, Tyler?"

Silence from the phone. Everywhere else was mayhem.

And there was nothing he could do. He was a sitting duck in here. He ran to the door and pounded. "Let me out of here. Let me the fuck out."

No answer from the other side. None from Tyler either when he redialed. Minutes passed, and the fighting continued.

Was that his team out there, forcing their way in? Christ, he hoped so.

The yelling drew closer, and his adrenaline ramped back up. He searched the room for something, anything, to fight with, and came up empty-handed.

When the door flew open to show Handles standing there, pointing that fucking Glock at his face, the only thing he could do was turn and dive.

Too late, though. Too fucking late.

The first bullet tore into his back, pinning him to the bed, and Clay Navarro was a dead man.

2

Five months later

THE DOOR TO THE CLINIC STOOD WIDE OPEN, INVITING IN A way Clay didn't entirely trust. It had all been too easy—the drive into town, locating the place, finding a parking space right out front. The few people he'd encountered on the sidewalk had been friendly, smiles so wide and open Clay developed an uncomfortable itch at the back of his neck—like the buildings were a facade and everybody actors, and he was the only one who wasn't in on it.

He was right not to trust, he decided when he reached the door, only to find a hand-written sign taped to the door. It read: CLOSED—No A/C.

Dead end.

Yeah, well—not good enough. They'd need a road-block to keep him out at this point. He tried the door and found it open.

Inside, the place was dark and stifling. There was a reception area, waiting room—what you'd expect from a doctor's office—all empty. He waited for his eyes to adjust and listened to what sounded like the scratch of pen on paper. He cleared his throat, and the woman hidden behind the reception desk jumped up like a jack-in-the-box.

"Afternoon," he said and walked farther inside, still squinting against the dark interior.

"Hi there," the woman said, her voice bright and warm. "Sorry to say we're closed. A/C's out, and we can't see patients in this heat."

"You the doc?"

She hesitated, looked to the side as if searching for reinforcements, then faced him head-on again. "I am."

"Any chance you could help me out?" He made his voice as light as possible, trying for friendly, even though it never seemed to work.

"Do you have an appointment? Cindy was supposed to call everyone and—"

He sighed. "No appointment. I hear you're the only place around that does what I need."

"Oh." She blinked, big eyes roving curiously over him from beneath blond hair that looked darker along her forehead. From sweat, he realized, before letting his gaze travel down the rest of her—not a large woman, but curvy in a way that he liked. Something about the heat, her flushed face, the way the fabric of her tank top clung to her belly, and her hair stuck to her slick neck woke him up a little. She swallowed, her vibe slightly nervous. That was no surprise, since he knew exactly how he looked: mirrored glasses, long-sleeved shirt, short dark hair, ink creeping up the back of his neck. Staring at her like some goddamned creep.

"I don't mind the heat," he said, taking a step back. *See how nonthreatening I am?*

"Yes, but—"

"I'll pay."

"Cindy takes care of paperwork and invoicing, insurance and all that. I'm just not equipped to—"

"Could you just take a look, Doc? Please?" he cut in, unable to keep the emotion out. "I could use your help."

She hesitated another beat, then softened. "What do you need looked at?" she asked, voice gentler. Warmer.

Stomach a goddamned fireball of nerves, Clay reached up and pulled off his aviators. He stood there and let her see what Ape had done to him, what he'd have done himself for the sake of the mission—and waited.

∿

The man who stood in her reception area didn't *look* like he needed help. But then he removed the glasses, baring eyelids marred by ink, and George squinted over the desk at him. Taking off those lenses transformed him from a hard wall of masculinity into something even more appealing, if just as intimidating.

"The eyelid tattoos?" she asked, moving to walk around the desk.

"Yeah. Others, too."

Up close, she felt the difference in their sizes more keenly. He was *huge*. "Lean down, please. Let me get a look." Lord, what had the man done to himself? "Ouch."

"Yeah." The word emerged on a half laugh, as if she'd surprised it out of him.

"You haven't had this long, have you?"

He shook his head, and George's brain filled with questions—some appropriate, some not. She went with the former.

"How long?"

"Few months."

"Any idea what was used?"

"Used?"

"What kind of ink?"

"No." He cleared his throat before going on. "Tattoo ink, I guess."

"They protect your eyes while they did this?" she asked, and he snorted in response.

"Not exactly."

"Did you consent to having your eyelids tattooed?" she asked, knowing this wasn't the sort of question you asked a man this big, this badass.

His eyes shot open, and George fought not to step back.

Oh dear God, his face.

"Have we met before?" she asked, wondering where she'd seen those eyes, the high, flat cheekbones, the perfectly shaped mouth, outlined by dark stubble that made her fingers itch disconcertingly.

"Don't think so, Doc. I'd remember if we had."

George blushed at what she thought might be a compliment even as she continued to study him.

Those wide cheekbones, a sharp nose, and an obstinate-looking jaw made her think this wasn't a man who'd easily ask for help. Layered over his striking features were the ravages of life: those lids marred by black ink, a scar bisecting a cheek and disappearing into short, dark hair.

But most intimidating—and appealing—of all, were the darkest eyes she'd ever seen, perfectly in keeping with those dark looks. They were wide and hard. Just like the rest of him, she thought, with a hiccup of something sharp and hot and previously dormant in her abdomen.

"You have others?" she asked, ignoring the unwanted twinge with a quick step back.

She wouldn't allow herself even a glance as he unbuttoned his shirt and shrugged out of it. She saw the ink on his arms only peripherally, barely looked at how it contrasted so dramatically with the bright white cotton of his T-shirt. He reached to take that off, too, and she stopped him with a hand on his arm, immediately removed.

His golden skin was covered in tattoos, starting at his hands and crawling over solid shoulders to seep through his tee, dark enough to look like a design on the surface of the white cotton. He was wide, his arms long and strong-looking. She didn't say anything for a time, caught up in ink and muscles and the crisp-looking hair of his forearms.

He finally broke the silence. "You get it now?"

"I'm sorry?"

He fisted his hands, knuckles up. "Kinda urgent. Ma'am."

Ma'am. She hadn't been called that in ages. It made her feel like she'd been bad, chastened—the way she'd felt the one and only time she'd gotten pulled over for speeding.

"I see."

"Can we get started today? I'm on a bit of a deadline."

She considered it, her feelings divided. On the one hand, she had the perfectly normal urge to make him better, to help. But on the other hand was this overwhelming whoosh of something…uncomfortable, disconcerting.

Attraction? Was that it? It had been so long since George had felt anything even remotely physical toward a man that she wouldn't recognize it if it came in and bopped her on the head. Or punched her in the gut, more likely.

She shouldn't bring this man into the back with her. Shouldn't be able to picture him splayed across an examination table, shouldn't feel the need to get a closer look, inviting intimacies with just the two of them here—all alone in the clinic with this beast of a man. Not only that, but once most patients found out how much it cost to get their ink removed, as opposed to put on, they got a little angry.

Would this man get *angry*? She narrowed her eyes at him, trying hard to picture that.

"I don't think that's a good idea, Mr.—"

"Blane. Andrew Blane."

"Mr. Blane, I'm alone here as you can see and—"

"Look, Ms.…"

"Doctor. It's Doctor Hadley."

"Right. Doctor. I'll pay you. I'll pay whatever it takes. I've just got to get these taken off. The sooner the better."

"I understand it's urgent, Mr. Blane, but tattoo removal is a long process. It's never instantaneous. And, even so, I can't guarantee that you'll—"

"Please. *Please, Doctor.*" The words, even in that low, coffee-rich voice, reeked of desperation.

And George Hadley was a sucker for desperation.

She glanced again at his face and saw, besides the obvious, no real threat there. Yes, he was big, tattooed and scarred, leaning on the counter, hands thick and capable-looking, but his vibe wasn't threatening.

With a sigh, she stood up and, as much as she could with their disparate heights, spoke directly to him. "You're an intimidating man, Mr. Blane. Forgive my hesitation."

"I won't hurt you."

"Is that a promise?" she asked in a voice too low to be hers.

A corner of his mouth quirked up slightly, and George had to look away from a smile that was positively annihilating.

"Yes, Doctor. I promise you're safe with me."

"All right, then, Mr. Blane. Let's get you taken care of. You can fill in the paperwork while I get things set up."

In an effort to recoup some sense of professionalism, she grabbed a new client packet and pushed through the swinging door, holding it open for him and then going back at the last minute to grab her lab coat off Cindy's chair.

❧

Clay watched as the doctor moved around the room, setting things up quickly and efficiently. That was how she appeared—like someone who didn't waste extraneous time on things. That hair, short and blond, looked easy to maintain rather than stylish, and her face was devoid of makeup. All business, which he kind of liked. And fresh in a way he didn't think he'd ever seen in real life.

Fresh like a shampoo commercial or toothpaste. Only more real.

And the way she looked at him… When was the last time someone had looked at him like that? Like he was just a guy. A man. A patient. In the hospital, he'd been an agent, under heavy guard, riddled with bullets, fighting for his life. But even the nurses and docs who knew exactly why he was there gave him a wide berth. Because of how he looked.

Bullshit. It wasn't his looks; it was his demeanor. No matter where you came from, spending every waking hour as a dirty-ass biker rubbed off on you eventually. But this woman—

With a loud crack, the doctor pulled one of those sheets of paper over the exam table and ripped it, breaking through his thoughts, then washed her hands at a sink before settling onto a stool and rolling it over to his side.

Even with those beads of sweat collecting along her hairline, she looked smart and in control. Not the kind of chick who'd ever touch him, under normal circumstances.

"Okay," she said, gathering the papers in front of her like a shield. "I'll have the receptionist get anything we miss here today. She can also deal with payment next time you come in."

"Don't have insurance," he said, thankful but a little surprised she'd actually agreed to take him in, alone like this. "Filled those papers in, but if we could…you know, keep this on the down-low, I'd be grateful."

"Oh." Her eyes flew up to his, full of concern. "Are you in trouble?"

"I can pay. Just rather keep this quiet." He swallowed,

reading her as too much of a straight shooter to go for it. "If you don't mind."

After a quick scan of his body, she looked at him again, everything about her serious. Whatever she saw must have decided her, because she grabbed the papers he'd just spent five minutes filling out with bullshit and ripped them in half before throwing them into the trash. Clay's brows lifted in surprise. Maybe not quite the Goody Two-Shoes he'd taken her for.

"Okay, Mr. Blane. Let's see what we're working with here." Her eyes ran up his arms. She was clinical now, in charge. "You want all of these removed?"

"No, ma'am. I'm keeping the sleeves." He indicated his face. "But I could use some help with these."

"Right. The eyes." She slipped on a pair of horn-rimmed glasses—sexy ones that framed her eyes, spotlighted the bright-green irises that he only now noticed—and stood, leaning in to stare at the ink on his eyelids. The neckline of her lab coat sagged enough for him to catch a glimpse of the skimpy tank top beneath. He ignored it, instead concentrating on her face, a perfect distraction from thoughts of the two deadly numbers etched onto his lids.

"It's a relief you only want a few of these gone. You've got so much ink on those arms, we'd be here for years." One small, white hand reached out, cupped the side of his face, and pulled at his skin. Firm and painfully gentle.

Trying not to breathe her in, Clay averted his gaze. None of the nurses in the hospital had looked at him with this much kindness. It made his throat hurt.

"These are quite crudely done."

"Ya think?"

She glanced at him, eyes wide with surprise, and he pulled it back. No point offending the person he'd come to for help. Why was he being an asshole?

Because she's pretty and nice, and I'm not used to that.

"Sorry. So, these too." He held up his hands, baring knuckles that had seen better days—knuckles that itched with the ink of his enemies. Ink that couldn't disappear fast enough, as far as he was concerned. One hand to his neck. "This one and a few more."

"Good. Black is good. And prison-style tattoos like this are generally easier to get rid of than professional work, so…I know it might not feel that way, but it's actually a positive." She smiled, cleared her throat, met his eyes, and held them. "I work with a lot of people who've been through some…hard times, Mr. Blane. And you…are you okay?"

"What? Yeah. Great," he lied.

"I don't want to pry, but if you're in trouble… If you need help at all—" Her hand landed on his arm, soft and comforting, and something tightened in his throat before he shook it off.

"I'm fine."

There were a couple of beats of quiet breathing as her eyes searched his. She was close to him now, lips compressed in a straight, serious line, and he could feel her wondering. Jesus, this was a mistake. He should go, before she freaked out and called the cops, who'd fuck everything up. "Where else, Mr. Blane?"

She sat back down and rolled a couple of feet away. When he caught her eye, expecting judgment, he was surprised to find more of that unbearable empathy.

In response, Clay stood up and pulled off his wife beater, looked straight ahead, and braced himself for the real judgment.

~~∾~~

Before she could stop it, a startled *Oh* escaped George's mouth.

He was beautiful. Beautiful, but tragic, his skin a patchwork of scars, old and fresh alike, intersected by ink that ran the gamut from decorative to distressing. After a few seconds, she felt the awkward imbalance of their positions and stood, which still put her only about chest high.

A chest unlike any she'd had the pleasure of seeing. Beyond the obvious—the ink and the damage—his shape appealed on a level her brain couldn't even begin to understand, but her body seemed quite eager to explore. She eyed his pectorals, curved and strong-looking, solid and sprinkled with a smattering of hair, and that vertical indentation in the middle, just begging a women to slide her nose in there, to run it up to a finely delineated set of clavicles, where she knew he'd smell like man, and down to the apex of a rib cage and belly carved in bone and muscle and sinew. She wondered how he'd gotten all that strength and unconsciously lifted a hand to touch…

With a start, George pulled herself back to the room, to her job, *to her livelihood, for God's sake*, and felt her face go hot.

Dear God, my ovaries are taking over.

Take George's professional trappings away from her—things like paper gowns and background music and attending nurses—and you might as well throw her into a barnyard or a zoo or whatever uncivilized place her overheated brain had escaped to.

This is a patient, she firmly reminded herself.

Not a man. *A patient*.

She cleared her throat, pushed her glasses farther up her nose, and leaned in. Still too close, too much. She thought she could smell him. Probably his deodorant, although it was more animal than chemical—very light, but inevitable in the stifling heat—and a hint of something less healthy. Alcohol?

"Please take a seat on the table, Mr. Blane." There, that would give her some much-needed distance. Doctor, meet patient. She waited as he stepped up effortlessly and settled himself with a crinkle of paper, perfect muscles shifting under tragic skin.

Burns and battle scars. Even the tattoos.

Most weren't professionally done, except for the arms and one word she could see, curved at the top of his chest in scrolled lettering that skimmed his collarbones. *MERCY*, an oddly poignant blazon fluttering above the mess beneath.

"This one looks professional," she said, reaching out toward the letters before stopping herself, her finger almost close enough to touch the crisp-looking hair. She'd have to touch him eventually, she knew. But better to do it with gloves on, laser in hand.

"That stays."

Good, she thought, with the strangest sense of letting go inside. Just a tiny slide into relief that the man wasn't all blades and bared teeth.

"And like I said, I'm keeping the sleeves. They're…

mine. Except for the clock." He touched his wrist. "We can get rid of that."

His hand moved to his chest, and he rubbed himself there. The move seemed unconscious, mesmerizing, the sound of his hand rasping over hair loud in the quiet room.

MERCY. What a strange banner for a man who looked like he'd been spared nothing.

"Got it. Keep *MERCY* and the arms," she said with an attempt at a smile. She eyed those arms, where death and destruction appeared to play the starring role. A skull, covered in some kind of cowl with a scythe and what looked like oversized earrings took up his right forearm. Higher, from shoulder to elbow, leered a mask, Mayan or Inca, and perfectly in keeping with his chiseled face. The other arm had darker imagery: a kilted man with a sword, wreaking havoc on what looked like a big wolf. A griffon sat, claws sharp and deadly, and around all of the violence, rooted in the clear-cut line of his wrist, was a complicated design made up of knots and what she thought were Celtic symbols. Crowning it all, an oversized cross covered his entire shoulder, overflowing into the ink on his chest and back, connecting the *MERCY* in front to his back.

"Yes, ma'am."

Doctor, she almost wanted to correct him, because anything was better than *ma'am*. It sounded old, dried-up, sexless, which, on second thought, was probably more than appropriate. Although she didn't feel sexless right now.

Christ, not at all.

For each tattoo, she went through her usual questions:

How long ago had he gotten it? Had it faded? Was it professional? What kind of ink was used?

He didn't know about the ink for two of them—the eyelids and knuckles—which wasn't good. She'd had people come in with tattoos made from soot—a lot of those ex-cons—but his didn't look quite so crude. People would use anything, anything at all, on themselves and each other. She'd once had a patient whose "ink" had been made from melted car tires. The memory made her shiver.

George glanced up to find him looking at her, his attention intimidating in its focus.

She ignored it. Back to his body.

Around his neck curved a black spiderweb, its lines thin and delicate, unlike the heavier areas where no ink had been spared.

"This should be faster than some of the others. The black and the…" She leaned in. "Huh. It looks sketched in. Very light. Interesting how shallow this one is. Looks professional." Which was *weird* for a prison tattoo. She'd seen spiderwebs like this before, and they were all prison tattoos.

He nodded, didn't appear surprised in the least, and quirked that eyebrow again—his version of a smile. "Good eye, Doc."

"And the rest? You want those gone?"

"All of 'em."

"I'm afraid it's going to hurt."

"Don't mind."

Across his body, front to back, her gaze traveled, taking in every pit, every crag, every heartbreaking curve. What a tragic story—she'd seen bits and pieces of ones like it, but this—

Her eyes landed on a swathe of discolored flesh marring his side—a burn, if she wasn't mistaken—an elongated triangle, curved at the top like an—

"Oh no," she gasped before her hand flew to her mouth to cover it. An iron. He'd been burned with an iron, the skin melted. "Who did this to you, Mr. Blane?"

When he didn't answer, she went on, cowed and embarrassed at her outburst. She should be professional, should keep her shock to herself. Lord, if she couldn't control herself enough to do that, she shouldn't be seeing patients at all, should she?

Okay. Slow down, concentrate. In an attempt to control her breathing, to rein in her pulse, she closed her eyes.

Now. Open, professional, serene.

She continued cataloging the man's sufferings. On his back were two perfectly round scars. *Don't react. Be a doctor.* She kept her voice calm, steady when she said, "You've been shot." *In the back.* "Are you safe now, Mr. Blane?"

"Yes."

"Do you need help? There are people who—"

"I'm fine," he interrupted, his voice harsh, the subtext screaming that she'd better let it rest.

After a few beats, she continued her perusal. An *S*, as intricate as the letters on his chest, but not nearly as dark, followed by a scrolled *M* along his spine and a *C* on his right shoulder blade, with a complicated set of symbols in between—a triangle, arrows, an eagle, a river. A skull. The whole thing making up a deadly coat of arms.

"They really laid it on here." Her hand skimmed the picture, gently, barely touching. With a shake of her head, she went on, "I'll be honest with you. This is a lot of ink. It's going to take months, with gaps in between to heal. And it's going to hurt. This red here, that's not good. Red's a lot harder to get rid of. The particles don't break down as easily and—"

"How long?"

"Several sessions, definitely. A few months, certainly. I would venture to say close to a year. Possibly longer." She'd seen tattoos take ages to fade. And some…some never went away. "There'll almost always be remnants, Mr. Blane. I just need to make sure you understand that. Your skin's never going back to how it looked before."

He nodded and sighed, that big back curving slightly, as if in defeat. Were he a woman, she'd put a hand on his shoulder, comfort him, but this man…no. Better keep that to a minimum.

"I've got a couple farther…uh…farther south." One wide, ink-blackened hand gestured vaguely to his legs, and she smiled nervously, nodding as if this were all just par for the course. As if she hosted half-naked bad boys in her office every day.

"Yes, well. How about we start with one session whenever we can fit you in, and we'll—"

"Start now."

"Oh. No. There's prep that needs to be done. We need to numb you for big surfaces like this. And then when you come in, we'll also ice you down. For the pain."

"Doesn't matter." He swallowed, his Adam's apple bobbing visibly, and she could feel his nerves or fear or whatever that edge was. "Clock's ticking, Doc." His expression grew impossibly harder: jaw tight, lips curving down into a sharp, pained sneer. "Just…" One of those big, rough-looking hands skimmed his chest. "At least my face and knuckles. Here, too. Whatever a suit can't cover up to start with, but…"

That surprised her. "A suit?" she asked before she could hold the question in.

He gave a tight smile, one brow arched high. "Yeah. Can't picture that, huh?"

"Oh, no, that's not what—"

"I know what you meant, Doctor." He caught her eye, held it, intimidating, but also human behind the markings. "Not offended."

"Look." She glanced at her watch, avoiding the parody of a timepiece etched into his wrist. "It's late on a holiday weekend and—"

"I don't need pain meds. I can do this. And I know you got family waiting. But maybe you could just…" He looked away before nodding once and turning back to her with a harshly expelled breath. "You're right. Not the best time. I'll let you get back to your life." He stood, swiftly and smoothly, and George couldn't help but stare at the mess of his skin, contrasted with the perfection of his body—the mystery of the man within.

All sorts of bodies came through her clinic, young and old, tight and saggy. She'd examined some whose scars were hidden and others whose damage was obvious. There'd been babies, fresh and new and already marred for life, and yes, there were sometimes men she admired. Next door, for God's sake, was a plethora of hard bodies to choose from. The MMA school overflowed with them—men who lifted and punched and fought and worked, but this… This was masculinity in its purest form. This man didn't primp in the mornings or even look in the mirror. He got up, he washed, he walked out the door. Only there wasn't a door in her musings. There was nothing but the great outdoors, savage and unkempt, or the mouth to a cave.

Hard and dark, his hair almost black, with brows that arrowed straight out from three deep frown lines. And his body—she stared, caught up in the *realness* of this man, which was the oddest thought, as if the rest of her patients were somehow *less* than this one. This wasn't just another epidermis to examine. This was muscle, undeniable in its curves and hollows. And even the damage was heartbreakingly appealing, layered as it was on top of that firm flesh, his energy palpable, tensile strength, so real that she could almost feel him vibrate with it.

Beneath her gaze, under the harsh white light, she could have sworn his nipples hardened, and viscerally, her body felt it, reacted as if separate from her doctor's brain.

Keep it in your pants, Hadley! The man is probably dangerous, possibly in trouble, and, if nothing else, completely inadvisable.

Out of guilt, as if to make up for her rogue brain or overactive hormones or whatever the hell was pushing her to skim the line between brazen and professional, she put a hand up to stop him.

"Fine. We'll do your knuckles and your eyes and see how it goes from there. Your face is… You'll need injections and metal eye shields. Would you like something to drink? Water or tea?"

"Tea?" he asked, that brow up again, and she felt herself flush.

Right. Not a man who drank tea.

"All right, well, I'll need to numb your lids first."

"No numbing."

"It'll be painful, Mr. Blane. Like being splashed with hot bacon grease." *I know firsthand*, she almost added but decided to keep that detail to herself. "And if you accidentally open your eyes, it's… Look, I don't recomm—"

"No numbing," he repeated firmly.

"Okay, then. But I'll have to insert eye shields. They're like big metal contact lenses."

"Sounds sexy." His voice was low with what might have been humor—an apology, perhaps, for his abrupt words before.

George's eyes flew to his to find him watching her, and rather than dwell on the way his gaze affected her, she looked quickly away and busied herself by collecting supplies. If nothing else, she could at least pretend to act professional.

She was, after all, a doctor.

Acknowledgments

When you first start writing a book, you might think it will be a solitary venture. And while there are certainly moments alone, by the time the book is out and the process is over, you look back, and what you see is an army of helpers strewn along the path to publication. A team so vast that you don't even know the name of everybody involved.

For me, it started off with teary phone calls to friends, whose only job was to tell me I didn't suck. To those friends—Abby, Radha, Marisa, and my patient husband—I send out a huge thanks. I'd never have gotten here without you.

Next, I have to thank my incredible beta readers, whose feedback made all the difference: Radha and Corey Jo, Callie Russell, Sara and Melissa. You guys rock. You helped make this book what it is today. Also, to Meredith Cole, whose advice on publishing and writing was always spot-on, as well as the multitudes of fabulous writer friends I've made along the way—Madeline Iva, Joanna Bourne, Kasey Lane, Sheila Grice,

Alleyne Dickens, Chan Cox Elder, Elizabeth Safleur, and Callie Russell, to name a few. Your support means the world to me!

Next, there are the unsung heroes, the contest judges, who took the time to read my work and provide valuable criticism. I learned so much from you. Thank you for the time and energy you put into other people's work. It really does make a difference.

This book no doubt has many errors, but none of them can be blamed on the amazing folks I had the pleasure of talking to along the way. Thank you to Stephanie Snell from Charlottesville Skin & Laser for sharing her vast knowledge of laser tattoo removal. You gave me so much more than facts! Also, a huge thanks to Gordon Emery of Charlottesville Brazilian Jiu-Jitsu, whose knowledge of Jiu-Jitsu and other martial arts is vast and profound and so inspiring. Also, to Joe P.: thank you for your insight into the life of a prosecutor. The character in this book is in no way based on you.

Thanks to Allison, the most supportive boss in the world.

To my agent, Laura Bradford: you are a superstar. Thank you for believing in this book.

This book would be a different creature if not for the tender attention of my fabulous editor, Mary Altman, whose thoughtful suggestions and praise were equally delightful to receive. I can't imagine a better partner in this process! And to the editors who polished up my prose: you are amazing.

Finally, thank you to my parents, Le Husband, and my kids, who supported this wild dream in more ways than I can count. I love you all.

About the Author

Adriana Anders has acted and sung, slung cocktails, and corrected copy. She's worked for start-ups, multinationals, and small nonprofits, but it wasn't until she returned to her first love—writing romance—that she finally felt like she'd come home. Today, she resides with her tall French husband, two small children, and a fat French cat in the foothills of the Blue Ridge Mountains, where she writes the dark, emotional love stories of her heart.

Visit Adriana at www.adrianaanders.com.

Like Adriana on Facebook: www.facebook.com/adrianaandersauthor.

Follow Adriana on Twitter @AdrianasBoudoir and Instagram at www.instagram.com/adriana.anders.